PRAISE FOR THE
JAYU CITY CHRONICLES

"*The Hermes Protocol* grabbed my attention from the get go. I found myself in a believable future world that left me torn between wanting to destroy the establishment and accepting my corporate branding in order to enjoy the enticing benefits available. Chris Arnone weaves a tale of intrigue wrapped around characters I found myself rooting for. As Elise revealed each layer of story and world, I lived the shock, anxiety, and everything else with her. Quynn and Bastion were a cyberpunk dream come true. If you're looking for a relatable adventure of cyberpunk mystery rather than misery, then this is the story you've been waiting for."

—H.S. Kallinger, *Author of the Lost Humanity Series*

*　　*　　*

"*The Hermes Protocol* has everything you could want in a story: adventure, mystery, and a heist! Following Intel Operative Elise through the twists and turns of her mission kept me on the edge of my seat, desperate to know what happens next. Movie material, for certain!"

—Stephanie Eding, Author of *The Unplanned Life of Josie Hale*

NECROPOLIS ALPHA

CHRIS M. ARNONE

CASTLE BRIDGE MEDIA

CASTLE BRIDGE MEDIA
Denver, Colorado

Cover art by Adrian Marc

NECROPOLIS ALPHA
© 2024 Chris M. Arnone
All rights reserved.

ISBN: 979-8-9895934-0-8

For Grandma and Pamma

You always read to me when I asked.

Chapter One

"MOTHER OF CORTO, THIS IS worse than getting a neural interface tuned," Nox whispered over my comms. He was standing on the stage, dressed in a gold robe trimmed in dark blue, the hood so big that I couldn't even see his face from my seat in the balcony. His dark hands held a box covered in ornate gold and blue carvings.

"Quiet on comms," Solomon said from somewhere in the audience below. I couldn't see him from my viewpoint in the front row of the balcony. The stage was brightly lit, a couple dozen meters wide, with navy curtains hanging from high above. The rest of the theatre was dark. Big enough for a few hundred people. The theatre itself wasn't ornate, either. The design focused on clean, sweeping lines from the arch of the proscenium to the sweep of the balcony. The gold, swirling embroidery on the curtains, however, was quite lush. It matched the trim on Nox's robe, the robes of the other four people on the stage, and the little box Nox was holding. "Sure," Nox said. "Stand still. Hold the box. Be quiet. Do whatever Solomon and Elise tell me to—"

"Cut the chatter," I whispered, careful to make sure the people sitting next to me couldn't hear. "New person gets the boring jobs. Prove yourself."

"But—" Nox started. "Silently," I interrupted.

I glanced left and right to see if anyone heard me. They were all dressed to impress and thankfully too focused on the spectacle of Josephine Toinette-Deus, superstar preacher of Toinette Holdings. She was front and center on the stage, dressed in a glittering gold robe, open in the front to reveal a nearly glowing, high-necked dress. Her arms were spread wide, addressing the crowd.

"My dear friends," she said. "I'm so pleased you're joining me tonight, whether gathered here before me in person or streaming this to your homes. Tonight is a special, holy night. I get to personally welcome more than a dozen new believers to the blessed paths of Shainette and Aphnette. My friends, please come join me on stage."

A dozen people filed up from the audience, each dressed in a flowing, unadorned, navy robe, their heads covered in voluminous hoods. I didn't know which, but I knew one was Solomon. Giving each one a hand to the stage was one of the largest people I'd ever seen, his heavily armored hands easily visible despite the blue and gold robe. Vert "The Hurt" Toinette. Famous retired fighter and Josephine's personal bodyguard.

"Raptor ready?" Solomon asked.

I refocused my attention on the stage, on the job at hand, and whispered, "Ready."

"Adam ready?" Solomon said. "Finally," Nox said.

Solomon audibly breathed in and out, loud enough for Nox to hear through comms. "Adam ready?"

"Yeah, I'm ready," Nox said, hopefully not too loudly.

"Pull ready," Solomon said, referring to himself. "We are go. On my cue."

The new initiates lined up on the stage as the music changed. It had been basic, nonintrusive tunes before. I'd forgotten it was even there, but now the music sounded boisterous and loud, full of deep voices and shrill strings. Someone in a robe of the already initiated walked a slow circle around the new people, spinning a small device over their heads that poured out steam, filling the air of the theater with a heady perfume.

"It's been a long journey for all of you," Josephine said once Solomon and the other hooded figures were in a line upstage of her. "You come from all over Jayu City, outside of Toinette Holdings, from places horribly unbalanced between Shainette and Aphnette, fate and chaos. Huginn Industries and Nexus Neuronics, so chaotic, bowing only to Aphnette. Kotega Systems and Corto Corporation, ruled too heavily by Shainette. By fate. And now you come here, to Toinette, to find balance in your lives.

"Will you strive, above all else, to find a balance between fate and chaos, our twin deities, progenitors of creation?"

"I will," the hooded figures said together, Solomon's empty promise ringing in my comms as well.

"Will you look for the hand of Shainette and Aphnette in all that transpires, in all that you do?"

"I will."

"Will you look to your superiors for spiritual guidance, defer to their wisdom, and recognize our CEOs, Pablo Toinette and Zurian Toinette, as the prophets of Shainette and Aphnette?"

"I will."

Josephine nodded to Nox, though if everything was going according to plan, she thought she was nodding to another faithful servant of Toinette, not a neophyte Intel Operative from Corto Corporation. Nox approached, taking measured steps and holding the ornate box out in front of him. He stopped a step away from her, and Josephine opened the box, reaching in. When she pulled her hands out, they were dripping with a bluish liquid that threw light all around the stage. She approached the hooded figure farthest to the right and said, "Your hood."

The person pulled back their hood. It wasn't Solomon. Not yet.

Josephine drew one hand across the side of the person's face and said, "May Shainette set forth your path." Then she painted the other side of the person's face with her other hand and said, "May Aphnette fill that path with more boons than blights."

Then Josephine placed a blue-tinted hand on either side of the person's face and said, "And may you find balance in this holy paradox. Now and forever." Then Josephine drew the person's face down and kissed them on the forehead.

The audience erupted in applause, and I joined to keep my cover.

Couldn't let the gathered crowd believe I was an Intel Operative from Corto Corporation, after all. I was just another corporate citizen of Toinette Holdings, applauding the ascension of a new citizen under Josephine, the latest superstar evangelist. I could pretend as well as anyone.

Josephine repeated the sequence on the next hooded initiate. And the next. When the fourth person drew back their hood, I saw it was Solomon, his skin darker than any visible face on the stage. Gray stubble was visible on his jaw and head, even from here on the balcony. He looked like he belonged right there, his expression one of reverence and humility. Less than a foot from the preacher, and she had no idea who she was looking at. That was why Solomon was the Cloak of Corto, the best Intel Operative in the company. It was more than an honorary title, too. It placed him above the managers in our Intel division, on par with the directors, answerable only to the VP of Intel. In an entire industry of closely guarded secrets, the identity of the Cloak was guarded at all costs. When the Cloak was on a job, he was in charge. No questions asked.

Josephine painted one side of his face blue. Then the other. But as Josephine drew Solomon's face down, the Cloak stumbled, arms dashing out, steadying himself against Josephine. Nox leaped toward them both, balancing the box in one hand and using the other to help Solomon to his feet.

Except Solomon wasn't clumsy. He wasn't prone to falling. He was the best pickpocket in the Corto Intel office, one of only a few who could cut a metaphorical purse on a stage in front of a live crowd and hundreds of thousands watching from home. The fall was planned, as was Nox's reaction. Now I just had to wait for confirmation to begin my part of the plan.

"Are you all right, my friend?" Josephine asked once Solomon was steady again. Solomon nodded, and Josephine finished her ritual, saying the sacred words and planting the sacred kiss. Josephine re-dipped her hands and moved to the next initiate.

"Pull confirmed," Solomon whispered through the comms. "Nasty dry lips."

I bit my own lip to suppress a laugh before I said, "Noted."

"Transfer secured," Nox whispered once Josephine started her ritual on the next person.

"Understood," I said, standing up from my seat and heading up the aisle to leave the auditorium. "In transit. Count them down."

"Eight," Nox said.

I was out the door in moments. I glanced left and right, but there was nobody in sight. I triple-tapped my ring finger and thumb on my left hand, and a keyboard appeared floating in front of my fingers. There wasn't really a keyboard there, but since my eyes were cybernetic replacements, a keyboard appeared in augmented reality as though it was. Likewise, since I'd long ago replaced my arms with mods, my fingers delivered haptic feedback so it even felt like the keyboard was really there. I typed out, "Directions, please."

"Gladly," Bastion said via text on my display. Bastion was an artificial intelligence, which, strictly speaking, was illegal under Earth Space law. Not necessarily in Jayu City or on this planet, Little Sekhmet Settlement, but even we were under Earth Space laws. Bastion was secretly developed by the CEO of Corto Corporation, but she'd decided to let me keep him to myself. It wasn't charity, though. Dr. Ariela Corto was going to call and cash in that particular chip at some point. Probably multiple points. But she hadn't yet. I couldn't have my fellow Intel Operatives knowing about him, either, hence the text conversation.

A glowing green line appeared on the floor below me, another AR projection, and I followed it with long strides. I crossed the foyer, lightly stepping on the plush carpet gaudily patterned in the hallmark blues and golds of Ibhalism, the Toinette Holdings religion that Josephine was going on and on about. I followed the glowing line down a hallway that ran the perimeter of the circular building two hundred and ten floors up. Outside the windows, the other skyscrapers of the Toinette borough were practically glowing with towering advertisements for herbal supplements, designer handbags, high-end narcotics, and so much more.

"Seven." Nox's voice carried through my comms.

The halls were blessedly empty, but that was the reason for the timing. Why were we doing all this during Josephine's livestreamed sermon? Her entire operation was in that auditorium right now. It was maximum effort for Josephine's big show, from camera operators to designers to computer techs to PR specialists. So this floor and the two below it were practically barren. The glowing line led to a nondescript door with a simple lock. No keypad or scanner, just a jagged little spot for a key. I deployed a pair of equally simple lock-picks from my right forefinger, and the door was open in a second. I closed the door behind me and flipped on the light, illuminating the small janitorial closet, reeking of a woody cleaning chemical. Hanging next to a pair of mops was my carbon nanoweave jumpsuit.

"Six," Nox said.

I quickly stripped out of the long skirt and billowing, long-sleeve blouse that were very much not my style. I kicked off the boots, too. No need for shoes when your legs from the hips down are cybernetic mods. The carbon-polymer skin didn't mind what I stepped on. I pulled on the black jumpsuit, which covered all of my biological flesh from the crotch to the neck, magnetically sealing to my modded limbs at the hips and shoulders. Once I had it zipped up completely, the jumpsuit sucked in, clinging to and protecting my flesh.

Now I was ready for work. Black, carbon nanoweave jumpsuit with my equally black, carbon-polymer limbs fully exposed, free to move in any direction unimpeded. My black hair was combed back and plastered to my head, the sides shaved close against my brown skin. Elise Corto-Intel. Intel Operative. Professional burglar. I finished double-checking all my systems and supplies right as Nox told me there were only two initiates left for Josephine to kiss.

"You ready?" I said to Bastion via text.

"Of course," he said.

I opened the door, glancing both ways to confirm the hall was still empty, and a new glowing line appeared on the floor. I followed it, checking my corners as I moved from hall to hall. I was no longer dressed like another citizen of Toinette Holdings, so I needed to be more careful. I turned one last corner, and the glowing line terminated at a bank of elevators.

I flattened myself against the wall opposite the elevator doors, sliding along until I was directly underneath the pair of security cameras keeping watch. I reached up one hand and snapped my fingers, triggering a mini-EMP that shorted out both of them.

"One," Nox said.

I checked the elevators. Of the three, the one on the right was the only one parked on a floor above me, so I quickly moved to those doors and pulled them open. Cybernetic arms: not just for picking locks. A burst of wind immediately hit me in the face, drying out my eyes and forcing my legs to compensate to keep me upright. I was looking out at the Jayu City night. No windows. No floor. These elevators were on the outside of the building, offering a tremendous view as they moved, but offering no protection for an industrious thief prone to climbing elevator shafts.

But I knew that before I opened the doors. I stepped out, holding onto the door and spinning to magnetize my hand to a thick, metal railing against the side of the building. Once I had both hands and feet on it, the door closed, and I started climbing like an insect.

"Elevator nine," I said in my comms, telling both Nox and Bastion which elevator "shaft" I was in.

"Nine," Nox said. "Understood. Leaving the stage now."

I was climbing to meet the elevator car, which seemed impossibly far above me. I kept glancing up, climbing, glancing, climbing, glancing—

Suddenly the car was much bigger than it had just been. And bigger still. The elevator car was moving down. I should have known the evening was going too well. I needed to move to the next shaft, and quickly.

My hip joints swiveled, and my knees bent in ways biological limbs never could, wrapping around the rail to which I was magnetized and sticking to the other side. I released my hands, and my legs did the work of whipping me out of the way of the oncoming elevator, though I felt the little hairs on my neck vibrate as it whizzed past. So much for elevator nine. I looked up shaft eight, and then down, spotting the car at least two dozen floors below. The drop was too far for my legs, and probably for the ceiling of the elevator car.

"I feel the need to remind you," Bastion said on my display, "that you are not a spider, no matter how hard you pretend."

Very funny. Clinging to the side of a building was practically a hobby at this point. Not that I didn't enjoy it at least a little. I thought of half a dozen retorts, but my hands were busy keeping me from falling. No texting.

"Offstage," Nox said, louder than a whisper for the first time all night.

"Correction," I said. "Elevator eight."

"Eight?"

"I'll explain later."

"I assume you have a plan?" Bastion said.

I nodded, a gesture lost on the AI that lived on an advanced neural interface chip hidden in a secret compartment in my right shoulder. Merely being in contact with him was enough to enable our interactions, but I hadn't brought myself to install the chip at the base of my brain. I had grown to trust Bastion, to become friends, but installation felt a step too far. Even though he's told me about all the benefits like reduced lag, I just couldn't do it. At least I'd had a special compartment added to my arm for him.

"Are you above or below?" Nox asked. "Going to be above," I said.

"Going to be?"

"Funny story," I said. "Just give me your turn-by-turn."

"Should we abort?" Solomon asked, still in a whisper. "Are you compromised?"

"No," I said. "Please do not abort. I just need to time this."

"Elevators in sight," Nox said.

I lined up my hands and feet for an even release from the rail, stretching my shoulders and keeping my focus on the elevator car far below.

"Pressing the button," Nox said.

After only a moment, car eight was moving up while the wind buffeted me.

"Car is here. Stepping on. Do you—?"

"You're three floors below," I said.

And then the car was moving, picking up speed as it closed the distance. In a blink, it was only two meters below me. Then one. I launched myself up and slightly away from the rail. In less than a breath, the top of the elevator car was under me, colliding with my feet as my legs absorbed the sudden lift.

I heard a shrill scream in my comms and through the ceiling of the elevator car at the same time.

"That was me," I said.

"Are you still spinning?" Nox said, his voice shaky.

"Spinning?" I asked.

Nox sighed loudly. "Are you okay?"

"I am." My legs did their work, compressing and compensating, finding balance before my fingers even came down to meet the top of the car. After a few moments, a panel on the roof of the elevator jostled. I grabbed it and pulled it open to find Nox's hand reaching up. I peered down inside, and there was the rest of him. A head shorter and almost a decade younger than me, he was standing on that ornate box he'd been carrying just so he could reach the ceiling. His skin was even darker than Solomon's, though his head and chin were shiny with a fresh shave. The Toinette robe was in a heap on the floor, revealing his black pin-stripe suit, complete with vest and silky tie. A ridiculous getup for an Intel Operative on a job.

"Hey, nice weave," Nox said, grinning like he'd already completed the job.

"The key?" I said. Spinning? Weave? It's like he was just making up words. I thought he was talking about my jumpsuit but didn't have time to decipher what he meant.

"Oh! Right!" Nox's eyes went wide. He jumped down off the box, turned it over, and slid open a hidden compartment on the bottom. Out came what Solomon had lifted from the preacher: a decryption key. Half the size of my hand, it was pinkish orange with visible circuitry inside. Nox gave me another goofy smile before he stood back up on his box and handed the key to me.

I grabbed it as I opened a compartment in my left thigh, the faux muscles sliding back on magnetic tracks. Nox was still looking at me like I was going to give him a cookie or something as I stowed the key. I just rolled my eyes and closed the roof hatch back up. I was never that annoying when I was the new operative. No way.

I barely had time to reorient myself to face the building when the elevator began to slow.

"What do I—?" Nox began to say in my comms. "Handoff complete," I said over comms.

"Thank you, handoff," Solomon barked. "Continue."

Seriously. I was surprised Gustin, my manager, ever thought Nox was ready for fieldwork. Whatever. He made his delivery between Solomon and me, so he was no longer my problem.

The elevator stopped, and I yanked the doors open, rolling into the building and across the hallway as quickly as I could. The doors were already closed again as I rose to my feet, pressed against the wall below another set of security cameras. I stood there silent and still, breathing in and out, waiting to see if any security guards came running. I had only been on camera for a second or two, but better to be safe. After a full minute, the hallway was still dim and silent.

"No open channel alarms. No emergency calls," Bastion said in my display.

With that assurance, I crept along the wall until I was clear of the cameras and then texted Bastion to ask for directions again. The familiar glowing line appeared, and I started following it in full stride, down the corridor that ran the perimeter. I turned a corner left and before I could even focus on what lay ahead of me, a human ball of muscle slammed into me, knocking me on my back and sending every particle of air out of my lungs.

Chapter Two

"I'M SORRY! I'M SORRY! I'M so sorry!" The person who had tackled me was practically crying, scrambling to their feet, fumbling with a number of tools and a bag of crackers as they tried to help me up.

But getting the wind knocked out of you has a funny effect on your brain. For a few seconds, all you can think about is how your chest hurts while your body is convinced that you're actively dying. Once I finally sucked in a big gasp of air, and then another, I started processing what I was seeing. The person standing over me was several centimeters shorter than me, with a similar skin tone to mine and a mess of shoulder-length, black hair. They had sharp cheekbones dotted with freckles and lips that looked too full for their face. Despite their substantial muscles, they looked too young to be wearing those gray technician's coveralls with "Valdo" printed on the chest.

And they were scared. I knew how to use that. I planted my hands on the floor on either side of my head and kicked up in the air, the force carrying my body off the ground so that I went suddenly from prone to standing in a slight, predatory crouch.

"Who are you?" I practically growled.

The stranger silenced and swallowed their ramblings. They glanced at me nervously and looked up and down the hall, probably looking for an escape.

"Don't make me ask again," I said.

They swallowed one more time, their Adam's Apple bobbing furiously before saying, "Valdo. Valdo Toinette-Sixteen. He/ him."

"Sixteen?" I said. Only sixteen years old. Just a baby. I softened my approach a little. "Awfully young to be here. Alone."

"What's going on?" Solomon growled in my ear.

"I can't find anything on a Valdo Toinette-Sixteen," Bastion said on my display. "Could be a fake name."

It probably wasn't. Toinettes, particularly the devout of Ibhalism, tended to be extra-protective of their kids. Didn't let them drink, vape, or ride with strangers, and kept them off social media. And since the public Net was all Bastion had access to, it didn't surprise me that he couldn't find mention of this child online.

"I...I..." Valdo said, stumbling over his words. "I work here. Computer technician."

"At sixteen?" I asked.

"I could do a lot more if they let me," he said with surprising force.

I took a step toward him, and what little force he had faltered. He tripped over his own feet and landed on his ass again. "Well, Valdo Toinette-Sixteen," I said. "Why don't you run home to your parents? Forget you ever saw me. That would be in your best interests."

To my great surprise, Valdo's face hardened at the suggestion. He swallowed again and then shook his head. "I can't."

"Can't? Or won't?"

"Both," he said as he rose to his unsteady feet. "I need this job. My mom needs…"

"Elise!" Solomon practically yelled over comms. "Mother of Corto, click your comms!"

Right. It had been so long since I'd done a job with someone else, clicking my comms hadn't even entered my mind. On an open channel like this, it was expected that an operative couldn't always talk freely. So we could click. Some people made little sounds with their jaws. Others tapped the microphones mounted near their ears. I made a complicated but discrete little motion with the finger of my right hand, a macro that opened a click program I had.

Two long clicks for all clear, no troubles. Two quick clicks followed by one long click meant to abort. A nonstop succession of clicks, short or long, was a distress call. I tapped my fingers together twice, long and clear.

"I trust you, but keep me informed, Elise," Solomon said.

Though my eyes had never left Valdo, my attention had. Now I focused on him again. He seemed to deflate at the thought of his mom. His previous sentence had trailed off, never finishing. It was so easy to intimidate someone when they were just an obstacle. So much harder when the layers started peeling back to reveal the person beneath.

"Mother of Corto," I whispered to myself.

"What?" Valdo asked.

"What are you doing here?"

"I told you, I work—"

"On this floor. I know. But right now, what are you doing here now?"

"Oh," Valdo said. "Upgrading the relay terminals. Has to be done overnight so it doesn't interrupt work. I was just getting a snack while the firmware was—"

"Anyone here with you?"

Valdo's eyes went wide, a level of fear I hadn't intended. He heard a threat that wasn't there, though I wasn't going to correct him. Fear was a great motivator. He shook his head briefly.

"Go back to what you were doing," I said, doing my best impersonation of my own mom's command voice. "Stay there for at least the next thirty-five minutes. Don't call anyone. Don't trigger any alarms. I'll know. You never saw me."

"I don't even know who you are."

"Exactly."

He stood there still, staring at me, waiting for me to do something, maybe. "Now, Valdo. Go now."

He nodded as he spun on a heel and practically ran down the hall, ducking into a room and slamming the door behind him. A small pile of tools and fallen crackers still littered the floor from our collision.

"Nervous fellow," Bastion said. I brought up my keyboard and typed back, "He's just young. That works in our favor."

"No alarms or calls, in case you were wondering."

"I was," I typed. "Keep monitoring. Directions."

The line appeared again, and I followed it past Valdo's little room, deeper into the center of the building until I arrived at a pair of double doors. They didn't look like any other doors in the building, tall and broad, covered in blue lacquer and dazzling gold scrollwork. Josephine's private offices. There were no nobs, no keypads or scanners, only a small metal panel with a slot exactly the size of the key Solomon had lifted from the preacher. I removed the key from my leg, fit it in the slot, and the doors slid open with the barest of whispers.

"Office breached," I said on my comms. By now, Solomon should have been at the exit point, and Nox on his way there, but they would remain silent unless I needed them. Still, I had to keep them apprised of my progress.

I'd seen documentaries on CEOs and influencers with more subtle homes than Josephine's office. The blue with golden scrollwork carried onto every surface from the patterned carpets to the pressed-metal ceilings. Faux wooden desks sat to either side of the doors, likely for assistants, while a few semicircular steps led up to a space as big as my entire apartment that was dominated by a large, real wood desk. Wood that could only come from another planet since trees didn't grow on Little Sekhmet Settlement, sixty-odd lightyears from Earth.

A painting dominated the entire wall behind the desk. Two figures, one clad in a bespoke gray suit, the other dressed in a mismatch of fabrics and colors and styles, were fighting or dancing in a beautiful, serene field. Far in the background, however, a volcano was erupting, foretelling of doom to come. Shainette and Aphnette, Fate and Chaos, forever entwined in the course of creation. That was Ibhalism. The Toinette religion. What Josephine preached.

Now I would really get to test the information Hessod, my analyst, had provided me. I moved to Josephine's desk, half of which was taken up by an unusually large and archaic computer. I knelt and felt along the inner left drawer of the desk until I felt a rectangle that didn't match. It was too smooth. I pressed it, and it slid to the side. There was another slot just like the one that opened the door to this room. I inserted Josephine's key again, and a gentle whirring started behind me.

The enormous painting was rising, rolling up into the ceiling to reveal another door. It was normal size, and the top half was glass. In nearly the same moment the painting rolled up enough to reveal the glass, and lights flickered on in the room behind it. Three server stacks stood in the room beyond, accompanied by a single computer terminal accompanied by yet another slot for Josephine's key. But something was missing.

"We have a problem," I said.

"What?" Solomon and Nox asked at the same time.

"The grown-ups are talking, Nox," I said.

Nox started to answer, "But I—"

"Quiet," Solomon barked.

"There's no lock on the private server room," I continued. "No handle."

"No key slot?" Solomon asked.

"I can see one at the server terminal inside, but not on the door. Or nearby."

"Checking," Solomon said. While he checked with our office, I looked around the door for any sort of hidden panels or scanners, but there were none. I gave the door a push just for good measure, but it didn't budge.

"Hessod doesn't have any record of special alarms or locks ordered since Josephine started using that office," Solomon finally said, talking about my analyst. "He thought the key would open the door to the server, but that must just be the server terminal itself. Do you need—?"

"Understood," I said. "I'll find a way."

The comms went silent in response. I knew Solomon wouldn't take it personally. He was the Cloak of Corto. He'd easily completed ten times the jobs I had. He knew when it was time to plan and discuss and when it was time to just do. I was glad he respected me enough to just let me do, though he was never one to hold someone's hand through a job. When I was just barely done apprenticing, we did a job at a plant nursery. Enormous place. Took hours to find the safe. He was gruff. Impatient. He also made me rely on my training to do my part, not just doing it himself. When things went a little sideways, though, he made sure both of us got home safe. He'd earned my trust dozens of times over since then, and I was always glad to have his.

I looked around one more time, just to see if my eyes had skipped over anything, but to no avail. I sighed, crossed back to the desk, and pressed a key on the computer.

The screen lit up in an instant and asked for a password. Not a biometric or cybermetric scan. Not a proximity key tied into an onboard processor. An old-fashioned password. I walked around the desk to the backside of the computer, looking for a data port I could plug into, but every port was far too old.

"Sparks," I said aloud. Then via text to Bastion, I asked, "Any ideas?"

"That computer doesn't access the public Net," he said. "I don't even see a Net routing in this room. It's just too old."

"Smart way to control a high-security door. Any guesses on the password?"

"That machine is running a Toinette operating system from nearly three decades ago. Nevertheless, it will accept passwords up to two hundred and fifty-six characters long. At that rate, it would take you—"

"Pet's names. Kid's names. Anything like that?"

"She has a robotic schnauzer named Sacred Balance."

"Ugh, that's horrible. Really?"

"The schnauzer features heavily in her social media feeds."

"How on-brand," I said, and typed in the fake dog's name. I hit enter, and the screen shook slightly. Large red letters informed me that it was the incorrect password. I had two more tries before the computer locked. Definitely not enough attempts to try permutations of the robot dog's name.

"I have an idea," I said aloud, not worried if Solomon or Nox heard me. I jogged out of the office, down the hall, around a corner, and threw open a door.

"Aah!" Valdo yelped, a half-eaten sandwich falling out of his mouth and splattering onto the concrete floor.

"You," I said to him. "Follow me."

"But you told me—"

"Not asking. Now." I turned and started walking back to Josephine's office with long strides. Sure enough, Valdo started following a few seconds behind me. I was already back at Josephine's desk by the time Valdo reached the door to the office, and then he just stood outside, his look incredulous.

"Over here," I said. "I can't," Valdo whispered.

"You can. I need you over here."

"I can't. This is her holiness's office. You can't be… who are you?"

"Valdo," I said as sternly as possible. I was losing my intimidation over him, his spine growing as he stood there. I needed to reign him in. "Get over here now, or so help me—"

"No!" he suddenly yelled. "This isn't right. I don't know what you're after, but if you're in there, then I'm not helping you. I won't go against her holiness. I'm going to call security!"

"And what did you think I was doing here, Valdo?"

"What?"

"Before. In the hallway. When you were all right with hiding in that little room? Whether I'm in this office or not, you know this entire floor is Josephine's. You were okay with everything then, but not now?"

He was flustered, obviously trying to work it all out, his brow sweating with the effort. "Who is that?" Solomon asked in my ear. "What's going on?"

I sent along two long clicks again.

"Valdo," I said, calming my voice. "I'm an Intel Operative. I'm here to do a job, just like you're here to do your job. I'm not here to profane your way of life or blaspheme your preacher."

"You're here to steal something," Valdo said. Each word was measured, calmer, working through the information.

"That's right."

"What?"

I pointed into the locked server room. "Just some data."

"What data?" he asked.

"I don't know."

"What are you going to do with it?"

"I'm going to turn it over to my boss, like handing in a report. Because it's my job. They tell me where to go and what to take, and I do it."

"But I caught you."

If he wanted me to play at his ego, fine. "Yes," I said. "You caught me."

"Then you can talk to Toinette Holdings' security." He turned and started to walk away.

"What do you want, Valdo?" I hollered.

He reappeared, still outside the office, the mellow light of the hallway spilling across his sharp features, giving him a melodramatic look. "What do I want?"

"I need your help," I said. "Surely there's something you need. You wouldn't be working late at night in this building, by yourself, at sixteen years old unless you needed something."

Several expressions flashed over his young face. I had him there, and he didn't know what to do with that.

"I can help you. I can find things. Get things."

"Steal things," Valdo whispered.

"Sometimes."

"Do you hurt people?"

"I try very hard not to."

Valdo nodded, but the gesture seemed more for his own benefit than mine. "Can you get Preg Vaxxus B?"

"A drug used in treating Cranial Starriazas," appeared on my screen from Bastion. "Expensive, but not difficult to obtain. It should be provided to any citizen of Toinette Holdings."

It was a strange request. I wasn't aware of any company in Jayu City depriving its citizens of medical treatments. Ever. But that was something I could worry about later. "Are you sick, Valdo?" I asked.

"Not me," he said quickly. "My mom."

I waited for the kid to finish, but he looked like he was focused on holding back tears, purposefully looking anywhere but directly at me. I felt for the kid. It was a terrible disease that ate away a person's muscles and brain at the same time, causing them to wither away while forgetting everything and everyone they loved. Preg Vaxxus B could stop it in its tracks, but otherwise, Valdo's mom would die slowly and painfully.

"Yes, Valdo," I said. "I can get you Preg Vaxxus B."

He finally met my eyes. "You promise?"

I honestly wasn't sure where or how or when, but I could get anything, really, so I said, "I promise."

Valdo swallowed hard and finally stepped into the office. "What do you need?"

"There's no lock for that door. I need to get in, and I'm guessing this old computer has something to do with getting me in there."

"Hold down both shift keys, tab, number two, the open bracket, and zero," Valdo said as he was crossing the office. "I'll tell you when to let go."

I did as he said. "Got it."

Valdo walked straight up to the back of the computer, put his hand on it, and made something click. The computer instantly powered off.

"Hey, what are—?"

"Keep pressing," he said. He made the click again and the computer powered back up, going through some startup sequence slower than any I'd ever seen. Valdo came around to stand next to me, watching the screen. Finally, the antique said STARTING UP IN DEBUG MODE. "You can let go now," he said.

"You're hacking into Josephine's system," I said.

"Hardly. A machine this old? It's mostly about tricking the hardware. I'm just bypassing her security. These old things are great for keeping out remote hacking, but useless when face-to-face."

"That's a shame," I said.

"Why?" Valdo asked as the machine finished booting up, and then he was opening and closing dozens of apps I didn't recognize with deft keystrokes.

"I can always use a good hacker."

"You have me," Bastion said.

"I didn't say I couldn't hack," Valdo said, and then pressed a key with a flourish. "Just that this antique doesn't need hacking."

The door to Josephine's private server unlocked with an audible clunk and then slid open.

"Well done, kid," I said. I took one step into the server room, and suddenly there was a hand on my arm, spinning me back around.

"The drug," Valdo said, his face uncomfortably close to mine.

"You promised."

"I did," I said. "Send me your comms link."

Without letting go of my arm, he reached into his pocket and pulled out a personal tablet.

"Are you an Orthodox Ibhalist?" I asked, referring to the small, splinter sect of Ibhalists that forsook all mods, spouting something about the human body being holy and born balanced or something like that. Whenever I was getting briefed from Hessod, I tended to focus on technical details for my job, not so much the cultural details unless I thought I would need them.

Valdo shook his head slightly as he tapped on his tablet a few times. "My grandmother is. My mom is. Sort of. She doesn't do mods and doesn't want me to."

"She can't stop you," I said.

"No," Valdo said in a whisper, suddenly much sadder. "She can't."

I decided not to pursue the conversation any further.

INCOMING DATA FROM VALDO TOINETTE-SIXTEEN, appeared on my screen, followed quickly by DATA RECEIVED.

"You got it?" Valdo asked.

"I got it," I said and tried to pull my arm from his grip, but he didn't let go.

"Elise," Solomon said over comms. "Josephine just finished the ceremony. I estimate you have five minutes to get what we need and get out of there."

"You promised," he said again, holding my gaze with an intensity I didn't know he had. "Don't forget."

"I won't," I said and pulled my arm free. "You should go back to your room. You don't want to get caught in here. And the less you know, the less you have might have to lie about later."

The nervous worry returned to his face, making him suddenly look like the teenager he really was. "When you leave," he said, "flip the green switch on the back of this computer off and back on. Without the keys pressed, it will reboot normally. Keep her holiness guessing a little."

"Thanks, Valdo. Now get out of here."

He did, though not without looking back once he was out the door and throwing me a sheepish smile.

"Livestream just went offline," Solomon said on comms. "Time to go."

"I'm not sure that was the smartest idea," Bastion said. "That young man could be running off and telling someone about what you're doing in here."

"I don't think he will," I said via text. "I think he's invested in my success. That has a way of rallying people to my side."

"Touché," Bastion said. I was glad he got my reference to our first meeting. He needed me. I needed him, and now look where we were. I plugged Josephine's decryption key into the terminal in the server room and it lit up. No password required. This terminal did have a data port I could use, so I pulled my data cable out of my right elbow and plugged in. In only half a minute, I'd copied everything Corto Corporation needed. I looked over my shoulder and the coast was still clear. "Time check," I said over comms.

"Maybe a minute," Solomon said. "I have no idea how much glad-handing Josephine is doing after the ceremony. Or did. She could be done by now and on the elevator."

"Going," I said, but I wasn't. Not quite yet. From the same compartment I kept Bastion in, I pulled out a microdrive, fit it into the same data port I'd had my cable in, and watched a flurry of programs run and close in quick succession. It took almost a minute but then it was done. I stashed the microdrive, yanked out the encrypted key, and was out of the server room. Then it was track-covering time. I flipped the switch on the old computer back and forth, the door to the server room sliding closed. Then I dropped the painting back down, walking out the door to the office before it was even finished. I closed the office door and pushed Josephine's key into its slot, leaving it there. With any luck, the preacher would think she'd just been absentminded enough to leave her key in the lock.

I blew out a breath and backtracked to the elevator. Past Valdo's room, the door closed once again. I turned the corner and nearly ran into Josephine Toinette-Deus, whose office I'd just broken into.

"Oh!" I said out of reflex, rocking back on my heel.

"Hello to you too, friend," Josephine said. She was still in her ceremonial robes. Her white hair fell around her shoulders, though flattened from all that time with the hood up. She was coated in a thin film of sweat as she stood there, towering over me with that too-friendly smile she was so good at.

"Hello," I said and tried to move past her without looking at her too much.

"Can I help you?" she asked.

"No, thank you."

"It's rude to not at least introduce yourself to someone." Josephine moved in front of me, hands placed on her hips like some obstinate tree. She was more than a dozen centimeters taller than me, her sleek, pale throat at my eye level. The reminded me a bit of Dr. Ariela Corto, the Corto Corporation CEO. That same soft, level speech. That same air of superiority. I could handle that.

But then an even larger figure soon strode up behind her, one that scared me to my core. Vert "The Hurt" Toinette. Over two meters tall, cybernetically modified more than any human I'd ever seen. His entire body except for his bronze face was covered in dark metal, heavily armored and powerful. He was wearing a black tracksuit that was straining against his bulk, his own robe draped over one shoulder. His black eyes fixed on me and narrowed.

"I'm Ellie," I said, and tried to dart around them both.

"Ellie." Josephine took one quick, long stride sideways and blocked me again. "No corporation. No division. No pronouns. That's fascinating."

"Elise?" Solomon asked over comms.

"I was just leaving," I said to Josephine.

"Shall I see them out?" Vert asked in a far more melodic voice than I had anticipated. I doubted being escorted out by him was as nice as it sounded.

"That won't be necessary, Vert," Josephine said, placing a gentle hand on his arm and purring his name. Her eyes never left mine, though. "I can see you're in a hurry. And dressed for a stunning night out, too."

That struck me. When most people saw the carbon nanoweave jumpsuit and my carbon-polymer limbs, they were confused. Too much black. Too much functional tech and not enough style. It wasn't an outfit for socializing, but for stealing, not that most people knew what it was for. Josephine barely glanced at all of it, and her only analysis was *dressed for a night out*. It wasn't inaccurate, just odd.

"Are you lost?" Josephine continued. "The ceremony ended almost ten minutes ago. The nearest landing pad was right on that level."

"I needed to use the bathroom," I said. "The ones down there were all full. Long lines."

"So you took the elevator eighteen floors up," she said with a tilt of her head. "Naturally."

I swallowed, caught off guard not only by how intimidating this woman and her hired muscle were but thrown further by just how much I was fumbling for a decent lie. Her eyes seemed to burrow into me, searching. They reminded me too much of another woman in another place, a woman who had nearly killed me and still wanted to. Roxy. I looked away from Josephine, unable to hold that hunting gaze.

"You were in the balcony, right?"

"Yes," I said, trying to hold by my surprise at her recognition.

"First row," Vert said. "Just to stage right of center." That wasn't frightening or anything. Not at all.

"You left early, though," Josephine said. "Not even halfway through the initiations. Was it something I said, friend?"

Vert must have told her. His eyes had been watching the room. That was the only logical explanation. She had her back to the audience when I left. "Cramps," I finally said. "Of course," she said with a sympathetic smile, but her eyes were all cold and calculating like she was peeling me apart with her gaze.

But this time I held her gaze, looking back at her as much as she was looking at me. I needed to get the upper hand or at least even footing. This wasn't like me, and I wasn't going to let it continue. Even if I was fumbling my words, I could at least look like I wasn't scared.

After a few long seconds, her eyes went wide with feigned surprise. "Oh, I'm so sorry for keeping you," she said, turning and gesturing toward the elevators. "Please, do go on."

I didn't wait for a written invitation but breezed past them both without further delay. I couldn't believe she'd seen me, that I'd just run into her, all in the name of my own reckless inquiries. I hoped it would be worth it. I reached the elevators and wailed on the call button. No point disabling the cameras when Josephine had already seen me.

The elevators dinged, and just as the doors were opening, Josephine called from down the hall, "Oh, be sure to thank Gustin for sending a pretty one."

The bottom dropped out of my stomach. Hearing my manager's name coming out of her mouth like that sent chills down my spine. For a moment, dread stole my breath. I took two more steps and composed myself. By the time I looked her way, I only caught one of her long legs vanishing around the corner, back toward her office. Vert was standing there, staring blankly before tilting his head to me slightly. A glint in his hand caught my attention. He was holding a decryption key just like the one I'd left in Josephine's door. Then he turned and followed the preacher down the hall.

If she knew Gustin, she knew I was Corto Intel. Not only was that not possible, it was terrifying.

Chapter Three

"SHE SAID WHAT?" QUYNN ASKED loudly enough for our neighbors to hear. Quynn Corto-Nano was my love, my partner in life. They were also a director in Corto Corporation's Nanotech division, hence their name. Today, they were a full head shorter than me with dark brown skin and a green mohawk a dozen centimeters tall. Yesterday, they were my height with slightly lighter skin, and about the same weight, but with long, blonde, frizzy hair. Quynn used nanobots to change everything about their appearance from day to day. Short, tall, light, dark, bulging in the pants or bulging in a bra, and every other variation and combination imaginable. The only thing they never changed was their eyes, which were like an anchor for me: one violet and one aquamarine. I flopped down on the oversized couch in our undersized living room. I'd changed out of my work clothes and work limbs to some stretchy pajamas and my everyday limbs. The limbs weren't anything special, practically the first cybernetic limbs I'd ever bought. A little stronger and faster than biological limbs and covered with a bad facsimile of biological tissue.

"She knows Gustin?" Quynn asked, poking at a console mounted on the wall in our kitchen to order some food.

"From the sound of it, yeah," I said.

"That can't be good."

"She made me. Was toying with me the entire time."

"How would she even know what an Intel Operative looks like?" Bastion said from a speaker next to our viewscreen. Since Bastion had come into our lives fully, we'd added speakers to every room just for him. He'd been pretty picky about them, too, wanting to make sure his scratchy tenor voice came through just right. "Let alone an Intel Operative specifically from Corto Corporation?"

"Our trade is in secrets. Secret locations, identities, operations. No clue how a preacher from Toinette would know who I work for just by looking at me."

"Curry?" Quynn asked while staring at the console.

"Green," I said. "Not yellow. The heartburn last time…"

"I remember. You tell Gustin yet?" Quynn asked.

I shook my head. "I don't even know if I should."

"Why?" Quynn and Bastion asked at the same time.

"The way Josephine said it," I said. "Not just that she knows Gustin, knows what I am, but like she knew I was going to be there."

Quynn sat down hard on the couch next to me. "You don't actually think Gustin could have betrayed you? Told her you were coming?"

"We don't exactly get along," I said.

"There's a wide berth between not getting along and setting you up," Bastion said. "Along with Nox and Solomon."

He had a point there, especially with Solomon, the Cloak of Corto. To sell out the Cloak of Corto to another company would destroy Gustin's career, maybe even get him tossed out of Corto Corporation altogether. Discommended. Still, it's not like those sorts of things had never happened before. I'd lost two important people in my life to discommendation, their names barred from my tongue.

"Do you think Gustin suspects?" Quynn said in a whisper and nodded their head toward Bastion's speaker. "That I'm working with an illegal AI? No," I said. "We've been careful."

"And I've seen nothing in Gustin's public Net traffic to indicate any suspicions," Bastion said.

"What about Nox?" Quynn said. "What about him?" I asked.

"How well do you know him?"

"Not well," I said. "He started a few months ago. He's been in deep with Toinette for most of that. I assume he went through our training programs before then. I hadn't really paid attention to him before this job." I ran through all of our conversations during the night, but nothing jumped out at me as probing or untoward.

"Gustin did assign him to this job," Bastion said.

"That would be a bold move," I said. "Sending a mole on a job with Solomon. Can't get much if anything by him." Still, it made me wonder. Who was this young man with so much bravado? Why was he sent on that job?

"You should talk to Gustin," Quynn said, putting their hand over mine. "Give him a chance to explain. We're jumping to conclusions here."

I nodded. They were right. I could at least approach cautiously and gauge his reaction. "We have a debrief scheduled for the morning."

"Are you certain this can wait?" Bastion asked.

I sighed, blowing hair out of my face. "I just got into my pajamas."

"And dinner is on the way," Quynn said.

"I require neither food nor comfortable clothes," Bastion said. "You could head into the office, sneak in, and plug into Gustin's data port. I could…"

"Bastion," Quynn said with an edge of authority.

Bastioned sighed, a disconcerting sound coming from an AI that didn't have lungs. "Couple time?"

I turned and smiled at Quynn, grateful for the gesture. I ran a hand along their cheek and kissed the spot.

"Couple time," Quynn said.

The speaker fell silent. In the few months since Dr. Ariela Corto had told me to keep the AI's chip, Quynn and I had adjusted our lives. Not just the speakers but tending to his needs like another member of the family. He was fairly analytical but just as prone to moods and emotions as any flesh-and-blood-and-mods human. We also had to tend to our own needs as humans and a couple, which meant setting boundaries. He'd agreed to respect our sleep schedules, refrain from speaking to me when I was using the toilet, and give Quynn and me some space when we asked for it. Not sexy time; we didn't do that. Couple time.

Quynn turned on our viewscreen, flipping through a couple of streams before they found the news. After several bright ads for apartments in the new Corto Cadmium high-rise, Nike sneakers, next-gen neural amphetamines, and an AR game called *Cyber Skelter*, our favorite Corto Corporation news anchor, Scarlett Corto-Media started talking about production ramping up on Corto's newest cybernetic hand. Funny enough, I'd stolen some schematics from Nexus Neuronics that went into that hand.

Our food arrived from a little noodle shop sixteen floors up from us, right next to a grocery store and a cafe that served the best lattes in the building. We ate in relative silence, absorbing the news and relaxing. It was perfect.

"Your window is closing to get tickets for the upcoming *Dregs of Osiris* tournament happening next weekend," Scarlett said with her trademark drawl. Nobody knew where Scarlett's accent came from, but Quynn and I both thought it was adorable. "For the first time in nearly twenty years, Little Sekhmet Settlement will be playing host to a major eSports event, broadcast live to three dozen planets, including Earth.

"Mother of Corto," Quynn said, leaning forward. "That's next weekend?"

"Major players like Grim3000, BossProcDox, Vitamin K, and Lady Entropy have qualified and are expected to draw big crowds as local favorites," Scarlett continued. "General admission tickets are nearly sold out for the two-day event, but there are still a few VIP and Elite passes for sale through the *Dregs of Osiris* website."

Quynn suddenly hopped off the couch and was in front of their workstation in a blink. "I need to grab tickets. Do you mind if I go in for VIP? You know what? I need to look at VIP versus Elite before I do anything."

"Wow," I said after swallowing a big bite of curry noodles. "I thought you hated that game."

"I'm terrible at it," Quynn said. "That doesn't mean I hate it. I like watching the pros play way more than I like playing myself. I don't have the mods or processors to be any good, let alone the skills."

"How did I not know you were this excited about it? I thought you were still obsessed with *Vlad's Return*."

Quynn shrugged and tapped away at their workstation, the *Dregs of Osiris* website dancing in a kaleidoscope of colors on their screen. "You don't game. Doesn't interest you. And I don't watch our shows when you're out on a job, so I play. I finished *Vlad's Return* last month. I'm usually playing *Galaxy of Grandiose* or *Bollywood Brawl*. But I love watching Dregs of Osiris. Lady Entropy is my favorite."

"Wow," I said, extending the word for effect. "This is a whole side of you."

Quynn glanced at me with a little worry on their face.

"No, no," I said. "I like it. I'm glad you're not bored while I'm off scaling buildings and staring down Toinette preachers."

"Oh, I definitely want an Elite pass," Quynn said, and then sucked in air between their teeth.

"Get it," I said, turning my attention back to the news.

"Really? You don't even know how much it costs."

"You're really excited," I said. "And I trust you. Do it!"

I slurped the last of the curry sauce from my bowl, and then took it into the kitchen. "I should head to the garage. Let Bastion get started on this data."

"I thought you were in for the night."

"You know how he gets if we don't give him something to do while we sleep," I said. "Besides, he might come up with something new overnight. Maybe some extra ammunition for my debrief with Gustin. And if I'm staying in the building, I can stay in my pajamas."

Quynn got up from their workstation and joined me in the kitchen, planting a kiss on my cheek. "Okay," they said. "You going to be long?"

"Nah. Just going to plug in the data drive and get Bastion started. I'll be right back."

#   #   #

I stood in the hallway before the door to my garage, letting the combination of biometric and cybermetric scanners verify my biological and mod configurations. As they did their work, a floor-to-ceiling ad for the newest Corto flesh-like mods lit up the door. LeGrand Corto, the face and body of Corto Corporation, was swaying her impossibly curved hips and dancing with modded limbs that didn't look modded. That was the point. After several long seconds, the ad flickered away, and the door clicked.

I entered, carefully closing and re-locking the door before I turned on the lights. Poe, my bike, sat under a tarpaulin in the garage bay nearest me, the glint of new hyperthrusters just poking out from underneath. On the back wall of the other stall ran a long workbench with four meters of viewscreen mounted on the wall above it.

Since Quynn's promotion to director, we'd decided to upgrade from the tiny one-stall garage to a double. It wasn't that we needed another vehicle. We needed the double-stall garage because I often couldn't sleep. In the process of recovering Bastion's chip from a particularly violent Huginn Industries Intel Operative named Theo, he'd blurted out that all five of the companies were connected. They were his dying words. Words that echoed through my dreams and screamed through my nightmares, his face blank and dead. Because it was my fault. Just thinking of him put my stomach in knots. He'd been trying to kill me, sure, but his blood was on my hands.

Maybe I was obsessed. Quynn looked at me sometimes like I was, but humored me, even helped when they could. The five companies of Jayu City were completely independent as far as I knew. Each with its own culture, its own leadership, and its own products sold all over Earth Space. Five roughly equal titans of industry competing nonstop for market share across the galaxy.

Three months ago, I broke into the apartment of an R&D director for Kotega Systems. I relieved her of a prototype for a new, hyper-compressed mini data drive, just like I was hired to do. I also plugged into her personal workstation while I was there and downloaded a host of Kotega data which I was not hired to take. Later that month, I spent four days infiltrating a Huginn Industries physical therapy center to coax corporate secrets out of a lab technician. I also lifted his apartment key, visited his empty home, and relieved him of some data. I'd done a couple of dozen officially sanctioned jobs for Corto Corporation in the time since Theo died, and I'd downloaded some very unofficial data on almost each one of them.

There were no official Corto regulations against this. No laws in Jayu City at all, let alone against theft. I knew of at least three Intel Operatives who always took small souvenirs from each job. The behavior was frowned upon, though. Unprofessional. Those three would never get promoted. I wanted to be the Cloak of Corto one day, so I was keeping this on the down low. I couldn't stop, though, not if I ever wanted to silence Theo's voice ringing around in my dreams.

Only two things sat on the workbench in front of that enormous screen. A small speaker and a computer even older than the one Josephine had been using. I crossed the half-empty shelves lining the wall of my garage and turned the antique on.

"Time to work, Bastion," I said aloud.

"All work and no play," Bastion replied from the speaker.

"What?"

"Sorry. From an Earth movie several centuries old."

"The things you get up to when Quynn and I need some alone time."

The old computer booted up, along with the extra-wide viewscreen, and it started to display my work. Our work. The four meters of viewscreen were divided evenly into five sections: Nexus Neuronics, Corto Corporation, Huginn Industries, Toinette Holdings, and Kotega Systems. The five companies. Pictures and clickable dossiers of CEOs, CFOs, CTOs, and every other C-suite executive ran across the top of the sections. Dozens of smaller pictures of vice presidents took up most of the rest of the space. The section for Toinette was a little sparse compared to the other four, but that was about to change. "Anything I missed?"

"Nothing important," I said as I watched all the pictures resolve in their places, hoping some connection would jump out at me that hadn't before. "Quynn is going to that *Dregs of Osiris* tournament next weekend. They're pretty excited."

"Are you going with them?"

"No," I said. "Not my scene. I'll either be working or—"

"Holding down the couch. I'm aware of your two modes."

"Funny," I said. I bent down and picked up the end of a data cable that sat on the floor next to the computer, bright blue against the gray concrete. "You ready?"

"I am."

I plugged the cable into a wall socket, and the machine was online, which meant Bastion was in control. Despite primarily existing on a neural interface chip I kept on my person at all times, Bastion was able to freely move about the Net so long as I was connected. So I made sure to stay connected at all times, going so far as to install a special antenna in this new garage so it wouldn't act like a Faraday Cage. However, I didn't want this particular computer connected unless I knew it had Bastion's full attention. He could block any hack or attack, so he said, but only if he was watching for it.

I pulled the little data drive out of my shoulder and plugged it into the front of the old computer. After a few seconds, I said, "What did we get?"

"There's a lot."

"Good a lot?"

"A great deal more than I would have anticipated from the preacher. I don't know if it is good or bad yet."

"We need to add a dotted line between Josephine and Gustin."

After a few moments of silence, Bastion said, "Agreed. Though she may just be trying to get under your skin."

"That's why it's dotted. That she even knew to give me that name is terrifying enough."

I looked across the screen, sweeping my gaze back and forth several times, lingering on Dr. Ariela Corto, CEO of Corto Corporation, wondering when she was going to call in one of her infinite chits. Thus far, there were no lines connecting any one company to another. No VPs of Kotega working or dining or golfing with VPs of Huginn.

No secret emails or buried family ties. Each company was a silo operating independently of the others. But Theo's dying words kept ringing in my ears. *You're going to lose. You're not even playing the same game as me. You're blind, don't even see how everything is connected. How the five companies are—* And then sparks blew out of his head as his eyes rolled.

Those words could have been pure manipulation. We'd been fighting, brawling across the deck of his father's ship, and those words could have just been another tactic. He could have been lying. He could have been telling what he thought was the truth, but someone else's lie. The possibilities abounded, and Bastion and Quynn and I had gone over them in steady rotation. But something about it felt true. There was more to Theo's words, we just needed to find it.

"Something is wrong," Bastion said.

"Wrong?" I asked.

"This data is corrupted. Or cleverly encrypted."

"What do you mean? What are you seeing?"

"I'm still trying to make sense of it."

That didn't bode well. Bastion had shown that he could process information and ideas faster than anyone or any computer I'd ever known. In mid-conversation, he would find information from the Net and put it on my display to help me. I no longer carried a dictionary of lock algorithms on me since Bastion could figure out any lock much faster. His grasp of the physical world was often lacking, but software was never confusing to him.

"I am eighty-eight percent certain this is encryption. Pieces of data are linked together that do not belong, but the pattern is not entirely random as it would be if the data was corrupted. I think it is designed to look like corruption, however."

"Can you decrypt it?"

"I can decrypt anything; the issue is how long it will take me. Given the volume of data here and the resources at my disposal, it would take me three hundred and twenty-two years, seven months, and a few days to complete the decryption."

"Mother of Corto," I whispered. "What did we miss?"

"Miss?" Bastion asked.

"In our research. In the office and that server room. How did we not know the data would be encrypted like that?"

"Neither you nor Hessod nor even your Cloak are perfect."

"No, but this is a big miss. A big waste of a job that took months of planning."

"You did retrieve the data," Bastion said. "It could be as simple as retrieving a decryption key."

"When is it ever as simple as that?" Bastion didn't say anything in reply.

I rubbed my temples, my brain too fried to consider my next steps. Maybe Hessod would have some ideas.

"Are you alright?" Bastion asked.

"I need sleep. And a shower."

"Do you enjoy sleep?"

"What?" I asked.

"Do you enjoy sleep? I've been meaning to ask for a while. What does it feel like?"

I rolled that question around in my head for a while before saying, "In some ways, it feels like shutting off the world. But there are dreams, or slightly waking when Quynn rolls or if I need to pee in the middle of the night. Time seems to pass in an instant, and then I awake refreshed, with the memories of my dreams falling out of my head in moments."

"Thank you," Bastion finally said after a long silence. "While cryptic, that clarifies somewhat the accounts I've read on the Net. Something to ponder."

"Need anything else?" I asked.

"No. Good night, Elise."

"Good night, Bastion."

Chapter Four

THE ELEVATOR DOORS OPENED ONTO the floor of the Intel offices for Corto Corporation, and I instinctively turned right. Only then did I remember, again, that our offices were to the left of the elevators now. The entire office had relocated to a different building as part of the Hermes Protocol several months ago when Bastion's chip was stolen from our vault, but the muscle memory still told me to go right. I turned around, walked back past the elevators, and up to the black glass doors. My display told me SCAN IN PROGRESS as a little sensor above the doors scanned me for the encrypted passkey embedded in my neck that was changed out every week. A lot of people put their passkeys in their mods, but I didn't like wearing my work limbs unless I was on a job, so neck it was. I was in my everyday limbs, wearing a loose-fitting shirt and stretchy pants. I was just here to debrief, after all. After several seconds, the doors silently slid open.

I still wasn't used to the new layout, with a second set of black glass doors that only opened once I stepped in and the doors behind me closed. From there, the office was shaped like a T, a long hallway twenty meters wide stretched on 50 meters before me, lined on both sides with waist-high cubicle walls. Intel Analysts sat in half the cubicles, silently intent at their workstations or having animated comms discussions with their Operatives.

As I got to the T-junction and the wall of windows in front of me, the morning sun glimmering against the sea of skyscrapers outside, I glanced to my left, into Gustin's corner office. He wasn't there, though I didn't know what I would have done if I'd seen him. *Be sure to thank Gustin for sending a pretty one* was still ringing in my head. I couldn't help but wonder if my manager was up to something. My debrief with him was in less than an hour, so I would find out soon enough.

For now, I took a right, past a few more rows of cubicles before I found Hessod's. My analyst was sitting there, typing away rapidly at his workstation, an oversized, orange, fizzy drink taking a prominent spot on his desk. Hessod was a big man. Tall, round, with hands bigger than my head. He was usually a jovial man, too, with a personality and laugh that dwarfed his body. Most of his desk ornamentation had made the move from the old office: pictures of his daughter, now almost twelve. A few of her drawings from when she was younger. Detailed miniature models of some of Corto Corporation's spaceships. There were no pictures of his wife. Soon-to-be ex-wife, I should say. The entire divorce had made him seem smaller, somehow.

"Good morning, Hessod," I said as I approached.

"Hey," he said without looking at me. He clacked away at his workstation for another dozen seconds before tapping the screen with a flourish and turning his attention to me. "How did it go?"

"Josephine's private server room didn't take that decryption key," I said, taking a seat next to his desk and quirking an eyebrow so he knew I was throwing him an accusation. I was smirking, though.

"So that key just opened the office?"

"It also accessed the servers, like you said."

"But not the door to the servers," Hessod said, his eyes darting as he thought. "You obviously got in or you would have led with that."

"I did," I said. "Can you guess how?"

"Would you just tell him?" Bastion piped up.

"Is there broken glass all over the office?" Hessod asked.

"No, I roped some kid into helping me," I told Hessod about Valdo and the kid's little reboot workaround. "I will never understand Toinette people," Hessod said. "Just as much access to technology as we have, and they embrace it most of the time. But then some of them go and use physical keys and ancient workstations to lock their doors."

"Maybe they know something we don't know," I said. "A state-of-the-art locking mechanism, I can deal with. I was clueless with that old computer."

"I could have helped you if you'd asked," Bastion said.

"Nearly foiled by Luddites. I'm surprised your little voice didn't help you."

I chuckled a little. Yes, Hessod knew about Bastion. "Nearly foiled." I leaned in closer and lowered my voice. "Or maybe entirely. The data is encrypted. All of it. Unreadable."

Hessod's face scrunched up, his eyes looking down and darting around like he was searching for an answer on the floor. He knew about my own data collection. Without my little side project, there would have been no reason for me to know anything about the data. He asked, "Encrypted? From both of you?"

I nodded my head.

"Encrypted how?"

I shrugged as a litany of technical details I didn't understand appeared on my display. Bastion obviously understood how the data was encrypted. I waved the details away and said to Hessod, "I'll send you what I have."

Hessod smiled briefly before his expression changed to confusion. Then concern. He said, "Better not. You shouldn't know, so I shouldn't know. I'm sure somebody else with a better title will figure it out soon enough."

"True, but they won't tell me anything."

Hessod sighed and crossed his arms, glancing sideways at the pictures of his daughter. "I can't. Not with this divorce. Zora is trying to take custody. I can't take the chance of doing anything off-book. I'm sorry."

"Come on," I said. "It's not like we have laws around—"

"No," Hessod interrupted. "We don't, but if the tribunal sees that kind of work, the kind of work you do, as an unnecessary danger for someone raising a child…I can't take that chance."

I opened my mouth to protest more, but Hessod held up a hand and said, "Have you thought about the Offworld Relay?"

I gave him a look that plainly said I had not. And I felt like an absolute fool. It was so obvious, right there all this time. All of the data that flowed to and from this planet to the rest of Earth Space went through the single, towering Offworld Relay stationed out on Cirilla Island, a little piece of land that was otherwise a giant resort. All of the data, including everything from the five companies of Jayu City.

"Why did I not think of that?" Bastion said in my ear.

"Neither of us did," I whispered. "But that makes so much sense. One relay. Five companies doing business across all Earth Space. It's a natural convergence."

"I don't know if there's anything natural about it," Hessod said.

"The security and technology there will be the absolute best, I'm certain," Bastion said.

It was my turn to sigh. I gave my analyst and friend a warm smile. "The Relay will be a tough job. I could really use you."

"Really?" Hessod said. "Don't you have your new little friend riding along?"

"I am not little," Bastion said in my ear. "I am currently accessing over three thousand servers across Jayu City."

"I do," I said. "Who apparently takes offense to the size comment. But we still haven't found any connections. You have certain... access privileges."

Hessod shook his head vigorously. "No way. I can't risk it. The tribunal can access everything I do, see everything. I'm sorry."

"They can always do that," I said. "They can see all of my Net traffic, too."

"But you're not fighting for custody," Hessod spat.

"What can you do?" I asked. The question came out brusquer than I'd intended, more like an accusation than an actual inquiry.

"Elise," Gustin hollered from the vicinity of his office before I had a chance to apologize.

I stood and turned toward the sound. There he was, leaning out of his office door. About my height, with a small gut and a shade paler skin than me, he was in a bright turquoise button-up shirt, a floral sport coat to match, and black slacks. His visible mods were low-end and minimal, though I'd heard that he had much better equipment when he was an Operative. Once I saw him, he beckoned quickly with one hand and retreated into the office. I turned back to Hessod, but he was facing his screen, a comically large pair of headphones over his ears, the tinny sound of some techno music drowning out the world.

Sparks. I would need to apologize to him later. This debriefing couldn't wait. I hurried to Gustin's office, several analysts' eyes on me after he'd called my name like that. I gave a few of them smiles, though none were returned. I think they were still sore with me for my involvement in the office relocation. But hey, I wasn't the one who broke into the old vault.

I entered Gustin's office unceremoniously and fell into a chair before Gustin had offered it. If he wanted to yell at me like a child in a playroom, I could abuse his furniture like one.

"I see you uploaded the data last night," Gustin said, scrolling and tapping on his own AR display. I couldn't see what he was seeing, of course, but I recognized the gestures.

"I did," I said.

"Quite a bit there." He didn't say it like a compliment, but coldly. He was building up to something, I was sure.

"Oh?" I was playing dumb. "I've got a team of three analysts still going over all of it."

"Our own analysts are looking at it? Not our client's?"

Gustin looked directly at me, but only for a moment before his gaze softened back into AR. "This job is internal. So yes, our analysts. Way more data than we anticipated."

I noticed he hadn't mentioned the encryption. If our analysts were looking at it, there was no way he didn't already know. But he wasn't telling me. "Lots of data is good, right?"

"Depends on what we find." Gustin made a big swiping motion with one hand, and his eyes settled on me again. "Any issues? Anything I need to know about?"

"A little issue getting into Josephine's server room, but nothing I couldn't handle."

"Solomon said there was someone else on the floor?"

My stomach leaped into my throat for a second, Josephine's intense gaze and parting words still fresh. But then I remembered Valdo.

"Just a kid," I said. "A computer tech. Didn't know who I was or what I was doing. Easily intimidated."

"You get a name for this kid?" I shook my head. No sense in getting the kid in trouble. Gustin could be dogged in pursuing possible leaks. Intel Operatives were experts at extracting data and goods from other boroughs. It was just as easy to plant false data, to make life difficult for someone who knew too much about our operations, no matter which company they worked for. I didn't want that for Valdo.

"Let's hope you're right, then," he said. Gustin looked over my shoulder, outside his office, and nodded his head at someone. I didn't have time to turn before his office door opened, and Nox stepped inside. Nox was in his usual outfit: a white sweater that looked three sizes too big even though the sleeves stopped midway down his forearms. White pants that were equally baggy, the crotch connecting halfway down his thighs, and a dozen centimeters of his dark skin showing before the stark white socks and shoes. No color, just the intense contrast with his skin tone.

"Hey, G!" Nox said to Gustin as he strode in with a swagger. "You told her yet?"

"Told me what?" I asked. Suddenly I felt trapped, outmaneuvered. The two people I suspected of betraying me were in the same room, very chummy with each other, and my exit was blocked. Lots of witnesses, though. The entire office. I took a deep breath and counted to three.

"Not yet," Gustin said. "I wanted you in here first."

"Told me what?" I repeated.

"Detox, E," Nox said, like we were best friends. Detox? I could never understand him. "It's good news."

"Elise," Gustin said. "You have your sights set on becoming Cloak of Corto one day, right?"

"Of course," I said and sat up straighter, suddenly feeling a fool for abusing Gustin's chair.

"Well," Gustin continued, "there are certain things you need to do.

Boxes to check."

"Safecracking, lockpicking, hacking, pickpocketing, so on and so on," I said. "I know my pickpocketing could use some work, but there's nobody better in the office at bypassing security systems."

"You have to *teach.*"

"Teach?" I glanced at Nox, who was grinning like the fool kid he was.

"It's past time you take an apprentice," Gustin said. "Almost two years past time, to be exact."

That got me on my feet. "An apprentice? You know I work best alone."

"You worked with two other operatives last night, and you just said the job went smoothly," Gustin said.

"As fresh-pressed carbon polymer," Nox chimed in.

Gustin clapped his hands and pointed to Nox, still looking at me. "There you go! You can be a team player. The Cloak of Corto is part of a team, not a solo act."

"Since when does teaching my skills qualify me for Cloak of Corto?"

"Do you know the best way anyone proves themselves at any skill?" Gustin asked, but he didn't wait for a response. "Teach that skill. Take what you've learned, what you've practiced, and distill it. If you can pass it on, then that proves just how skilled you really are."

I recalled my time as an apprentice, my own impatience and unwillingness to learn. I hadn't been the easiest apprentice. I always thought I knew better, knew the best escape routes, or was hip to the newest locking tech. My mentor, he, well… Solomon was my primary teacher once I was done as an apprentice. He took me under his wing, a strange move for him, but I've been forever grateful. When he was named Cloak of Corto, I couldn't have been prouder of anyone.

I opened my mouth to protest, but nothing came out. I wanted Gustin to be wrong, but he wasn't. I also knew it was part of the job, just a part that I'd hoped I could skip.

"Nox is going to be your apprentice," Gustin said. "Starting now. For the next six months, he goes where you go. Every job. Every research trip. Every jaunt you take down into The Mist to gear up. You teach him what you know, and you'll be that much closer to Cloak."

"The best learning from the best," Nox said in a sing-song voice. "Maybe I can teach you a thing or two along the way!"

Nox was smiling like a madman, glancing back and forth between me and Gustin. Gustin was smiling, too, an expression I wasn't used to seeing. They shared a silent exchange like they were friends. Like they were working together. Like Gustin has just hitched me to his little spy. *Be sure to thank Gustin for sending a pretty one.*

Maybe Gustin was tethering me to his own eyes and ears, his own spy.

"This will make our personal inquiries more complicated," Bastion said in my comms. His words were an understatement. I still didn't have any connections between the five companies, but how was I going to keep gathering my own intelligence with this obnoxious little man on my hip?

"Well?" Gustin said.

"Are you asking me if I want to do this? If I want an apprentice?"

Gustin's smile faded. "It would make everything easier if you did. This is happening either way."

"This is going to be better than a neuro-sync rave!" Nox said, extending his arms like he was going to hug me. I took a step back from him, and his face fell.

"Elise," Gustin grumbled. "This will be a much better experience for both of you if you can at least be civil."

I threw my hands up. "I'm civil. Perfectly civil. I don't know what a neuro-sync rave is, but I'm civil. We're just not at the hugging stage."

Nox started to say, "It's—"

"I don't actually want to know," I said.

"Touchy, touchy," Nox said and extended a hand toward me. "This more your speed?"

I took Nox's offered hand and shook it. "It is."

I looked at Gustin again, who looked entirely too pleased with himself. I wasn't sure what he was playing at, what he was doing contacting Josephine, or if he even was. If I confronted him without any proof and he was conspiring with an agent of Toinette Holdings or any other company, he would slap me down lower than Nox and bury me in a back corner of the office. If I made the accusation and was wrong, I might not even work in

Intel after that. I had to dig into this, to get proof one way or another. And for now, that meant playing his game.

"Welcome to the team, apprentice," I said.

Impossibly, Nox's smile grew even wider.

"Excellent!" Gustin said and then his fingers were flying over an AR keyboard I couldn't see "And I have your first job for you. The data from last night, it was encrypted."

"Wait," Nox said. "We messed up?"

Gustin threw him a look that was somewhere between *shut up* and *aren't you precious*. Then he continued, "None of our preliminary research indicated this level of encryption, but our analysts are fairly certain there is a second decryption key like the one you used to download the data."

"Binary system," I said like Bastion and I hadn't discussed this on the ride to the office this morning. "Smart. And their closed system kept us from figuring it out ahead of time."

"Can somebody explain this to me?" Nox whined.

I ignored him. "What's our time frame?"

"How confident are you that nobody knows you were there?" Gustin asked.

"Not very," I said. Between literally running into Valdo and my encounter with Josephine and her oversized bodyguard, it was the least stealthy I'd been in a long time.

"Then we need to move quickly," Gustin said, rising from his chair. "We're already looking into possible targets for the second key. Hessod should know what we know soon."

"Understood," I said. Nox was looking back and forth between us in utter confusion. Without waiting, I left Gustin's office.

"That's it," Gustin said to Nox. "You're with Elise now. Go on."

"E and N!" Nox said once he jogged to catch up to me. "El and X. Elnox. No-ise. The newest, baddest operative pairing in Jayu City."

I had to give it to him, he had enthusiasm. His approach to language needed work, though.

"So what's first?" he asked. "Where do we start looking for this key?"

"I've already seen the key," I said.

"Why didn't you tell G?"

"Gustin oversees several dozen operatives. The details of each job aren't his to worry about. He needs to know I'm working on it. He'll want to know when it's done and if there were complications."

"Like we had to shuffle elevators."

"No," I said, stopping in the middle of the office to face him directly. "I mean like if Josephine had made one of us. If Toinette security had shown up. If something happened that compromised our office or our mission. Nobody cares about the stupid elevators."

"Sorry," Nox said.

I sighed. "Don't be sorry, just take in what I'm telling you. The quicker you learn, the quicker you'll be out from under my wing."

Nox nodded but didn't look happy about it.

I turned and kept walking. I sat down at Hessod's desk, leaving my new apprentice to stand there.

"New job," Hessod said as he was reading several large blocks of text on his screen.

"Vert has the second key," I said.

Hessod's head slowly turned toward me, one eyebrow cocked up. "And how do you know that?"

"Let's just say I have a very reliable source."

Hessod frowned but nodded. He probably thought I meant Bastion. I'd make sure he knew the full story later, but I didn't want Nox to know I'd seen Josephine and Vert face-to-face last night.

"That guy could pop my head off with one hand," Nox said. "Now we have to steal something from him?"

"You should tell him about the Targa Freehold job," Hessod said to me with a smirk.

"Or the Trumbo and Hilde Nexus job," I said.

"Ooh," Hessod said. "Or that thing with those twins and the space elevator."

"Mother of Corto," I said with a chuckle, watching Nox's eyes grow wider out of the corner of my eye. "That one about killed me twice."

"What?" Nox finally blurted out.

Hessod and I both laughed before I patted Nox's arm and said, "You've been my apprentice for five minutes. There will be plenty of time to tell you all my best stories."

"Why not now?" Nox asked.

"Because now," I said, "we need to track down our target, find out where he sleeps, eats, works. Where he likes to hang out and who his friends are."

"Isn't that what analysts are for?"

Hessod raised both eyebrows and turned back to his terminal.

"Would you like to explain this one to my apprentice?" I asked him.

"He's not *my* apprentice," Hessod said with false disdain. At least I knew it was false.

"Let's go, apprentice," I said, standing up and heading toward the doors without waiting.

"Did I say something wrong?" Nox asked as he caught up.

"Hessod is messing with you," I said. "But also yes. Operatives and analysts are a team. My job isn't just to act on the data he digs up but to help him before the job. Hessod is a wizard with research—"

"A wizard who sits in an office all day," Nox said with disgust.

I stopped and looked directly at my apprentice. "Now that kind of comment will get Hessod and every other analyst genuinely angry with you. What they do is critical. Hessod can find information from that terminal that would take me days to find on my own."

"I…" Nox started to say.

"What we do is hard," I said before he uttered another syllable. "But it would be impossible without analysts. Maybe I'm biased, but Hessod is the best. I would have been dead or discommended dozens of times without him. You'd be lucky to have someone half as good as him."

"I'm sorry," Nox whispered.

I let him wallow in his self-pity as we walked out of the offices and rode the elevator to the nearest landing pad. Once his regret started shifting to nervousness, I said, "You hungry?"

He looked at me like he was confused before he slowly nodded.

"Let's get some food. I'm buying since it's your first day as my underling. By the time we finish ordering, Hessod will probably have a lead we need to track down."

"Elise?" Nox asked as we stepped out onto the landing pad, wind whipping my hair and the loose t-shirt I was wearing. There were a few different flying cars on the pad, most of them Stryders, the biggest autonomous rideshare service in the city. Nox's confidence seemed to be steadily returning.

"Yeah?"

"If Gustin put me with you as some sort of punishment or payback, that's on him."

His words punched me in the gut. I thought it was just me who saw this pairing as a punishment, but if this neophyte could see it, if it was that obvious, was Gustin trying to make an example of me? If he really was in Josephine's pocket, what did such a public punishment mean?

Nox continued, "I know you two don't really get along. I'm just here to learn. And you're one of the best. A star. What's that old Earth saying? Something about hooking to a star?"

"Hitching your wagon to my star," I said. I smiled a little despite myself, despite still wondering exactly why he was hitched to *me*.

"Yeah, that sounds like it. I'm hitched to you, Star Girl. I just don't want you to see me as a punishment."

"I don't," I said. Which was true. I saw him as a potential spy for Gustin, but not punishment. Maybe all of this was some sort of punishment, though. I was a good Intel Operative. A great one, but I didn't prop up Gustin's ego or talk him up to anyone else. I didn't go that extra mile to get on his good side. And when he wasn't able to pin the Hermes Protocol on me a few months ago, I could tell it angered him. He didn't scream at me or punish me. He couldn't, but I could tell he wasn't happy about it. Maybe this was all part of his payback.

"Princely," Nox said, bouncing on the balls of his feet. "Princely. I'm glad we cleared that up. I'm excited about this."

"Gray BMW," Bastion said to the unasked question. "Thanks," I said to Bastion via text. "What do you make of all this? You think Gustin is trying to play me?"

"I think he is constantly trying to play everyone to his benefit. Whether he's particularly honing in on you is yet to be determined."

The door to the BMW swung up and open as Nox and I approached.

"What do you like to eat?" I asked Nox as I lowered myself into the car. He entered the other side and the doors swung down behind us.

"There's a new bistro down by the cliffs that is using this new hybrid breed of peppers I've wanted to try," Nox said.

"You like spicy food?" I said. The car hummed and shuddered slightly as it lifted off the landing pad.

Nox started to say, "I'm in mad deep for spicy—"

"Elise Corto-Intel," a vaguely familiar voice said over the car's speakers. Too loud. A second later, a hologram of Josephine Toinette-Deus appeared in the seat across from me, dressed in a gold suit, her legs crossed, hands steepled together.

"What in the—" I started.

"Is that—?" Nox stuttered.

"This is a recording," Josephine continued. "But the last thing you're going to see. You took something from me, something valuable and important. Your Corto associates should have known better than to get anywhere near me, and I have to remind them of that."

"Bastion," I texted. "What is happening? How is she—?"

"I don't know," Bastion said. "I don't have access to the car's systems."

"If there is anyone you love, call them now. I'll make sure Gustin knows why you crashed into The Mist."

"What?" Nox yelled, his eyes wide with terror.

The hologram blinked out along with every light, screen, and readout inside the car. And then the hum of the engines suddenly stopped. In an instant, the flying BMW was a falling BMW, and my apprentice and I were trapped inside.

Chapter Five

I WAS UP AGAINST THE back window in an instant, the heavy engine at the front of the car pointing the nose down toward The Mist hundreds of meters below. I dug in, the fingers of my everyday limbs poking through the faux leather as I hauled myself back down into the seat. I quickly pulled the seatbelt across my chest, buckled it, and reached down between my legs for the emergency ejector. Every car, no matter the make or model, had the same ejector design. Reach down, grab the handle, and pull. But the handle came away in my hands, the cables connected to the ejector mechanism cleanly sliced.

"Elise? You need to eject!" Bastion said in my ear.

"I know!" I yelled. "I need ideas, not stating the obvious!"

"I didn't say anything!" Nox yelled, his own hands scrabbling with his seat belt.

I yanked a panel off the door next to me, looking for the bright, red lever that would quick-release the door. Not in this car. I could see where the handle should have been, where it would connect, but there was no handle.

"Nox?" I yelled. I looked toward him and he'd had the same idea with the same result. Panel removed. No red handle.

"No good!" Nox said, panic writ large across his face.

"Can you do anything?" I asked Bastion aloud. No time for the discretion of text. "Override the thrusters?"

"Not before we meet the pavement below," Bastion said.

"I don't know how to override anything in this car," Nox said as though I'd asked him.

With the seatbelt still engaged, I turned and gave the window next to me a hard kick, the impact reverberating up into my biological pelvis. I tried again anyway. Three, four, five times. Not even a scratch. My everyday limbs weren't my work limbs. They weren't quite as strong, but they should have been sufficient to shatter glass. Whatever Josephine had done to this car, she'd been thorough.

"What about the pneumatics in your legs?" Nox asked. "Or some other Intel Operative gizmo you have hidden away?"

"Wrong limbs," I said. "I don't have any of my tools!"

I unlatched my seatbelt but held onto it. I spun completely in the seat and slammed both feet into the rear window while pulling on the straps. The tiniest of cracks appeared under my left heel, so I did it again. And again. And again. The crack was growing, along with another tiny one under my right heel.

"Two hundred meters to impact!" Bastion shouted.

I bashed my heels again and again, but there was no way I was going to get through that window in time. Even once I did, I didn't have any magnetic grapples or glide wings or anything to save me. I kicked again. Again. I swallowed hard and kept kicking, not knowing what else to do.

I pulled my legs up for another kick when suddenly the back window burst out. Tiny pebbles of glass whipped around me as the air suddenly became a whirling, seething presence in the car. Something gripped my ankle, and I was yanked out of the car through the now-open space. I barely had the presence of mind to let go of the seatbelt. Still falling and disoriented, hands were moving on me, turning me or moving around as I turned.

Then Nox's dark face was close to mine, his eyes intense, his hands on my shoulders. He yelled, "Hold on, Star Girl!"

I did as he said, not knowing what else to do, and his arms wrapped tightly around me. Then my vision was flooded with a glowing, sparkling magenta. The air suddenly wasn't whipping at my hair or clothes. Every sound seemed to deaden, though I could still see floor after floor of buildings whipping by. Then the buildings were gone, everything was just that blinding color, Nox's arms still around me.

A boom. Muted. It sounded far away, though the magenta grew brighter in the same instant. The air felt warm. And a moment later, our fall stopped. There was no slam into the ground, no splintering of bones or crushing of cybernetics, all of my internal organs knew we'd stopped falling, though the jolt had been cushioned immensely.

Then the magenta vanished. Sound and heat and the smells of burning metal and meat rushed in on me. Nox stood up, pulling me to my feet by my hands. We were standing amid the wreckage of the fallen car. A broken thruster was near my feet, blue flames flickering. Twisted pieces of metal and plastic ranging in sizes from pebbles to boulders were scattered around an area a dozen meters across. One person was helping another hobble away from the wreckage, both dressed in mismatched clothes and both bleeding. Three people were using blankets to try and put out the flames on a food stall, hollering to coordinate their efforts. Someone was screaming. Through the haze of heat and tendrils of smoke, I could see people running in all directions. Some toward the wreckage and some away. A young child, no more than ten, was on their knees and crying, a gash on their forehead sending a stream of blood down their face.

"Silent circuits," I whispered.

"We need to get out of here," Nox said, his hand on my wrist.

I wrenched free and said, "Call emergency services."

"What?" Nox said.

"On it," Bastion said at the same time. I didn't care who was calling, so long as someone was.

"Corto Corporation emergency services," a deep voice said in overly pleasant tones. "My name is Hendricks Corto-Support, he/him. With whom am I speaking?"

"There's been a crash," I said as I trotted over to the child, weaving through the wreckage. "A Stryder went down."

"I'm sorry," Hendricks said. "I didn't catch your name."

"That doesn't matter! There's been a crash!"

"This is emergency services for Corto Corporation. I need to verify your corporate citizenship. Your name, please?"

I swallowed a curse. "Elise Corto-Intel."

"Thank you," Hendricks said. "How can I assist you?"

"I already told you, there's been a crash!"

"Which building?" Hendricks asked.

"Next to Corto 88." I knelt in front of the child, putting a hand on their shoulder and looking them in the eye. They wore stained clothes, the shirt from Nexus and the pants from Toinette, both too big for them. Their hair was cut unevenly, by shaky hands. They didn't seem to register my presence.

"Next to Corto 88?" Hendricks asked. "Did the car crash into one of the neighboring buildings?"

"No," I said. "In the street."

"In The Mist?"

"Yes! In The Mist!" I yelled. Less than ten meters over my head, a dense fog blocked out everything above, ever-present down here at ground level. It blew in from the bay, stuck around like an unwelcome visitor, and made a clear separation between the corporations above and these people below, the people without companies. The Mistwalkers. I said, "There are people hurt, maybe dead. I can't even—"

"Are there any Corto Corporation citizens injured?"

"Elise, what are you doing?" Nox said, his voice still close behind me.

I looked my apprentice up and down. He seemed no worse for wear. I wasn't injured, either. I told Hendricks, "No, not down here."

"Is there any damage to Corto Corporation property?" Hendricks asked. "Any potential for damage to Corto Corporation property?"

I glanced around, but the lower levels of the buildings looked unaffected. "No, nothing like—"

"Then will you be paying for this visit from emergency services?" Hendricks asked without a trace of pity.

"Paying?" I asked. "People are hurt and dying. You have to…"

"This is Corto Corporation emergency services. Unless Corto Corporation citizens or property are in danger, then we have to know where to send the bill for our services."

"Fine!" I yelled, startling the child into finally seeing me. They looked terrified and then pointed to a large piece of rubble nearby. A bloody arm the same color as the child's was sticking out beneath it.

"Oh, Mother of Corto," Nox said.

"How much for the service?" I asked.

"Our basic emergency response package is a single emergency medical vehicle," Hendricks said, his voice suddenly chipper. "That comes with two medical technicians and a state-of-the-art mobile clinic. A single destination to assess is eighty thousand Corto credits, plus reimbursement for supplies used, and a twenty percent surcharge for any trip below thirty meters in altitude."

That was more than I made in a year. Definitely more than Quynn and I had in savings. There was just no way I could do that.

"Our basic plus service," Hendricks continued, "includes—"

I double-tapped my right earlobe, disconnecting the call. I looked at the child, moving my face between theirs and the arm they were staring at. "Are you okay?"

The child looked at me, confused, and blinked. "Are you hurt?" I asked.

The child pointed to the gash on their head. Of course they hurt there. Come on, Elise.

"Anywhere else?"

The child shook their head.

"Stay right here, okay?"

The child blinked again but said nothing. That would have to do. I turned around and grabbed the wrist of the arm poking out from the wreckage. It felt biological, so I felt for a pulse. I didn't find one.

"If that arm is badly damaged, it could impede blood flow," Bastion said. "The person could possibly be alive underneath."

There really didn't look like enough room for a living person to be under there, but I had to try.

"Nox!" I yelled. "Help me."

Nox was by my side in an instant, but he stood there looking dumbfounded. "Help you what?"

"Lift this," I said, putting my hands under the charred metal hunk pinning that arm to the ground.

"Are you kidding? These mods are—"

I let go of the rubble and stood, my face only a couple of centimeters from his ear. "You see that child? Staring at that arm? What if that was your parent under there?"

Nox swallowed hard, his throat wobbling.

"Help. Me."

Nox nodded slightly, and we both put our hands under the wreckage and lifted. It was terribly heavy, but soon three strangers joined us, ran to us, and our combined modded limbs were lifting it. I didn't even have a chance to look underneath before I heard the child scream behind me. I looked to them, still holding the twisted chunk of BMW in my hands, to see the child had gone pale, still staring at what we'd revealed. Without a word, we set it back down.

I knelt back down in front of the child. "Is there anyone you can call? Anywhere you can go?"

A big, pale hand was suddenly on the child's shoulder. I looked up to see a thin figure a in loose-fitting, patchwork dress glaring down at me. One of the Mistwalkers who'd help lift the rubble. They said, "Not with you, Corto. You've done enough."

"I wasn't flying the car, I didn't—"

The tall figure spat, barely missing my foot. The child leaned in close to this new person as I stood. Still, the child stared at the lifeless arm on the ground.

"I'm sorry," I said. "I will find the person responsible. I'll make sure—"

"Nothing you do will help us. Will help her," the pale person said, and then picked the child up and hurried off.

I watched them go for a few moments, weaving through the street vendors and crowds that were quickly dispersing. What had I gotten myself into? Who was this Josephine, really? She had to have known this kind of carnage could ensue, sending a Stryder into The Mist. I felt guilty, yet again, for a death. Probably more than one. I turned back to the crash site, looking for anyone else that could need help, but the Mistwalkers had quickly cleared out. The whines of thrusters started as a whisper then, up above, muted by The Mist.

"What just happened?" Nox asked. He looked horrified, standing there, his immaculate suit stained in dirt and soot, eyes wide and taking in the wreckage all around.

"Josephine happened," I said. "But why?"

"Why?" I said. "We stole from her."

"You steal from all sorts of people."

"You'll find people take that differently."

"It's just our job, though."

"There's no convincing everyone of that."

"It's just our job," Nox repeated, no emotion in his voice, unblinking.

I grabbed him by the shoulders and shook to break his stare. He finally blinked and looked at me. I said, "This isn't normal, none of it. It's terrible, and it's always a possibility with what we do."

"So Josephine," Nox whispered, tears gathering in his eyes. "She's going to kill us? She's crazy?" "Don't throw that word around. She's seemed perfectly sane so far, just far more dangerous than we'd anticipated." Whoever was involved, this had nearly killed Nox, too. He certainly wasn't anyone's plant, and he at least deserved this nugget of truth. "She's not after you. She saw my face."

Nox's eyes widened. "It wasn't some kid you saw up by her office, was it?"

"It was, first. I ran into her and Vert on my way out."

His eyes grew even larger. "And you're still pulling air." He looked back out over the wreckage. "Mother of Corto."

"It's not normally like this," I said.

"How did she drop a Stryder like that?"

"Good question," I said, still scanning the wreckage as half a dozen vehicles descended from The Mist, thrusters swirling vapor and whipping the scattered flames. They each bore the Stryder logo, but they weren't passenger cars. They looked more like construction vehicles. Two had large beds with high walls. Two had huge, articulated arms folded down and ready for use. The last two had four doors for the passenger cabin, but behind that cabin was a box with dozens of small doors on it, compartments for equipment, certainly. I continued, "She obviously is a skilled hacker or knows someone with skill. Even scarier, she knew exactly where I was and when."

"What kind of preacher knows all that?"

"That, my apprentice, is the real question."

More than a dozen people in Stryder uniforms piled out of the vehicles once they landed, all outfitted with industrial-grade mods. They doused flames with chemical powders and picked up small debris. The articulated arms unfolded, moving and clearing away the wreckage with practiced efficiency. Two Stryder employees were walking every square meter of the crash site, surely scanning everything for their lawyers.

"Should we help them?" Nox asked, his tone truly unsure of how I would answer.

Before I got the chance, a familiar figure emerged through the smoke. Heavily armored. Powerful. Vert Toinette-Deus was taking long strides, looking over the scene as he walked. I grabbed Nox by the shoulders and pushed the two of us down behind the wreckage we'd just lifted.

"It's The Hurt!" Nox whispered.

"Here to make sure I'm actually dead, I'm sure," I said.

"We should get out of here," Bastion said. "You will not survive an encounter with that man."

Still, I stared, looking for survivors and watching Vert move around the bulk of the wreckage. He ignored commands from the much smaller Stryder workers, who were obviously not willing to do more than politely ask Vert to move away. The big man stared at the largest chunk of wreckage for several seconds before touching the side of his head. Nanobots quickly formed a skull-like mask over his face, and then he sauntered into the still-smoldering rubble. He threw pieces of pavement and ruined car around like they weighed nothing.

I knew I should run, should put as much distance between myself and Josephine's muscle as possible, but that child's scream was locked in my brain. I kept looking for someone I could help, and my eyes kept coming back to that child's fallen parent, the limp arm only centimeters away from me. Josephine had attacked me. Because I stole from her. Because I was too slow and she saw me. This was my fault.

"Should I call a Stryder?" Nox whispered. Half a laugh escaped my lips before I could help it.

"Sorry," Nox said. "I didn't mean—"

"It's fine," I said. "But even if I was okay getting back into one right now, they don't do pickups down here."

"Good thing I called for help," Bastion said in my ear. "Help?" I whispered.

"Elise!" Hessod whispered from behind me. "Thank Corto you're okay."

Nox and I both turned, and Hessod was kneeling a meter away, his car hovering another dozen meters back. His face flitted between worry and awe. He sat behind a desk for a living. He'd told me many times he wasn't cut out for fieldwork, and that was written plainly on his face. He swept a shaky hand toward his too-tiny car. For a man who relished his size, his love for compact flyers always surprised me.

"Come on," Hessod said, waving us over and running back to his car.

I looked back again. Fire and smoke. Wreckage everywhere. Vert tossing aside pieces of the broken car, looking for signs of my body. Stryder employees cleaning up their mess. I saw a flash out of the corner of my eye. Copper-colored, and I flinched, but Roxy wasn't there. It wasn't one of her coppery, spider-like, bladed limbs coming at me. Just flames reflecting off of a scrap of metal. Roxy wasn't here. She was an assassin who nearly killed me twice. I'd been looking over my shoulder for her ever since, whether consciously or not.

Nox's hand was on my elbow then. Gently. "We're as useless down here as wheels on a car."

I gritted my teeth and then nodded sharply. Despite his weird metaphor, he was right. There was nothing either of us could do. But Josephine was going to pay for this. I could do something about that.

"Hessod flies his own car?" Nox whispered as we moved toward said car, staying low and out of Vert's sight.

I just nodded and said nothing.

Nox looked half-terrified, but he climbed into the back seat as I climbed into the passenger side.

"Are you okay?" Hessod asked before I'd even closed the door. He was sweating and looked pale, his eyes focused intently on me.

"I'm okay," I said. "Thanks to my apprentice back there."

"Thank Corto," Hessod said, but I could tell his mind was elsewhere. "What happened?"

"I'll tell you all about it later," I said and pointed at Vert. "For now, we need to follow that man out of here once he's done searching.

"Follow him?" Hessod sputtered. "You were just in a crash. Shouldn't you be going to a clinic or—?"

"That's our target," Nox said. "Vert 'The Hurt' Toinette-Deus."

"Did you both hit your heads?" Hessod half yelled. "That man could kill all three of us without breaking a sweat. Silent circuits, he's probably so modded he doesn't even sweat anymore. And in case you had forgotten, I'm not an operative. I've taken the tests. The psych evaluations. You can follow him all you want, summon your bike and ride off—"

"He's starting to leave," Nox said.

"No time, Hessod," I said, watching Vert touch his metal ear and walk back in the direction he'd come from.

"I don't do this," Hessod was practically whimpering. "I sit in my chair and gather information and—"

"Hessod!" I grabbed my analyst's face with both hands and looked him straight in the eyes. "I will not let anything happen to you. We're going to ascend out of The Mist and then follow Vert to his next location. From a reasonable distance. Then I'm getting out and you are going home."

"I'm getting out with you," Nox said.

"This isn't up for—"

"He's our target. I'm your apprentice. I'm with you."

I growled, frustrated with everyone in this car, but I didn't have time to keep arguing. "Fine! Nox stays with me. You drop us off and go home."

Hessod was working his jaw, his eyes wide, but he finally nodded. Then he took a deep, shaky breath and the little car started to ascend through The Mist.

"We're following the hall-of-fame fighter to his secret lair," Nox said. "Then what? We going to swipe us a key?"

"Maybe," I said. "We don't have a lot of time, even less with Josephine trying to kill me. But we need to do this right so Vert doesn't kill us both."

"Then what's the plan?" Hessod asked. In almost the same moment, another vehicle lifted out of The Mist a few dozen meters ahead of us, already on a trajectory out of the Corto Corporation borough.

"For now," I said and pointed at that vehicle. "We follow that. Try to keep about a quarter kilometer back. Drive normally, but don't lose him."

"And then?" Nox asked.

"I do what I do so well," I said. "I wing it."

"Mother of Corto," Hessod whispered.

Chapter Six

"NOT SO CLOSE," I SAID to Hessod. "As long as we can see him, we're close enough."

Hessod mumbled something incoherent and slowed a little, staying just to the right of a main flood of traffic moving through the Huginn Industries borough and on to the Toinette Holdings borough. Thus far, Vert hadn't been flying like he suspected anything. No erratic steering or sudden changes in altitude. It looked like he was just going from one place to another.

"Hey," I whispered to Hessod. "I'm sorry." Hessod said nothing, not even glancing at me.

"I shouldn't have pushed like I did back at the office."

"You're not the only one going through things, Elise," he said.

"I know. You're right. I'm sorry."

"Something I should know?" Nox asked.

"No," Hessod and I said, rather forcefully, at the same time.

We rode along for a few minutes in silence, Hessod focused on following Vert.

"Is it always like this?" Nox asked. "People trying to kill you just because you were doing your job?"

"No," I said. "This is extraordinary."

"Not so extraordinary," Bastion said as Hessod threw me a meaningful glance. Okay, there was that one other time. That didn't make it a pattern.

I turned partway in my seat so I could face Nox and change the subject. "What was that back in the Stryder? That purplish light?"

Nox smirked. "What? You aren't up on all the latest tech?"

I closed my eyes and counted to three. Hopefully, he didn't see my eyes roll with each number. "It's not a competition. What was it?"

"Anti-inertial field," Nox said like he'd been the one to invent it. "Just had it installed last week. I have a friend over at Cyber who hooked me up. Only the third one installed."

"What does it do?" Hessod asked.

"It…" Nox said, his confidence flagging. "Absorbs inertia."

"Oh, is that was anti-inertial means?" Hessod said with a massive dose of sarcasm.

"Is that even possible?" I asked my analyst with a smirk.

He glanced at me, smiled himself, and said, "Doesn't seem like it."

"That's not really how physics work, right?"

"Don't think so."

"Hey!" Nox said in an open-mouthed protest. "It worked, didn't it? We were in freefall, and this little baby absorbed the impact. And the impact of that exploding Stryder!"

I looked straight at him and smiled. "I know."

"You know?" Nox stammered, and then his incredulity melted. "You know. You two were messing with me."

"You *are* the new guy," Hessod said, the nerves still apparent in his voice.

Nox shook his head and looked out the window with a huff. "You would be a splatter on the street without me. Without this."

"And I thank you for that," I said. When he didn't respond, I reached back and put a hand on his knee. He turned to face me.

"I mean it," I said. "Thank you."

"Gotta watch out for my teacher. I got you, Star Girl."

"Star Girl?" Hessod asked.

"Yeah," Nox said. "Because she's a—"

"Don't say it," I said, slumping back into my seat and training my eyes on Vert's vehicle.

"—superstar."

"Sparks," I whispered.

"Is that right?" Hessod said. His laugh was barely suppressed.

"Pretty good nickname, right?" Nox asked with far too much pride in his voice.

"Sure," Hessod said to Nox. "I guess that makes you Star Girl Junior."

"What?" Nox said in a pitch two octaves higher than he normally spoke. "No, that's not—"

"He's descending," I said, watching the thrusters on Vert's car simmer down and the vehicle shed altitude.

"What do I do?" Hessod asked.

"Stay with him," I said. "Keep back, though."

"Where are we?" Nox asked as he craned his neck around to look.

"Closing in on the docks in Toinette," I said. Jayu City occupied all of Drakon Bay, named for how it was shaped like the head of an enormous dragon. The bay was the mouth and each corporation had the same access to the shipping and receiving that happened there. Originally built for all the mining that happened on Little Sekmet Settlement, the docks were repurposed when technological advances rendered the mines worthless.

Now the docks were used to receive the various natural resources harvested around the planet and to ship out items the rest of the planet needed to live in the modern era. Over two billion people lived on Little Sekhmet Settlement and more than half lived in Jayu City. The people in the villages and towns elsewhere wanted viewscreens and cybernetic mods and luxury cars just as much as we did here. Despite the incredible advancements in space travel and cold fusion engines, travel by sea was still the most cost-effective way to ship goods on-planet.

Now Vert's car was descending toward the docks, The Mist falling away, held back a kilometer from the docks by the persistent sea winds that swept across the bay. When the shoreline came into view, I told Hessod, "Hold here."

Hessod hit his brakes a little too hard, and another vehicle blared their horn as they dodged around us. "Sorry!" he yelled to the passing vehicle.

Then quieter, to those of us in the car with him, "Sorry."

I didn't take my eyes off the twinkles of Vert's thrusters, however, as they descended toward one of the medium-sized warehouses right on the docks.

"What is that?" I said. "What is what?" Nox said.

In my display, the distant outline of the building lit up yellow and Bastion said, "One of Toinette Holdings' deep-sea maintenance facilities. They coordinate shipping and receiving parts for vessels that dive deeper than ten kilometers. Designation Toinette DS Warehouse Four."

I repeated the name aloud and then told Hessod, "Set us down here."

"Here?" Nox asked. "We're still half a kilometer away. How did you even see which building we're going to?"

"Maybe you're not the only one with really great tech," I said.

Hessod started to lower his car to the street and said, "You know you're not in your work limbs, right?"

I glanced down at the flesh-colored limbs. The t-shirt and fashionably patched denim. Everything was covered in grime from the crash. I had, in fact, forgotten that I wasn't equipped for work. Too late now. "You have a better lead on this guy?"

Hessod frowned. Then he continued moving the car down to the street, landing moments later with a gentle shudder.

"Hessod," I said with my hand already on the door handle. "Find me any connections you can between Vert and that building. The company that runs it, friends or family he has there, anything."

Hessod nodded and said, "Don't do anything stupid."

"Nox," I said, giving Hessod a little grin. "Stay with me. Follow my lead. If I tell you to do something, don't ask why or argue, just do it. You can ask me why tomorrow."

"You got it, Star Girl."

"You know my actual name," I said and opened the car door. "Let's go."

#   #   #

The building was a low hulk of brown stone broken up every few meters by slivers of mucky windows that ran from the ground to the roof several stories up. It was boring, looked eternally dirty, and pretty much like every other building for blocked around. It was dizzying to be standing on the street, no Mist, no towering advertisements, and the dimming sky so easily visible above these squat buildings. The air felt different, denser, saturated with salt and moisture blowing in off the ocean. Living high up in skyscrapers, you grew accustomed to the slight and gentle sway of the buildings. Down here on solid ground, even with cybernetic legs, everything felt too still. Nox and I peered around the edge of the neighboring building, still cautious of our line of sight.

"From what I can find online," Bastion said in my ear. "Their hours of operation go on for only ten more minutes."

"What could Vert Toinette-Deus want with deep-sea diving equipment?" I asked.

"Josephine planning to convert the whales to Ibhalism next?" Nox said.

I blew the faintest chuckle out of my nose. "Wouldn't that make our lives easier?"

I zoomed in on those windows, but the dirt or whatever that was coating them made it impossible to make anything out. I could see vague silhouettes moving inside the building, but any of them could have been Vert. Or not.

"Come on," I said to Nox. "Stay close."

My work limbs were designed to move as swiftly and silently as modern technology allowed. Each joint was magnetic, holding the parts micrometers apart so the only friction was with the air. Those same joints could bend and extend in ways biological ones could not, allowing me to move close to the ground at a full sprint. Combine them with my carbon-nanoweave bodysuit in the exact same shade of black as the limbs, and I could slide along the side of a building in perfect harmony with the shadows.

My everyday limbs, however, moved pretty much just like the biological limbs I'd had removed when I was seventeen. A little stronger. A touch faster. The same light brown as my skin, but obviously not skin. My baggy, light-colored clothes didn't even blend in with dock workers, let alone the shadows creeping over the streets.

But these were what I had to work with, what I had to use when I just couldn't let a flimsy lead get away. I crept along as best I could, the slight squeak in my knees screaming in my ears. I only hoped nobody else thought they were so loud. I stayed close to the outside wall of the building, checking behind me periodically to make sure Nox was still there. He was on me like my own shadow.

"Eighty-two people inside," Nox said. "Minimal cybernetic modifications to most. Some arms and a few legs. Nothing major."

"How do you know that?" I asked in a whisper.

"A new app I'm running. Peekabuu. Takes my ultrasound and x-ray and thermal into a single viewing algorithm. I can't see faces or pick out one person from another, but I can see the shapes of everyone in that building. Cybernetics look different from biology, of course."

"Of course," I said, though I didn't really know what he was talking about. Peekabuu? Was he running homebrew software on his systems? Whatever it was, I really wanted it for myself. I didn't have time to go into that right now.

"Lot of them are just standing around," Nox said.

"Closing time," I said. "Probably about to—"

Before I even finished my sentence, several dozen Stryders swooped down, the whines of their landing thrusters filling the streets with dissonance.

"Oh!" Nox said. "They're all moving now! All—"

"Leaving?" I said. "Time for them to clock out and go home."

In moments, dozens of people filed out of the building, laughing and waving and hopping into Stryders that instantly took off in different directions, deeper into the Toinette borough.

Once the last Stryder was gone, I asked Nox, "Anyone left in there?"

"A dozen. No, fourteen."

"Can you tell if Vert is one of them?"

"How would I—"

"He'll look like the most modded person you've ever seen. And he's taller than he has any right to be."

"Maybe," Nox said. "It's like the people with the most mods are the ones who stayed."

"Come on," I said. "Let's get a closer loo—"

I was interrupted again by Stryders, but only a pair this time. They landed near the same door so many people had poured out of only minutes ago. Two people climbed out of the first one, both heavily modded, hulking silhouettes. Someone even taller than Vert exited the second car. A small, wiry person and another figure about my build followed after. All five people entered the warehouse as the pair of Stryders flew off.

"We need to get inside." I took off in a sprint across the street. I put my hands on the building, ready to climb, but the color of my hands reminded me that there was no magnetism here, no sticky goo to deploy.

"What now?" Nox asked.

"Can you climb this?" I asked.

Nox looked at the wall from the ground up, staring up and taking a step back as he did. "No, but I can fly."

I gave him my most incredulous look. "Fly?"

He sighed. "Jump."

"Silently?" I asked.

Nox grinned and instead of answering me verbally, he hunched down and launched into the air with barely a hiss from his legs. I awaited the boom or bang of him landing on the roof, but none came.

INCOMING CALL FROM NOX appeared on my display. I opened the channel.

"Like landing on a cloud," Nox said in my ear, though I could see him leaning over the edge of the building, looking down at me.

"When I ask you a question," I growled, "I expect a verbal answer."

"Oh," Nox said, deflation on his voice. "Do you want me to …?"

"I want you to look around up there for an entrance. Roof access. Ventilation. Open window. Anything that gets us in."

"What are you going to do?"

"Worry about you," I hissed. "Tell me what you see."

"Right." Then Nox's head disappeared from my view.

"What *are* you going to do?" Bastion asked.

"Walk around," I said, making up the answer as I spoke. "Pretend I'm just casually out for a stroll or something. A tourist."

"A tourist in an industrial part of the city?"

"I don't have a plan right now, okay?" I said.

"That much was obvious," Bastion said. "I've been looking at Stryder traffic patterns for this building. Outside of the expected comings and goings of workers like you saw at the end of shift, three to five Stryders arrive as the workers are leaving three days each week. On those same days, ten to twelve Stryders pick up passengers here at 27:30."

"Now what would that many people be doing here between closing and thirty minutes to midnight?" I said.

"Of that," Bastion said. "I'm not certain."

I walked around the perimeter of the building, trying to look as casual as possible. The building was unremarkable. Just one of the dozens of warehouses sprawling out from Drakon Bay. The smells of hot metal and plastic dust permeated the air, punctuated occasionally by the sea breeze. In addition to the door so many people had poured through not long ago, there was a similar one on the other end of the building. Next to it were a pair of towering doors at least a dozen meters wide. I guessed some of the deep-sea parts were rather large.

What I didn't see was a single soul walking or even standing around. Nobody was guarding the doors. No cameras, either, which was exceptionally odd. It was hard to step or fly anywhere in Jayu City without a camera seeing it. I had to zoom in on a building two blocks away before I finally spotted a decade-old security camera watching the street.

"I have a way in," Nox said, and his voice suddenly in my ear made me jump.

"What is it?" I asked.

"Skylight with a busted lock."

"Anybody directly below?"

"I'll check," Nox said.

"Carefully," I said. "Use a fiberoptic camera or—"

"Nobody beneath. Looks like a small office."

I looked up at the roofline of the building. Six stories tall. Twenty meters or so. No ladders or any other way up. But I couldn't just stand around out here blindly leading my apprentice inside. I felt useless as I let out a heavy sigh and asked Nox, "I don't know your mod loadout, but is there any way you can get me up there?"

I kept watching the roofline, occasionally glancing around to make sure I was still alone out here. And of course, during one of those glances, Nox landed next to me with a gentle whuff and a flutter of his clothes. I didn't scream or pee myself. Not even a little.

"Mother of Corto," I said with a growl. "It was a 'yes' or 'no' question."

"Not really," Nox said. "How much do you weigh?"

"What?"

"I know I can make that jump with my weight plus sixty kilograms. Give or take. So how much do you weigh?"

"Less than that," I growled. I was pretty sure. My everyday limbs were heavy, but not that heavy.

"You're sure?" Nox was eyeing me. "Those limbs—"

"Just get us up there."

Nox turned and knelt. I climbed on his back, careful not to choke him as I wrapped my arms around his neck. I felt like a child and hated it. He turned to face the building again, crouched, and I felt his legs spooling up beneath us. Then we suddenly launched as Nox gave a little grunt.

In a breath, I knew we were going to be short. Thankfully, so did Nox. I reached up and grabbed the edge of the building right before his body slammed into the side, one of his hands clinging to the edge of the roof as well. Nox coughed a couple of times and said, "After you, Star Girl."

Nox grabbed the edge with his other hand, and I climbed up, being as gentle as I could planting my heels in his hips and on his shoulders. Then I put out a hand, but without my added weight, Nox pulled himself completely onto the roof.

"Less than sixty kilograms, huh?" he asked.

"Where's the skylight?"

Nox smiled and rolled his eyes, but he started walking across the roof. I fell in behind him. The roof was flat and dotted with skylights, each one a meter long and half a meter wide. A hulking air conditioning unit took up residence in the middle of the roof. We walked around it and kept going to the opposite corner before Nox finally knelt next to one particular skylight and lifted it.

I knelt next to it and looked in. Just as promised, it was a small, dark office. A cheap citrus cleaning chemical and a candy-flavored vape hung in the air down there, making a bad combination. Nevertheless, I grabbed the edge of the open skylight and flipped down inside, landing on the floor with a louder thud than I liked. Nox followed and walked straight over to the door.

I moved to him and slapped his hand just as he was grabbing the door handle. "Right now," I whispered, "This is reconnaissance. I'm not equipped for a real job and neither of us has the information we need to actually steal anything. We're looking for Vert. Why is he here? Does he come here often? Is he meeting someone?"

"And what if he has the key?" Nox said. "What if he's waving it around or sits it on a table and goes to the bathroom?"

"You take nothing unless I say so," I said. "Good operatives get killed when they aren't patient."

"But what if—?"

"The answer to any *what if* you have is: Only if I tell you to. Got it?"

Nox grimaced but nodded.

"We're here to gather information and get out without ever being noticed. I don't care if that key is sitting on the floor in an empty room, you don't try for it unless I say so. Clear?"

"As the sky," Nox grumbled.

I opened the door and crept out. The air was stuffy and smelled of hot metal in the narrow hallways outside the office. There was a nondescript door across the hall just like the one I'd opened. To my left, half a dozen meters away were similar doors. Then the hallways ended at the outside wall of the building. To my right, however, the hall opened into stairs only a few meters away. Sounds of voices and scuffling were echoing up from that direction. I started in that direction as silently as I could manage.

I stayed low as I approached a small railing to the side of the stairs, Nox right on my heels. There were no walls around the stairs, just open metal framing suspended over the warehouse floor. I gazed down and took in the scene. Tall, wide shelves ran up and down the building, which was all one big space below these offices. The sounds were still echoing, coming from somewhere below us and out of sight. I motioned to Nox to stay low and stay quiet.

He looked at me like I was speaking a different language.

I looked at him and made the hand motions again, this time whispering what they meant as I did them.

Nox nodded and smiled like I'd let him in on a joke. I continued forward, taking each step slowly and silently, checking corners to make sure nobody was coming up the stairs or coming into view. We reached a landing, a U-turn in the stairs, and as I moved down and around, I saw the source of all the voices and ruckus.

Back in one corner of the warehouse, still partly obscured by towering shelves stuffed with equipment, was a makeshift fighting ring. Circular with a plain, black mat for the floor, it was a few meters in diameter. Stanchions and ropes surrounded the space as a pair of people were circling each other. A couple of dozen other people were standing around the ring in small groups, occasionally cheering or booing.

"A brawl?" Nox asked from very close to my ear.

"Looks like it."

"Vert couldn't quit the fight life."

I shrugged. I wasn't very familiar with the professional fighting circuit. A few months ago aboard a Huginn Industries yacht was the closest I'd ever been, and that was just a Huginn Rite of Youth in which teenagers fought each other. Even then, it was a bloody, violent affair. Too violent for me. From what I'd read and heard, the professionals were far nastier. People lost limbs. They died. Regularly.

I zoomed in and scanned for Vert but didn't see him. I asked Nox, "Do you recognize anyone over there?"

After a few moments, Nox said, "No."

"I'll work on facial recognition," Bastion said.

"Let's move closer." I continued down the stairs. My apprentice and I descended slowly until we reached the warehouse floor. Then we moved quickly and quietly through the stacks of equipment. For once, Nox was careful to follow my directives, only moving as I moved.

Once we were only one aisle away from the fighting ring, I climbed up onto a shelf that was as tall as me and squeezed into a space between two large, metal objects that looked vaguely like the whale fins. The spot gave me a decent view of the ring while keeping me in the shadows. It also had enough room for Nox to join me, but only just. It was a tight enough squeeze that I could smell my apprentice's body odor mixing with something spicy he'd eaten for lunch.

"Okay, okay, okay!" a bald, paunchy figure said with a growl, stepping into the ring and ushering out a pair that had been lazily sparring. "Let's get this show going. I don't have all night."

The haphazard crowd answered with a smattering of claps and a few whistles.

"Who is fighting tonight?" Growler asked.

A hand went up.

"Violet!" Growler said. "Get in here. Don't be shy."

Violet stepped out of a small group and into the ring. They were tall and gangly, looked to be still a teenager, and not quite in command of their limbs. But there was significant vascularizing on their thin muscles. Pale skin. Short hair that matched their name. They stepped between the rope and into the ring without a bit of hesitation.

"Who else?" Growler asked.

I didn't see the hand, but Growler looked off to my left. Then he said, "Little Vert!"

"Little Vert?" Nox and Bastion repeated.

A compact, muscular figure walked into my view. Sandy hair was in a braid down to their waist. A bouncing gait. They ducked between the ring ropes and said in a clear voice that couldn't decide between tenor and baritone, "My name is Larsen."

"I know," Growler said, "but until you can actually win a fight and make your own name, you're just Vert's little boy."

"Vert's little boy?" Nox echoed. Now that was something I could use.

Chapter Seven

"I SEE VERT," NOX WHISPERED.

"Where?" I asked. I followed Nox's extended finger to a tall figure, hooded, leaning up against a large crate. The hood was the characteristic blue and gold of Ibhalism. The exposed forearms and hands glinted with metal. He was a dozen meters away from anyone else, standing in the shadows with his arms crossed.

"How do you know that's Vert?" I asked.

"The etchings on those arms," Nox said. "I'd know them anywhere."

As the fight in the ring commenced, Vert remained passive. He didn't react to a particularly nasty haymaker Larsen took to the jaw. Nor did he react when Violet flipped over Vert's son and planted a vicious jab into Larsen's kidney.

"Why are we being so quiet?" Nox asked. "They're pretty loud by the ring."

"Quiet is our way of life," I whispered. "You never know how acute someone's aural mods are. Someone like Vert."

Nox's eyes widened and then he nodded.

"We need to separate Vert from the crowd," I said. "Find a way to discretely plant a tracker on him."

"You have a tracker on you?" Nox asked.

"I—" I started to say. Then I remembered these stupid everyday limbs. I felt like an absolute fool for forgetting again. I was so accustomed to my work limbs while, you know, working. "No. Do you?"

Nox shook his head.

"Mother of Corto," I said. "All of those fancy mods, and you don't have a tracker. We might have to rob him after all. And not get beaten up in the process."

"Beaten up? He'd probably kill us."

"You a fan?"

"Of his in particular?" Nox said. "Not really. I've been watching the fights since I was six or seven though. Vert really was one of the best ever. Undefeated as a professional. Killed a few people in the ring."

"Vert," Bastion chimed in. "Was thirty-six-oh. Twenty-two knockouts. Four of those victories were by opponent death. His punch holds the league record of twenty-five thousand sixteen Newtons of force. He was capable of delivering up to twelve of those punches per second."

I sucked in air through my teeth. Without appropriate armor, there was no way I could withstand a single punch from Josephine's bodyguard, let alone twelve. Even with my work limbs and helmet, I wouldn't stand a chance.

"We need a distraction," I said. "Something to pull focus in about a billion directions at once, give us a chance to get in close without being detected."

"We could make a fire," Nox said.

"No," I said. "I don't want to burn everybody up."

"I mean the fire suppression system. Make a little fire and the place will fill with suppressive gases."

I glanced up to the ceiling but didn't see standard gas lines and dispensers. "I see pipes," I said. "But they look different. Too big. And those dispensers…"

"This building uses a water-based fire suppression system," Bastion said in my ear. "Likely pumped in from the bay itself."

"It's water-based," I said, parroting Bastion's words.

"Why would they—?" Nox started to say.

"Good question. That's archaic, why would you…" Then it dawned on me. "Because everything in here is for deep-sea submersibles. Everything they store and sell is built to go in the water. So why not? Might even be cheaper."

"Still," Nox said. "These people would leave if it started raining in here, wouldn't they?"

In the ring, Violet landed another nasty blow on Larsen, sending the youth to his knees as a spray of blood flew out of his mouth. Both fighters were dripping with sweat.

"Maybe," I said. "But Vert would likely leave with the rest of them." I kept watching the bout, which didn't last much longer. Larsen was swinging his fists wildly, missing as Violet kept bouncing around on their toes and laughing. After several of those embarrassing misses, Violet finally came in, leaped, and planted a knee right under Larsen's chin. Larsen came up off his feet and landed on his back. The announcer jumped in between the fighters, waving their hands in the air. The match was over.

"Not really a spark off the old man's armor, huh?" Nox asked.

"Not at all. Never going to be popular if he…" I trailed off, an idea creeping up on me. "You said Vert was popular. One of the best?"

"Yeah."

"How popular was he? Is he? On Little Sekhmet specifically?"

Nox shrugged. "He was one of the top three fighters for about a decade. He had fans all over Earth Space. I bet in Toinette alone—"

"If we were to put a call out to his fans, say that he was giving autographs or something?"

Nox's eyes went wide. "An exhibition fight! Against Cordelia the Crippler!"

I twisted up my own face at the suggestion.

"She was his biggest rival!" Nox said with a new level of excitement. "She tore something in her back a few years before Vert suddenly retired. The fans had been all-capping for a title clash between them for years, but it never happened. If there was a pop-up fight between them—"

"Fans of both would descend on it like gearheads on the newest BMW."

"But how would we—?"

I moved my hands forward and triple-tapped my left thumb and ring finger together to call up my AR keyboard. At least, that's what I made it look like. I actually didn't complete the third tap but pretended to type furiously all the same. Bastion knew the signal.

"I've found a number of fan forums," he said in response. "Several of which are dedicated to Vert and Cordelia. Their userbases are significantly large enough on our planet that a few legitimate-looking posts should have the desired effect."

I stopped "typing" and looked around. A handful of people were cleaning up the ring while everyone else moseyed about and chatted. Vert was still leaning up against his crate, unmoved.

"I think we can be ready in twenty minutes," I whispered to Nox, though really it was for Bastion's benefit. Nox grinned and said, "How are you getting people here?"

"Fan forums," I said.

"Twenty minutes," Bastion said. "Posting now. I have access to some social media bots I can leverage to boost the signal as well."

"And social media posts," I said to Nox.

"Screaming!" my apprentice said.

I blinked at him. I truly didn't know what he meant.

"It's good," he said. "Really good."

I shook my head and pretended to type up the posts for several more seconds. Then I asked Nox, "How are you at picking pockets?"

Impossibly, he grinned even harder. "I've been taught by the best."

"I doubt that," I said. Solomon was the best, and he didn't train neophytes. "But it'll have to be you. Vert has seen my face."

"You said that before," Nox said. "When? How?"

I sighed and pretended to finish my typing. "Outside Josephine's office."

Nox's eyes went wide. "You didn't say anything over comms. Didn't tell me or the Cloak."

"No, I didn't. I had it under control and I didn't want Solomon to panic and abort."

Nox shook his head but didn't say anything.

"What?"

"You are an enigma," he said, focusing his gaze back on the ring as two new fighters were entering. "I'm supposed to follow you, obey without question. I can get into that. But then you go against orders in the field. Against the Cloak."

"Nox," I said. "I've been doing this a while. I have my own instincts and experience to fall back on. I trust the Cloak and his orders, but I also know myself and what I'm capable of. I had it under control, so I made the call."

Nox didn't look back at me and didn't respond.

"But probably best not to tell Gustin or the Cloak about all that," I continued. "I don't think they'd agree with me."

Nox shook his head slightly as he watched the next fight get underway. I watched with him for a few minutes, though I wasn't really paying attention. "Elise," Bastion said. "Response to the forums and social media has been impressive. I would estimate that several hundred fans will be arriving in less than seventeen minutes."

I grabbed Nox's shoulder, gave it a gentle squeeze, and then told him my plan.

#   #   #

I was positioned right next to the large, sliding front doors of the warehouse, standing in shadows and waiting for the little countdown timer on my display to hit zero. I could hear the footfalls and voices of the crowd gathered outside, practically stamping the ground to get in.

"I'm in position," Nox whispered over comms. "They don't suspect?" I asked. "Clueless. The fight is too loud over here."

"Target is still in reach?"

"He hasn't moved," Nox said. "His kid came by earlier. Looked like they mumbled a little, but he's gone now."

"Good," I said and glanced at the timer. "Thirty seconds."

"Thank you, thirty seconds."

I ended the comms connection and visually confirmed my route once. Twice. Then I put my hand on the big, green button that would open the doors. I'd already bypassed the lock. I crouched a little just to give my everyday limbs a little extra boost. As the timer hit 0:00, I pressed the button and leaped up onto the nearest crate, pulling myself up to make up for what my legs lacked.

A loud claxon rang out from above the doors, jangling as green lights flashed and the doors screeched and started to slide open. Those doors weren't even a third of a meter apart when the first fans started to squeeze through, sprinting in and searching for the fighting ring.

"There it is!" one of them shouted, pointing, and the entire herd rushed in that direction.

I moved as fast as my limbs could, climbing stacks of crates to get a bird's eye view of the scene, to give my apprentice what visual support I could. For the first time since we'd been in the warehouse, Vert was no longer leaning against his crate. He'd drawn his hood back, his armored scalp glinting. The fighters around the ring were looking in the same direction as Vert, toward the rowdy stampede of fight fans suddenly flowing into the warehouse. Even the pair in the ring had stopped to gawk.

I watched my apprentice peel off from behind a crate, out of the shadows, and into the flow of the crowd just as someone yelled, "Look! There he is! The Hurt!"

Soon the crowd was chanting *The Hurt* and flowing directly toward Josephine's very surprised bodyguard. To his credit, Vert Toinette-Deus crossed his arms and allowed the crowd to surround him. Tablets and action figures were suddenly thrust in his face, begging for autographs. To my surprise, Vert didn't scoff or yell or throw a punch. He patiently took hold of the first pen and tablet near him and gave the fan an autograph. Then he did it again. And again. He smiled, shook hands, and posed for selfies. He was like an entirely different person. As he gladhanded, I watched Nox move through the crowd. He bumped Vert and then moved away.

"Anything?" I asked him over comms.

"Nothing in his pants pockets," Nox said. "Going back in." "Change your appearance," I said.

"He didn't see me. I came up behind—"

"Never underestimate your mark," I said, cutting him off. "He could have cameras or sensors or something. Never hit twice in the same look."

Nox grumbled, but then ended the connection. I watched him move through the crowd in little circles before he finally traded his suit jacket with someone in the crowd for a pink hoodie. He pulled it on, threw up the hood, and made a second pass. This time, he wound up around Vert's front, practically knocking over two fans in the process. It looked clumsy to an untrained eye, but I could see the purpose of each little movement. He had been trained well.

Once Nox was a couple of meters away from Vert, he said over comms, "Front pockets and jacket are empty. He's not carrying anything. What did I miss? I'm so sorry, Elise, I tried, but—"

Then I realized my own error. My own foolishness. If I was carrying something that was that important, a key that literally safeguarded a trove of data for my employer, I wouldn't keep it in some flimsy garment pocket. I had magnetically sealed compartments in my work legs that I used for carrying items I'd pilfered. I had a small compartment in the right shoulder specifically for carrying Bastion's chip. If I was Josephine's bodyguard and carried her precious decryption key, I'd keep it inside.

"Nox," I said in a rushed whisper. "You did nothing wrong. This is on me. Vert is modded more than any human I've ever seen. He's definitely carrying that key, but internally. There's no way of lifting it from him."

I waited for Nox to reply, to keep apologizing or agree or something, but no reply came over comms. I could see him, still in the pink hoodie, standing still as the crowd of fans flowed around him. Vert was still politely signing autographs. The fighters had left the ring, and I didn't see any of their crowd now, either. Must have slipped out in all the commotion.

"Nox?" I said. "Did you hear me?"

"I heard you," Nox said. "This can't be it. We need that key."

"We'll get it. Just not tonight. Abort. Meet me out back in two minutes." I turned and started to climb down.

Nox said, "I have a plan."

"A plan?" I asked, stopping in my tracks.

Nox said nothing. I climbed back up but couldn't see him in the crowd. "Nox?"

Nothing.

"Nox, respond! Where are you? What's your plan?"

"On the move," Nox finally responded. He sounded a little winded now. "Dockside in two. We're going to need a quick escape."

"Nox, what are you doing? What's your plan?" My apprentice didn't respond.

"Bastion, do you have any idea what he's doing?"

"I don't," Bastion said. "I'm reviewing your own visual record from the last thirty seconds, but I do not see him."

"Nox?" I said again as I started climbing back down toward the front door of the warehouse. To my amazement, people were still squeezing in through the front doors. Nevertheless, once I hit the ground, I started moving upstream. I had to push a bit, but finally forced my way out onto the street, then broke into a full sprint. The docks were only two blocks away. I turned the corner of the neighboring building, the glare of the still-setting sun glimmering on Drakon Bay right into my face. My optical mods adjusted quickly and I didn't break stride. Soon enough, the street ended with a large, concrete dock jutting into the bay and Nox was down near the end of it. He wasn't alone, though.

I kept running, unable to make out who Nox was standing over or what my apprentice was pointing at the fallen figure. In a dozen strides, the tableau clarified. Larsen, Vert's son, was on his stomach, holding his hands out in surrender as a trickle of blood seeped from an open gash on his cheek. Nox was standing over him, a matte-black handheld rail gun pointed at Larsen's face.

"What are you doing?" I yelled over the rolling waves.

Larsen started to turn his head toward me, but Nox screamed, "Eyes on the ground!" Larsen obeyed.

"What are you doing, apprentice?" I said again.

"I'm making him call his father," Nox replied.

"So he can kill you?"

"He won't hurt me so long as I have his kid," Nox said with far too much confidence.

"This isn't how we work! We don't threaten people. We don't kill them."

"You should listen to her," Larsen said, his voice quivering as he stared at the concrete.

"You should call your father. Tell him to slip out of that warehouse and get over here." Nox shook his rail gun a little, the sound making Larsen flinch. "Now!"

"Let him go, Nox!" I yelled. "Walk away. This isn't how—"

"I have this under control," Nox said. The crack in his voice said differently. "There's no other way."

"There's always another way. There are dozens of other ways, none of which involve you holding this kid hostage or a very dangerous man taking your head off."

"Too late, Star Girl!" Nox said with a shaky smirk.

I glanced down and saw Larsen's lips were moving. I couldn't hear him, but I was quite certain who he was talking to.

"Chatter on social media is indicating some confusion as to Vert's whereabouts," Bastion said. "Fans at the warehouse have lost track of him."

"Sparks," I whispered to myself. Vert was going to be here any second. If he saw me, he would know this was a Corto Corporation plot, as would Josephine. I needed time to think my way out of this, but I didn't have it. I said to Nox, "What can I do? How do we—?"

"Overwatch, Star Girl. Watch my back."

As I opened my mouth to protest, Bastion said, "I can think of seven ways in which your presence here makes this situation worse. You need to leave now. Vert will certainly be here in seconds."

"Mother of…" I said, the curse trailing off my tongue. "If you live through this, apprentice, I'm going to have your neck." I didn't wait for a response. I turned and sprinted to the nearest building, grabbing hold of a maintenance ladder and scrambling up as fast as I could.

I was only halfway up when I heard Vert bellow from below, "Let go of my son!"

I finished my climb and turned to see if my apprentice was still alive.

He was still there, now standing less than a meter from the end of the dock and holding Larsen in front of him like a shield, the rail gun up against Larsen's temple.

"I just want the key," Nox said.

Vert was approaching them slowly, open hands wide at his sides. "What key? Who are you?"

"You want to play stupid with your son's life?" Vert stopped walking. "You. I know you."

"Hardly."

"Beltran. You helped with the initiation last night. You've been with us for months. Why are you doing this?"

"Not my real name and not the point here. Give it to me and we all leave here alive."

Stupid apprentice. Giving up his alias so easily. He could have used that to diffuse the situation.

Vert slowly rolled his shoulders, letting the long, hooded jacket he was wearing slip down onto the dock. His torso was all metal armor, like stainless steel musculature. With his left hand still held out and open, he gently reached his right hand across his front. I couldn't see what he was doing from my vantage point, his back to me, but a moment later, he held out something small and pinkish orange. The decryption key.

"Set it down," Nox said. "Step back."

"I can't do that," Vert said, holding the key aloft in his right hand.

I couldn't see Vert's face but when I zoomed in, I could see Nox's face twist up in what may have been confusion or surprise. Then Vert tossed the key into Drakon Bay.

Chapter Eight

NOX'S EYES WERE WIDE AS saucers. The rail gun he had trained on Larsen's temple was shaking. "Why did you do that?" he yelled.

"What you need is down there," Vert said, nodding his head toward the water. His hands were held out wide by his sides. His voice was even calmer than the placid water around him. "You have no need to hold my son. Maybe if you dive in right now, I'll let you live through this."

Nox sputtered.

Larsen smiled weakly.

"You should know," Vert said, taking one slow step and then another toward my apprentice, his voice unchanged. "I am a violent man. I've seen your face now. Memorized it. I'll look you up. Learn your name, your parents' names. Sisters. Brothers. Cousins. Aunts. Uncles. Whoever. Contrary to popular belief, I do not enjoy violence. But I am a violent man, and that is my son. If you hurt him, I don't care what company you work for, I'll hunt you down and everyone who shares a drop of your blood."

I hurriedly typed a message to Nox and sent it, "Get in the water, Nox. Go now. You've already lost."

But as Vert slowly approached, Nox just stood there, the gun still shaking in his hand. I needed to do something and fast. I really didn't want to go down there myself, since that would likely mean both of us being beaten to death. The roof was hot, even as the sun was setting. Black and waterproof with occasional metal gadgets that normally dot an industrial roof. Nothing immediately grabbed my attention as a surefire way to diffuse the situation on the dock. But Vert was still approaching a terrified Nox.

I grabbed one of the vent covers, a hollow ball covered in slits that slowly turned as air moved through it. I grabbed and pulled. The bracket holding the ball tore loose. It was surprisingly light, which was both good and bad. I could throw it, though I hoped it wouldn't catch in the sea wind and fly away as I did. I took two big steps, spun the ball on the end of my arm, and flung it at Vert.

The metal ball sailed, whistling slightly as it arced off the roof and bounced with a loud clang less than a meter behind Vert. The tall, armored man spun, looking down at the wreckage of the ball with hate in his eyes, and then looking around for where it came from. Fortunately, I'd dropped to my belly as soon as I'd thrown the ball, peeking just over the edge of the roof to watch.

The ball hadn't hit Vert like I'd hoped, but it broke the trance Nox had been under. His eyes darted around, and then he let go of Larsen and holstered his gun in his right thigh in the same motion.

"Father!" Larsen yelled as he rolled away from Nox. Even though my apprentice was moving toward the water, he was just too slow. Vert spun back on him, took a single step, and then his meaty, armored left hand launched from his wrist, flying through the air and slamming into Nox's chest a moment later, laying him out hard. The fist came right back, reeled in on a thin metal cable. Vert didn't wait, he started closing the gap on my apprentice, who was gasping for air like a fish on land.

I couldn't wait or make a better plan. Even if Vert saw me again, I couldn't just let Nox be turned into a splatter on the pavement. I grabbed the ladder back down and started descending to the street with all the speed I could muster, nearly slipping off the rungs more than once. Finally, my feet hit concrete and I turned to start running. But Nox was nowhere to be seen. Vert was now standing by Larsen, who was holding his ribs in obvious pain. I turned up the sensitivity of my aural implants to listen.

"First you get beat by that weak fighter," Vert said, his voice surprisingly soft. "Then you let that little bedwetter take you hostage? You do not have to be a fighter, you know?"

"I know, but—"

"You cannot be weak. Artists and musicians and poets, for them, vulnerability is a strength. For a fighter, you cannot have vulnerabilities. No weaknesses. No cracks in your armor."

Larsen mumbled, "I just, just—"

"Do you want to be a fighter?" Larsen nodded silently.

The gesture was interrupted by a brutal slap to the face that sent Nox sprawling. Vert's hand was so quick that I didn't even see the slap coming. And the change from loving father to violence was dizzying.

"I'm sorry, Father, I'm sorry!" Larsen was doing his best not to cry and barely succeeding.

"You want to be a fighter, then don't be sorry. Don't cry. Next time, don't let me strike you." Vert didn't wait for a response. He strode toward his son, grabbed the back of his jacket, and bodily hauled Larsen away as he strode back toward the warehouse. I ducked into the nearest doorway, scanning for any sign of Nox, but saw none. Once Vert had passed me and the building I was hiding by, Larsen sputtering the whole way, I launched myself toward the dock, toward the last spot I'd seen Nox.

"Did you catch anything on my auditory sensors while I was going down that ladder?" I asked Bastion.

"Too much noise," Bastion said, "I was not able to make out any of their conversation if there was any. I heard no fighting or screaming."

"Okay, what did you hear?"

"Other than your hands on ladder rungs, some splashes, bird calls, nothing out of the ordinary."

"Splashes?" I asked, turning my gaze to the water since I didn't see any blood on the concrete dock.

"Yes, but nothing out of the ordinary."

"Can you pinpoint where the key went in the water? The key Vert tossed in there?"

"To your left," Bastion said, and sure enough, a yellow circle was superimposed over the water in my display.

"Please be right," I said to myself, took two long strides, and dived into the water. I have a whole diving add-on for my work mods. Propellers, rebreather, the whole works. Not that they did me any good right now, hanging neatly in my power closet at home. Instead, I held my breath and kicked my way down. My optical mods adapted to the growing dark and my auditory mods changed to submersed mode for clearer hearing. I'd descended half a dozen meters before I realized I hadn't taken a big enough breath. I hadn't found any sign of Nox or the key yet, but I had to go back up. I flipped and kicked hard, letting my buoyancy do the rest.

"Did you account for any tidal movements with your AR circle?" I asked Bastion between gulping breaths. "Would it have moved before sinking to the bottom? Hell, how far down is the bottom here?"

"It should not have moved more than a meter in any direction," Bastion said. "And the bottom is fourteen-point-six meters according to the port's website."

"Okay," I said. I did my best to slow my breathing, slow my pulse, still looking around in case Nox suddenly appeared. That was a long way to dive without help breathing, but I didn't see another choice. I took the deepest breath I could and dived back down. I paced my kicks this time. Even though my legs and arms were cybernetic, my core and back were not. I still had to expend calories and air to dive and keep diving.

As I passed twelve meters and my lungs were tightening, a shape started to clarify down at the bottom. Contrasting shades of black and white and that ridiculous pink hoodie. I swam down another meter, and I could see the shape was moving. Nox. Not only was he alive, he was actively digging around the bottom of the bay. Looking for the key, no doubt.

I grabbed my apprentice's shoulder and he turned, a roil of bubbles that threw me upward half a meter. His eyes were wide with panic until he saw it was me, then his look turned quizzical. I didn't know what to do other than return a quizzical look of my own. Then he pulled aside his collar to show a set of cybernetic gills working on the side of his neck. The little fool really did have all the best mods. And I was running out of air. I pointed up toward the surface and then followed my own suggestion, swimming gently with my own buoyancy until I was able to draw breath once more.

I expected Nox to come up right after me. I wanted to yell at him and bounce his head off the concrete for nearly getting himself killed. But I was alone next to the dock, treading water for a full minute. Then two. Then five. Was he trying to annoy me further? Just when I was about to dive back down, a dark-skinned hand holding a pinkish-orange key emerged from the depths followed by Nox's arm, head, and shoulders.

"Who's the greatest apprentice Intel Operative in all of Jayu City?" he whooped.

I opened my mouth to unfurl a very long string of expletives at my apprentice, but I was so relieved that he was not only okay but that he'd actually retrieved the key, I couldn't. Plus, the more I thought about it, the more it seemed like something I would have done. Instead, I pulled myself out of Drakon Bay, started walking away, and just muttered, "Not you."

"Ouch," Nox said. "I got the key! I actually got it!"

My vintage t-shirt was ruined by my swim. Maybe I should bill my apprentice for it. Without looking at Nox, I told him, "Enjoy the moment. You have the mother of all lectures coming. And not just from me, I'm sure."

I heard Nox follow me out of the water. Then I stopped. Something else struck me, something I would never do. I spun on Nox and said, "We don't take hostages. Where did you even get that gun? Who do you think we are?"

Nox's right thigh opened, and he drew the gun out again, keeping the barrel pointed at the concrete. "This? It's not even loaded. I never would have—"

I yanked it out of his hand. It took me a few moments and some instructions from Bastion, but I was finally able to verify that yes, it was unloaded.

"I would never have shot him," Nox murmured.

I worked my jaw and stared at my apprentice. I was glad he wasn't the murdering type, but this still wasn't acceptable. Once he looked sufficiently contrite, I hauled back and threw the gun into the bay.

Nox opened his mouth, maybe in shock or to say something, but he thought better of it. I held out my hand and nodded to his left hand. He handed me Vert's key and said, "So we need to get this back to the office, right?"

I stared at it. We did need to get it to the office, but I also needed to copy the decryption algorithms for myself. Bastion needed them. With a complicated hand gesture, I summoned my bike's autopilot to come get me. I turned the key over in my hand and finally found a small, covered data port in one corner. I asked Nox, "Are you hungry?"

#   #   #

Abreu's Belt was one of the greasiest, grimiest diners in all of the Corto Corporation borough. From the outside, it looked like a mostly nondescript corner of a building, one hundred and twelve floors up in a working-class section of the borough. If it weren't for the two large, though decrepit landing pads on the corner, you wouldn't even realize there was a business there.

"I've never heard of this place," Nox said as I spun Poe, my bike, around and descended to one of the sturdier-looking places to land.

"You wouldn't unless you lived off the sweat of your brow," I said.

"So how do you know about it?"

I wasn't sure if he'd meant it as an insult, so I decided to ignore the barb. I parked Poe and turned off the thrusters. "I came here after my first job as an operative. The first one where I wasn't just observing."

"Your first success?" Nox asked as he stepped off my bike.

I didn't answer him but instead walked inside. A little bell rang over the door and a combination of smells I hadn't encountered in years overwhelmed me. Grease and coffee and burned rubber and dried sweat. Stained tiles covered the walls. Some sort of peeling, taupe polymer was trying to cover the concrete floor. Booths ran along the windows, all cracked and peeling vinyl set in severely tarnished chrome. A long, L-shaped counter of white polymer and the same dingy chrome was dotted with only a few sad stools. Empty quartets of holes in the floor showed where many more had stood long ago. A dozen faces lifted from their meals, all of them splattered with grime. We didn't really belong here and they knew it, but after each gave me a brief look of confusion, they went back to their food.

"Mother of Corto," Nox whispered from behind me.

"Be nice," I said.

"Sit wherever is clean," a raspy voice called from somewhere to my left. We found a clean table soon enough and a menu appeared on my display as soon as I sat down.

"You come here a lot?" Nox whispered.

"No," I said. "Not since that first job. Consider it tradition."

The owner of the raspy voice then walked up to the table. A hard couple decades older than me, dressed in dirty black slacks and a spotless white shirt. They walked up to our table looking like they were already tired of Nox and me. They took my order as though I was ordering them to stand before a firing squad. Under the table, I silently opened the compartment in which I'd stowed Vert's key, extended my data cable, and plugged it into the key.

"This is a surprising amount of information for a decryption key," Bastion said. "I will have to copy bits of it to different cloud storage options so as not to overload your internal data stores."

Nox ordered food.

Bastion continued, "It does appear to be the complementary encryption information needed to read all of the data you secured from Josephine, though. I won't know for certain until I can try to use it back at the garage."

My tea and Nox's coffee arrived. My apprentice said, "Pretty good job for my first time, huh?"

I took a sip of my tea, which was terribly bitter. Then I said, "Eight years ago, I was on a job. Kotega. One of the last jobs I ran as an apprentice."

A little progress bar in the corner of my display showed Bastion was seven percent done copying the data from the key. "I don't remember who we were taking it from," I continued. "Doesn't matter now. What matters is we went in, got past a few doors. Quietly subdued a security guard. I had to drop down a ventilation shaft to get what we were after."

"Nice!" Nox said.

"Just listen for a moment," I said as the progress bar passed fifteen percent. "My mentor, he stayed behind while I went down the shaft. Once I got down to the bottom and entered the target residence, I found a kid in the room. Maybe five or six years old."

Nox's eyes widened.

"They were playing. Wide awake well after midnight. As soon as they saw me, they screamed." I took another sip of my tea and held Nox's gaze. "My mentor said to abort, to drop some knockout gas and just get out of there. But I saw the target. A blue, metal polyhedron just small enough for me to palm with one hand. So I grabbed the kid and put one hand over their mouth. I grabbed the polyhedron with my other hand. Then the kid's parents came in.

"I did the stupidest thing I've ever done. I panicked. I shifted my hand from the kid's mouth to around their neck. The kid started screaming, and I squeezed. The parents were yelling, pleading, but I just squeezed that kid's neck and backed toward the vent."

Our food arrived then, and I paused my story as Raspy Voice practically threw the plates in front of us without a word. The progress bar on my display was at thirty-one percent.

"Did it work?" Nox asked. "Did you complete your job?"

I took a bite of eggs. Sausage. It tasted worse than I remembered. "Looking back, I still can't understand what I was thinking. Maybe I wasn't. At some point, I would have to have let go of the kid and gotten back in the ventilation shaft. Then what? Maybe a parent was armed. They certainly would have called security."

"They didn't?"

"Not on me," I said. Then I couldn't hold Nox's gaze as I continued. "My mentor came crashing down through the ceiling, right on top of the parents. Detonated a charge or used some cybernetic super-strength, I don't know. He screamed at me to go. To run. I let go of the kid and finally followed orders."

"What happened to…?" Nox's words and face were tinged with worry.

"I moved up back up that ventilation shaft as fast as I could. Their screams, items crashing and breaking, all that echoed up the shaft the whole way."

"And your mentor?" Nox asked in a whisper.

I still couldn't meet my apprentice's eyes. The word to answer him held in my throat like acid.

"Who was your mentor? You've never told me his name." I finally moved my gaze up just as Nox's eyes grew wide.

He said, "You…you can't say his name, can you?"

I squeezed my eyes shut and shook my head. I didn't even try to think about my mentor's name. That's what happens when someone is terminated from Corto Corporation. Discommended from the company. From that day on, we do not speak their names. Not since the moment before I scrambled back up that ventilation shaft have I uttered Ilya Corto-Intel's name aloud.

"Because he helped you?" Nox asked.

"Because I disobeyed him," I whispered. "I was still his apprentice. I should have turned and left the second I saw that kid. But I didn't. My mentor saved me. He was detained by Kotega security. They demanded what I stole in exchange for him, but the higher-ups at Corto Corporation refused. So Kotega burned him. Blasted his name and face all over the livestreams in Jayu City."

Nox said nothing, just pushed greasy food around on his plate without looking at me.

"The stupidest part? That polyhedron I stole? It wasn't some brilliant new nanotech or neural interface or aural implant. It was a toy. The hottest toy in half of Earth Space for the next three years. Recorded parents' voices and answered questions using those voices based on algorithmic learning or something like that. I can't speak my mentor's name because of a toy."

Now Nox and I both moved our food around a bit. I hadn't thought about my mentor in a long time. Too busy with life or whatever, not that it was a good excuse. I wondered what he was doing now, if he had landed with another company or if he was somewhere down in The Mist, squeaking out a feeble existence. The progress bar on my display read sixty-eight percent.

"I get it," Nox finally said. "But at least it wasn't just a toy this time."

"It's not," I nearly yelled. I took a breath and brought my voice back under control. "That's not the point. You got the key, sure, but there are other ways. When I say abort, or any leader says to abort, you abort. Trust that they know better, that there will be another opportunity. If we didn't get the key today, we would have tried again."

"What if there wasn't a next time?"

"What's worse?" I asked. "Losing a target or your parents never being able to say your name again?"

Nox's dark skin paled just a little at that, then his jaw set and he nodded.

"Plus," I said as the progress bar hit eighty-five percent and started moving even faster. "Now Vert knows your face, too. Josephine sent a Stryder into The Mist with me in it after she saw my face. Now we're both their targets."

"At least she thinks you're dead," Nox said.

"I'm not counting on that." I glanced at my food, which looked even less appetizing than it tasted. The progress bar on my display hit one hundred percent, and I said, "Enough story time. Let's get to the office before Hessod starts to worry."

"Elise?" Nox said, looking more sheepish than I'd ever seen him.

"Yeah?"

"I'm sorry."

"Don't be sorry," I said. "Be careful. And do what I say. For your own good."

Chapter Nine

DROPPING THE KEY BACK OFF at the Corto Corporation Intel offices was non-eventful. Poe didn't fall from the sky. Neither Gustin nor Hessod nor Solomon was there. I handed the key to an analyst I didn't know, gave Nox a list of Toinette locks to research as homework, and flew home. I turned on the garage workstation, connected Bastion to it, and fell into an old chair.

"The key is working," Bastion said over the speaker in the garage. "I'm accessing the data now. This is going to take a while."

New pictures started popping up on the Toinette Holdings section of my digital conspiracy board. Ali Toinette-Cyber, VP of Cybernetics. Sasuke Toinette-Intel, VP of Intel. Four Intel directors.

"Intel?" I said. "Those aren't common knowledge to just anyone."

"No," Bastion said. "They're not. Josephine has access to a surprising amount of…"

I waited a few seconds, and then said, "What? Amount of what?"

"I am sorry. A surprising amount of confidential information for other companies."

"Did something happen? Something distract you?"

His voice was suddenly quiet and somber. "You remember Roxy?"

My heart shuddered. Remember Roxy? She was impossible to forget.

Every time I rounded a corner, I had a flash of her raging stare, her bladed copper mods coming at me. She'd been sent to get Bastion's chip from me all those months ago. And that was after she'd massacred the lab in which Bastion was developed, stealing his chip before I'd stolen it. When I'd not only escaped but embarrassed her, she made it her personal crusade to murder me. Painfully. I'd shaken her off, but I still worried I'd run into her on some job, in some dark corner. I still woke in a cold sweat once a week, memories of her turning a Nexus Neuronics cafe into a bloodbath.

"Yeah," I whispered. "I remember."

My woefully under-connected web of companies slid away, and a pair of headshots with accompanying names popped up on the display. Aurelie Toinette-Cyber, she/her. Her face was plump and dark, with a large poof of black hair. Hode Toinette-Deus, he/ him. This man was pale, with gray and brown hair cropped tightly to his head and face.

"Who are they?"

"I found a collection of files," Bastion said. "Not on Josephine's terminal or private server, but in the servers of these two. For some reason, Josephine has access to them. My algorithm copied the files."

"Okay…" I let the last syllable drag out. It felt like Bastion was hesitant to speak or keeping something from me.

"There is a video."

The pictures faded away, replaced by a video clip, frozen. It showed what looked like security footage from a home, the angle high and the lens fish-eyed. The walls were a dark emerald, with plush orange carpet and furniture. A garish color scheme. A large shrine to Shainette and Aphnette took up residence in one corner of the room. There were no people in the frame, not until the video started playing.

What looked like a family entered, two tall, well-built, masculine figures with dark hair. They were wearing suits. Between them was a feminine child, maybe ten or eleven. Even young, I could recognize the frizzy red hair and piercing eyes of Roxy. No murderous, coppery mods, just the bright optimism of a girl with her parents.

The family entered and appeared to be talking to each other.

"Why can't I hear them?" I asked.

"There is no audio on the file," Bastion said.

The parents put down some bags, kissed, and went out of the frame in different directions. The young Roxy hopped over the back of a couch and appeared to give a voice command, the light on her face changing like a viewscreen had turned on. Right as the parents re-entered, the front door burst open and I jumped. I knew what was coming. I just did, and I didn't want to see it. "Stop this," I said to Bastion.

"You need to see this."

"All of this? I can only imagine what happens—"

"Trust me," Bastion interrupted. "You need to see all of this."

The video resumed as two younger figures rushed in, both gaunt. One had dark skin and tight-cropped black curls. The other was pale, with brown hair pulled up in a tight bun. They were both wearing masks, the overdrawn smile and frown of comedy and drama. The parents created a wall between the intruders and Roxy, who scrambled down off the couch, cowering low on the video. There appeared to be a heated verbal exchange for several seconds, and then the pale intruder took a baton or something similar and slammed it into one of the parents' heads. It was so quick and brutal that I flinched and bit down on one of my knuckles. The suited parent crumpled to the ground, and then the darker figure pointed another of the bludgeons at the other parent. More words were exchanged, the masked people gesticulated wildly with their weapons, and then the dark figure hit the second parent. And hit. And hit. Both masked assailants were beating the parents, who had fallen out of sight behind the couch. Roxy crawled out of frame to what was surely the morbid sounds of her parents being beaten to death. I looked away.

"Mother of Corto," I whispered.

"It goes on like this for several minutes," Bastion said. "Then the attackers appear to rummage around the house but leave without taking anything. It was not until after they had both left that young Roxy emerged from where she was hiding."

"That poor girl."

"I suppose so," Bastion said. "But considering what she became, what she's done, I have trouble feeling any sympathy for her."

I nodded but didn't say anything more on the matter. She'd been hired to steal his chip, killing everyone in the lab in the process, including the one friend Bastion ever had before he met me. Roxy scared me and I certainly didn't like her, but Bastion hated her. I needed to get back on task. "Those were her parents?"

"Kazuo Toinette-Nano and Gregory Toinette-Deus, yes." Bastion's voice was cold.

"Why did that happen?"

"I don't know. I found files on the investigation. Toinette Holdings security never named any suspects or motives. Nothing was stolen, though the house was ransacked. There are files on Roxy's subsequent years of failed foster attempts and corporate group homes. Multiple reports of her assaulting other children. Once she came of age, she vanished from Toinette's files."

"So who are Aurelie and Hode? Were they the people in the masks?"

"Nothing in the files says that directly, but I believe that is the implication. The build, skin tone, and heights from the video back up that implication."

"This goes a long way to explain how someone can become the murderous woman we encountered. If I'd watched my parents..." I couldn't finish the sentence. Just thinking of that happening to my mom made me cold all over. "I cannot fathom what that would do to anyone."

I gently touched the scar on my cheek. A memento of Roxy's rage as I was pinned to the ground. She embedded one of her long, spider-like, bladed limbs right next to my face, drawing the faintest trickle of blood.

"Not to sound callous," Bastion said. "But this could be useful to you."

"That is callous."

"Roxy wants you dead, but this appears to be information that was kept from her. Information she likely wants. Information you might be able to use to lure her into a trap. Or at least trade for a reprieve from her wrath."

I gritted my teeth. "Aurelie and Hode, are they still alive?"

"They are."

I sighed and dragged a hand over my face. I was tired. I also didn't like the idea of trading my life for these two, even if they did murder Roxy's parents. Because if I gave Roxy this information, that's what would happen. But Bastion was also right. This was a lead worth following, even if I didn't use it. "Fine," I said. "I'll look into it. But for right now, I need some sleep. And I need you to analyze all this new data."

"Don't ignore this," Bastion said with surprising force.

"I won't. I know what she did to you. She's going to answer for that."

Bastion was silent. I waited for a reply, any reply, but none came. After a few minutes like that, I left my garage and weaved through the halls until I was home. An advertisement for the newest Kawasaki flying motorcycle suddenly covered my entire front door. I watched it for a few seconds. It did look really cool, but I had no intention of replacing Poe. I swiped the ad away and entered the apartment. Quynn was relaxed on the couch watching an old episode of a sitcom we both loved.

"Been for a swim?" they asked when they looked at me. My clothes were soaked from the bay. Torn and stained from the crash. "And a fight with a truck?"

"Yes, and surprisingly close to the mark. Neither was my idea," I said. "I have an apprentice now."

Several looks of surprise crossed Quynn's face. They knew everything about me, including the story I'd told Nox at the diner. They also knew how that event shaped my views on having an apprentice of my own.

"You okay?" Quynn asked.

I nodded. "I need a shower."

"Want me to warm up dinner?"

"I ate." I leaned over the back of the couch on my way to the bathroom, planting a kiss on Quynn's cheek. They squeezed my hand.

The shower was as hot as I could stand it, my brown skin reddening a little under the heat. I breathed in the steam, scented heavily with artificial Earth flowers, and tried to work out the knots in my neck and shoulders. If I wasn't careful, Nox was going to put me in an early grave from stress alone. I scrubbed away the day, noticing rips in the artificial skin of both arms and one of my legs. Add that to the list of things I needed to take care of. But that's what happens when I'm in a car crash and go on an impromptu job while wearing limbs designed for sleeping and lounging.

Feeling warm and refreshed, I plopped down on the couch next to Quynn. Despite my lack of hunger, I grabbed a handful of nuts and dried fruit from the bowl sitting between us.

"Tell me about your apprentice," Quynn said as they turned down the volume on the viewscreen. "Anybody I've met?"

I told Quynn everything about Nox. His penchant for words and phrases that didn't make sense to anybody else. His strictly black-and-white fashion. His bleeding-edge tech that had saved my life, but he relied upon too heavily. His seeming inability to listen to my instructions and penchant for putting his own life at risk.

"Sounds like somebody I know."

"You never knew that version of me," I said. "She grew up the day my mentor went away."

Quynn sighed. "I know. I just mean you need to be patient while you're being firm. I know the latter comes easier for you than the former. He's young."

"Very young."

"He has a lot to learn from you. From the world. You might have to take some lower-risk jobs and bring your profile down a bit while he's under your wing."

"Lower my profile?" I asked and then put the entire handful of snacks in my mouth.

"You followed Vert after the crash," Quynn said. "And we're definitely going to talk about that crash and this Josephine lady, by the way. Anyway, you followed Vert. Took advantage of the timing."

I nodded while I chewed.

"That was dangerous. I know you're careful. Mostly. But you're used to looking out only for yourself in the field. Now you have him. Maybe you shouldn't have followed Vert with your apprentice in tow and these flimsy limbs on. Before you dive headlong into a situation like you do, remember you have him, that he doesn't know how to be as careful."

I swallowed and took Quynn's hand. "Why are you always right?"

Quynn shrugged and smirked.

"It's annoying."

"Well, nobody is perfect," Quynn said and shoved some of the nuts and dried fruit in her own mouth.

I leaned my head back on the couch cushion, watching the dysfunctional, fictional family on the viewscreen get up to some familiar antics. All of the characters were drinking a special edition cola that was super-popular three years ago, the bottles prominently displayed in their hands. Then everything started shifting, growing darker around the bottle, and then the dark hand crushed the bottle. But the can didn't just crush, it exploded, shards of clear polymer slowly spiraling out, bathed in green light.

Green light. Pulsing. Thrumming. Filling my vision in the shape of a hammer. A glowing, green tattoo etched on Theo's face.

"Five companies," he said, his voice a hoarse whisper, like his mouth was filled with dirt.

I tried to speak, to tell him I was sorry, that I hadn't meant for him to die, but nothing came out of my mouth.

"Five companies," he said again, more forcefully. Mud bubbled from his gaping mouth as he did.

I startled awake, Quynn's hand on my shoulder. The viewscreen was off. Only the lights of the advertisements outside lit our apartment in dim, moving colors.

"Let's go to bed," they said.

I nodded, rising off the couch. I really hoped Theo wouldn't visit my dreams again tonight, but I knew he would.

#   #   #

I sat backward on Poe, eating from a box of white gruyere crackers. I'd tossed the tarp on the floor. Quynn sat beside me on a stack of totes, reaching out for crackers on occasion. We munched in relative silence.

After sleeping in, catching up on news, and eating a light breakfast, Quynn decided to join me in the garage. I wasn't the only one curious about what would turn up on Josephine's enormous data files. We were both looking at the ultra-wide viewscreen. On the left side, Josephine Toinette-Deus' picture was surrounded by other pictures and documents. A few of her close associates. Lists of the people she'd evangelized to Ibhalism not just from Corto Corporation, but from all four of the other companies outside

Toinette Holdings.

"Funny enough," I said, "this is a connection between the five companies."

"You think it's what Theo meant?" Quynn asked.

I shook my head. "This feels too small, too one-sided. This is Josephine pulling people to her, not really connecting the companies. I could be wrong, though."

On the right side of the viewscreen were several pictures of the Offworld Relay that dominated the Cirilla skyline. I still felt like a fool for not thinking of it. Hessod was right. We all learned about it in school. Every communication or data stream that came to Little Sekhmet Settlement from anywhere else in Earth Space ran through that tower. Same with every communication or data stream leaving our little planet.

"So why is there only one of those on the whole planet?" I asked.

"Something about rare metals?" Quynn said.

"The Amana Translight Data Relay System," Bastion chimed in, "uses seventeen kilograms of thorium, eleven-point-three kilograms of mercury, nine kilograms of highly pressurized platinum dust, and a titanium-rhodium weave that—"

"We get it," I said. "Lots of science. Hard to get."

"None of these elements exist naturally on Little Sekhmet Settlement," Bastion said. "Thorium can be refined on-planet, but the rest of them have been fully mined out on Earth and the rest of the Sol system. Shipping costs alone to replace our relay would be billions of credits."

"So all five companies have to use it if they want to send data offworld," Quynn said.

"Which they do," I said. "I remember Dr. Corto telling me the vast majority of Corto Corporation's business happens offworld. I'm sure it's the same for the others."

"It is," Bastion said.

"Then Hessod is right," Quynn said. "They all connect there. Worth checking out."

"And practically impossible to," I said, standing up from my bike and handing the box of crackers to Quynn. I walked to the viewscreen, pointing at the picture of the tower. "There's a convention center and hotel complex attached to the tower. Three stories tall. That's where your game tournament is happening this weekend. The next several floors of the tower are basically a museum for the Offworld Relay and Little Sekhmet Settlement.

"Above that, the security is so tight, I can barely get any information on it. One elevator. I have no idea what's between floor six and the top, almost two hundred floors up. No windows. No landing pads. Just black, semi-matte metal."

"Then there's the top of the relay," I said, and all the rest of the pictures and documents fell away on the viewscreen, Bastion pulling up an enlarged picture of the relay, which looked like an enormous lotus blossom of glimmering blues, blacks, and reds. The "petals" of the relay spun slowly like a complicated series of rings moving in opposite directions.

"Pretty," Quynn said.

"Yeah, but I have no idea how to get there. Earth Space enforces a no-fly zone around the tower. I'll need to scout the place before I can do anything."

"Nobody in the city has information on it?"

I shrugged.

"Surely someone does," Bastion said. "But all I've been able to find are licensing agreements between three of the companies and the Offworld Relay. They were all digitally signed by Horus McLaughlin. No pronouns."

"Company name?" I asked. "Horus McLaughlin does not have a company name."

"A freelancer?" I asked.

"Not in the way you think," Bastion said. "He does not live in The Mist, but he does not work for any of the five companies. He lives on Cirilla and represents the relay, which is operated by Earth Space Coalition."

"Sounds like a place to start," Quynn said. "What does all this have to do with Josephine?"

"Nothing," I said, turning back to the viewscreen. Bastion put the preacher's picture and her associated people and documents back up. "Absolutely nothing. And I know I shouldn't be worried about all this since she's trying to kill me."

"Perhaps she thinks she already did kill you," Bastion said.

"She knew at a glance that I worked for Corto as an Intel Operative. She knows Gustin. She found my name, the building that the Intel division had moved to not even three months ago, and then hacked into the exact Stryder I hired to fly home. Oh, and her bodyguard has seen my apprentice's face. I'm pretty sure she knows I didn't die in that crash."

"I don't like this," Quynn said as they rose to their feet.

"I don't either," I said.

"No," Quynn said, taking me by the hand and making sure I was looking at them directly. "This isn't right. After Theo, you said it wouldn't be like this anymore. Back to normal. Do your job and come back home to me. This is all feeling a bit too much like before."

"But it's not," I said.

"Oh?"

"This isn't even about me. Whatever Josephine is after, it's more about her and Corto than me. I'm in the middle by accident."

"You're still in the middle." I nodded, conceding the point. "So don't go after her, after this preacher," Quynn said. "Just get out of the middle. Let Gustin handle this fight. Come with me to Cirilla. You can scope out the relay while I attend the convention."

"That does sound nice." We kissed. Bastion stayed wisely silent.

"So you walk away from this?" Quynn asked, nodding toward the picture of Josephine.

"I'll try," I said.

"I'm going back to the apartment," Quynn said after they pulled away. "I can't keep looking at all this."

"Okay."

"Are you going to be long?"

I shook my head.

"Good," they said, and then looked at the viewscreen. "And I expect you to help her untangle from this mess, Bastion."

"I'll do my best," the AI said over the speakers.

Quynn pecked me on the cheek, and then left the garage, snagging the open box of crackers on the way out.

"So how do we get you out of the middle?" Bastion asked.

"I don't trust Gustin to do anything other than throw me into the fight even more," I said. "So we need to shut it down."

"I don't think that's what Quynn had in mind."

"Probably not, but if Josephine could find me outside of the Intel offices and put a Stryder into The Mist, how long before she finds my address and goes after Quynn?"

"So to extract yourself from this problem, you intend to dive even deeper into it."

"Temporarily," I said. "For it to work, I'm going to need leverage."

"There is nothing leverageable in the files you took from her office."

"Then we'll have to visit Josephine at home."

"In Toinette's Deus Quarter?"

"Yeah. In the only no-fly zone in Jayu City."

CHAPTER TEN

ONLY A FEW BLOCKS FROM my apartment, I pushed the handlebars of my bike into a nearly straight dive, The Mist rushing up to meet me. Then I remembered to ease off the throttle. I still wasn't used to the upgraded thrusters. Rumor was they could put my Kawasaki up over three hundred kilometers per hour, but the very thought of that made my face itch.

"Text Echo, please," I said.

"The usual?" Bastion replied.

"Yes."

Poe and I passed into The Mist, and I watched the altimeter on my display. I had no intention of crashing into the street again. Twenty-five meters. Twenty meters. Fifteen. At twelve meters, I pulled back on the handlebars and the bike leveled out just as The Mist cleared ten meters above the street. Below me was the familiar hive of Mistwalkers, people who had tossed off the corporations above. This was how it was supposed to look, without broken Stryders burning in the middle of the street. People going about their lives, struggling without the safety net of a corporation.

Most citizens of the corporations never came down here. Some of them only thought the Mistwalkers were a myth, that there was no way anybody would live in the sunless, disused streets at the foundation of the city. The

Mistwalkers I knew were pretty cagey about why they lived down here. I heard mumbles about freedom and identity, but it seemed terrible to me. My Corto Corporation citizenship guaranteed me work, a place to live, good food, and healthcare. And I belonged to something a lot bigger than me.

Despite all of that, I needed to come down here at least every couple of weeks. The Intel Office could get me all sorts of great toys and gear I needed for jobs, but only items officially in production from Corto Corporation. If I needed to get something bleeding edge or experimental, or something from another corporation without showing up on their security cameras, The Mist was the place to go.

The street was lined with little stalls selling food and all sorts of wares. A couple holding hands and wearing mismatching faux denim were shopping last season's handbags. A teenager with half their head shorn and the other half flowing with green hair down to their knees was perusing homemade optical implants. The oldest person I'd ever seen was leaning on an ancient cybernetic leg like it was a cane while they haggled over discarded and reprogrammed nanobots. If the corporations above threw it away, it wound up down here. Mistwalkers could get just about anything.

And Echo was my go-to supplier. Maybe he was a friend, too. It was hard to tell with Echo. We were loyal to each other, so maybe that was enough. I truly had no idea how he felt about me or if he had any friends.

I took a wide and careful approach around a corner and immediately started scanning the area around Echo's landing pad. A few rodents were scurrying around, but otherwise, the landing pad was empty. I cruised on in, keeping a watchful eye as I set Poe down close to Echo's front door. Inevitably, my eyes were drawn to the small puncture in the middle of the landing pad. That was where I'd met Roxy the first time. The first time she tried to kill me. I absently rubbed the scar on my cheek again.

I shook off the memory and stood in front of Echo's door. After a few seconds, the heavy thing slid open. I stepped in, and it slammed shut behind me.

"Feet," Echo called from back in his shop. "Feet. Feet."

I grabbed a pair of fuzzy, pink slippers from a bin next to the door and put them on the carbon-polymer feet of my work limbs. I wasn't going to be caught off guard by Josephine again, and I felt safer with them whenever I visited The Mist.

I walked up an aisle of pristine shelves nearly three meters tall. This particular aisle was well-stocked with clothes from Huginn Industries, cybernetic hands and fingers, and a wide selection of handheld tablets. I never understood Echo's organizational system, but I knew he had one. I also knew that if I ever asked, I'd probably never get him to stop explaining it.

Echo was standing behind his wide counter at the back of the shop, pale, bald, and shirtless. I'd never seen him with a shirt on. A cybernetic leg was arrayed in front of him, the calf completely disassembled. Each little gear and wire and plate was spotless and carefully aligned to some imaginary grid. Echo's metallic fingers were open, multiple tools extending out of each one so it looked like a couple of dozen screwdrivers and soldering irons and whatnot were crawling over the leg.

"No spider," Echo said without looking up from his work. "No spider. No spider."

He meant Roxy. I'd texted. He'd checked. The usual. Maybe I was being paranoid, but at least I was in good company here.

"I'm making a run at Toinette's Deus Quarter," I said.

Echo's eyebrows moved up by a couple of millimeters, but he didn't stop what he was doing. "No-fly zone. No landing. No Poe. No Poe. No Poe."

"I know," I said. Toinette's Deus Quarter was the core of their spiritual life. It was home to all the Ibhalism clergy, those with the Deus division name. No personal or commercial craft was allowed to fly in. I'd never been but from the pictures I'd seen, all the landing pads had been converted into green spaces. Footbridges crisscrossed the gaps between buildings. It was beautiful but seemed like an unnecessary bit of asceticism. There was a lot I didn't understand about Ibhalism.

"Forty-two buildings. Thirteen thousand floors. Eight thousand. Eight thousand. Eight thousand kilometers of bridges." Echo shook his head while he rattled off the numbers.

"I'm not planning to walk," I said. As I told him my plan and what I needed, he finally stopped tinkering with the leg.

#   #   #

Every borough of Jayu City had a company-regulated maximum altitude for personal vehicles. In Corto Corporation, that was fifteen hundred meters. The others were all around the same number. For Toinette Holdings, it was eighteen hundred meters. Higher than that was reserved for commercial travel and shipping lanes. It was also the limit of the Deus Quarter's no-fly enforcement. I was riding Poe through the Huginn Industries borough, heading for the Toinette borough, and climbing past thirteen hundred meters. I'd never taken her this high, but the hyperthrusters were having no issues thus far.

I passed fourteen hundred meters as I crossed into Toinette at 25:00, well after sunset and three hours until midnight. For the first time in my life, the height made me nervous. Just me, Poe, and a whole lot of sparkling city below me.

I passed fifteen hundred meters and felt a little lightheaded. The air was thinning.

"It's time for your helmet," Bastion said.

I reached back and tapped a plate magnetically attached to my upper vertebrae. Nanobots swarmed over my head and neck, a slight tickle and itch, but more noticeably, the air stopped touching my skin in spots the nanobots built the helmet around my head. The little robots blocked off my mouth and nose, and I held my breath for the few seconds it took them to finish. Then the bots crept up to my eyes, temporarily blinding me as the helmet structure solidified. After a long three seconds, my display came back, the nanobots working in conjunction with my visual implants. Less than a second later, I took a deep breath of air augmented by the first of Echo's new additions: an oxygen supplementer installed in the helmet. According to him, I would be able to go into low orbit without losing consciousness with it.

It was a pretty view, Jayu City, the jewel of Little Sekhmet Settlement spreading out below me. I always thought it was a little funny that our planet, populated by humans for over two centuries, was still called a settlement. That felt impermanent, somehow. But it was an Earth Space distinction. Settlements were planets founded and settled by private individuals and corporations. Colonies were controlled by Earth Space government. In school, I learned that Hiromi Jayu founded Jayu City under a single corporation. In the century that followed their death, the companies split and split until one became five.

Sixteen hundred meters went by, and then seventeen hundred soon enough after. Now it was time for Echo's next trick. I flipped the little manual switch mounted next to my right hand on the handlebars. The hyperthrusters immediately shut down, putting Poe and me into freefall for a moment before a different set of thrusters came online. I didn't feel or hear them, but my ascension resumed instantly. They were a smaller version of the escape thrusters used by starships. Very experimental. Something about gravity inversion waves. Too technical for me. In his own way, Echo made it clear that these were loaners and that the price would be a detailed account of how they performed. More importantly, they wouldn't set off any scanners searching for personal vehicles above Toinette's altitude limit. Combined with the matte black paint specially blended to absorb radar and lidar I already had on Poe, hopefully, it would make me invisible.

I passed eighteen hundred meters, Toinette's regulated limit, and I leveled Poe off. I waited for an incoming security transmission or a pursuit vehicle.

"How do you feel?" Bastion asked.

"Fine," I said, more focused on the airspace below and around me.

"How is the air?"

"Good. Doesn't feel thin. Do you hear any chatter on Toinette's security frequencies?"

"Plenty," Bastion said, "but nothing regarding you."

"Good," I said, turning Poe a full one hundred and ten degrees to my left, toward the Deus Quarter. I wanted to make sure that if anyone was watching my trajectory before I turned off the hyperthrusters, they wouldn't know my final destination.

"Are you certain this is the right plan?" Bastion asked.

"I've never jumped from this high, but I think the plan is good."

"That's not what I mean. I mean keeping yourself in the middle of this fight. Going after Josephine. You know it's the opposite of what Quynn wants. And…"

"And what?"

"I hate to say this, but I'm not enough backup. I have my limits. I don't think you can outmaneuver Josephine without someone physically there to help you."

"You sound like Quynn," I said. "We both care about you, so I take that as a compliment."

Now I just felt bad. I said, "What alternative do I have? I feel like Gustin is throwing me to a wolf here. Nobody else is going to get me out of it."

"What about Dr. Ariela Corto? She could certainly pull some of Gustin's strings, make sure her star Intel Operative isn't killed off."

"So instead of one person I'm not sure I can trust," I said. "You want me to ask someone I know I can't trust. You and I both know that the CEO doesn't care about me. She's looking out for herself. Maybe the company, too, though I think that's just part of watching out for herself."

"She is invested in my success," Bastion said.

"She's invested in the world and Earth Space not finding out you exist. I'm not sure how or if your success comes into play."

Bastion said nothing.

"We need to take care of this," I said. "Just find a way to get Josephine to leave me out of whatever she has with Gustin and Corto Corporation. Then we can get back to important business."

"And you believe this visit to her home will accomplish that?"

"Everybody has skeletons in their closets. Some secret, something they're ashamed of. I just need something to give me the leverage. Something I can hold over her to make me a less viable target."

"A little blackmail."

"Exactly."

"Assuming she doesn't see you as an even bigger threat and come after you even harder," Bastion said.

"That's always the risk with blackmail."

"This is a terrible plan."

"It is," I said. "But it's the best plan I have."

I crossed into the Deus Quarter of Toinette Holdings. At least that's what my GPS said. From this high up, it was indistinguishable from other parts of the borough. Vehicle thrusters were barely pinpricks from this far away, so it just looked like more twinkling nighttime city.

"No Toinette security chatter about a vehicle entering the no-fly zone," Bastion said.

"Good," I said. "Can you bring up AR guidance?"

Then hovering in the air before me was a blinking green line, curving slightly to the left and vanishing a hundred meters away. I followed the line on my display. I needed to be exact for this next part. As I proceeded, the end of the curved line came into view as it turned sharply into a sheer vertical, disappearing a hundred meters below. In moments, Poe and I were hovering directly over that vertical.

"This suddenly feels very stupid," I said as I looked over the side of the bike, my destination unrecognizable from this far away.

"Because it is very stupid," Bastion said.

"Yeah," I said, and then threw a leg over Poe's seat and dived headfirst from eighteen hundred meters up.

CHAPTER ELEVEN

I STARTED JUMPING OFF BUILDINGS when I was twelve. Back then, my only modifications were pretty basic aural and communications implants. My mom bought them for me as a tenth birthday gift, though I think it was more for her own peace of mind so I would have no excuse for not calling her.

My friends and I found surplus glider suits on the Net, and we would jump from landing pads, freefalling for a couple of dozen floors before deploying the glider wings. We would weave through buildings and land on lower landing pads a dozen blocks away. Then we would take the elevators up and do it all over again.

I was grounded, literally and figuratively, for months when my mom found out.

My love of adrenaline was part of why I became an Intel Operative. Not that every operative leaped off buildings or bikes to get in and out of places, but there were no rules or regulations or worrying mothers telling me I couldn't. Jumping from my bike eighteen hundred meters up into literally thin air was different. My various ailerons and flaps on my limbs were making small adjustments so I could stay on that AR line, and I had been at terminal velocity for almost a minute already.

"Fifteen hundred meters," Bastion said even though my altimeter was in the upper right of my display, quickly counting down. I still wasn't sure how an AI could be worried, but it was nice.

In the span of only a few breaths, the Deus Quarter below changed from indecipherable cityscape to clearly defined buildings. Outside the Deus Quarter, little dots of thruster lights moved between the buildings like an ever-flowing sparkle of waterways. Inside the Quarter, the spaces between buildings were empty other than the omnipresent advertisements towering on the sides of buildings.

In three more breaths, the Deus Quarter filled my vision, the green AR line pointing at a building directly in the middle.

"Twelve hundred meters," Bastion said. "Less than two hundred meters to landing."

"Ready," I said. I was focused on my landing point, a green space atop the center building, which was growing larger and larger by the nanosecond. The surrounding buildings were zooming out of my peripheral vision. Exactly thirty meters above the top of the building, my entire display flashed red. I pulled my knees and elbows into my chest and yelled, "Canopy! Canopy! Canopy!"

A sparkling blue light surrounded me, similar to what Nox had used, though a different color. I brace myself for impact, for the knock-off anti-inertial field to fall short of the brand-name one. But just like on the street in Corto, my internal organs felt a sudden stop. A wave of nausea hit me, but nothing else did. The sparkling light fell away and I was kneeling in the middle of a garden. Nothing bent or broken except a few flowers beneath my feet.

I tapped the plate on the back of my neck, and the helmet disassembled. Green was everywhere, along with bright splashes of floral color here and there. Little paths made of sand-colored pebbles wound through the green like a spiderweb. The air was heavy with humidity. Green spaces weren't unheard of on the rooftops of Jayu City, but they weren't common, either. I'd certainly never seen one as vast or well-maintained as this one. I took a deep breath, flooded by the perfume of real flowers. I sneezed.

"Gesundheit," a voice to my left said. It was raspy, deep, and had an accent I couldn't place.

I turned to see a pair of people dressed in dingy brown robes, roughly the same height, though the robes made their bodies shapeless. Both figures had shaven heads with golden tattoos in similar, swirling patterns.

"Thank you," I said. "And good evening."

The pair looked at each other briefly before the raspy one spoke again. "You are not supposed to be here."

"I'm just visiting."

"Leave now, please," one of them said.

"I believe those are monks from the Siblinghood of Aphnette," Bastion said. "They tend the gardens. The tattoos denote some sort of rank, though there's nothing on the Net that deciphers them."

"Gardeners," I whispered. "And here I was worried."

"Please leave," Raspy Monk said.

"I'm just visiting Josephine," I said. "I wanted some fresh air. It's so beautiful up here. Am I not allowed?"

The pair of monks glanced at each other again, and then Quiet Monk produced a device from their robes that quickly extended into a two-meter staff. Raspy Monk did the same a moment later.

I held my hands up and took a step back from them. Since I'd barely survived a string of fights with Roxy and Theo a few months ago, I'd taken precautions. When I repaired my work limbs, I added expensive alloy reinforcements. My joints were now able to bend an extra fifteen degrees. Despite Echo's pleas, I didn't add any weapon mods. I wanted to defend myself, not kill anyone. To that end, I'd also been taking classes on Corto Capoeira and Jeet Kun Do. Both martial arts had given me the same guidance. The quickest way to end any fight wasn't a pressure point or well-aimed kick. It was just to run.

So I did just that. I turned on my heel and swept my eyes across the roof of the building. Before I could blink, the exit down into the building highlighted yellow on my display. Thank you, Bastion. I took off toward it, the extra fifteen degrees in my hips, knees, and ankles making me noticeably faster than I'd been before the upgrades. I could hear the footfalls of the monks behind me, but they were slower, losing ground with every step.

Before I even reached the door, I could see it was locked, but only with an old-fashioned deadbolt. My lockpicks were out of my fingertips before I even reached the door, and I had it open in less than a second, pulling it shut hard behind me. In an instant, I swapped my lockpicks for an arc-welder, and in a pop of bright heat, welded the deadbolt into the locked position. I was able to take three full, deep breaths before the door finally shuddered with the monks' efforts to open it.

"Not so difficult," I said. "You have arrived surprisingly un-punched," Bastion said.

"Very funny," I said, taking in the small stairway descending before me. The stairs were concrete and narrow. A dim light illuminated the landing half a dozen steps down from me. "This looks like a service stair."

"Security offices or server rooms are frequently close to service stairs," Bastion said.

"I know. Makes me worried." I started my way down the stairs two at a time.

"Why?"

"Whenever I feel like I'm getting lucky, it usually means a very bad thing is just around the corner."

"It seems to me that very bad thing is exactly who we're heading toward."

"I like that," I said as I kept descending the stairs, looking for the first door that would open. "Like reverse karma."

"Whatever puts you at ease."

I finally found a door, though it had no window. I slowly turned the handle and opened it a couple of centimeters. I deployed a fiberoptic camera from my left pinky. As soon as I had it through and turned left, I saw a dozen monks jogging directly toward me. I retracted the camera, let go of the door, and jumped straight up. My feet and hands spun on their joints, and I stuck to the ceiling like an insect. I crawled backward a little just as the door below me burst open, the monk squad pouring in and up the stairs. The pair on the roof must have called their siblings. As soon as the last of the monks had moved past on the landing directly above me, I dropped back down and darted through the door. I wasn't sure how long that weld would hold all of them, but there was a chance that they wouldn't be able to break it. That meant they would all be coming right back down. No time to waste.

The hall looked like any other apartment building in Jayu City. Boring, patterned carpet ran the length in navy and gold. The walls were painted an uninspired beige. For the first time in years, I was on a job and had no idea where I was going. No analyst support. No blueprints. Nothing but the public information that Josephine Toinette-Deus lived in this building.

"Thermals," I said, already jogging down the hall. "Deep penetration."

The normal visual spectrum changed to a rainbow gradient of shapes with a white wireframe overlaid so I didn't run into the walls. Most inanimate objects were blue or green, taking up most of my vision with the penetration this deep. I was seeing through multiple walls and rooms at once. People were moving around. Human-shaped blobs of yellow and orange. Lines of black ran in straight horizontal and vertical lines. Those were water pipes in the walls, just like the thin green lines were electricity.

"What are you looking for?" Bastion asked.

"A server stack or very large terminal," I said. "Given how much data we pulled from her job site, I'm guessing she has some significant hardware at home, too."

"A rather large assumption."

"Educated guess based on years of dealing with people like Josephine."

"You've dealt with lots of preachers who know an Intel Operative on sight?"

He had me there. "Just help me look."

Bastion had access to all of my sensors, just like I did, but he wasn't constrained by a human brain. I could only focus on one thing at a time, no matter how sophisticated my tools were. Time and again, he'd shown that he could take in all of that data, review it in real-time, and re-review it at the same time. He could spot things I'd missed. A handful of computer terminals on this level gave off the heat I was looking for, but nothing concentrated enough for my needs. I stood still a moment and swept my gaze down, searching through several floors below, but still didn't see what I needed.

"Normal vision," I said, and my visual display snapped back. I hustled along another fifteen meters to an elevator bank, which was surprisingly devoid of security cameras. I slapped the down button, and in a few moments, stepped onto an elevator.

"Back to thermals, please," I said, and I was scanning the area around me as the elevator began its descent.

"Is it possible this building doesn't have security?" Bastion said.

I shook my head, momentarily forgetting that he couldn't see the gesture. "There's no way. I can't think like that."

"Why?"

"Because that's an assumption that gets us caught or worse."

While I was still scanning, the elevator started to slow and I heard a faint ding in the hallway outside.

"Elise," Bastion said, immediately flipping my display back to normal vision.

"Sparks," I whispered. I looked up and quickly located a maintenance hatch. I scampered up, gently lowering the hatch beneath me just as the doors opened and the car shook with entering bodies. Muddled voices were speaking in the elevator as it started to ascend, but I couldn't make them out. I pressed an ear to the elevator and let my aural implants do the rest of the work.

"…just appeared on the roof?" one person said. Their voice was low, rumbling through the ceiling.

"That's what Tasha and Hoyimm said," another voice said, quieter and wispy. "There was a flash of purple or something, and then this stranger all in black was standing on the roof in the middle of the spiral lilies."

"Are you sure Tasha and Hoyimm weren't smoking the spiral lilies?" the deeper voice asked.

"There was definitely someone there," the wispy voice said. "Abrim is still trying to get the roof door opened. The lock is welded shut."

"By Aphnette's holy hands. And they said they were visiting Josephine, the gall. As if anyone ever visits her outside of one of her parties."

"As if she is ever even here otherwise."

"They may know where Josephine's apartment is!" Bastion barked, too loud for how sensitive my implants were at that moment. Right. There were times when running was the best option available. And there were other times when a fight was really the only option. I had a feeling I was closing in on the latter. I took a breath and carefully lifted the maintenance hatch just enough to fit my camera.

"Careful what you say about Josephine," the deeper voice said, and I could see the person speaking was short and squat. Built big like Hessod, though a head and a half shorter. Another monk. Did anyone actually live in this building beyond the monks?

"It's just us," the wispy voice said, another monk, tall and lanky. They seemed to limp a bit whenever they shifted their weight. "And she is the darling. Nobody is bringing in new followers like she is."

"Evangelism has never been our way, sibling," the deeper voice said. They moved a bit, leaning against a railing directly beneath the hatch.

That would have to do. I wrenched the hatch fully open and yelled, "By Aphnette's holy hand!"

Both monks gaped up in astonishment. More importantly, the one with the deeper voice lifted their weight from the railing. I dropped straight down on them, landing awkwardly on their shoulders. The monk went down to a knee with a grunt, but I held on, squeezing their head with my thighs. Then with a slap to the top of their head, I deployed my tasers at half-charge.

The monk crumpled entirely beneath me, but I wasn't able to clear my legs in time. The heavy, unconscious monk rolled onto my right leg, pinning it to the floor at the knee. It didn't hurt since it was all cybernetic, but the monk was even heavier than they'd appeared. I was stuck.

The lankier monk took a swing at me, wild and wide. With my leg pinned and my torso leaning hard to one side, I was barely able to get a forearm up in time. The monk hit harder than I would have anticipated, but my upgraded mods took the blow without complaint. The lanky monk, however, grimaced and held their arm where it had met mine.

Finally, I grabbed the heavier monk by the back of the collar and lifted, freeing my leg. At my full height, I found myself eye-to-eye with the lankier monk, who looked terrified. I slapped the stop button on the elevator and said, "I won't hurt you if you answer one question."

Lanky Monk nodded.

"But if you lie to me," I said. "I'll hurt you much worse than I hurt your friend."

Lanky Monk glanced down at the heap behind me, and then back to me. They paled and nodded again.

"Where is Josephine Toinette-Deus' apartment?"

#   #   #

After the near violence of the roof and stairwell and the actual violence of the elevator, breaking into Josephine's apartment was simple. I'd seen no security cameras in the building. No security office or guards, for that matter. Just the monks and other residents, or so Lanky Monk told me. They said there was no need for other security in this building, at least not before now. They told me right before I stunned them and dragged both monks into a maintenance closet. That was exhausting.

Josephine's door was standard-filled fiberglass with a thumbprint scanner lock. A Toinette AX18, common enough that I had the bypass codes stored in my onboard memory. I hacked it wirelessly in less than five seconds, and I was in. Lights immediately came on when I entered. After a tiny moment of panic, I realized that meant nobody else was here. The lights were just triggered by motion, which was unusual for a residence.

I took a breath and looked over the enormous, expertly decorated room before me. I'd seen pictures of it online from various social and evangelical events held here, but it was even grander in person. Swirling glass chandeliers hung from the vaulted ceiling, throwing a mosaic glow around the clean, white walls. After the initial awe, I noticed it didn't look much like a living room, though. There was no viewscreen. No comfortable chairs or luxurious couches. Instead, the edge of the huge space was dotted with tall cocktail tables and a smattering of stylish but uncomfortable-looking chairs.

It was set for a party, but nobody was here. Strange. I crept through the space, keeping an eye out for cameras but not finding any. I went through a door and found the kitchen. It was spotless. Not just clean, but clear of clutter. Oddly so. I opened the refrigerator. Empty. Not even a condiment bottle. I opened the cabinets, and found them well-stocked, but only with tiny, high-end plates and scores of drinkware.

"It's like this is just for parties. Nothing else," I said aloud.

"The place is very clean for an unoccupied residence," Bastion said. "Not even dust."

"Easy enough to pay to have the place cleaned every week. What I don't understand," I said as I left the kitchen, "is why keep this place? It's huge. Expensive."

"It is an excellent place for social gatherings."

"Sure." I crossed the living room and turned down a hallway. "But she could rent a space like this. A lot bigger than this and it would still be cheaper than just keeping this place year-round."

"Maybe this was a perk of her job?" Bastion asked. "Or a gift from the monks?"

"That would make a lot of sense if she had another address where she lived."

"Another address available in a database I can access."

"Fair point," I said and kept moving through the apartment. Both bathrooms were well-appointed, looking absolutely normal at first. But when I opened the drawers, I found no medicines or hygiene products. Finally, I found the master bedroom at the end of the hallway. Again, it was huge and gorgeous, but missing all the personal touches to indicate that anyone ever slept here even a single night.

"Perhaps this is just how she chooses to live," Bastion said. "All things in balance with Ibhalism, yes? Private and public? Luxury and asceticism?"

"No painkillers or toothpaste in the bathroom?" I asked. "No clothes in her closets or places to charge her mods? No, this isn't just balance. Even those monks mentioned she's never here. This is something else."

"It could be that she's extremely private. Private enough to keep this as her public home, but actually lives somewhere else."

"Then why lie?" I asked as I wandered back to the living room. "She could keep her home address private without keeping this charade. There's something else going on. Give me thermals again, please?"

My vision switched and I looked around. Everything looked positively normal. Electrical and data and water conduits snaked through the walls, floor, and ceiling. Wide ducts showed several degrees warmer than the room itself. No secret servers. No odd gaps in the wiring or water to reveal a hidden door. I searched every room, tried every likely hiding spot and several very unlikely ones. Frustration was making my guts bubble.

"Normal vision, please," I said with a sigh. "There's nothing here."

"I have to agree," Bastion said. "Whatever Josephine is doing, she isn't doing it here."

"Mother of Corto," I cursed under my breath, and then I left Josephine's apartment and started back toward the elevators.

But then I stopped. Something was off. I turned back and saw it. I'd been so focused on reaching Josephine's apartment, I hadn't really been looking at the other doors before. Across the hall and one door down from Josephine's was a door unlike any others. The texture was impossibly smooth with absolutely no visible lock or handle. The door frame was subtly bulkier than all of the rest, too. I smiled.

"Now that, you don't see every day."

"What?" Bastion asked.

"You have the Net at your disposal," I said. "What do you see?"

"One moment," Bastion said. Several seconds passed before he continued. "This door is produced by Huginn Industries."

"Not just that," I said, passing my hand over it. "It's the Huginn Arctic One. The most advanced security door in Jayu City. I haven't encountered one before, but according to our reports, Huginn Intel Operatives were consulted in its design."

"Can you get through it?"

I shook my head. "It's made from a new metal alloy that absorbs virtually all vibrations. And the locking mechanisms, I only know the ad copy. They're made to repel Intel Operatives."

"So this is a dead-end?"

"No," I said. "I just have to go around it."

Chapter Twelve

HIGH-END SECURITY MEASURES LIKE the Huginn Arctic One were obviously designed to provide security. And they did, to an extent. What they really provided was a *sense* of security. And that sense could often undermine actual security. When I'd been looking around Josephine's apartment using my thermal imaging, I'd tried various depths. In doing so, I'd noticed there were no other people on the entire floor. Or the floors above or below this one. I had filed it away as curious, but not really relevant. Now it was a blessing.

"Are you going to shimmy through the air ducts?" Bastion asked.

"No," I said.

The Huginn Arctic One was built to be impervious to all but a high-powered directional charge, and the hinges would likely have given way long before the door would. The lock was likely a combination of biometric, cybermetric, and dynamic algorithmic keys. Those first two were pretty common, but the last was like the chip in my neck that allowed me into the Corto Intel offices. That was my best guess, at least. It's how I would design a door to keep out people like me.

"Going outside to come back in through a window?"

"No."

As a very good Intel Operative, I knew how to get past the first two with a face-to-face visit with my mark on the day of the heist. That code, though, was different. Several analysts in our office had been working on how to get those codes from a potential mark, but to no avail yet. However, when you bought a state-of-the-art security door that was basically unhackable, you often ignored some other possible entry points, like the wall right next to the door. Drywall. Fiberglass studs. Sound-dampening insulation that was little more than foam. Someone—and I would have bet good money that someone was Josephine—had installed an impenetrable security door in an old, cheaply-made building.

"Are you going to break into the neighboring apartment and cut a hole in?" Bastion asked.

"Going through my greatest hits?"

"What?"

"The answer is no," I said. "But you're close." I moved half a meter to the left of the door, hauled back, and punched my fist straight through the wall. Don't be too impressed. That wall didn't really have a chance against reinforced carbon-polymer cybernetics.

"Oh no," Bastion said.

"What?" I punched my other arm through the wall right next to the first.

"Every security channel in Toinette just lit up. High-level alert to this building."

She didn't reinforce the wall, but she'd installed sensors I couldn't see with thermal imaging. I felt a little stupid, definitely outsmarted, but I didn't have time to dwell on it.

"I guess we found the right place," I said. "Just have to work quickly." With a twist of my wrists, both arms started to vibrate. The movement was small, but very fast, giving both forearms a blurred quality. Then I moved, both arms acting like saw blades, and ripped a hole in the wall a meter in diameter. As I pulled my arms back, I grabbed the disc of the wall and tossed it aside. Then I dived in, rolling on the floor of the room beyond and popping to my feet.

I flipped a light switch. A bare bulb hanging from the ceiling lazily illuminated a space much smaller than Josephine's showpiece apartment. It was only about the size of the bedroom I shared with Quynn. No windows. Two of the four walls were plastered with plastic printouts. They were pictures next to printed pages, paired up corner to corner from floor to ceiling. In the darkest corner of the room sat a professional atomizer. The Corto Intel offices had a couple for disposing of highly sensitive materials.

I didn't have time to examine the contents of the room, but I didn't need to right now. "More light," I said, and a pair of headlights lit up on my exposed shoulders. Then I started blinking rapidly while I moved my gaze across the first wall, triggering the camera function of my optical implants. In less than a minute, I'd taken dozens of photos, capturing every millimeter.

"Status update on security," I said.

"Four teams inbound," Bastion said. "The closest team is a little over a kilometer away, though they're having trouble wrapping up a domestic situation."

"How much time do we have?"

"Maybe three minutes before one of the other teams arrives."

I stopped taking photos, my gaze hung up on a face I recognized. Gustin. There was his picture, his usual scowl locked in place, hanging on the wall. Why? What did it mean? Were my suspicions right? Was he in league with Josephine?

"Elise," Bastion said.

That broke me out of the trance. I looked around the room, glanced back to Gustin's picture once, and then I took pictures of the next wall and snapped a few shots of the atomizer and the undecorated walls.

"A team just landed on the rooftop," Bastion said.

"Oh, the monks must be livid about their flowers."

"Yes, but I have a feeling the security forces won't have a problem with the welded lock like the monks did."

"I think you're right there," I said. "Lights off. We're out of here."

The lights on my shoulders flicked back off as I ducked through the hole in the wall. Just as I did, the elevator dinged, and half a dozen monks poured out of it. They didn't look like the ones from the elevator or roof, though. These six were heavily modded for combat. Oversized arms, optical arrays made for targeting, you name it. They were here to take me down.

I redeployed the first rule of any fight yet again. I turned in the other direction and started running. I'd made it only three steps when my left foot was suddenly yanked out from underneath me. I sprawled, my arms barely catching me before my face planted on the hallway carpet. Then I was being dragged backward nearly as fast as I'd been running. I spun to my back and pushed out my three free limbs, embedding my hands and foot in the walls and halting my movement. There was an articulated cable like a long, metal worm wrapped around my left ankle, and the other end of that cable was attached to the arm of a monk. The monk pulled, but even their hulking mods couldn't quite overcome the grip I had on the hallway. Only barely. I actually heard the motors in my shoulders whine with the effort and my left hip hurt where my mod attached to my pelvis.

"I have no fight with you lovely people," I yelled. "It seems Josephine has been using your building for some questionable activities. You should have a cable around her ankle. Or maybe her neck."

Four of the five monks who didn't have a hold of me glanced at the fifth, and I knew which one was in charge. Then that one said, "Josephine is a sibling of faith, of righteousness. What she does in the privacy of her own home is in service of the great balance."

"Is that her home?" I nodded my head toward the hole I'd made in the wall. "Or the one behind me with the giant party room? I don't think she lives there, either."

"And you," the lead monk said. "Do not live here at all. We will turn you over to Toinette Security. They can listen to your story." Then the lead monk nodded, and the other four who weren't holding me started advancing.

Bastion started, "Elise, we really need to—"

"On it," I said. I pulled my hands and foot back from the walls and rolled forward, hitting the cable with my finger-deployed arc welder. In a flash of heat and light, the cable snapped, sending its wielder sprawling into the wall behind them. I kept rolling until I was up in a kneeling position, facing the oncoming monks with my arms crossed in front of my chest, hands toward me. A sparkling yellow shield erupted from my forearms.

Before the monks had a chance to notice my shield, I turned my hands out toward them, and then pushed them forward, breaking the cross on my chest. With an immense boom, the monks were tossed backward. Lights shattered. The once-pristine walls were now webbed with cracks. My nonlethal sonic weapon—another mod courtesy of Echo—had the desired effect. I stood there for a moment, glancing at every monk, watching each chest rise and fall. They would be fine.

Another elevator dinged and an armored foot stepped out. I was ninety percent sure that was Vert, but I didn't wait to make sure. I spun and returned to my sprint, not giving the monks, Vert, or what was probably a small squad of Toinette security a chance. I knew the door I was heading toward, the one I'd gone through before. While I was still two meters away, I sent along the already-broken bypass codes, and the door to Josephine's so-called apartment opened with a simple twist of the knob.

"We need to leave the building, Elise," Bastion said. "Not hide."

"I'm not hiding." I weaved through the assorted cocktail tables, sprinting directly toward the wall of windows overlooking the garden terrace outside. Thundering footsteps weren't far behind me.

"I knew you were still alive!" Vert yelled from behind me.

I saw sliding glass doors to my right, but Vert was already in the room, running straight through the door I'd slammed behind me. The noise was horrific. I pulled back my right fist and twisted it to the right twice. A little whir emitted from it, and just before I would run right into the window, I punched. Another upgrade I'd made in the last few months. A loud pop sounded when my knuckles hit the window, a charge of focused sound and pressure firing as they made impact. The window blew outward in a dramatic shower of glass.

And I kept sprinting as the shards rained down. One foot landed in the middle of a flower bed, some tall, purple bloom crushed beneath my heel. My next foot landed in the middle of a large melon.

"Stop right there," Vert growled from behind me, closer than before. Popping sounds filled the air.

My next step landed in the middle of a narrow, shallow, fake creek. Without slowing down, my fourth step out of the apartment landed on the top of the railing, meant to prevent people from falling over one hundred and fifty stories to The Mist below. I felt a sting and a tug just above my right hip, but I ignored it. I used that railing to launch myself off and into the night.

"Again?" Bastion screamed.

I giggled. I couldn't help it. The feeling of my stomach floating up as accelerated toward The Mist made me giddy. Well, when I was the one doing it, not so much when I was trapped in a Stryder. The wind whipped at my eyes, so I reached around and re-deployed my helmet, watching the altimeter on my display gleefully drop.

"Did you call her?" I yelled. "Call who?" Bastion asked.

"I thought you were designed to anticipate needs." In a blink, I'd dropped a dozen floors, my arms and legs sprawled to catch the wind.

"You never tell me your plans," Bastion said. "How am I supposed to anticipate anything?"

"Aw, you're no fun," I said. "Call Poe."

"You don't want me to do that."

"Why not?"

"Toinette security is alerted to your presence. There are two units on the roof. Their comms channels are awash with your description, your leap from that balcony, and trying to determine how you arrived."

"So?" I said as my altimeter dipped below six hundred meters.

"The moment Poe dives below the altitude limit, Toinette security eyes will see its thrusters. Your prized Kawasaki will be impounded before it gets below the level of the rooftops."

"Sparks!"

"This is why we should really talk through your plans if you're not going to include Quynn or Hessod."

"Lecture later," I said. I was approaching only three hundred meters above the street. I snapped my ankles together and my wrists to my hips. Once I saw green lights appear on all four corners of my display, I went spread-eagle, deploying my glider wings. My drop turned into a high-speed glide, and I aimed south, back toward the Huginn Industries borough and Corto beyond.

"You will make it to the street below well before you make it to the Huginn borough," Bastion said.

"I know."

"Security throughout the entire Toinette borough is now on high alert."

"I guessed as much."

"I calculate our odds of escaping the Toinette borough to be roughly—"

"You do realize none of this helps me, right?" I barked.

I glided between bright, towering ads and under another footbridge before Bastion said, "You do know I am trying to help? I don't wish to see you detained, or worse."

I chewed on the inside of my lip. It wasn't his fault that I was in this position. "I know. I just need to think."

"And I am giving you data, trying to help your thinking. And I am not without my own imagination or thoughts."

"You have an idea?" I asked as I fluttered silently over the top of a footbridge, this one bursting with plants.

"You have friends. People who will help you."

"Who?" I asked. "Hessod wants nothing to do with this. Quynn can't find out I made this extracurricular trip. Nox? That kid will get himself killed before he gets me out of here."

"Have you no friends in Toinette?"

I opened my mouth to protest, and then thought of someone. Maybe not a friend. Not yet. But not an enemy. I glanced at my altimeter. I didn't have time to keep brainstorming. "I think there's someone I can leverage."

"That doesn't sound like a friend."

"No, and I don't feel good about it, but leverage can often be more reliable." I pulled up my contact list, found the name, opened a channel, and hoped I was right.

"Hello?" the young man's voice said on the other end of the line.

"Valdo?" I said. "It's Elise. Elise Corto-Intel. The woman you met in Josephine's office last night."

"Oh," Valdo said. "You didn't give me your name."

"No, I didn't. I have trust issues. But I'm trusting you now."

"You need something."

I swallowed. "I do, yes."

"Do you have my Preg Vaxxus B?"

The kid was sharp. Straight to the point. "Not yet," I said. "But I will.

I just need—"

"I did you a solid last night in exchange for a promise," Valdo said, his voice tight. "And now you're asking for more. More what? Time? Credits?"

"This isn't a good idea," Bastion said in my ear.

"I understand," I said to Valdo, diving twenty meters before redeploying the wings so I could skirt beneath a large hanging garden and the people wandering around on it. "I really do. I asked for a lot and promised a lot. Now I need more. Probably a bigger favor."

Valdo made a noise of disgust.

"But I swear to you," I continued, "I'm good for it. I need your help. Once I get clear of this threat, getting your Preg Vaxxus B will be my highest priority."

Several long seconds passed in silence. My altimeter ticked below one hundred meters. Soon, even in the dark, I would be able to see The Mist creeping up below me.

"This isn't going to work," Bastion said. "He is sixteen. We don't know him, his motivations, or his allegiances. He could turn you over to security or Josephine just as easily as help. I would likely do him more good, in fact."

Bastion was right, but in my gut, I felt differently about Valdo. There was something about him that made me think he was on my side. Or wanted to be. I was about to say something more to the kid, find some new way to beg, when Valdo spoke again.

"Tell me something, something personal," he said.

"What?"

"You want me to trust you, to help you, so give me something meaningful. Something I could use against you if you don't hold up your end of these promises."

"He's too good at this," Bastion said. "Don't—"

"I live at Corto Building 29. Apartment 25344. I live there with my partner, Quynn Corto-Nano."

"An address? A partner?" Valdo said. "How is that…?"

"I'm an Intel Operative. Our addresses and personal information are kept secret from public records. We anger a lot of people, make a lot of enemies in our line of work. Look up my name, see what you find on the Net."

The Mist was coming into view before Valdo spoke again. "Okay, Elise Corto-Intel. I'm going to need two full-year treatment cycles of Preg Vaxxus B."

"That's nearly a quarter of a million credits," Bastion said. "More than you make in three years."

"Agreed," I said to Valdo quickly. I meant it, too. "What do you need?" Valdo asked.

"I need help getting out of the Deus Quarter."

Valdo whistled on the other end of the line. "Where are you?"

I gave him my coordinates and vector.

After a few seconds, he said, "Two blocks south and three blocks east of you, there's a section of the building that's under construction. Find a place to hide and stay put. I'll meet you there."

The link disconnected. I took the turns Valdo had described, gliding soundlessly between the Toinette buildings. Above, the no-fly zone had become less so, with at least one security drone or vehicle moving above me constantly. I guess the flying restriction didn't apply to security.

In about a minute, I found the building Valdo had mentioned. It mostly looked like any other, but dozens of floors were surrounded by scaffolding, The Mist wafting gently into the lowest levels of construction. The problem was I was nearly to the bottom of the scaffolded floors already, and still a block away. I deployed my ailerons and tried to make my body as concave as possible, attempting to slow my descent as much as I could without slowing my horizontal speed.

"I need distance to that building," I said as I steered to point directly at it.

"Three-hundred-twenty-six meters and closing," Bastion said.

"Visually, please."

The yellow number appeared at the top of my display, really a three with the last two digits quickly decreasing. I kept my body rigid while monitoring my distance and altitude together. Once that number ticked below two hundred meters, I pointed my left pinky at the building and fired a magnetic grapple.

I knew the electromagnetic firing mechanism was strong and that the magnetic grapple was traveling quickly, but it felt like three very long breaths before the grapple made contact. GRAPPLE ATTACHED flashed in green on my display, and then I started reeling it in as fast as it would go, keeping my glider wings deployed to help me gain altitude as I zipped through the air. It was a wobbly ride that ended with me slamming up against the building between bars of scaffolding. I stuck my hands to the glass with my familiar climbing goo, surrounded by The Mist, and then methodically retracted my grapple and wings.

"Glad no one saw that," I said.

"I saw that," Bastion said.

"That doesn't count. You see everything I see."

"You wound me."

"You'll get over it." I climbed sideways to an opening. It didn't take long to find a way into the unfinished building, just as a security drone floated by, a spotlight searching over the shell of the building, but not finding me.

The space inside seemed too large for an office space or apartment. Maybe it was the lack of walls. Maybe it was the flapping plastic tarps around the outside. Bare concrete floors, occasional concrete pillars, and rippled metal ceiling at least six meters above my head. Wires poked out of holes. Various building supplies sat around in piles. But I could see all the way to the other side of the block-sized building. It was like walking through an industrial cave. Another security drone flew by, its spotlight moving over the translucent plastic tarp in a methodical search pattern.

"What do we do now?" Bastion asked.

"We wait."

"Do you feel all right?"

"A little tired. Cold. But I'm fine," I said. "Why?"

"Your blood pressure is dropping, and your heart rhythm and breathing are irregular."

I was feeling dizzy, too, so I leaned up against one of the huge pillars. Instantly, a sharp pain bit into my back. I reached back and felt wetness. My hand came away bloody.

"Mother of Corto," I said. "I've been shot."

CHAPTER THIRTEEN

"IS THERE AN EXIT WOUND?" Bastion asked.

I was already unzipping my jumpsuit, though, trying to even my breathing and focus as I started to feel dizzy. I yanked the black fabric down off my shoulders, and then slowly rolled it down to my hips. As I did so, I saw blood plume out of my abdomen only a couple of centimeters above my modded hip joints. Pain shot through me like I'd pulled away my own skin.

"It went all the way through me," I said. "I have to stop the bleeding."

"There could be internal damage. Your bowels and kidney. If the bullet splintered off before it left, there could be damage to—"

"I'm not a doctor, Bastion," I yelled. "All I can do is stop the bleeding. Your panic isn't helping me."

The blood seemed like it was everywhere, even though the flow from the little hole in my stomach was slow. It had to have happened before I jumped, before I glided all the way here. Too long. The stabbing sensation was thrumming to the beat of my heart. Adrenaline was great until it wore off. I knelt and pressed fingers to the underside of my left thigh, which promptly opened.

I pulled out a device shaped like a pizza cutter, but instead of a circular blade, the oval head was plain polymer on one side and dark glass on the other. A handheld imager and medical suture. HIMS. I pointed the HIMS over my gaping wound and an image appeared on my display. It was my abdomen overlaid with a wireframe. The HIMS identified the wound and I pressed a button.

A searing, itching pain bloomed on top of the already painful wound as the device stitched my skin back together. I screamed as my abs spasmed. The HIMS wasn't actually growing skin but applying a skin-like polymer. It did nothing for internal damage, but it stopped the blood from leaving my body. Once the hole was closed, I moved the device to my back, using my display for guidance, and repeated the process.

Once the holes were closed, I put the device away and then pressed a sequence of hidden buttons on my left shoulder. Half a liter of my own blood was stored in there and it was now transfusing back into me. Another button and a standard dose of healing nanobots were deployed into my bloodstream. Not enough to fix me completely, but hopefully enough to keep me alive. I sat in a heap on the floor in a puddle of my own blood and jumpsuit. The night air blew in through openings in the tarp, cold on my bare chest and back.

"How am I doing?" I asked.

"Your vitals are improving," Bastion said. "I cannot tell how much blood you lost, and I'm not sure the tank in your shoulder will be enough."

"It's all I've got," I said.

"You need to get to a doctor. You are likely bleeding internally."

"I know." I gingerly leaned back against the pillar again. "I need to get out of this borough first."

I don't know when I fell asleep or how long I'd been unconscious when my comms rang in my ears. I blinked my display back to life, quickly getting my bearings back before I saw that it wasn't Valdo calling, but Quynn.

"Sparks," I whispered.

"They don't know where you are," Bastion said.

"I know."

"It's after three in the morning. They woke up to use the bathroom and noticed you weren't in bed. They asked me about it, but I didn't know what to say."

"So you told them to call me."

"I didn't have to."

I gritted my teeth and opened the comms channel.

"Where are you?" Quynn asked before I could even greet them.

I swallowed, quickly deliberating the truth or some lie, but I didn't have anything prepared. And I hated lying to Quynn anyway. "I'm in a husk of a building in the Toinette Holdings Deus Quarter."

"The Deus Quarter. I'm guessing that's where this preacher woman lives."

"Sort of," I said.

"Sort of?" Quynn yelled.

"She doesn't actually live—"

"Stop," Quynn said. "Just stop. Are you safe?"

I glanced around. I was alone. No searchlights roamed the outside of the building. No security officers in sight. I wasn't bleeding anymore, at least not on the outside. So it wasn't entirely a lie when I said, "Yes. I'm safe."

Quynn sighed loudly. "I have one very important question for you. Is there any chance that your office called after I went to bed? That this is an official job that came up last minute and you just happened to forget to tell me? Because that would be the only way you won't be sleeping in that damn garage for a few nights."

Yeah, that would have been a plausible lie. Part of me wished I'd thought of it, but a bigger part was glad the truth was already coming out.

"Elise?" Quynn asked.

"No," I said. "Nobody at my office knows I'm here. This was all me."

"You said you would leave this preacher be, but you went after her anyway."

"It's complicated, but yes, I came here because Josephine keeps an apartment here. Believe it or not, I was following your advice."

"My advice? My advice?" Quynn was on the verge of yelling, and they were not a yeller. "My advice was to extricate yourself from this whole situation, from anyone who tries to kill you. That does not mean you go right at them."

"I just thought—"

"I can't right now, Elise," Quynn cut me off again. "I can't. You need to think long and hard about this. You can't go running off with some shortsighted plan like this, whatever the plan was. I know you have good intentions. You always do, but you're going to get yourself killed."

"Quynn, I'm sorry."

"I know," Quynn said. "But find somewhere else to be sorry for a while."

"Quynn, please."

"No. This isn't up for debate."

"How long?"

"I'll call you," Quynn said.

I was about to say something else, some other protest, at least an *I love you*, but Quynn disconnected before I had the chance.

To Bastion's credit, he stayed silent for several minutes before he said, "I'm sorry."

I wanted to curl up in a ball and cry. I wanted to call Quynn back and beg, plead for their forgiveness. But I also knew my love. When they said they needed space, that was exactly what they needed. I was only able to mope for a few minutes before my comms lit up again with an incoming call from Valdo.

"Are you here?" I said after I opened the link.

"I am," Valdo whispered. "Where are you?"

"The third floor of the construction area."

"There's a stairway in the northwest corner. I'll meet you there. Eight or ten floors up."

"Okay," I said, but the connection ended before I could say anything else.

"He's not happy with you," Bastion said.

"No," I said as I got to my feet. "Can you look into Preg Vaxxus B? Someplace I can acquire it in sufficient enough quantity?"

"You don't have the credits to make that purchase."

"I didn't say purchase." I pulled my jumpsuit back on, sticky with my own blood. Blood was still splattered all over my arms and legs. I had a whole new reason to be glad I was all in black.

"I…of course," Bastion said. "I'll find out what I can, though the public Net isn't likely to provide security details or exact quantities of drugs on hand at any location."

I started taking the stairs two at a time, though each step felt like a dull knife rummaging around in my intestines. Things were moving that weren't supposed to move, and the pain ripped through me with each movement. "No, but as you said, it's a start. I don't know why this kid needs this drug, but he's certainly putting in the work for it."

Eight floors up, I found Valdo, his eyes buried in his handheld tablet, tapping furiously. He wasn't in his technician's uniform but wearing a gray t-shirt covered in printed computer code over well-pressed khaki pants.

"Nice night for wandering through empty buildings," I said.

Without lifting his eyes from his tablet, he turned and started walking away. "Follow me."

"Where are we going?" I asked as I fell into step with him.

"Out of the Deus Quarter."

"Care to expand on that?"

He tapped even faster, flitting between several apps far too fast for me to follow. After several seconds, we stepped up to a windowless footbridge and he dropped his tablet to his side. We both peered around, checking to see if any drones were flying nearby. I still felt tired, which probably wasn't a good sign. Too much blood loss.

"Let's go," Valdo said. He started crossing the bridge in a strange half-run, half-crouch like he'd seen people sneaking in movies and was trying to do the same. I followed in an utterly silent walk, relying on my mods to keep me stealthy.

"You're angry with me," I said once we were across.

Valdo said nothing. He pulled up his tablet again, tapped out a sequence, and the door to the next building unlocked and slid open. The hallway on the other side was clean and white, though dimly lit. Each door was a light gray, simply labeled with small numbers in large print. An office or medical facility of some sort, not apartments.

"You don't think I'm going to get you that Preg Vaxxus B."

"Why would you?" Valdo grumbled.

"Because I said I would."

Valdo made a dismissive noise and opened an unmarked door which led down another hallway just like the first.

I needed to get in this kid's good graces before he decided to lead me into a trap, so I changed tactics. "How do you know where you're going?"

"It's Toinette," he said.

"Okay. I've lived my whole life in the Corto borough, but that doesn't mean I know my way through several miles of buildings all on foot."

He held out the tablet briefly, his eyes still affixed to it. "I have access."

"It's more than that," I said.

After a few seconds, he said, "I grew up around here. My mom is devout. She brought us to church down here a couple of times a week. She even considered changing to the Deus life, moving the family here, and really focusing on her faith. On the family's faith."

"You close to your parents?"

Valdo shrugged, the openness he'd been displaying suddenly shutting back down. He opened another door and started climbing a desolate concrete stairwell.

"I don't mean to pry," I said.

"Then don't," Valdo spat back.

Each stair was reminding me that a little piece of metal had passed through me only a couple of hours before. I expected the pain to lessen at some point, but that hadn't happened yet.

"Are you okay?" Valdo asked. He had stopped and turned to look at me, worry on his face.

"Yes," I said. "Why?"

"You're breathing hard. And you look like you're in pain." His eyes moved over me then, purely in assessment, and his eyes widened. "You're covered in blood!"

"I'm fine."

"If you're trying to tear down walls with the boy," Bastion said in my ear. "Perhaps tearing down some of your own will help."

Valdo was still looking at me like I was about to bleed out in front of him, so I said, "I patched up the wound. The skin, at least. But a bullet went all the way through me."

"By the prophets," Valdo whispered.

"Yeah," I said. "And I'm a little low on blood."

"What type are you?"

"AB negative."

"Seriously?"

"Yeah."

"You're joking."

I grunted. "Not really in a joking mood here."

"Your lucky day, then."

"You're AB negative?"

Valdo nodded.

"Now's not the time to tease me."

"I'm not." Valdo stepped down a couple of steps to join me. "Isn't that, like, the rarest blood type?"

"That's what I hear," I replied.

"Do you have anything for a transfusion? Something in your mods?"

I shook my head.

"Maybe there's something in this building," Valdo said, looking up the stairs. Then he continued, mostly to himself. "Or the next building to the north. There's a long-term care facility about twenty floors up."

"I'm okay. Just tired, but I can keep going. The sooner I get back to the Corto borough, the better."

"You would only require two needles, a small tube, and gravity," Bastion said. "Surely you could manage that."

"Let's just keep going," I said to both of them. "I'm good now."

Valdo didn't look happy, but after a few seconds, he nodded. Then he pulled my hand over his muscled shoulders and continued the hike up the stairs, helping me along. I let him. It did make things easier. We climbed four more stories before Valdo opened a door, peeked out, and then ushered me through it. This hallway was wider, with a patterned carpet and maroon walls.

"Apartments?" I asked.

"For clergy with family," Valdo whispered.

I nodded. Valdo tried to help me along again, but this time I waved him off. Flat surfaces were much easier for me to handle than stairs. We loped along in silence, though this time it was less awkward or angsty. We crossed another footbridge into another apartment area, down one flight of stairs, and repeated the process. After yet another footbridge, we entered a building with metal walls and a tile floor of gray stone.

"Creepy," I whispered.

"The Tower of Shainette," Valdo said at a normal volume. "I never thought of it as creepy, just boring."

"What happens here?"

"Nothing."

"Being cagey now?"

"No. Literally nothing." Valdo started walking down the gleaming hallways, his steps echoing strangely. "The epitome of fate, of order. No one lives here. No one works here. No one and nothing to add chaos. Whatever happens, happens."

"That's ridiculous."

Valdo laughed, but not in a way that said he found what I said funny. Then he said, "Somebody tell my father that."

"Did he build this or something?"

"No. He programs neural interfaces."

We took a couple of turns, never passing a single door or any other noticeable demarcation in the hallway. Valdo approached a section of wall, pushed, and what had appeared to be a seamless wall slid open to reveal a stairwell.

"Up or down?" I asked.

"Up," Valdo said with a wince. "Twelve floors. Need help?" I nodded, and then he was helping me up the stairs again. Once I'd endured six stories of increasingly painful ascension, I said, "I need to rest."

Valdo nodded and helped me sit down on the steps. "Do you need anything?"

"Probably surgery," I said and tried to laugh, but that hurt.

"More than probably," Bastion said.

"I'm no help there," Valdo said as he sat next to me. "Unless you mean those mods. Or any computer, really."

"You do seem to be pretty handy there. And you're only sixteen?"

Valdo nodded sheepishly. "I wish I was older."

"No, you need to enjoy being sixteen while you can. Few responsibilities. No need for a job." Then I remembered how we'd met. "Why do you have a job already?"

His face darkened, but he said nothing.

"The Preg Vaxxus B. You need money for it, that's why you're working."

Valdo nodded, his jaw tightly clenched.

"The Cranial..." I trailed off, trying to remember the name of the disease. Helpfully, Bastion put the name and symptoms of the disease on my display. "...Starriazas. You obviously don't have it, so it must be someone you care about. Someone you lo—"

I stopped short when I glanced at Valdo. Tears were streaking his defiant face.

"Oh, Valdo," I said. I put an arm around him this time, pulling him in. He didn't lean in, but he didn't pull away, either.

"My mom," he whispered.

"I'm so sorry."

We sat there for a few minutes in silence. Valdo defiantly wiped away every tear that escaped his eyes.

"I hate to intrude," Bastion said, "But I've been looking through Toinette Holdings' medical protocols. According to what I've found, anyone with a level four or higher occupation would qualify for a full treatment of Preg Vaxxus B. I don't know what Valdo's mother does, but if his father is a neural interface programmer, that is at least a level six occupation. There should be no need for Valdo to seek out the drug."

I bristled. Was this kid lying to me? I gritted my teeth and took a breath, ready to lay into the kid, but then he used a fist to brush away another tear. What if he was telling the truth? He'd opened up to me, trusted me with this terrible thing. If I accused him falsely, I would be hurting him. Badly. So I tried a different tact. "It's not fair," I said. He shook his head.

"It's not fair that you're having to get this med for your mom. Why isn't your father helping?"

"Because that isn't Shainette's will," he said with a scoff.

"I don't—"

"Of course, you don't understand," he spat. "You're from Corto."

I remained silent.

"I just mean," he started to say with venom, and then took a breath and continued, "you're not from Toinette. Not raised in Ibhalism."

"I get the gist, though," I said. "Shainette and Aphnette. Fate and chaos. The never-ending quest toward balance between the two."

"A gross oversimplification," Bastion said.

Valdo nodded. "That is the gist, sure. But some people put more faith in deity one or the other. My father," he said, spitting the word like a curse, "very much puts his faith in Shainette."

"In fate?" I said. Valdo nodded.

"So your mother is sick, and your father just thinks—"

"As Shainette wills it."

"And your mother doesn't get a say?"

Valdo shook his head. "She hasn't worked in five years."

"So she doesn't get full citizenship rights," I said. "Just like in Corto Corporation."

Valdo nodded. "Toinette only lets her remain a citizen by marriage. Dad has total control."

"That is cruel," Bastion said. "Denying his own wife life-saving medicine because of some backward beliefs? How could he let someone he loves suffer like that?"

I shook my head slowly, silently agreeing with everything Bastion said.

Valdo took a deep breath and blew it out. He stood and said, "Are you ready? We need to keep going."

I stood up next to him and nodded. He pulled my arm over his shoulders again, and we continued up the stairs.

"Hey," I said. "I really am going to get you that Preg Vaxxus B."

Valdo didn't say anything, didn't even acknowledge that I'd spoken.

"Just imagine me as an agent of fate guiding your mother back to good health."

Valdo smiled a little and kept right on moving up the stairs.

"You are much more an agent of chaos," Bastion said. "You leave confusion everywhere you go."

"Shut up," I whispered.

"What?" Valdo asked.

"S…Sh…Step up!" I said after a momentary fumble. "Just reminding myself to keep pushing through the pain."

"Just let me know if we need to stop," Valdo said. "Though we probably shouldn't if we're going to make it out of the Deus Quarter before dawn."

#   #   #

The skyscrapers of Jayu City were just starting to shimmer with morning light as we exited onto a landing pad on the hundred and twenty-fifth floor. The edge of the Deus quarter. After all those halls and stairs and footbridges, it was nice to see a circle of pavement surrounded by open sky and vehicles flying past.

"We made it," I said.

Valdo pointed directly south. "You're still about three kilometers from Huginn Industries airspace, and I'm sure our security is still on alert for you."

"Guaranteed," I said. "But it's been hours and we're a few kilometers away from the scene. I know how to keep my head down the rest of the way."

"How are you going to get the rest of the way—"

As if on cue, Poe's thrusters roared from straight overhead, quickly descending from the holding pattern she'd been keeping all night over the Deus Quarter.

"That would be my ride," I said.

"Fantastic," Valdo said, suddenly grinning like the teenager he was as he watched my bike swoop down and land on autopilot.

"You need a ride home?" I asked, pointing a thumb at Poe.

"I wish. There's no way my dad would be okay with me showing up on that. With you. I left quietly last night. Best if I come back in the same way."

I swung a leg over Poe, grimacing with the effort. Before I put my hands on the handlebars, though, I said to Valdo, "Thank you. Seriously. I don't know how I could have gotten out of there without you."

Valdo smiled sheepishly, his dark cheeks reddening a touch.

"And I'm going to get you those meds. I promise. You're not losing your mom anytime soon."

Valdo looked up and away for a moment. Even from several meters away, I could see a glisten in his eyes. Then he took a deep breath and looked back at me, locking eyes. "I'll hold you to that."

Before I could say anything else, Valdo turned and walked back into the building we'd just left. I checked traffic and took off for the Corto Corporation borough.

#   #   #

It was almost three hours later when I finally pulled Poe into my garage. Leaving Toinette had been easy enough, if slow. I stayed in regular traffic lanes and kept to the speed limit, changing lanes and altitude precisely according to Toinette regulations. I then zipped through Huginn Industries, which didn't even have air traffic regulations to worry about, and called ahead to the medical clinic two blocks from my apartment.

After waiting there half an hour, I'd gotten in to see a doctor. They examined me, gave me more blood dosed me with medical-grade nanobots, and had me wait an hour to make sure the little robots were on target. My abdomen was still sore, still telling me whenever I accelerated too hard, and I was going to have two big bruises for about a week, but everything inside and out was patching up nicely.

I threw the tarp over Poe and stumbled toward the door to the hallway.

"Where are you going?" Bastion asked.

"Need bed," I said.

"Aren't you forgetting something?"

"Probably. That's why I need my bed."

"Quynn said—"

"Sparks!" I yelled. Right. I wasn't allowed to go home. "Should I find you a hotel?" Bastion asked.

"No," I said. It felt like I was processing Quynn's rejection all over again. "I...ugh. Tell Quynn I'm sleeping in here. Too tired to fight. They can yell at me later if they need to."

I scrounged through our boxes, digging through old computer and cybernetic parts to find things that were marginally softer than the concrete floor. A few old blankets and a box of shirts became an impromptu bed, and I quickly fell into an uncomfortable sleep next to Poe.

Chapter Fourteen

AFTER SIX UNCOMFORTABLE HOURS OF sleep, I really needed coffee. But I was still wearing my work limbs and jumpsuit. While the clinic had helped me clean the blood off my limbs and torso, they did nothing for my jumpsuit. My skin was sticky with dried blood after sleeping in it all night. My limbs were all below ten percent charge. I wasn't sure I could make it to a cafe and back before my limbs went dead.

I slowly peeled out of my jumpsuit once again, the fabric sticky with blood. The wound was an angry pucker, though it looked better than it had before I slept. At least the professionally programmed nanobots had reduced my gunshot wound to an annoying itch.

"Give me some good news," I said to Bastion as I stood at the long bench in front of the viewscreen. I shivered as I scrubbed the inside of my jumpsuit with car shampoo and a few shop rags. I made a mental note to upgrade the climate control in the garage sometime soon.

"I've been poring over the photos you took," Bastion said. "I have a lot of information, but I'm not certain any of it is good or bad news."

"Then just show me the information," I said through gritted teeth.

"I just ordered you a coffee delivery. You might want to cover up before it arrives in seven minutes."

I growled and kept scrubbing. The blood was proving rather resistant to my cleaning efforts.

"Right," Bastion said. The viewscreen was suddenly populated with all the photos I'd taken the night before. Photos of people from every borough in Jayu City except for Toinette. Next to each photo was a printed letter. Not a screen. Not email. These looked like hand-typed letters printed on semiflexible epaper. I glanced from one to another, looking first for patterns. Each one was in a traditional letter format.

"Each one is addressed to G," I said.

"Correct," Bastion said. "Not J or Josephine."

"No."

"Makes me wonder if that room was hers at all."

"I can't say for certain," Bastion said. "But given how cryptic the letters are, it's entirely possible that whoever is sending them is trying to hide her identity."

"Any leads on who the mystery sender might be?"

"Not yet, but the letters appear to be from different people. Each one is signed with a single letter, though not all the same letters. A, M, N, and X. The distribution is relatively equal."

Inevitably, my eyes focused on the one familiar face in the crowd of strangers. "Read me the one next to Gustin, if you would."

"Are you sure?"

"Just read it, please."

Bastion paused for a few seconds while I dug into a stubborn splash of blood near a seam. Then he started reading.

G—

Target 144. Gustin Corto-Intel. Oppositional management 12 years. Son of Target 92. Premium intel access. Married with four. Ambitious. Antagonizer above and below. Minimal social. W/ L 80/20. M8, C6, E6, I3. Individual 32. Access 90. Assets in play. Advise before approach.

—N

Little of that made any sense to me. It was part biography and part resume but descended into gibberish as it went along. I felt more confused than ever about my manager. "Who is Target 92?" I asked.

"Unknown," Bastion said. "Each of the eighty-six photos is labeled with a target number, but 92 is not among them. That's also fewer than Gustin's Target 144 or the highest number on the wall, 182. There does not appear to be a logical ordering to their layout, either. None that I can decipher."

"Target," I said, rolling the word around in my mouth. "Not asset. Not ally or coconspirator. Target."

"Perhaps Gustin is not on the side of our opponents, after all."

I sighed and scrubbed the blood even harder. CRITICAL BATTERY WARNING flashed across my display. I threw the shop rag across the garage and cursed. My jumpsuit needed a nanobot cleanse, but I wasn't even mad about that. Or at least, it was just one small pebble on the mountain of my anger. A conspiracy was going on between Toinette and the rest of Jayu City that had nearly gotten me killed. Twice. The closer I looked into it, the more convoluted it appeared. My boss was caught up in it, possibly as a target or conspirator or both. I had an apprentice who was either my new best friend or Gustin's special spy. And I'd been kicked out of my own home. I dropped my forehead down on the section of jumpsuit crushed in my hands and tried not to cry.

"Elise?" Bastion asked.

I grunted.

"Gustin does not appear to be the villain you think he is. I think it's time to go to him with this."

I stood up straight and looked at the viewscreen, finding his face and staring it down. "Or he's just on the opposite side from whoever put all those pictures on those walls."

"The opposite side of what?"

"That's the real question, isn't it?"

"You're going to get a chance to find out very soon."

"Why?"

"Gustin just sent a text. He wants you to come into the office."

"I'm sure he does," I said. I pulled the still-bloody jumpsuit on, cold from my futile attempts to wash it. "But he's going to have to wait."

"For what?" Bastion asked. "Is Quynn gone? Off to work?"

"They are."

"I'm going to shower and wash this nasty thing," I said as I zipped up the jumpsuit, the inside still sticky. "And sleep in my own bed while the nanobots do their work and my limbs charge."

"Your coffee is arriving in five minutes."

I sighed. "Coffee first. Then all the rest. I have to go home, though."

"Quynn will not be happy," Bastion said. "They will certainly figure out you were there."

"Quynn isn't the only one who pays the rent."

#   #   #

The Corto Corporation Intel offices were quiet. Not as quiet as when I dropped off items in the middle of the night, but most of the cubicles were empty. The lights were already dimmed, and the sun was setting outside. I'd only slept for four hours after cleaning myself and my clothes. I woke to find a voicemail from Gustin.

"Elise," he'd said, spitting my name like a curse. "I'm leaving at 22:00 hours. If I don't see you in my office before I walk out the door, consider yourself demoted to apprentice. Maybe Nox can teach you a thing or two about following orders."

So I was here, in the office, well after office hours. That voicemail had come in only minutes after I'd fallen asleep, so I expected a very angry manager. I rapped on Gustin's office door twice and then opened it. The lights were on but he wasn't there. I checked around the outer office but didn't see him. So I gently closed the door behind me and went for his desk drawers.

None of them were locked, but they were all useless to me. The largest one was filled with snacks and energy drinks. Another held a few printed portraits of what must have been his family. Gustin, smiling in a suit, arm around another adult and four kids. He never mentioned them, at least not to me. No pictures hanging or sitting on display, just these in this drawer.

Married with four. The last drawer held only the handheld tablet I'd seen him use frequently. I leaned back quickly as the screen lit up, a little light next to the camera glowing as I opened the drawer. Smart. If you wanted to keep someone from breaking into your tablet, put a motion-sensing camera on it. That camera was likely linked to Gustin's optical mods. Any face other than his popped up, or if someone tried to unlock it and that camera didn't see Gustin's face, he would know. Hopefully, I'd moved out of the way in time.

"I literally oversee a team of thieves," Gustin said, suddenly in the room with me. I jumped. I hadn't even heard the door open. "I have to protect myself against the very tendencies we hire you for."

"Gustin, I—"

"Save it," he said and closed the door. He gestured to the chair on the other side of the desk. "Sit."

I did, and he took his chair.

"You wanted to see me?" I asked.

He stared hard at me and took a deep breath before he spoke. "Why is a blurry picture of you on every news feed in Toinette Holdings?"

I started to say, "I—"

"I sent you there two days ago to get files from Josephine Toinette-Deus," he said through gritted teeth. "You did. I have not given you an assignment since."

"I know, but—"

"I spoke with Hessod, and he wasn't aware of any activities that would have taken you back to the Toinette borough. You didn't call him for support. Though I know you two are close. He could have been lying."

"He wasn't." I held my jaw tight, trying not to give away my rising anger.

"Wasn't what? Involved or lying?"

"Either. Hessod had nothing to do with my latest trip into Toinette."

"And why should I believe you?" His control had slipped. He was on the verge of yelling, his face red, a growl in every syllable. "You used your considerable skills for an off-book trip into Toinette's Deus Quarter. You can go wherever you want, but when your picture starts showing up on feeds, that puts our entire operation in danger."

"But my name—"

"Of course they don't know your name!" Gustin interrupted. "If they had your name, we wouldn't even be having this conversation because I wouldn't be speaking your name. As it is, my director was just screaming at me, the end of a long chain of screaming that started with our CEO screaming and on down the line."

"I'm sorry. I—"

"Now you need to tell me why I shouldn't be screaming at you. What in Corto's name were you doing in Toinette last night?"

I sat there staring at my boss, gritting my teeth. I was the one being played, kicked out of my own home, and shot. I should have been the one screaming. I took two deep breaths before I answered. "Josephine tried to kill me."

"That's the only reason I'm not screaming. The only reason my director didn't order me to demote you immediately. But it's also not an answer to my question. What were you doing there?"

"I was going after her," I growled.

"Revenge?"

I shook my head. I couldn't keep the venom out of my voice. "Trying to get leverage. To get her to lay off me. Her issue isn't even with me. She's targeting Corto. I'm just the center of the bullseye."

"Let me get this straight," Gustin said, leaning forward and resting his elbows on his desk. "She goes after you, tries to kill you as a direct result of a sanctioned job. In response, you don't tell me or your analyst or your apprentice. Instead, you go off on your own with no support to get leverage on a woman who is very obviously dangerous?"

"Not entirely without support," Bastion said in my ear.

"It was between me and Josephi—"

"You just said this is between Josephine and all of Corto Corporation!" Gustin yelled, slamming his hands on the desk. "Especially this office. Everyone here works to support everyone else. I know we don't get along, Elise, but I'm your manager. I will always have your back, but I can only do that when you use this office, when jobs are sanctioned and we can bring our considerable resources to bear."

"Because sometimes the problem is in this office!" I yelled back, instantly wishing I hadn't.

I expected a defensive posture, for him to suddenly become guarded. The shock that flashed across his face wasn't something he could fake, though. He glanced through the windows to the outer office. Even though nobody was out there, it was like he was looking out there for a traitor. He sat back down. When he spoke again, he was quiet, his anger now a simmer. "In this office? Our office?"

I stared at him, trying to read him for a lie, for some sort of deception. I'd heard he was a pretty good Intel Operative before he went into management. Lying comes with the territory. I didn't see it, though. He looked genuinely surprised and worried.

"Elise?" he asked, his tone imploring.

"There was nothing in Josephine's apartment," I finally said. "She doesn't even live there, but I found another room down the hall. More secure. It was filled with pictures and letters."

Gustin's brow furrowed. "Pictures of what? What did the letters say?"

I only had two choices before me. I could lie to him or come out with it, force him to deal with his picture on that wall, whatever that meant. Corto help me, I didn't think he was in on this now. If I was wrong, I'd be making another daring escape. I swallowed hard and said, "Pictures of people from every borough except Toinette. I think the letters were research, maybe guidance. One of the pictures was you."

The color ran out of Gustin's face. I should have felt bad for him, but at that moment, I just felt relief that I'd been right to tell the truth. He said, "Who else knows about this?"

Paranoia ran amok through my mind again. That wasn't a question that innocent people usually asked. It was usually a question looking for loose ends. I wasn't about to put someone else in danger, though, so I said, "I haven't told anyone, but I have the data backed up on a secure site."

Gustin nodded and gazed back out at the outer office. He looked contemplative, like he was thinking hard, but not in a how-do-I-get-rid-of-this-body sort of way. Then he looked back at me, his face set. He nodded again and took a deep breath.

"Gustin?" I asked.

"This is good work," he whispered. Then he spoke in a normal voice. "You should have gone through proper channels, but this is really good work."

"Thanks?" I didn't know how else to respond, my head spinning from his sudden change in tone.

He stood up from his desk and started for the door. "Come with me."

"Come with…" I started to say, but he was already out the door and walking, not waiting. I followed. Without a word, we walked out of the entire Intel office and to the elevators. He hit the call button for down.

"Where are we going?" I asked.

"Nowhere bad, if that's your concern," Gustin said.

"It is, a bit," I whispered. He either didn't hear me or ignored me. In moments, we were out of the office and on the elevator. He didn't press any buttons. Instead, he placed his modded palm on a metal panel that looked just like part of the wall. Then an ascending trio of chimes played and the elevator started descending.

"Neat trick," I said.

Gustin smiled just a little as the elevator descended. And kept descending farther than seemed possible, not just below the floors on which most business happened, but down through the low-income floors, down through The Mist, and down farther. The numbers on the elevator display eventually hit 1 and then just showed a pair of zeroes. Was there a subterranean Jayu City? I fought to keep a straight face, to not give Gustin the satisfaction of my surprise. That was a hard fight.

Finally, the elevator car stopped. Gustin was walking before the doors had fully opened. The hallway beyond was nondescript. Thin, beige carpet and beige walls. White ceiling regularly interrupted by squares of cheap lighting. It went on farther than the edge of the building or even the next building.

We took no turns, nor were there any we could have taken. No doors, either. It was just a long, straight corridor until it ended with another beige wall. Gustin stopped about a meter away, just staring forward.

I was about to ask if we'd taken a wrong turn when the wall ahead of us slid to the side in absolute silence. The space beyond was dark. So dark that the light from the hallway seemed to just give up and die right at the threshold.

"Come on," Gustin said as he stepped into the darkness, vanishing instantly.

I swallowed hard and did as I was told. In the course of two steps, I went from a poorly lit hall to not being able to see my own hands in front of my face.

I started to say, "How—"

The darkness vanished and I found myself standing in a large, warmly lit room. An enormous viewscreen took up the entire far wall, easily ten meters across and half that tall. The entire thing was filled with white static. The space between the viewscreen and me was filled with tables, each piled with plastic printouts, empty energy drink bottles, coffee cups, and discarded food wrappers. There were computer terminals every meter or so, and they, too, were showing static. There were roughly a dozen people scattered throughout the room, all of them staring at me. It was a little dizzying trying to take it all in.

"This," Bastion said in my ear, "is easily four million credits worth of computing power. And I have no information on most of the faces here."

"What is all this?" I asked.

"This is where the real work of Corto Corporation's Intel division gets done," Gustin said. For the first time since I'd known him, there was joy in his voice.

"My work is very real, Gustin," I spat.

"You're good, Elise. But we don't work for the breaking-and-entering division of Corto Corporation. We're Intel. Welcome to Necropolis Alpha."

Chapter Fifteen

"NECROPOLIS?" I SAID. "LIKE A graveyard?"

Gustin looked at me with a smug smile. "Like where the skeletons are buried."

"Cute," I said. The alpha part was curious, though. It implied there was at least a beta. How many of these rooms were there in Corto?

"She doesn't have clearance to be down here," a deep, familiar voice said from the corner of the room.

"Hello Solomon," I said.

"Elise," Solomon said, though he was looking at Gustin.

"Nice to see—"

He moved past me to focus on Gustin again before I'd even finished the sentence. "Explain this."

"She has information that we all need to see," Gustin said, though he seemed flustered to say the words.

"You couldn't just send it down? Call? You have to bring her down unannounced?"

Gustin worked his jaw and then seemed to find his confidence. "She's part of my team. My call."

"I'm right here," I said.

"Not now," Gustin and Solomon said at the same time. Gustin had barked the words, though Solomon had been just slightly kinder.

Solomon held Gustin's gaze for an agonizing few seconds.

"What?" Gustin said to Solomon. "You don't trust her?"

Solomon's voice softened considerably. "Of course I trust her. That's not the issue." Then he spared me the briefest of glances before saying to Gustin, "Give her credentials before she leaves." He started walking away, and then barked to the room at large, "Get those screens back on! We're not paying you to stare at digital snow!"

"Come on," Gustin said, following Solomon.

"Are you in trouble?" I asked with a barely suppressed chuckle.

"Laugh while you can," Gustin mumbled.

The screens in the room blinked and switched away from static. First, the small terminals stationed around the room, and then the wall-sized viewscreen. Every piece of tech in sight was the newest you could find. Not all of them were buyable in the Corto Corporation borough, either. Right in the center of the big screen, much larger than in real life, was a picture of Josephine Corto-Deus. Except that wasn't the name in large print below her photo.

"Who is Tazia Toinette-Intel?" I asked.

Solomon whipped his head around to Gustin and said, "I thought you said she had useful intel."

"I didn't say she had all the intel," Gustin replied. Then to me, he said, "The woman you and most of Jayu City know as Josephine Toinette-Deus is actually Tazia Toinette-Intel."

"Intel?" I asked, walking down closer to the screen. "So this whole preacher thing is a grift?"

"Yes," Solomon said.

"Or not," a birdlike voice said from the back of the room.

Solomon grumbled. "Which is it?" I asked.

Solomon started to say, "Mione has a pet theory—"

"A working theory," the person who must have been Mione piped up, though I still couldn't see them, the voice carrying from the other side of a row of terminals. "It's not a pet that you stroke and ignores you half the time.

It's a theory that has merit as a very real possibility."

"Mione," Solomon growled and rubbed his temples. "Not again," Gustin whined.

"There are far too many assumptions, too many complexities, and not enough motivation behind any Intel Operative from any corporation running a job like this for this long," Mione said, finally popping up above the terminals.

They were a substantial person, both taller and wider than Hessod. Their skin was so pale that I could see a crisscrossing pattern of veins, arteries, and circuits just below even from several meters away. They moved toward the center aisle of the room in three long strides, bouncing and talking the whole way.

"We've already heard—" Solomon started.

"If this was a high-level recruitment effort," Mione said unperturbed. "The targets would be of much higher quality. In Tazia's two years, two months, and fourteen days as Josephine, she's converted a hundred and twelve people from other companies to Ibhalism. Of those, only nine have scored high enough in our research to be deemed viable targets.

"All nine of those have taken on positions in the Deus sector of Toinette. They haven't gone back to their old occupations, and no significant technological advances have been made as a result of their defections, nothing that would point to those defections resulting in intelligence leaks."

"Then why would she be doing this?" I asked.

"Oh no," Gustin mumbled. "Don't ask Mione questions."

"The simplest explanation is that Tazia found religion," Mione said.

"At forty-two years of age," Solomon said like he thought that was a point against Mione's theory.

"There are numerous documented cases of people," Mione said. "Particularly in Toinette, latching onto Ibhalism well after forty years. Thirty-eight of the hundred and twelve that Josephine has converted are over that age.

"It also explains her name change. She was in Intel. You know as well as anyone how secretive that line of work is. If you wanted to change careers, particularly into something so public, wouldn't you consider a name change?

Keep the past in the past, as it were?"

"Makes sense," I said.

"Not you, too," Gustin said as Solomon growled.

"It also makes sense to take a fake name if you're going to run a long, highly visible con," I said.

"That's what I said," both Gustin and Solomon said at the same time.

"That's one possibility, I suppose," Mione grumbled.

"Then," I continued, "there's what I found in Toinette last night."

Now the Cloak looked at me with genuine interest. "What did you find?" Mione asked.

"Is there somewhere I can plug in?"

Mione came down the aisle the rest of the way and took my data cable, plugging it into the nearest terminal. I started transferring all the photos from the creepy little room.

"I paid a visit to Jos—, I mean, Tazia's apartment down in the Deus Quarter last night."

"Her party pad," Solomon said.

"Right," I said, trying to suppress my surprise that the Cloak of Corto already knew that apartment was a sham. "But just down the hall was a much smaller room that had far better security."

Solomon glanced around the room at different faces before settling on mine. I swore he smiled just a little.

I looked over to Mione, who had been typing furiously on the terminal. Then their eyes went very wide and they said, "Oh!"

"On the big screen, please," Solomon said. It wasn't a request.

In an instant, all the photos I'd taken were arrayed on the oversized viewscreen, pieced together in a mosaic to perfectly recreate the two-wall spread of portraits and letters.

"What is all this?" Solomon asked.

"Targets, I think," I replied. Then to Mione, I said, "If you could zoom in on—"

Before I'd finished the sentence, the portrait of Gustin enlarged to fill the middle of the screen, including the letter.

"Mother of Corto," Gustin whispered. Though I'd told him about his own portrait on that wall, I guessed seeing it himself hit a little deeper.

"You see that?" Solomon asked Gustin without taking his eyes off the screen.

"G," Gustin said. "Addressed to G. Are they all addressed to G?"

"They are," Mione said with breathless reverence.

Solomon was smiling.

"What?" I asked. "Who is G? Isn't her name Tazia?"

"Add that to the list, Mione," Solomon bellowed. He was still smiling, still fixated on the screen. Gustin was staring at it, too, working his jaw. Mione was chewing a fingernail and burrowing holes in their terminal with their eyes.

"Will anyone tell me what's going on here?"

"Tazia Toinette-Intel is a high-level Intel Operative," Solomon said. "Maybe the highest in Toinette."

"The…" I stuttered. "The Ghost of Toinette?"

"That's my theory," Solomon said.

Pieces from the last several days started falling into place. How could a livestreaming, evangelizing preacher know I was an Intel Operative for Corto who reported to Gustin just at a glance? How had she hacked into a Stryder I was climbing into and overridden all of its safety protocols to send it into The Mist? Why didn't she actually seem to live in the very expensive Deus Quarter apartment she was known for? Why did she have this very secret room?

Because she wasn't a preacher at all. The Ghost of Toinette could do all of those things, though. I suddenly felt very lucky to have survived her wrath.

"Just a theory, though," Gustin said. He seemed unconvinced.

"These letters are addressed from four different people," Mione said. "Or at least four different initials."

"Could be names or just monikers," Solomon said. "If she's really the ghost, then they're likely analysts or her superiors in the Toinette Intel office."

"What is she doing?" I asked. "Why all these people?"

Solomon looked at me like he'd forgotten I was in the room. Then he said, "Thank you for this information. You can go."

"Go?" I said. "But I—"

"Solomon," Gustin said. He was the last person I expected to stand up for me, but there it was.

Solomon grunted and inclined his head, beckoning me to a corner of the room. Once I joined him, he whispered, "You're not ready for this."

"For what?" I asked.

"All of this, this spy stuff. You just took on an apprentice. You can't mix him up in all of this."

"I'm already in this, whether you like it or now. I can keep my apprentice out of it."

Solomon smirked and shook his head. "You don't know Nox."

"And you do?"

Solomon sighed, his mouth flat. After too many long seconds, he said, "Fine. Call this a trial run. Prove that you can handle this and keep your apprentice in the dark."

"Thank you."

"Don't thank me yet," he said. "This is all about to get much more dangerous for you."

I stood there processing the warning as Solomon walked back to join Mione. I wondered how much Solomon knew about how dangerous things had already been for me recently. More dangerous wasn't what I was after.

"Those photos and letters on the two walls," Bastion said in my ear. "They're different groups of people."

"What?" I whispered.

"Different groups!" Bastion practically yelled. "Tell them."

"The people on those walls," I blurted out. "They're different groups."

Mione stopped typing and looked up at me. Solomon turned to fully face me. "Different how?" he asked.

"Like they said," I gestured to Mione and started speaking aloud the concepts that Bastion was pouring into my ear. "The letters on that wall, the wall with Gustin, those are opposition research. Looking for perceived weak points, possible points of leverage."

"Right…" Gustin let the implied *so what* hang in the air between us.

"But the wall on the right, those letters aren't research. No thinly veiled discussions of kids or debts or sick relatives. The codes are denser."

Solomon narrowed his eyes and then looked hard at Mione, who had resumed typing as I was speaking.

"She's not wrong," Mione said. "But I don't know why. They have more in common than different. From all corners of Jayu City except Toinette Holdings. In positions to acquire actionable intelligence from their companies. No obvious ties to Tazia, Toinette, or Ibhalism."

Mione and Solomon and Gustin kept discussing while Bastion prattled on in my ear at the same time, but I drowned them all out, lost in the sea of pictures in front of me. I hadn't had the chance to look at any of these photos when I was in that little room. Now was the first time I was really looking, and a number of them were familiar. I'd been working as an Intel Operative for several years all over the city, and that resulted in running into all sorts of people. While the people on the left wall—like Gustin—seemed to have no connections, I was able to piece together a rough network between most of the people on the right wall. They didn't all know each other but were within a few degrees of separation.

An idea struck me, so I turned to Mione and said, "Have any of the people on the right wall had any contact with Tazia?"

"None are known associates of—" Mione started to answer.

"Not associates," I said. "Just contact. Have they been in the same place at the same time as her in the last few months? Last year, even?"

Solomon shot me a look that I didn't understand. Surprise and maybe fear?

Mione looked inquisitive and then turned back to their console, back to typing.

"What are you after?" Gustin asked.

"Do you know any of the people on that wall where your picture is?" I asked.

Gustin scanned the wall and then shook his head. "No, I've never met any of them."

"A group of perfect strangers," I said.

"You can't know that," Gustin said. Solomon was oddly silent.

"No," I said. "But I'm pretty sure everyone on that right side knows each other. Or at least know of each other."

"What does that prove?" Gustin asked.

"That it might be—" I started to say.

"—a network," Mione said, finishing my sentence. On the enormous viewscreen, all the portraits from the left wall faded away. The portraits on the right moved, rearranging with thick, red lines connecting them like a web. "Every single one of these people has been in the same location at the same time as Tazia at least twice. Some, half a dozen times. Nothing official or scheduled, just same place at the same time. While none of them know each other directly, they're all connected through known associates by no more than two degrees."

"Mother of Corto," Solomon said and then whistled. "It's a network outside of Toinette. That's how I operate, how I build and maintain my own network. She is the Ghost."

We all stared at the big screen for a while, everyone in the room, letting Solomon's words echo.

Finally, I asked, "A network doing what?"

We all stared at the viewscreen in silence for a few long minutes. I traced the lines from one picture to another. They were from all over Jayu City, many in high-level positions. I'd run into many of them on jobs, but those jobs had been varied and spread far apart not only geographically, but by months and years. The disparate dots didn't come together to form a cohesive whole.

"I have no idea," Solomon said. "But it can't be good for Corto Corporation. We need to find out what she's up to. Mione, which three of these have been in the same location as Tazia the most?"

After a little typing, all but three of the portraits faded away, and those three enlarged. "Brock Nexus-Neuro, Elizabeth Huginn-Sec, and Twila Kotega."

"You want to hit them?" Gustin asked.

"I do," Solomon said. "Silently. Without any trace of intrusion. We look for commonalities in their personal files, private communications, anything that gives us a clearer picture."

"Why three?" I asked.

"One tells us nothing," Mione said. "Two only shows us coincidence. Three reveals a pattern. You'd be amazed how many jobs you've gone on after or before two other Operatives have done similar jobs on similar targets."

"Which one are you hitting first?" Gustin asked Solomon.

Solomon shook his head and finally turned away from the screen to face Gustin. "All three at the same time. We can't afford to tip our hand. I'm heading to Kotega. You're sending Elise and Val into Nexus and Huginn."

Gustin nodded. "I'll need a few days to—"

"We go tomorrow night," Solomon said. He spun back around to face the oversized viewscreen again. "I'll be breaking into Twila Kotega's office at 27:00 hours. Make sure your two are on schedule to do the same."

#   #   #

After sitting around for another hour while Gustin increased my security clearances, I finally left Necropolis Alpha a little before 26:00, hungry and even more tired. Sleeping half the night on my garage floor and then only a few exhausted hours in my bed hadn't quite cut it. I also needed to be back in the office, the main upstairs office, by 06:00 tomorrow.

A series of notifications popped up on my display after I'd been riding the elevator up for about twenty seconds. Eight missed texts from Quynn.

"How did I miss these?" I asked Bastion since we were alone.

"You weren't able to receive texts down there."

"But you were able to talk to me."

"It's not a Faraday Cage," Bastion said. "They have hardware blocking non-secured communications."

"And you're secured?" I asked.

"With my chip riding around in your shoulder, yes. Though I did have to bounce around several routers to stay in contact. I missed eight floors of the initial elevator ride down. It would be easier if you were to install me as your primary neural interface."

"So you've told me," I said. He hadn't mentioned it often, but often

164

enough. He made a compelling case for reduced lag and optimize cybernetic performance. But having him actually in my brain felt invasive, like I would be giving up a part of myself. I wasn't prepared to do that.

Instead of saying more, I brought up my AR keyboard and moved through Quynn's messages.

22:31: Were you in the apartment? 22:38: You could have asked first. No need to leave a mess. 22:42: Ignoring me won't make this go any faster. 23:18: Your mom called. I just told her you were on a job. Didn't want to worry her.

23:40: Please just check in. I'm still mad, but I still worry.

23:48: Bastion isn't responding either. Hessod doesn't know where you are. Please call or text or whatever.

24:10: I love you. 24:45: Fine. Going to bed.

"Is Quynn already asleep?" I asked.

After a few seconds, Bastion said, "Yes."

"Please send a silent message for me, then," I said as the elevator stopped and the doors opened.

"Go ahead," Bastion said.

"I'm fine. Was just out of communication. The next couple of days are going to be a lot for me. All on the books. I'll call when I can. I love you, too."

"Do you want me to read it back?"

I shook my head. A useless gesture for the AI living in my shoulder. "No. Just send it."

"Sent."

Bastion and I didn't speak much the rest of the night. I rode Poe to an all-night diner down by the Corto docks of Drakon Bay. Pancakes and eggs. Comfort food. Green tea because I wanted to sleep soon. After the meal, I checked into a hotel in the same neighborhood as my apartment, paying extra for a room with a power closet. I wanted my limbs at full capacity for the day ahead. The bed was too soft, the pillow too flat, but I fell asleep in minutes.

Chapter Sixteen

I WALKED BACK INTO THE office at 6:02, and it was like stepping into a circus. Analysts were running around and shouting over each other. Gustin was standing on a chair and barking orders across the room. Before I'd fully gotten my bearings, Nox grabbed me by the arm, excitement written in all caps across his face.

"This is wild!" he said. "Can you believe this?"

"More than you know," I said.

"Come on. I'm supposed to bring you to the conference room."

I stopped in my tracks and gently pried his hand off of my arm, and he turned back to me, looking wounded.

"I know how to get to the conference room," I said. "I don't need my hand held."

"Sorry," he said, though he didn't sound like he meant it. I moved past him and headed straight for the conference room. Hessod was standing in the hall along with Val, the smallest adult person I'd ever met and one of the best Intel Operatives in the business. They were barely over a meter tall, their growth stunted by some childhood medical issues. Rather than use cybernetics or nanotechnology to grow taller, they used their size to their advantage. Their blonde hair was worn in a short mohawk with a long braid trailing down their back. Their dusky gray suit looked perfectly pressed.

Standing next to Val was their analyst, Irene. Irene was roughly my height and build, though a few shades darker. She kept her head shaved and was drop-dead gorgeous, peering at her portable terminal with a slight squint.

"We waiting on something?" I asked Hessod.

"We are," he said. "You're supposed to go in."

Right. I'd been "read in," as they said. For years, I'd been the one standing out in the hall, though I never imagined the discussions were about secrets of this nature before I was let in. This was a line I was going to have to walk for a while. I pressed the button on the wall next to the door and after a few moments, Solomon opened the door.

"Get in here," he grumbled.

I slid past him, and then he put out a hand to stop Nox from following.

"Not you," Solomon said. "Wait in the hall."

To my surprise, Nox gave no protest or witty quip. He visibly shrunk away from Solomon and moved back from the door.

"You're late," Solomon said with a scowl once the door closed.

I shrugged and took a seat. We were the only ones in the room. "Why isn't Hessod in here? If I'm read in—"

"His divorce," Solomon said, taking the seat across from me. "No point in having his wife sign updated confidentiality paperwork when she won't be his wife much longer. Plus she could use this as leverage. Or he could. It's happened before."

"So I can't discuss things with him?"

"Nothing regarding Josephine's real name or occupation as an Intel Operative. Same with Nox. You know what it's like to be in the dark regarding why we do what we do, now you're the one with the light switch."

"I don't like it."

"Welcome to the club," Solomon said with zero sympathies. "Our official line is that these three people are friends. They'll tip each other off, so we have to run the three ops at the same time."

"Other than the friendship, that's all true, though," I said.

"You'll find it's easier to lie when we stick as close as we can to the truth. Just remember what we're keeping secret. We don't even need to mention Josephine Toinette-Deus. Any questions?"

I thought about that. As far as Hessod or Nox knew, these were three normal ops that had to happen quickly and at the same time. It'd happened before. I'd stolen data from countless people without knowing what the data was about, who it was about, or how it was used. It was strange being behind the veil, but so gratifying, too.

I shook my head. "No questions."

Solomon stood. "Bring everyone else in, then."

I did, and we all took seats around the table. Solomon stood by the screen at the head of the table. "You all know we have three high-priority targets we're going to hit tonight. You've seen the intel on them, now let's finalize our plans."

He swiped his hand across the screen, and images of three people appeared. He pointed to the first one. "I'll be going after Twila Kotega. She's the Chief Financial Officer for Kotega Systems. As such, she'll be the hardest nut to crack. You two are skilled, but we can't take any chances here."

"The Cloak gets the hardest nut," I said with a chuckle. "Got it."

"Very funny," he said in a tone that clearly meant he didn't think it was.

I held up my hands in surrender. "Just trying to keep the mood light. We're all professionals here."

"Then act like it."

I glanced at Nox with *what's his problem* eyes, but my apprentice didn't seem to share my view. At least Irene smiled a little.

"I'll take Nexus," Val said. "Brock Nexus-Neuro's building is over seventy years old, tucked away in the lower east end of Nexus."

"Notoriously tiny maintenance tunnels run all through those buildings," I said. "An architectural oddity they abandoned once they realized their maintenance workers kept getting stuck."

"Exactly," Val said. "But not a problem for me."

"Makes sense," I said. "That leaves me with the Huginn target."

"Elizabeth Huginn-Sec," Solomon said. "A director in Huginn's security division."

"How do you propose we hit three targets in different boroughs of Jayu City all at the same time?" I asked.

"On my lead," Solomon said. "We'll get in place before 27:00 hours, and we'll go when I say go. You'll both stay in constant communication with me. I want to know about every picked lock, every cracked safe, every misplaced step. If I say abort, you both get out as fast as possible. Clear?"

"Clear," Val said. "Clear," I repeated.

"As I said before," Solomon said. "Our highest priority is to gather as much information as possible without tipping off our targets that we were ever there. I'll be pulling a classic Sandman with Twila Kotega. That will give me free rein of her apartment, as well as allow me to communicate with both of you."

The Sandman was an effective technique for ransacking someone's place while they were still home, though I'd never used it. The principle was simple: use a drug to make a sleeping target into a comatose target, at least temporarily. I knew locks and freefalls, but the fine chemistry of mixing chemicals with human biology made me nervous.

"Val?" Solomon said.

"Drugs aren't really my bag," they said, echoing my own concern. "So I'll use The Shade. It's what I'm best at, anyway."

"That's true," I said. And it was. I was good at sneaking around, but not compared to Val. The Shade was the first heist taught to any upcoming Intel Operative. Under cover of darkness, sneak in and out of a place, taking whatever was required, and never waking the target or disturbing even a dust bunny. It was basic. It was also very difficult.

"Elise?" Solomon said, turning his scowl toward me. I ran through a few good options in my head. The Spider. The Daybreak. The Get Help.

"Yeah?" Nox said, reminding me he was still in the room. "What are we going to do?"

"We?" I asked. "I'm sorry, kid, but this job—"

"The Doppler would work," Solomon said. "And it requires two operatives."

I cringed and said, "You said no chances. You really want to send my apprentice along when you don't want to take any chances?"

"I think you'd be pleasantly surprised," Solomon said, "by how useful my nephew can be."

Several things clicked in my brain at once. Solomon's mention of Nox down in Necropolis Alpha. The young man's inclusion on a high-priority job. It all made sense now. I wasn't sure if I should be worried that I'd been saddled with such a beneficiary of nepotism or flattered that of all the Intel Operatives to train the Cloak's nephew, Gustin had chosen me. Or had Solomon himself chosen? I would have to unpack that mountain of questions later.

"Fine," I said. "Does Elizabeth even have a balcony?"

Hessod said, "Yes, she has a balcony."

"That settles it," Solomon said. "Get everything in order. Every analyst and tech in the office has been reassigned to our three teams. Irene, Hessod, and one of my analysts will lead. Research. Plan. Upgrade. Get some sleep if you can. I expect both of you in position by 27:00 tonight."

The Cloak of Corto then swept out of the room without a backward glance or a goodbye.

"He's fun," Hessod said once the door closed. Then he noticed Nox still in the room, his eyes wide.

"Fun or not," I said, putting one hand on Hessod's shoulder. "You don't get to be the Cloak without being the best."

"Yeah," Nox said. "But Uncle Solomon is still a hemmy sometimes."

"Hemmy?" I asked.

Nox rolled his eyes and said, "It's not a compliment."

Even if I didn't understand the word, I'd probably called Solomon worse things over the years, even if I respected him more than just about anybody on the planet. Maybe Nox and I were going to get along after all.

#   #   #

27:00 hours had come and gone several hours ago. I was sitting in a server room three doors down from Elizabeth HuginnSec's apartment. She'd gone to bed at 27:20. From the building across the street, Nox had seen her breathing fall into a deep pattern of sleep just before midnight at 27:54. Twila, the Cloak's target, had fallen fully asleep at 0:20. Finally, at 01:22, Val's target was brushing his teeth. "Double-check your loadouts," Solomon said through comms.

Since 27:00, he'd asked us to check our loadouts six times. I wasn't going to do it again. I silently counted to fifteen, and then said, "Checked. Good to go."

"All loaded," Val said right after.

"Loaded," Nox said.

"Not you, apprentice," the Cloak growled.

After several seconds of silence, Bastion said, "What can I do to help?"

I muted myself on the open comms channels to talk only to Bastion and said, "Watch my back. See if you can watch out for Nox, too."

"I've spotted him on a few security cameras."

I shook my head. "Fool can't even duck a camera yet. He's not ready for this."

"To be fair," Bastion said. "He only appears as a blurry shadow on camera. I only assume it is him because I know he's in that building on that floor right now."

"He does seem to have the best toys," I said. "Target is asleep," Val said.

"Chatter to a minimum," I told Bastion. "But definitely chime in if you see anything worrying."

"Understood," Bastion said.

Just as I unmuted the open comms channel my fellow operatives were using, Solomon said, "Morpheus ready."

"Casper ready."

I stood up and rolled my neck out before I said, "Banshee ready."

"On my mark," Solomon said. I put my hand on the doorknob. "Three, two," Solomon counted down.

I took a deep breath and blew out, emptying my lungs.

"One. Mark."

I opened the door silently and slid down the empty hall, checking for cameras that weren't there. I knew they weren't but training and habit kicked in, so my eyes checked every nook and cranny for digital eyes. I reached Elizabeth's door and deployed the first of the upgrades that Solomon insisted upon. Instead of my standard combo of data cable and fiberoptic cable side-by-side, I unfurled a single carbon-fiber tentacle from my wrist. Only one centimeter wide and two millimeters thick, it slid under the door and back up to the locking mechanism smoother and faster than my old combo.

I didn't understand how, but the new cable showed me a near-three-hundred-sixty-degree view inside the room, while the end of the tentacle was able to morph into over three hundred different shapes including every type of data connection currently in use in Jayu City. I checked to make sure the apartment was quiet and dark and then plugged into the pinhole port on the inside of the door lock.

"Banshee lockpick ready," I whispered.

"Go for doppler," Solomon said after a small grunt. "Apprentice," I whispered.

"Ready," Nox said.

"Go."

I breathed in and out. In and out. I held my position. Waiting. Through the fisheye lens on the end of my data cable, I saw half of the top floor of the building across the street bloom in rolling fire. An instant later, an enormous boom shook the entire building, sending chandeliers swaying.

In short order, voices from the surrounding apartments started waking up.

"Apprentice?" I said. "Not yet," he answered.

I glanced left and right, knowing any moment, someone might pop their head out of their apartment and see me standing too close to a door that wasn't mine.

"Apprentice?" I asked through gritted teeth.

"Almost."

To my left, a door opened. It was now or never. I started running the algorithm to open the door. Three seconds later, my display flashed, UNLOCKED. My heart leaped. If I opened this door too early, Elizabeth could discover me. Too late, and somebody else in the building might. I froze in place.

"Now!" Nox practically yelled over comms.

I silently swung the door open and closed it behind me as gently as I could. None of the lights were on, but the blaze across the street lit the apartment like midday. Before I could keep moving, a sound started, one that gave The Doppler its name: faint sirens of responding emergency vehicles.

"Position?" I said as I moved toward Elizabeth's bedroom, staying low and swerving between a vast kitchen counter and a cluttered dining table.

"Right outside her bedroom."

Elizabeth was on the balcony. That was the idea of The Doppler, after all: misdirection. Create some sort of huge emergency, like an explosion and raging fire across the street, complete with swirling lights and wailing sirens, and almost everyone would get out of bed to watch the spectacle. So long as the show kept going, they wouldn't glance back even as an Intel Operative crept through their home.

Before I reached Elizabeth's bedroom, I spotted a handheld terminal on a side table in the living room. Time for one of my other upgrades. I turned the terminal over so it was facedown, and then placed the middle finger of my left hand gently against it. I tapped out a particular rhythm with the fingers and thumb of my right hand until FILM DEPLOYING lit up on my display. Then I slowly dragged my finger across the back of the terminal for two centimeters until the words on my display vanished. I checked my work, cranking my visual zoom up, but I couldn't see the film I had laid down. Two centimeters long, half a centimeter wide, but only three micrometers thick, it was invisible without a microscope. It would dissolve in a couple of days, but before then, it would ransack the terminal and transmit every scrap of data to Corto Intel servers.

Best of all, once I'd laid the film in place, I flipped the terminal back over and continued through Elizabeth's apartment. Much faster than standing around with my data cable plugged in uploading a worm or waiting to download all the data. I gently pushed open the door to Elizabeth's bedroom and stepped inside.

The space was wide, but not terribly deep. The bed was a meter to my right and against the same wall as the door I'd just opened. The windows and door to the balcony lay beyond the bed. Thankfully it was an automated door, so it had slid closed behind Elizabeth, whose silhouette seemed rapt in attention staring at the fire and the buzzing emergency services drones and workers. The wall across from the bed and door was mostly occupied by vibrant, framed artwork, though there were a couple of small dressers. I opened the door the rest of the way and found what I was looking for: Elizabeth's power closet tucked against the wall farthest from the windows.

I glanced at Elizabeth again to make sure she was still in place, and then slunk over to her closet, looking for her limbs. I opened the doors and had my first surprise of the night. I knew Elizabeth had modded her forearms by choice and her entire right leg after a childhood accident. Instead of two or three sets of limbs, though, there were a dozen. One was an approximation of her light brown skin tone. One jet black and another pearl white like the keys of a piano. Every color in the rainbow was represented, too. This was why the research phase conducted by analysts usually lasted days or weeks. Even with a third of our office's analysts working on Elizabeth, they couldn't get every detail in a single day.

"We only have two full sets of replacement joints," Bastion said.

"I know," I whispered. Most people have two, maybe three sets of cybernetic limbs. Not twelve.

Bastion began to say, "They need—"

"They need to match," I interrupted. "I know."

These joints were the nodes of metal and circuitry that connected the cybernetic limbs to implanted interfaces. I had brought enough joints to replace the stock ones on two full sets of limbs. There was no mixing and matching. If I only replaced one joint on a set, Elizabeth's neural interface would instantly detect the mismatch.

"Give me pictures of Elizabeth," I whispered to Bastion. "Half a dozen, at least."

"Any particular pictures?"

"Random."

"I see little benefit in random—"

"No time to explain. Now."

Six pictures of Elizabeth Huginn-Sec appeared on my display. In one, her modded limbs were green and she was wearing a mauve suit with lapels to match her limbs. In another, the jet-black limbs with a silky white dress. Red limbs with a blue paisley top and white pants. She was stylish, but there was no simplistic pattern to discern.

Blue and red lights played across my field of vision. I glanced back to see a cadre of fire suppression drones arriving. I needed to hurry before Elizabeth lost interest in the spectacle or the drones put out the fire. I put my attention back on the power closet and took a deep breath. I glanced around at the various limbs hung there. I knew there was a solution, something that was just out of reach but was definitely there in front of me.

"Is there a way to hijack her neural interface?" Bastion asked. "Perhaps you could tie into her home data connection to intercept all data going in and out?"

"Hush," I whispered. "I need a moment." I kept looking around, knowing the answer was here. Bastion's suggestions wouldn't work. Neural interfaces were notoriously difficult to hack and if done incorrectly, could cause brain damage. Tying into the home data connection wasn't hard, but Elizabeth spent ten to fourteen hours a day in her office. The quantity and quality of data on her home connection would be poor.

My eyes moved over the maintenance panel near the floor of the power closet for the tenth time, but this time, something rang familiar. I tapped furiously on the control panel for the closet. All limbs except the navy blue set were one hundred percent charged. Meaning Elizabeth wore the navy blue set today. I gently wobbled all three navy blue limbs ever so slightly out of their cradles. Just enough so they looked like they were properly seated but wouldn't charge.

Then I crouched, deployed a screwdriver from my finger, and gently pried the maintenance panel off. Beneath were a series of fuses and a number of brightly colored wires.

Bastion started to say, "I can pull up the schematics—"

"No need," I said. "I have this under control."

Two years ago, I woke one morning to find all of my limbs were at zero percent power. Completely drained. After four hours of work, I discovered a failed surge protector on our floor and a lightning strike had fused three wires in my power closet together. My limbs hadn't just stopped charging, but the malfunctioning closet had pulled the charges from the limbs and into the battery backup system. While Elizabeth's power closet wasn't the exact same model, the principle was the same. I grabbed the same three wires in

Elizabeth's closet, mashed them together, and then hit them with my taser at twenty-five percent charge.

The wire casings were a little melted but didn't look anything like what had happened to my power closet.

"Banshee," Nox said over comms. "The fire is dying. You'd better wrap this up."

I tried it again with a fifty percent charge. The results were nominally better, but after checking the control panel on the closet, everything was functioning normally. I checked on Elizabeth and didn't see her at first. My heart leaped into my throat, but then I found her sitting on a chair on her balcony, still captivated by the dwindling fire across the street.

"Banshee," Nox pleaded. "Almost there," I whispered.

"What's going on?" Solomon barked.

"Two minutes," I said. I knew it would take longer than that, but I needed people to stop talking in my ear. I knelt once more and hit the wires with a full charge, not leaving anything to chance. Visible arcs of electricity hit the wires and sent sparks flying in every direction. Little flames jumped up at the edges of the now-fused wires. I patted them out and checked the control panel. All the limbs that were properly cradled were showing ninety-nine percent charge and an error message was blinking at the bottom of the screen. Finally.

I closed up the maintenance panel and got to work on the navy blue limbs, working as carefully and quickly as I could to replace the interface nodes with our hacked replacements. I just needed to make sure I hung them back gently, still just out of their cradles so they wouldn't be drained overnight. She would have no choice but to re-wear her navy blue limbs.

I'd just started working on the second forearm when Nox said, "Banshee, target just yawned and stood up from her chair."

"Sparks," I whispered. "She's going back inside."

"Abort," Solomon said with a hiss. "Abort."

But I was so close, I wasn't about to give up now. Instead, I stepped into the power closet, closed the door behind me, and kept working. I pocketed the factory interface node on the forearm and started attaching our modified version. I could just wait until she was asleep and sneak out.

"Banshee!" Nox pleaded over comms.

I ignored him, placing the forearm just out of seat and grabbing the leg. One more limb to modify.

"I gave you an order, Banshee," Solomon said. "Abort now. We cannot risk discovery."

I ignored him, too. I heard a door close out in the apartment, but too close to be the balcony door. I kept working and listening as hard as I could. Just as I was starting to attach the replacement node in the leg, a toilet flushed. Then water started running. If I hurried, maybe I could slip out while Elizabeth was in the bathroom. Maybe I could—

An enormous BOOM rattled the entire building, much bigger than Nox's distraction, and light erupted through the spaces between the closet doors. I nearly dropped the limb.

"By Thor's hammer!" Elizabeth said from out in the apartment, practically yelling over the suddenly louder sounds of an inferno.

I finished with the last limb and placed it back in its cradle, but not seated properly. Then I snaked my camera out. The building across the street was ablaze even more than before. Three full floors were roiling with orange flame and billowing smoke. Elizabeth was back out on her balcony.

"Apprentice?" I said over comms. "Apprentice? Was that you?"

No response came.

"Apprentice! Respond!"

"Nox?" Solomon said, a worry I'd never heard in his voice suddenly present. "Nox, respond immediately."

A static blared in my comms, popping and fizzing, followed by Nox in barely a whisper, "…too much…fire…operative down."

Chapter Seventeen

I BOLTED OUT OF ELIZABETH Huginn-Sec's power closet, not even worried if she saw me. She was standing in front of her bedroom windows again, looking out at the newly engulfed building across the street. From my vantage point, every visible floor was ablaze, the fire suppression drones outmatched. I was tempted to run right past her, to undermine all the work I'd just done, so I could take the shortest line to the other building, to pull Nox out of there.

"Situation!" Solomon yelled over comms. "Banshee, have you completed your assignment?"

"What about your nephew?" I whispered. I gently closed the closet door behind me, still thinking about running directly past Elizabeth.

"He knew the risks," Solomon said. "As did we all. I love that kid and you'd better damn well help him, but not without finishing your assignment. This is bigger than you know, bigger than I can explain right now. But you must get those nodes in place and get out of there unseen."

I growled, my eyes transfixed on the blaze before me. Nox was there, right there, somewhere in that inferno before me. I could do it, disobey again. Run straight past Elizabeth and launch myself across the street. I could save him. If he wasn't already... Mother of Corto. If he'd just sacrificed himself, I couldn't let it be in vain. I ducked out of Elizabeth's bedroom with all stealth. "Fine," I said. "Assignment complete. Leaving the apartment."

I hurried back through the living room and out of the apartment door, making sure it locked behind me.

"I'm clear," I said. "I'm going for Nox."

"Keep me—" Solomon said before I closed the connection. Then I broke into a full sprint, darting through the hall, around the corner, and into the stairwell. Elizabeth's apartment was only a dozen floors down from the roof, so I launched myself up the stairs, extending my cybernetic legs so I was taking them four at a time and rebounding off the walls of the landings. Even with my mods doing most of the work, I was winded when I finally burst through the door to the roof.

The heat, even several dozen meters away, was intense. Smoke was hazing the air, and I coughed when I tried to take a deep breath.

"Nox?" I yelled over comms. "Nox? Where are you?" Silence answered. Not even static.

"Bastion, what was his last location?"

"Seven floors down from here," Bastion said. "Last visual of him was entering a room labeled 13552B."

"AR guidance, please," I said.

"You are not fireproof."

"NOW," I said.

A green line appeared before me, flying over the side of the building, down and to my left, right into the raging blaze. I glanced around, searching for an option. At least eight floors of the building were fully engulfed. Fire suppression drones were buzzing around it like bees at a hive, their chemical sprays creating little cones of darkness in the fire but having no real effect on the larger blaze. Large fire suppression vehicles were keeping their distance, their hoses spraying the same chemicals around to little effect.

"I estimate your odds of surviving confrontation with that fire to be minimal," Bastion said via text. "None of your mods are built to withstand that heat. In all likelihood, Nox is already dead in there."

"This isn't up for debate, Bastion. I'm getting him out of there." With that, I took one step back and then took off at a full sprint again, right toward the edge of the building. I used the pneumatics in my legs to launch myself from the roof. No parachute. No zip line. No glider wings. The pneumatics were enough.

"That is not the vector I gave you!" Bastion said.

He was right. It wasn't the vector he gave me because that would have been suicide. I would not have survived jumping straight into that fire. Instead, I leaped and landed right on top of one of the fire suppression drones, which dipped and swayed with the sudden and unexpected passenger. It never stopped spraying, though. Unlike a security drone, this wasn't programmed to deal with people. Its job was to find fire and spray. It was kind of stupid in that way, which was exactly what I needed.

"I need control of this drone!" I yelled.

"Programming ports are on the underside."

Holding on with my other hand and my feet, I deployed that new camera and data cable combo, running along the backside of the drone and down to the underside. Within a few seconds, I spotted the ports. I shifted the cable's shape to match the main data port and plugged it in.

"Just a moment," Bastion said.

In less than ten seconds, a number of augmented reality controls for the drone appeared on my display. Pitch, yaw, roll, and dozens of fire suppression settings were right there for me to use. I didn't have time to decipher them, though.

"How do I cover myself in that chemical spray?" I asked.

"I have an idea," Bastion said. "Deploy your helmet and hold on."

I did as he'd asked, tapping the plate on my neck and making sure both hands and feet were firmly attached to the drone, and then the chemical spray changed to a wide-angle.

"How does that—" I started to say, but then the drone started spinning wildly up, down, and sideways. It was nauseating, but in short order, I was covered in the sticky, sweet-smelling chemical.

Once my vision stopped spinning, I said, "Well done. Now put the sprayer back to a forward cone and give me control."

I took a deep breath, held it, and moved the drone forward into the fire. Giant, red flame symbols started blinking in the corners of my display.

Even though the fire suppression chemical was keeping me from bursting into flames, the heat was horrific. I moved the drone quickly through the billowing orange wall and into the melting shell of the building. It was hard even to see the green AR line leading to Nox's last known location and even harder to see anything inside the building other than flames and smoke. I almost ran into a wall, barely ducking the drone through an open doorway in time, the side scraping hard and splintering the door frame.

I flew down the hall, still spraying a cone of chemicals to create a path. Flames rushed back in after me. Before I even reached the last place Bastion had seen my apprentice, the chemical spray cleared away a dark spot on the floor in roughly human shape. Hairless. Dark skin. Clothes half burned away. I halted the drone, keeping the spray going directly on the figure, and leaped down next to it. The fresh spray on my skin and mods was like jumping into a cold pool.

I grabbed the figure's face and turned it toward me. It was Nox. His face, his arms, his everything that wasn't cybernetic was burned and blistered. Somehow, he was still breathing. Barely. I poked around on his cybernetic arms, opening every likely compartment until I found what I needed: a med kit. Two hypos of heavy-duty painkillers and two hypos of emergency medical nanobots. They were no match for the sheer amount of damage he'd endured, but maybe they would buy me just a little time. I gave him all of it.

I hauled Nox up onto my shoulders, jumped back onto the drone, and told Bastion to get us to the nearest Corto emergency clinic as fast as this hijacked thing could manage. In a flash, we were out of the burning building and racing through the Huginn borough back toward Corto Corporation. "Solomon," I screamed once I reconnected to him via comms.

"Elise?" Worry was painted across Solomon's voice in an uncharacteristic quiver.

"I have Nox. On my way to an emergency clinic in Corto 228."

"How?" Solomon said and then paused before he continued. "How bad is it?"

"It's bad, sir. Very bad. I gave him every painkiller and nano he had, but he's barely hanging on."

"ETA?"

I glanced around at the blur of Huginn buildings I was speeding past. I was still several kilometers from the border to Corto Corporation, and then Corto 228 was another half kilometer in. "Four minutes," I said. "Maybe five."

"I'll meet you there," Solomon said and then cut the connection before I could say anything more.

#   #   #

The clinic's waiting room was bigger than the one in my building. But our emergency clinic was only level three. Level one emergency clinics like these, ones equipped to deal with the worst trauma, weren't in very many buildings. I'd brought Nox in fifteen minutes ago, the nurse looking at me with as much worry as they looked at Nox. I scanned my palm and the nurse helped me scan his, and then half a dozen people emerged with a stretcher and whisked my apprentice away through green double doors. When I tried to follow, the same nurse stepped in my path. "He's my apprentice," I said to them.

"It doesn't matter if he's your son," they said. "You have to wait out here."

I worked my jaw, standing on the tips of my toes to watch as Nox was wheeled around a corner.

"Besides," the nurse said, rising to their own toes to get in my way and holding out their left hand, palm up. "I need to take a look at you. You've been coughing since you walked in and I'd bet there are some burns under all that soot and…whatever you're covered in."

"I'm fine," I said.

"That's wonderful," the nurse said. "Now let me read your vitals."

I sighed. This nurse was unmoved. Unmovable. I pulled up my medical diagnostics app and pressed my palm to theirs, sending the information over.

The nurse, Amethyst, she/her, determined that I was suffering from dehydration, heat rash, exhaustion, smoke inhalation, and mild burns in my lungs. She helped me fit a nasal cannula in my nose and turned on a nanobot-infused oxygen feed, which instantly helped with the cough. Then she led me to a medical shower, replete with lukewarm water and astringent soap.

I was back in the waiting room, still taking the deepest, slowest breaths I could manage from the cannula when Solomon finally entered the waiting room, his head on a swivel until he saw me, pivoted on one foot, and was suddenly standing far too close to me.

"How is he?" he barked.

"I don't know," I said. "They haven't told me anything."

The Cloak of Corto pivoted again toward the nurse's desk, took two steps, and suddenly stopped. His shoulders eased just a few millimeters. He looked back at me. "How are you?"

I nodded. "I'm okay."

He nodded curtly and said, "Thank you." Then he practically ran up to the nurse, and the two started discussing something in animated if hushed tones. Maybe they could keep me and my bum lungs from seeing my apprentice, but woe be it on whoever got between the Cloak of Corto and his nephew. I closed my eyes, leaned my head back, and took more deep breaths.

I didn't know if I'd been asleep for seconds or hours when I was jostled awake. Solomon had flopped into the seat next to me looking wearier than I'd ever seen him. The rest of the waiting room was largely unchanged. A few people had left and a few new people were sitting around. The air from the cannula in my nose no longer had the metallic tang of nanobots.

"How is Nox?" I asked.

"Floating in a bath of emergency medical gel," Solomon grumbled.

I pulled the cannula from my nose. "That doesn't answer my question."

He sighed. "No, it doesn't." We sat in slightly awkward silence for several minutes.

"How are you feeling?" Bastion asked.

I brought up my AR keyboard and responded, "Much better." I stared at the words for a while, wondering what else to say. I wanted to know how effective our three-pronged mission had gone. I wanted to know how Nox was really doing, and what his chances were. Inevitably, though, my mind wandered back home. I typed, "How is Quynn?" and send the words along.

"They are home," Bastion said. "In bed. They have been worried about you, asking after you. At least I was able to reassure them you were on an assignment tonight, which eased their anxiety a bit."

"Did you give them any details of tonight's mission?"

"No. I told them it was of a more classified nature than even most of your assignments, which is the truth."

I chewed the inside of my lip for a moment before I typed, "Have they asked me to come home yet?"

"Not yet," Bastion said. "I'm sorry."

"Who are you texting?" Solomon suddenly said, his voice too close to me. "Your partner? Quynn, isn't it?"

"Trying to write them an email, actually," I said. The lie came easily enough. One of a hundred or so I'd told to hide conversations with Bastion. Solomon and I hadn't seen much of each other in the last few years, so he wasn't on top of every aspect of my life. That made the lie easier.

"Old fashioned," Solomon said.

"Something like that."

He sighed. "I didn't teach you to be old-fashioned."

"Guess I came by that on my own," I said. "I didn't learn everything from you."

"No, I supposed not. Especially not the last few years."

I dismissed my AR keyboard. We sat in silence for a while after that. There'd been no falling out or fight or anything like that. Work just pulled us in different directions, especially after his promotion to Cloak.

"I get it now," I said.

"Get what?"

"Now that I've been…" I paused, wondering how to refer to Necropolis Alpha in public before landing on, "downstairs. I understand why I haven't seen as much of you."

Solomon nodded slowly. "You're starting to understand. I'm glad you're read in now. I hated keeping things from you. It was easier to just give you your space than lie all the time."

"Now I just have to lie to Nox." Solomon deflated at the mention of his nephew.

I said, "How are you holding up?"

The Cloak of Corto worked his jaw for a moment before he spoke.

"You know I'm pretty much all that kid has."

"Nox?"

He nodded.

"I didn't know that."

"He's about all I have, too. Well, and the Division."

It was my turn to nod this time. Solomon was a holdover from a time when the very existence of the Intel division was a corporate secret. "The Division" was a common moniker for referring to us when strangers were around. Funny that he held onto the term after all these years.

"They let me go back there to see him," Solomon continued. "Nox. He's burned everywhere. Everywhere. He's going to need some new cybernetics whether he wants them or not. They've got him hooked up to all these tubes and wires. Looks like he's submerged in liquid metal, like mercury. And his lungs… How did you even get him out of there?"

I shrugged. "Hijacked a fire suppression drone."

He made a face that was maybe surprised, maybe impressed. "A drone?"

"A big drone. Sprayed myself and rode into the building."

Solomon shook his head. "You could have gotten yourself killed in that."

"I did what I—"

"You were right," Solomon continued like he hadn't even heard me. "I should have never let him come along. Too soon. Far too soon. He wants to be an operative so badly, though. Has since he was little. You seemed like the best choice to teach him."

I was glad for my burns at that moment. Made the blush in my cheeks invisible. I said, "So that was you, not Gustin. Why did you pick me?"

"Nox talks like he already knows everything, but his instincts have always been terrible. Hesitant when he needs to be bold. Too bold when he needs to exercise caution."

"Caution is good."

"Sometimes, but you know in this job, sometimes you have to take radical steps to get it done."

"I do know," I said, thinking of too many bold or radical decisions I'd made in the last two days alone.

"I know you know! You do it more effectively than anyone in the office. Mostly, it pays off. Mostly. He needs to see that, learn to take those chances at the right times."

"Seemed like he took one crazy chance tonight."

"It does," Solomon said with a sigh. "I may have underestimated him there. I thought if I paired him with you, made him learn from the best—"

"The best?" I blurted out. "Me?"

Solomon finally smiled a little. "You can't have my cloak yet, Elise, but one day. I'm sure of that. I see a lot of myself in you. We taught you well, me and, you know. You do what it takes. Whatever it takes. Not the healthiest respect for authority. And you're almost as skilled as I was at your age."

"Almost?"

"You do jump off a lot more buildings than I ever did," Solomon said with a chuckle. The sound died as he looked up, his eyes hanging on the door through which I'd seen Nox disappear.

"He'll be okay," I said, placing a careful hand on his.

"I hope so. I hope so. I'd never forgive myself if—"

"There's no *if*," I said, cutting him off. "He's going to be fine. He'll heal up. He'll buy the fanciest new mods with a thousand little toys neither of us has ever heard of, most of which will be useless, and he'll talk about them all using a bunch of words we don't understand. Just like always."

The Cloak of Corto was chuckling, almost laughing. He squeezed my hand gratefully and I saw a single tear escape his eye, which he quickly wiped away and looked away from me. "That kid is going to be the death of me."

"Me first," I said. "You made him my apprentice. Now I have to take him everywhere with me."

Solomon barked out a laugh, slapping me on the knee and rising as a person who looked remarkably like him walked into the waiting room. "Too true, though I think he's going to be here for a little while longer."

I started to rise to follow, but he stopped me.

"This won't take but a moment," he said. "My sister. Then you and I need to leave."

"Leave?" I asked.

"Our targets should be starting their days in a few hours. We need to get some rest and you need another shower or three. Once our analysts see something actionable, we need to be able to move immediately if necessary. We'll both be useless if we don't get some sleep."

"But—"

"That's an order. Go on home. And thank you again."

Chapter Eighteen

BY THE TIME I GOT back to my garage, I was able to breathe almost as deeply as normal, though my chest stung if I tried too hard. The nurse had told me that healing lungs was a slow, gentle process. The nanobots would take several days to get me back to one hundred percent. Before I'd even turned off Poe's thrusters, I noticed a box of pizza on the workbench by the terminal.

"Quynn?" I asked Bastion.

"As if you didn't already know," he replied. "Of course, though it's likely cold by now."

Tears welled up in my eyes, blurring my vision in an instant. I missed their eyes, violet and aquamarine. Their kisses. Hugs. Just sitting around and watching bad movies. Talking about Corto Corporation politics like we could save the company over dinner. And there was a box of pizza. Cold and edible proof that even if Quynn wasn't ready for me to come home, they were still thinking about me. Still worried.

I wanted to text them, to ask if we could talk, but I knew how that would go. Quynn would ask if I was still wrapped up in this whole Josephine business. And now that I'd been read into Necropolis Alpha, I was more in it than ever. My apprentice was barely hanging onto his life. Once the analysts found what they were looking for in the data of Elizabeth Huginn-Sec, Twila Kotega, and Brock Nexus-Neuro; I was going to be involved with whatever came next. All that amounted to one giant keep-sleeping-in-the-garage non-starter.

"I need something to do," I said.

"You should rest," Bastion said. "It will likely take many hours before tonight's heists present any actionable information, and hours more for the analysts in your Intel office to determine what to do with that information."

"I feel rested," I lied. "I need something to do instead of worrying about Nox and Solomon and my relationship with Quynn."

"There are several reputable hotels in the vicinity. Combined with a mild sedative, I think you could get the rest you need and take your mind off those—"

"Preg Vaxxus B," I said, interrupting him. "Valdo needs it. Have you found leads on it?"

Bastion said nothing.

"I know you have. I know you heard me."

"Fascinating," Bastion said. "Since it appears that you did not hear me."

I sighed and ran a hand through my hair. "I hear you. I do. I just, I can't rest. I need to do something, anything. I can rest when this is over, when I can welcome Nox back to the office and tell Quynn that all of this is behind us."

"You are not as effective at your job when sleep deprived."

"I know, but I have you, a second set of eyes and ears to help keep me on pointe."

"I can only use your eyes and ears, actually," Bastion said.

"And numerous security cameras, open communication lines, et cetera, et cetera. My point remains."

Bastion sighed over the speakers in the garage, a sound that still unnerved me since Bastion didn't have lungs. "There are three companies in Jayu City that manufacture Preg Vaxxus B."

A map of Jayu City replaced my digital conspiracy board on the viewscreen. The five boroughs were clearly outlined. Nexus Neuronics in the southeast, Corto Corporation in the southwest, Huginn Industries taking the middle of the map west of Drakon Bay, Toinette Holdings in the northwest, and Kotega Systems in the northeast. Three glowing dots appeared. One in Kotega, one in Toinette, and one in Corto Corporation.

"I'm not stealing from my own company," I said. The dot in Corto disappeared.

"And I probably should stay away from Toinette Holdings for a little while, at least while their security is looking for someone roughly matching my description."

The dot in Toinette vanished, and then the map spun and zoomed in on the remaining dot in Kotega Systems. A wireframe model of a large building took up the center of the viewscreen. The wireframe was accompanied by a dozen photographs of that same building, orbiting like electrons. The building was a pyramid of sorts, tapering toward the top like large steps. Depending on the sunlight, it gleamed copper or green or dull beige. Many of the buildings I'd seen and broken into in Kotega were ornate, embellishing rooftops and landing pads and window frames and cornices whenever possible. Aside from the unusual shape, however, this building was incredibly plain, like it had been built in Corto Corporation rather than Kotega.

"Why is this building so fortress-y?" I asked.

"This is the main building for Kotega's pharmaceutical division," Bastion said. "Executives, research and development, and manufacturing all take place in this facility. Pharmaceuticals are forty-three percent of Kotega's gross corporate product, and they have sixteen percent of the pharmaceutical market share of Jayu City."

"That doesn't answer my question."

"Doesn't it?" Bastion said. "The security demands seem to necessitate the design."

They didn't, actually. I'd seen high security and fanciful design together plenty. Was Bastion dodging my question? I made a mental note to look into it myself later. Discreetly, if that was even possible for me anymore with this AI literally living in my shoulder.

"How do I get in?" I asked.

"According to the information I've found, the facility has never been breached."

"Ooh, a challenge!" I scooted forward in my seat. "Though that could also just be the company line, not the truth."

"There is a landing pad on the small roof."

"But no door," I said, squinting at a photograph of it. I was just a flat space.

"It is a door," Bastion said. "Aerial footage indicates that it has a two-stage elevator system. What appears to be a landing pad lowers and meter-thick doors close behind it."

"We're not getting in that way," I said. I was familiar with the two-stage landing elevator. Corto used them in high-security facilities. Once the elevator lowered and the first doors closed, a second pair of doors had to open before the elevator could continue. Those systems had lots of humans and hardware checking who and what was going in. And there was no forcing my way in. A meter thick meant nothing short of orbital bombardment would get them open without proper access.

"I've only been able to find a few photographs of the other access doors to the facility," Bastion continued. Those images appeared, all of them hazy, showing very large doors and at least half a dozen armed guards at each. "There are six of them, all down in The Mist."

"That's unusual. Who uses them?" I asked.

"Personnel transports enter and exit each Monday and Thursday, always accompanied by a heavier rotation of guards. Armored transport vehicles also exit from these doors."

"They don't enter through them?"

"No. Those same transport vehicles return through the elevator on the roof."

"Meaning they're carrying too much weight to come up the elevators, so they have to exit in The Mist and gain altitude the old-fashioned way."

"A plausible hypothesis."

"Not hypothesis. Experience. I hit a Nexus heavy metals refinery four years ago. That's how they worked."

"Understood."

"What about the rest of the facility?"

"It is a black box."

I blew out a breath. 'Black box' was Intel Operative parlance for a building with absolutely zero visibility inside. No schematics, security footage, or stray social media images to give even a clue.

"Maybe we're looking at the wrong end of this," I said. "What about hospitals?"

"Preg Vaxxus B is not addictive, but since it is rather expensive, hospitals keep it in secured areas," Bastion said. The photos and wireframe of the Kotega facility faded away, replaced by a couple dozen photos. They were obviously from social media posts. Nurses celebrating a birthday. Families and friends huddled together for various pictures. In the backgrounds of each, closed doors with SECURE printed in large letters could be seen.

"Locked doors aren't a problem," I said.

"No, but these doors are in brightly lit hallways with regular foot traffic and access occurring twenty-eight hours a day."

"Meaning I would need passable medical credentials and would have to act the part of a new doctor or nurse on the floor to get access. Not impossible, but that kind of thing takes time." I paced the floor of my garage, weaving through stacks of boxes, shining toolboxes, and shelves of spare parts for Poe. I knew the obstacles weren't created by Bastion, but he seemed intent on pointing them out without solutions.

"Might I again," Bastion said, "recommend rest? Perhaps a shower?"

"The transports that leave in The Mist," I spat, tired of his derailments. "Are those ferrying drugs to the hospitals and clinics?"

"I do not know what else they could be ferrying from that facility," Bastion said as though he didn't really like where I was going.

I waited for more information, which he didn't give. I gritted my teeth and asked, "What can you tell me about them?"

Again, the images on my viewscreen changed. A large schematic and a number of pictures appeared of a transport vehicle. "They are using a variation on the Kotega—"

"The Kotega Atlas," I said, interrupting him as I looked over the schematics. "Standard armor and locking. Electromagnetic shielding. Looks like the thruster configuration is for fragile loads, not speed or handling. Are those extra air conditioning units?"

"Standard and ultra-low-temperature refrigeration units," Bastion said.

"Definitely transporting drugs, then."

"What are the chances that one of those is carrying Preg Vaxxus B at any given point?"

"While I cannot access patient records or drug supply records for any clinic or hospital remotely, I know for a fact that the next shipment to Kotega's Northeast Emergency Clinic #4 will include a large quantity of the medicine."

"How do you know that?"

"Analysis of 1215 social media accounts, four hundred and thirty open-channel communications calls, a keyword search through unsecured email and text conversations that has returned over—"

"I get it," I said. "And I'm both impressed and a little scared that you were able to do that."

"Thank you."

"When is this shipment happening?"

"Tomorrow evening."

"Sparks," I hissed. "When is the next shipment leaving that facility? Any shipment?"

"There is no guarantee that the next shipment will contain Preg—"

"I don't care!" I yelled and slammed my fists on the table. My breathing was hot and fast. My heart was beating a quick tattoo against my ribs. Tomorrow evening. Tomorrow. The word felt like a cage closing in around me, the bars pressing into all the softest parts of me. I grabbed the nearest item, an old exhaust port for Poe, and flung it across the garage. I kicked a box, whatever was inside clanging hard against my cybernetic foot. Tears threatened to fill my eyes, but I denied them, screaming from somewhere down deep in me instead.

Bastion started to say, "I'm sorry—"

"You're doing this on purpose! You're so obsessed with me resting, with stopping! I'm not going to sleep in this forsaken garage again! I want my bed and my life and my…my…my…" I fell to my knees, the sentence dying in my throat. My Quynn. I missed them, missed our talks and watching stupid programs and their terrible cooking and just, just being with them. I dropped my head into my hands and finally let the tears go, a sobbing wail crawling up out of my throat at the same time.

I don't know how much time passed like that, little puddles of tears and snot forming on my thighs down there on the garage floor, before a pair of arms wrapped around me. Soft and comforting, smelling faintly of lilac and curry.

"Shh," Quynn whispered near my ear. "I'm here. I've got you."

"I'm sorry," I said.

"I know. I've got you. I've got you."

"I'm so sorry."

I went home. We went home together. Quynn told me to shower and change my clothes since I smelled like smoke and look like I'd run through a burning building, which I had. Then we had one of the longest and hardest conversations of our relationship. Quynn felt betrayed, felt that I'd put my job before them and our relationship. I'd been trying to make things better but had obviously made things much worse. I apologized. Apologized again. We never raised voices, but some words definitely had venom in them. Both of us emotionally exhausted, we ordered food and sat in uneasy, but familiar silence.

"So what are you going to do?" Quynn asked after swallowing a bite.

"I need to get the Preg Vaxxus B for Valdo," I said. "Though the office could call at any time with our next move against Josephine."

Quynn nodded and took another bite.

"I don't see how Valdo is relevant," Bastion chimed in over the living room speaker for the first time all evening.

"I made a promise," I said.

"There are larger issues in play right now," he said. "Maybe once all this is done—"

"No," Quynn said. "Elise made a promise. This child's mother is in jeopardy. He needs the medicine for her. To me, that's the highest priority."

"Her disease is slow-progressing, surely she has some time."

"Time for what?" I asked. "Time for me to wait, make other things a priority until I forget Valdo and my promise and she succumbs? Getting you and dealing with Theo nearly killed me. Now Josephine and her bodyguard have done the same to me and my new apprentice. What's next that can't wait? What if something happens to me before I can help Valdo?"

Quynn's hand was suddenly on my arm. They gave a gentle squeeze and a bright smile. "That's the woman I love."

I smiled back. Corto, I'd missed that smile.

"I'm not sure who scares me more," Quynn said. "Vert or Josephine."

I chewed slowly and considered that. I weighed the threats. I couldn't decide, either. "I don't like the thought of Nox unconscious in a hospital bed. I can just imagine Vert finding him, helpless and tied to machines. My apprentice wouldn't get lucky a third time."

Quynn worked their jaw and stared at me before finally shaking their head and whispering, "Mother of Corto, Elise."

"You see my problem," I said. "I can't just walk away from this, can't just hand it off to Gustin."

"No, but you could have before. You didn't need to follow Vert to the docks without a plan or your work limbs. And you had no business going into the Deus Quarter alone. Did Hessod even know you were doing that?"

I shook my head and set down my now-empty plate.

"You have to be the stupidest smart person I know, Elise," Quynn said. "I can't believe you keep running around like this without a plan or a thought to what might happen after. It's like once Bastion showed up, you misplaced your mind."

"I assure you," Bastion said. "This is not my doing. I advised her against this course of action."

"That's not even relevant," Quynn said to the speaker and then turned back to me. "Maybe he gives you a false sense of security or something. I don't know. But I want my old, patient, thoughtful Elise back."

I nodded again. I didn't know what to say. Quynn was right, though. I'd been reckless ever since I pulled Bastion's chip out of that safe in the Nexus Neuronics borough.

"Well?" Quynn asked. "Don't just nod your head. What are you going to do?"

"You're right," I said.

Bastion started to say, "Pardon me, but I'm not—"

"This isn't about you," I said and then focused on Quynn. "I don't know why, but I've been taking too many chances since I got Bastion. Now my recklessness has put more than me in danger. I need to fix this, eliminate the threats of Vert and Josephine, and then slow down. Figure out why I've been acting this way. I'll see a therapist or whoever you want me to see. But I have to fix all this first."

"And not alone," Quynn said. "She is never alone," Bastion said.

Quynn worked their jaw again. "I know, but that's not what I mean. Elise has an analyst in Hessod, a boss in Gustin, a whole operation backing her up when she needs it."

"And I do a better job when I let them do their jobs," I said.

"Exactly."

I nodded again and reached a hand across the couch to grab Quynn's. They squeezed my hand slightly, but then pulled back and stood up, taking their plate to the kitchen. Not both our plates, just theirs. Things were definitely not okay between us. My own plate suddenly felt so heavy even though it was empty. "There's nothing I can do tonight," I said. "Except rest and make sure my gear is ready. Can I—?"

"Stay here?" Quynn hollered from the kitchen. "Yes."

"Thank you."

Quynn re-entered the living room and stood over me. "But you're sleeping on the couch. I still love you, I hope you know that, but I've never been angrier with you."

"I'm sorry," I said for the millionth time that evening.

"I know," Quynn said and started heading toward the bedroom.

"Why did you come for me?"

"What?" Quynn stopped and turned back.

"In the garage," I said. "Why did you come for me?"

Quynn's frustrated look changed to one of compassion mixed with disappointment. "Because I love you. Even if I'm mad at you, I'm not going to let you crumble. You should have already known that."

Chapter Nineteen

"WE HAVE TO GO AFTER Vert," I said. After an amazing eight hours of sleep, full charge on my limbs, a deep cleaning of my jumpsuit, and more time for the nanobots to heal my lungs, I'd been in Necropolis Alpha all morning, listening to a small army of analysts I didn't know droning on and on about the information they'd gathered from Twila Kotega, Elizabeth HuginnSec, and Brock Nexus-Neuro. The analysts were thorough. Too thorough. At least Hessod knew how to give me only information that was pertinent to me. Instead, I knew what all three of these people had for their meals, who they talked to, and even when they used the bathroom.

Sprinkled in all that information were a few nuggets, mostly mined from extended contact to their onboard computers, that gave us anything useful and actionable. The most important information we received was that all three of them had tickets to attend the big gaming tournament on Cirilla that coming weekend, the same tournament Quynn was attending. A little more digging turned up that more than seventy percent of the names on that wall in Tazia's secret room were also going. That was odd since most didn't have *Dregs of Osiris* accounts, gaming consoles, or any history of gaming. Most importantly, Tazia had also purchased travel and tickets under her Josephine moniker.

None of their information dealt with Vert and the threat he posed.

"Vert isn't our priority," Solomon said from the back row, his arms crossed.

"Vert is a major problem if we want to get to Tazia," I said.

"We've dealt with bodyguards and hired muscle before," Solomon said. "This is no different."

"The easiest way," Mione chimed in from the gaggle of analysts at the front of the room. "Is to buy him off. We send an anonymous transfer to his account asking him to stay behind and not attend the tournament."

"That's assuming he's really just there for the money," I said.

"He was raised a true believer of Ibhalism," Mione said, "But his behavior over the last few years has resembled more of a mercenary. It is a solid inference."

I turned in my seat to look up at Solomon and said, "None of that is going to help Nox, however."

The Cloak of Corto fixed his eyes on mine, his posture changing subtly but definitively to one more defensive. "What do you mean?"

"Nox," I said. Part of me wanted to tell the whole story, to tell how he'd disobeyed me and it wasn't my fault. But as his mentor, everything was my fault. And he'd endured enough. I could take this on. "When we got Vert's decryption key, Nox held Vert's son hostage. Vert saw Nox's face and threatened him. Now Nox is laid up in a hospital, in a coma."

Solomon's face turned dark and he said, "And with Tazia's resources, he surely knows Nox's identity by now. He might already know where Nox is."

"We can move Nox," Gustin said. "The priority here—"

"The priority is making sure that Vert 'The Hurt' Toinette is no longer a problem," Solomon growled and jumped to his feet. "We have two days before the tournament starts. Two days to make sure that Vert is taken off the board completely, not just staying home and away from Cirilla."

Gustin stood and smoothed down the front of his shirt. "Solomon," he said. "May I speak with you privately?"

"No," Solomon said. He worked his jaw and sat back down.

I'd never understood the relationship between Solomon and managers like Gustin. Managers reported to directors. Directors and Solomon reported to the Intel VP, but managers didn't report to Solomon. Solomon was always in charge if he was on an op, but otherwise, it was murky. It made these power struggles rather common occurrences.

"Solomon—" Gustin tried again. "Say what you have to say!" Solomon barked.

Gustin glanced nervously around the room, holding my gaze a little longer than most before he found his footing and looked directly at Solomon again. "I know you have a personal, very personal stake in this. You and Elise."

"He's my nephew, Gustin," Solomon said. "Everyone here knows what you're dancing around."

"Fine. He's your nephew. You care for him. I understand that. We can protect him without losing sight of the bigger—"

"The bigger picture?" Solomon bellowed and moved to his feet again, this time moving toward Gustin with every word. "The bigger fish? What? You don't think I know the threat that Tazia poses? She's built a network spread across all five boroughs. She's been evangelizing people all over the city. We don't have a clear picture, but when we look at a worst-case scenario, we could be seeing a destabilization of Jayu City. And yes, Vert is just some big, stupid fighter. But if we don't take care of our own, don't protect every analyst and operative and," Solomon was in Gustin's face by now and he poked him in the chest as he said, "manager in our outfit, then what the hell are we doing?"

Gustin swallowed hard, but he stood his ground. "I wonder if our vice president would agree with you?"

"Fine," Solomon said, moving past Gustin and bumping his shoulder in the process. "You go talk to Ivan. Bring him down here. In the meantime, we're going to deal with Vert." Solomon reached the front of the room and addressed all of us. "Now, who has a plan for the guy who can punch through walls and rip cybernetic limbs right out of their sockets?"

Everyone shifted uncomfortably in their seats. Everyone except Gustin, that is, who walked right out of the room. Maybe he was going to get the VP of Corto Corporations' Intel division. Whatever. I hoped he got stuck in the elevator on the way out. Nox needed our help.

"Anyone?" Solomon asked again.

I wracked my brain for ideas, but I kept gravitating back to the Preg Vaxxus B that Valdo needed. The Kotega pharmaceuticals building, the transport moving medicine tonight, and how to break into a moving, armored vehicle. It was like my brain couldn't let go of the puzzle. Then it hit me.

"I have one," I said.

I could have sworn I saw the tiniest smile crack Solomon's lips before he said, "Oh?"

"I happen to know, completely unrelated, about a very hittable medical transport moving through Kotega tonight. What if someone were to steal something from it?"

"What does that have to do with—?"

"What if that someone is, very publicly, Vert 'The Hurt' Toinette-Deus?"

#   #   #

"Entering Kotega borough," Solomon said over comms. He was sitting right next to me, manually piloting a transport identical to the one we were getting ready to intercept. "Report in. Text only."

No verbal response came, as he'd requested. With one hand, though, he flicked the air, scrolling through several text confirmations that I couldn't see. After fifteen or twenty seconds, he stopped.

"How is Nox?" I asked.

"Still in a coma," Solomon said with a softness I only heard him use in private. "They don't know how long it will take him to come out of it. The medical gel is doing its job, healing his burns, but…"

I didn't rush him, just waited for more to come, for Solomon to work through it.

"There might be neurological damage. From the explosion and oxygen deprivation. We'll know more when he wakes up."

"No unexpected visitors?"

Solomon glanced at me briefly before returning his gaze to the lanes of traffic. "No. We've tripled security at the hospital. Though if this goes well, Vert shouldn't be focused on Nox."

"He took my call," I said. "He said he would meet."

"I still don't know how you managed to get Vert's communications code," Solomon said. "Or if he really values that key as much as you think he does."

"The Intel Analysts obviously haven't been able to analyze Josephine's data as quickly as I have," Bastion said in my ear. "Or they would have found his communications code as well."

More than a dozen of the top analysts in Corto Corporation couldn't work faster than Bastion. No wonder the Corto CEO, Ariela, had him developed. He could put them all out of work.

"I don't think Vert cares that much about the key," I said to Solomon. "I think he doesn't want it getting out that he lost it."

"You think he's that proud?" Solomon asked.

"Maybe pride. I know he's smarter than people think. I also think that Tazia is a dangerous woman. And Vert's meal ticket. Whatever she's paying him, it was enough to draw him away from a life of fame and fortune in the ring. I don't think he wants to lose that."

"Now that," Solomon said. "Is the smartest thing I've ever heard you say. Why didn't you tell the room that when we were planning?"

Because I didn't think of it until after the planning meeting was over. Quynn was right, I didn't think strategically nearly often enough. Or at least I needed to give myself more time to think strategically. At least this time, I'd done what they had said and made sure to bring the full force of the Intel division to bear on the problem.

Before I had a chance to answer Solomon's question, though, Bastion highlighted the target transport vehicle on my display. Roughly ten meters long, three meters wide and tall, calling it boxy would have been an understatement. The entire vehicle was gray except for the Kotega Systems logo, a swirling K and S intertwining in vibrant red and gold. Standard Kotega: ornate buildings and thoroughly dull vehicles.

"There it is," I said to Solomon, pointing. "Get in position," he said.

I nodded and opened my door in midair. In normal flying vehicles, the doors were automatically locked upon takeoff and could only be opened by emergency override. Fortunately, this was a very convincing replica customized for this very mission, including allowing me to open the door without any objection or alarm.

The wind buffeted me, but my carbon-polymer limbs, carbon nanoweave jumpsuit, and shellacked hair were undisturbed. Amazingly, my limbs and jumpsuit had made it through the fire relatively unscathed. Those chemicals had done their job, even keeping my exposed skin from the bullet holes unburnt.

The sun was half-set, casting an orange glow over the streets of Kotega Systems. Like in every other borough, enormous ads took up most of the vertical space on the buildings, casting their own myriad artificial light everywhere. Expensive flying cars, dozens of flavors of vape juice, high-end designer dresses, carbonated beverages, and Stryder's newest rideshare options flashed and danced on screens around every corner.

Using the magnets in my hands and feet, I climbed out, shutting the door behind me, and scrambled up onto the side of the transport. I flattened out my body, my limbs twisting and contorting to bring me flat against the side. Then I said to Solomon over comms, "I'm in place."

"Acknowledged," he said.

The towering ads, orange sky, and blinking lights of other vehicles all dimmed around me. I couldn't see it from inside, but I knew a holographic projection of the side of the transport had just been activated. From as little as half a meter away from the transport, it looked entirely normal. I was hidden completely.

"The Kotega transport is behaving normally," Bastion said. "Though I still do not like this plan."

With a flick of my fingers, I muted myself on the Intel channel and said to Bastion, "I know, but at least I brought in help this time."

"You always have my help."

"And I would have been dead several times over without it, but both of us need more than each other. No way we could do all this alone."

"I do not like being out of contact with you, though. I will be unable to assist."

"This time, you'll have to trust that Solomon is watching my back."

"I do not trust anyone except Quynn to prioritize you above their objectives."

"Aw," I said. "So glad you care."

"My chip is hidden in your shoulder."

"Way to ruin the moment, Bastion."

I held tight as Solomon piloted the transport through traffic, weaving between Stryders and other flying cars. I glanced up and saw another identical transport doing the same thing. Within a couple of minutes, both of our duplicate transports were pulling up along either side of Kotega's official one. I held on though, waiting until we were right up next to it before I demagnetized one hand, reached out, and touched the Kotega pharmaceutical transport. A dull thrumming shot to my shoulder and the battery level for that arm started blinking on my display, the charge depleting from eighty-nine percent to eighty percent in a matter of seconds. I quickly pulled my arm away.

"What in the Mother of Corto?" I said aloud to myself.

"Inductive shielding," Bastion said. "Draws power away from anything that tries to contact it. A clever deterrent against anyone with mods or nanobots."

"Good for them," I said. "But their cleverness happens to be a problem for me. I need a solution, not compliments to their engineers."

"Inductive coils of any type generate heat while they work. Considering how fast the power draw was from you, the coils powering that shield would need significant cooling to keep from overheating."

"So I need to take out their cooling mechanism," I said. "Got it. Switch my display to thermal."

"You misunderstand," Bastion said. "The cooling system will be complex and large, requiring significant damage to the hull in order to compromise. I believe overloading the coils and their cooling system would be easier."

"And how would I manage that? Do I even have enough juice to—?"

"You do not," Bastion said. "That shield would siphon all four of your limbs to zero percent in less than a minute. The backup thruster system on this transport, however, can provide the necessary power if you follow my instructions."

Bastion can be very informative when he has a mind to. In less than a minute, he walked me through bypassing half a dozen security and emergency systems and the necessary crossing of wires. Schematics on my display helped a lot. After I felt like I understood what I needed to do, I unmuted myself on the Intel comms.

"Any chance you'll need emergency thrusters today?" I asked Solomon.

"What?" he said. "There's always a chance. That's why they're called emergency."

"I need to disable them to take out some inductive shielding."

"Inductive shielding?" he barked. Then after a few moments of silence, he said, "You're going to bypass the CPU and bridge the power cells to the main feed cable, right? Hit it with the entire power cell load in one burst?"

That was why he was the Cloak of Corto. He'd distilled exactly what Bastion had just explained to me but in two sentences.

"Yes," I said.

"Do it," Solomon said. Then after a couple of seconds, the maintenance hatch on my side of the transport released, popping up a few centimeters. I unlatched it the rest of the way and got to work following Bastion's instructions. It took me several minutes, including nearly doing it wrong several times, with Bastion gently correcting me as I went along. Finally, I crawled out of the hatch with the splintered end of the main feed cable in my hand. I made sure I was securely magnetized to our transport with my three other limbs, took a deep breath, and started to reach out to the Kotega transport.

"Elise," Bastion said.

I froze, my heart leaping in my throat a little. "What?"

"Be careful," he said. "You do not want to touch the exposed end of the cable or any part of that vehicle when the cable touches it. The burst of power would blow every circuit in you and kill you in seconds."

I swallowed hard. None of that information was surprising, nothing I hadn't thought of, but hearing it put so bluntly jangled my nerves.

"Thank you for your concern," I said flatly. I took one more quick breath and without pausing again, I pushed the cable against the side of the Kotega pharmaceutical transport. In an instant, my vision was flooded with light. A loud pop temporarily overloaded my aural implants, and the cable jumped in my hand. In short order, though, my optical and aural implants adjusted. The transport was still right there, flying along, looking untouched other than a black burn scar. I still held the main feed cable in my hand.

"Did it work?" I asked Bastion. "You will have to test that manually," he said.

I dropped the cable, which hung off the side of my transport and fluttered like a dead snake in the wind. I reached out and pressed a single finger to the side of the Kotega pharmaceutical transport. No warnings of sudden power depletion showed on my display. I pressed my entire hand to it, and everything seemed in order. I magnetized that hand and quickly transferred myself completely over and started scuttling down to the bottom of the Kotega transport.

I wormed between a pair of thrusters, squeezing and bending before I was able to work my way toward the front of the vehicle. Once I was beneath the passenger cabin, I said over comms, "I'm in position for phase two."

"Acknowledged," Solomon said.

I wasted no time deploying a welder from my right hand and cutting into a spot that Bastion had pointed out on my display. The metal hull was thick, though, making the cutting take longer than I would have liked. I tried to shield my welding with my body so it wouldn't attract the attention of cars flying by below. Sparks flew out, my display compensating for the brightness and little bits of hot metal bouncing off my carbon polymer limbs. The small, bright bits that hit my carbon nanoweave jumpsuit made a sizzling sound and smelled vaguely of burning polymer.

After two full minutes, I finally finished cutting a circle fifteen centimeters across. I grabbed the disc of metal and tossed it. Then I reached my hand up inside, guided by my fiberoptic camera, and found what I was looking for: an angular contraption about the size of my fist with several blinking lights on it. I grabbed hold of it and squeezed, crushing it until all the lights went dead.

"Phase two complete," I said over comms.

"All ops," Solomon said, speaking to more than just me now. "Bring down the sky."

In the span of only a few breaths, all the traffic flying through this part of the Kotega Systems borough suddenly stopped moving, switching en masse to hover mode. Every vehicle in Jayu City, on the entire planet actually, talked to each other and a sophisticated system of satellites. Through some really brilliant programming, it allowed all the vehicles to fly through the city, weaving left and right and up and down through various lanes of traffic to their different destinations.

Of course, any system can fail. Or be blocked by several dozen well-equipped Intel Operatives. If just one vehicle loses satellite connectivity, it can get the information it needs from nearby vehicles and fly to a service station. If a whole area, say six square blocks, loses connectivity, then the safety protocol that kicks in tells every vehicle to go into emergency hover mode.

A little research showed our analysts that armored vehicles like this one were equipped with a two-way backup system, giving them communication and emergency navigation. Fortunately, I'd just reduced that backup to a twisted ball of circuits.

"The board is black," Solomon finally said to me. "Proceed."

I had already started crawling back before he said that, but now I moved between the thrusters again, up along the side of Kotega's transport, and onto the roof. Our duplicate transports had hemmed in this one on either side, pushing in less than half a meter away on each side. In front and back, a few Stryders and personal vehicles were crowding in as well. I knew, though I'm sure the Kotega employees in this transport didn't know, that Intel Operatives were driving those as well. We didn't want Kotega taking manual control and flying their way out. Not yet.

In the eerie quiet of the halted Kotega traffic, I could just barely make out shouting from the front of the transport. I didn't know if the Kotega pharmaceutical employees knew they were under attack yet, but they had to be worried about all traffic stopping and their backup not working. I took three quick strides, trying to be as quiet as possible until I was just behind the passenger cabin. With a somewhat complicated pattern of my fingers and wrists, the bottoms of my forearms opened and flat, round, matte-black discs became visible. I crossed my arms, grabbed one in each hand, and then put a foot forward. I leaned hard to the left and placed the first one on the top of the pilot's door. It tapped gently against the metal hull and then emitted a deep thunk as powerful magnets energized. I leaned hard right then, and the door on the other side started to open. A biological hand came into view, reaching up onto the roof, and I smashed it hard with the magnet in my right hand. A high voice screamed, the hand retreated, and I pushed the door back closed and applied the second magnet.

Now they knew they were under attack, but at least they would have a much harder time getting out of the transport. I needed to work quickly. I deployed twelve micro-charges along the perimeter of the transport's cargo area. I sprayed some magneto-gel in specific areas of the roof, checked, and doublechecked everything. Once I was prepared as I could possibly be, I stood tall on the top of the transport, pulled Vert's decryption key out of the compartment in my thigh, and waited for the fighter to show his face.

Chapter Twenty

"ODD CHOICE FOR A MEETING," Vert said. He had just stepped out of his car to stand atop the Kotega transport with me, just behind the passenger cab. I was facing him, standing near the rear of the transport, his decryption key still visible in my right hand.

"Neutral ground," I said.

"And all this?" he said, gesturing in every direction at once. I'd watched him pilot his own small, nondescript car through the unmoving traffic jam, his face plainly confused and impressed at the same time. He still looked to be confused and in awe of the strange, quiet stillness around us.

"Your boss made her point," I said. "Showed me, showed Corto exactly what she's capable of. It nearly killed me. I want to make sure you see that I'm not helpless, nor is Corto Corporation."

Vert stared at me, the confusion and awe giving way to a cold, hard expression.

"And then," I said, "you met my apprentice at the docks of your own borough."

"Apprentice? Beltran or whatever his name is?"

I nodded.

"You are a poor teacher," Vert said.

"Probably. But this one we can chalk up to naïveté." I held his key up. "I've brought this in hope that we can come to a truce."

"While that is certainly my preference, Josephine is not so inclined. She said if I see the opportunity, to end you here." He looked around, spreading his hands wide. "Sadly, I do see the opportunity. Even if I didn't, we could find you again, and Josephine does not miss twice." He sighed and looked a little sad. "And I already know where Nox Toinette-Intel is, exactly what clinic room he's sleeping in right now. He was a pretty good spy up until he wasn't."

I swallowed, trying not to show how much that scared me. "Look around. I'm not without my own resources. My own tricks. I found Josephine's room. How long had she kept that a secret? How many more secrets do I need to uncover? Do I need to shut down the entire Toinette borough?"

Vert glanced around, taking in the hundreds of Stryders and other vehicles hovering, but otherwise unmoving. In a city that never truly slept, that never had empty or still streets, the effect was unnerving for any of us. Then he narrowed his eyes and looked back at me. "A cute trick. I can think of at least three ways to accomplish this. None of which can shut down a borough or threaten our plans."

"Our plans?" I asked, changing tactics. "You talk like you have some say in things. We all know Josephine is the brains, the boss. You're just the hired muscle."

"I am the right hand of a prophet," Vert said, his face suddenly stern.

"Prophet?" I said.

"Yes," Vert said. "She is a prophet of Ibhalism, perhaps the first true prophet in a century."

I hadn't heard anyone call her that before. The implications were immense. Did she believe she was a prophet of Ibhalism? Had she just tricked this former fighter into believing she was something she wasn't? I saw another tactic unfolding before me. "I don't know anything about prophets, but she's not who you think she is."

Vert smirked and said, "Oh?"

I shook my head. "Josephine isn't even her name. Deus isn't her division, either."

Vert's smirk wavered. That was more like it.

"Her name is Tazia Toinette-Intel. An Intel Operative. This has all been a big con, a grift. She's no evangelist, no priestess or prophet or anything else religious. She's after something else, something bigger, and you're just a pawn she's hired to watch her back."

The smirk dropped away completely. I had him, had delivered a killing blow to his belief in this false prophet. But then he smiled. Not smirked, but fully smiled broader than I'd ever seen him.

"My eyes are wide open, Elise Corto-Intel," he said. "And I know exactly who I work for."

"Do you? How can you—?"

"Do you understand nothing of Ibhalism? Of the sacred balance between Shainette and Aphnette? Fate and chaos? How can this balance possibly be achieved with your own company so bent on structure and politics? With Kotega so obsessed with honor? Huginn and their glory or Nexus and their lack of discipline?"

"Sounds like balance to me," I said.

Vert scoffed loudly. "Tazia will spread Ibhalism to every corner of Jayu City. Then the rest of our little planet, and then on to the rest of humanity."

"She doesn't care about any of that!" I said. "She has her own agenda, manipulating people all over the city. Spreading Ibhalism is just a tool, but whatever she's really after, she's not afraid to kill people to get it. That doesn't sound like sacred balance to me. She's taking the beliefs you hold so dear and twisting them to her ends. That can't be what you want. But you can stop, you can help us stop her."

The last shreds of humor drained from Vert's face. "Help you? Help you? When Tazia is so close to bringing an entire borough into the fold?"

Entire borough? Which borough? How? That was new and dizzying information.

"I told you," he continued. "I know who I work for. I know her mind, her intentions. And yet, she calls out in the name of Ibhalism, and from all over the city, people answer. They come. They find the sacred balance even if their prophet does not see herself as one. Ibhalism is truth."

"So the ends justify the means?"

"They do when the stakes are high enough," Vert said. "But you didn't come here to test my faith. Give me the key."

"And you'll walk away?" I held the key out even farther, the lights from the surrounding buildings glinting off the pinkish-orange rectangle. "Tazia will leave me be?"

"I do not speak for her."

I pulled the key back, wrapping my hand completely around it. "You don't speak for yourself either?"

"Give me the key," Vert said, taking a heavy step forward. His armored foot clanged loudly against the top of the transport. "And I will let you leave here with your life. I don't want to hurt you. Please don't make me."

"I came here for a trade, not to cater to your demands."

"Please." He was practically begging. "You cannot stop me if I have to use violence."

"I'm more nimble than my apprentice."

"Of that, I have no doubt. But you are a thief, not a fighter. You might be able to pick my pocket, but if we come to blows, you are outmatched."

I worked my jaw, glancing around for a better option than handing him the key. Vert smiled. Finally, I tossed the key forward. It skittered to a stop on top of the transport, roughly halfway between us. Vert took another step forward and several things happened all at once.

Solomon, who had been listening in on the conversation, broadcast to all the other operatives on this job, "Light it back up."

In a few moments, the jamming we'd been doing to satellite communications cleared up. Personal devices and satellite-connected mods all over the area started reconnecting all at once. Similarly, all of the Stryders and other vehicles hovering in the area regained their connections. The transport, along with the rest of the vehicles hanging in the air, lurched forward. Vert tilted in my direction but stayed on his feet. If Vert had mods anything like my own, he noticed his connection return.

What he didn't know was more than forty optical mods were watching us. Watching him, really. They were all Corto Corporation Intel Analysts, all watching what was about to happen, and all started live-streaming under various proxy accounts the moment their satellite connections resumed.

At that same moment, Vert reached down, put his hand on his key, and Bastion triggered the directional charge I'd placed right on that spot. It was only a millimeter thick, exactly the same color as the hull of the transport, and strong enough to punch a hole in the armored vehicle, which Vert's extended hand fell into as the big man was put off balance. Punch was the key word here since Vert also had the strength in his mods to break through that armor. To any casual observer, it would appear that the big man had punched through the top of the transport. And given that this was Vert 'The Hurt' Toinette, a famous, hall-of-fame fighter, there were undoubtedly a lot of people watching.

Vert snarled, blinking wildly and looking back and forth between me and his fist now buried in the top of the transport. Then I saw the armored plates on his back shift.

"Now!" Bastion yelled.

I was already moving, squatting briefly before launching myself straight up. I heard a rapid-fire series of pings as Bastion fired the magnetic charges that I'd placed around the perimeter of the transport's cargo area. As I was in mid-air, flipping backward and reaching out my hands, I heard wrenching metal. Halfway through my flip and fully inverted, I saw the entire top of the transport ripping away with Vert's enormous fist still punched through the center of it. But that wasn't why I had my eyes wide open. In the brief moment available to me, I glanced into the exposed cargo area of the transport and blinked. It was basically a blur of containers and racks to me, but I knew it was enough for Bastion to look over the single image I'd captured.

I finished my flip, falling and grabbing the back of the transport at the last second. The sudden jolt pulled at my biological ribs and shoulders, but only slightly. I clung to the back of the transport and waited as it shuddered and shook, Vert practically roaring above me as he wrestled with the twisted metal still partly attached to the vehicle.

"I found it," Bastion finally said. "Four meters from the front of the cargo area. Right side. A green case twenty-five centimeters by twenty centimeters by three centimeters."

"You ready?" I asked him.

"Of course."

I pulled myself up, leaping into the now-exposed cargo area. Polymer and metal crates of various sizes were stacked against the sides, a narrow space winding down the middle. I could feel the cold of the cargo area, even as the refrigeration was rapidly escaping. The roof was still attached to Vert as he wrenched it back and forth, grunting and cursing loudly. I pushed forward, squeezing between two large crates and hurdling a third. Then suddenly the enormous piece of metal made a terrifying screech, and Vert flung it off. It slammed into something I couldn't see, making more racket of thundering metal.

"Deceiver!" Vert bellowed.

I hurdled another large crate and spotted the green case Bastion had told me about. Without me asking, he highlighted it in an even brighter green in my display. I took another big step, reached for it, and something flashed down from above, glancing off my extended arm.

"What the—?" I yelled and looked up just as Vert's right fist finished retracting. I couldn't believe how fast it had moved or how lucky I'd been that it had only grazed my arm. My reinforcements to my limbs held just fine, but I couldn't just ignore the fighter looming over me. He cocked back his left arm and launched his fist straight at my face. I lurched to my right, both away from his incoming punch and toward the case of Preg Vaxxus B. The heavy metal fist slammed straight through a crate of some medicine, jolting the entire transport. Metal and glass and glowing blue liquid splashed everywhere as a cloud of something suddenly filled the area around me.

"You can't dodge me forever!" Vert yelled.

I glanced up but couldn't see him through the fog. That meant he couldn't see me, either. I took advantage, moving blindly through the quickly dissipating gas to where I knew the green case sat. I grabbed it with my left hand, but as soon as I turned and started toward the back of the cargo area, a blow to the back of my left shoulder drove me down and forward, crashing into a metal crate that didn't give and sending the green case flying out of my hand. I turned, expecting Vert to still be above me, but he was down in the cargo area with me. He hauled back and threw another punch with his right hand. I tried to raise my left to guard, but the arm was unresponsive. At the last possible second, I leaped and dived down and under the punch, which rattled against the crate that had held me up.

I scrambled, ducking under a half-fallen container, squeezing through tattered coolant lines, and rolling over another crate. Behind me, I heard Vert bellowing and everything around him being torn apart. The green case was at the very back of the cargo area, sitting atop a jumbled stack of medicine. I reached for it again, this time with my right hand when suddenly I was thrown backward along with everything around me that wasn't tied down. I landed on my back, and then several heavy things landed on me. I pushed aside a few canisters and glanced around for the big man, watching for the next blow. By Corto, he was fast.

I hauled more crates off of me, a process made slower by my dead left arm. As I reached up to pull myself up, a large, heavy hand grabbed my wrist and pulled me up bodily off the floor. Vert had caught up to me.

"You are wirier than your apprentice," Vert said as he brought my face up level to his own. "But you never really had a chance."

"I'm still breathing," I said.

He tilted his head a little and smirked. "I admire that. You surprised me. I think you could have escaped, but you came back for that green thing. What is it?"

"Nothing to do with you."

"I'll be the judge of that." Still holding me aloft with his right hand, he shot his left out, much slower than when he'd been punching me from afar, and the hand returned a moment later with the green case. He looked at it, reading it and glancing at me occasionally. "Preg Vaxxus B? What is this?"

"A medicine," I said. "I need it."

"You're lying. This must contain something else, something to use against Tazia. You could steal medicine at any time. This is something more." Then Vert focused on me. "I'll just have to take it with me and find out. After I finish what Tazia started with that Stryder. Do you have any last words? Anyone I should notify of your death?"

"You need to stop being so nice to me," I said, failing to squirm out of his grip. "It's really messing with my head."

Faster than I could register, his right hand released my right wrist and was on my neck before my toes touched the ground again. Then I couldn't breathe. Vert's enormous hand was squeezing my completely unmodified neck, compressing my windpipe and sending jolts of pain down my spine. I uselessly flailed at him, my carbon-polymer right fist and forearm clanging against his thick arm. I couldn't even reach his face. I tried kicking, even winding up and delivering a solid blow to his groin, but the thunk of solid metal against my reinforced shin didn't even make Vert flinch. With a few flicks of my fingers, I engaged the taser in my right palm and slapped his arm as close to the shoulder joint as I could reach. Nothing. None of my tricks made a scratch or made Vert blink. Without my left hand, the explosive shield generator I'd used against the monks in Toinette's Deux Quarter was out of my grasp.

I looked around, trying to find anything that could help me, that could disengage this brute from my neck. Broken crates. Jars and syringes and hyposprays and so many meds with names I couldn't even pronounce. Bent and twisted cables and coolant lines.

"Those hyposprays half a meter down and to your right are loaded with anesthetic nanobots," Bastion said in my ear. "The bots are designed to deliver metered doses of propofol and Aurelium 7. Two or three of those injected into Vert should render him unconscious in a matter of seconds."

I looked down and to my right, but I had a hard time struggling as Vert was crushing my windpipe. As if Bastion knew what I was thinking, the syringes in question suddenly glowed yellow in my display. I reached out, fumbling and finally grabbing a handful of them. If two or three were enough, surely a handful would do the trick.

But then where could I press them? Vert was the most modified person I'd ever met. His face was flesh, but even that was framed in gleaming metal. Both arms and legs had been replaced like mine, but so was his torso, the metal plates and cords flexing and shifting as he moved. I saw no flesh exposed between plates, none except his face that I couldn't reach.

"O2 LEVELS DROPPING," appeared on my display, blinking in red. As if I didn't know.

I kept kicking, knowing it wouldn't do any good, but refusing to die without a fight. No one was coming to help me, either. No one could even see me. It was a big part of the plan. All the live streams of Vert on this cargo transport were from Corto Corporation Intel Analysts, and they were all running the same program that was actively deleting me from their video. I wasn't just deleted from the outgoing streams but their own optical displays.

"I don't know what to do," Bastion said. "I'm contacting Quynn, Hessod, anyone who might be able to help."

Quynn and Hessod weren't here. By the time either picked up and Bastion explained, I would be unconscious. By the time either of them reached someone who could help, I'd be dead. The thought brought to mind the last time someone with oversized arms nearly killed me. Theo Huginn-Intel. Only a few months ago, we fought in a pool on his family yacht. It was through pure luck that I survived. And he died. But then, it wasn't entirely luck. There was a moment when I let Bastion take over my limbs. It was a frightening but necessary experience, and it was a move that might help me now. I couldn't do it all on my own, so I had to hope that Bastion would catch on as I moved.

I pulled my legs up, my core screaming in protest. Those muscles were working hard enough trying to suck in air and didn't appreciate the extra load. I twisted and spun my knees in directions that biological limbs could not, pushing my right heel into the inside of Vert's elbow. He immediately grabbed my leg with his other arm, but I was bendy. I spun and twisted the left leg in and around, near to the maximum flexibility allowed. I dug my left heel into his elbow. This was when I needed Bastion, and he delivered, firing every pneumatic in my leg. They were designed to give me burst jumping but could deliver a terrifying blow when needed.

Vert's grip didn't loosen. He didn't drop me or stagger. But that massive elbow bent. Not a lot, but enough to bring me closer to his face. I slammed the handful of hyposprays into his face, catching his forehead and his right eye. All of them emptied in a loud hiss, and then his free hand batted them and my hand away.

Vert looked at me, confused and still enraged, straightening his arm back out as his right eye twitched and watered furiously.

"O2 LEVELS CRITICAL," blinked rapidly on my display.

For a few seconds, I thought the hyposprays hadn't worked, that Vert had some systems for filtering meds and toxins. That I was going to die right here and now, but then his face went slack. His confusion multiplied, glancing from my face to the emptied hyposprays on the ground. Then his eyes rolled up, his jaw fell, and he crumpled, finally releasing my neck.

I sucked in air, my throat aching with each ecstatic breath. I nearly wretched but held my stomach in check.

"You have to go now," Bastion said. "Right now. You have only seconds."

I nodded, not trusting my larynx to make sounds, and wobbled back to my feet. I grabbed the case of Preg Vaxxus B and then switched my comms back to Solomon. Hopefully, he hadn't left when I took too long.

"Ready for evac," I croaked.

"On your mark," Solomon said, and I breathed a shaky sigh of relief.

I scrabbled up onto the crates, moving all the way to the back of the cargo area as fast as I could and said, "Mark." I leaped up and out of the cargo transport, feeling gloriously free after literally being imprisoned by a metal fist. I cleared the transport in a breath, my flaps and ailerons deploying to guide me down between dozens of flying vehicles. Then the edges of my vision blinked a calm blue. I spread my legs and my right arm, and Poe swooped down from above. She had been stowed in the back of the transport Solomon had been piloting and caught me in her gentle embrace.

"See you on the beach," Solomon said.

Chapter Twenty-One

I TUCKED THE CASE INTO one of my hard polymer saddlebags, locking it up as I flew just above The Mist through the streets of Kotega Systems. My throat and neck ached, but I was free of Vert and his grip.

"Kotega security is swarming Vert," Bastion said. "Do you have a live stream?" I asked in a hoarse whisper.

A small rectangle of live video appeared in the corner of my display as I set coordinates in Poe's navigational computer.

Vert was back on his feet, wobbling amidst the wreckage of the Kotega cargo transport, which was now stopped. His hands were up as dozens of Kotega security drones hovered, large taser prongs extended and arcing electricity.

"…exactly why this famed fighter was destroying this cargo transport is still unclear," a bright, chipper voice said over the video. Then the image of Vert with his hands up shrank down into one corner of the video, which was now filled with earlier footage. Vert, still standing atop the passenger cabin of the transport, ripping the detached roof to shreds with his enormous hands.

"I can't see me at all," I said. "Not even a pixel out of place."

"You were right to bring in Valdo," Bastion said. "The deletion program the Intel Analysts wrote was good, but it did leave a distortion that would not have held up under close scrutiny."

"I'm just glad he agreed to help." It wasn't unheard of for Intel Operatives to use outside resources, which meant nobody asked who I was using to help clean the video feeds. "He seemed eager once you told him you were actually following through with your promise."

"I was always going to follow through," I said.

Bastion said nothing to that. I knew I would have followed through eventually, but his silence was right. When would I have made it a priority if it hadn't intersected with bigger problems?

"Vert 'The Hurt' Toinette arrived during an inexplicable satellite blackout," the streamer's voiceover continued. "And when communications were restored, he drove a fist into the vehicle, tore the roof off, and began to ransack the insides. We have no details at this time regarding what he was after or why he targeted a shipment of pharmaceuticals."

"So it worked?" I asked.

"It would appear so," Bastion said. "Forty-two different live streams captured Vert destroying the cargo transport. Kotega security has taken him into custody."

"Any stray images of my involvement from outside sources?"

"None that I've found. The Corto analysts were thorough in blocking all other views from the altercation."

My shoulders relaxed involuntarily, releasing balls of stress I hadn't even realized I was carrying. "Then Nox is safe from one threat, at least."

A Kotega Systems security vehicle came into the frame on the video, moving just above and to the side of the hovering transport. Three heavily armed security officers jumped out, their dark green, full-body jumpsuits a stark contrast to Vert's gleaming metal arms and torso. Vert was bigger than any of them, but he didn't resist. They brought his arms down, bound them, and placed servo limiters on his shoulders to reduce his extraordinary strength and speed.

"Close the video, please," I said.

Bastion did as I asked, returning my normal vision to me. This low, there was no other traffic. I leaned back on Poe's seat and stared up. Headlights were coming on as hundreds of vehicles flew overhead in every direction, making orderly lines of traffic between the towering buildings gleaming and glowing with advertisements.

"I am surprised you aren't piloting," Bastion said.

"I'm exhausted."

"Your throat?"

"Hurts. But we took care of Vert and got what Valdo needs at the same time."

"Should I contact the young Toinette hacker?"

I rolled the question around for a few moments before I said, "Text him our destination. See if he'll meet us there."

My messaging app appeared on my display, the message appearing as though it had been typed in a single instant and flying off into the ether of satellites and technology. Bastion had really gotten the hang of making texts and emails sound like me at this point. It was impressive. Or scary. In a few seconds, Valdo texted back, agreeing to meet us at the Toinette docks.

#   #   #

I'd always enjoyed the docks of Jayu City at night. It's never mattered which borough, just the rolling waves, the breeze off the ocean, all gently lit by the towering skyscrapers a few blocks behind. I loved Jayu City, all the traffic and endless possibilities, but the quiet of the docks after sunset was something I savored.

I had landed Poe one dock over from the small yacht I would be taking to Cirilla. Since we'd eliminated Vert as a problem, Solomon decided it would only be he and I going to stop Tazia from whatever she had planned on the resort island. He was flying out tonight on a party bus that Cirilla constantly ran back and forth between the city and the island. I was going to be on that boat before it left in the morning. I still hadn't told Quynn that I was going to be there, at the same game tournament they were attending. I wasn't sure how to break the news. They were looking forward to the time away to let things cool down between us.

"Everything go according to plan?" Valdo said from behind me. I'd been so caught up in the ocean and thinking about Quynn, I hadn't even heard him approach.

I turned to look at the young man approaching. "I've never done a job where everything goes according to plan."

"But you got it?"

I opened the hard saddlebag and pulled out the green case, dangling it like a golden treat. The movement was awkward with only one functional arm. "I got it. And great job."

For the first time since I'd met Valdo, I saw his face open up in a big, unbridled smile. "Thank you. It was actually kind of fun."

"You ever been to Cirilla?" I asked.

He shook his head, eyeing the case and still standing a meter away.

"You want to?"

"You need something else from me," Valdo said, his voice and face crestfallen.

"I do."

"And let me guess. If I want that case, I have to say yes."

"Not at all." I tossed the case to him. He caught it easily. "You went above and beyond for that. Besides, if your mom needs it to survive, what kind of heartless creature would I be to keep it from you?"

Valdo didn't say anything. He opened the case and seemed to marvel at the tiny vials inside, enough to treat half a dozen people.

"But I do need your help, I think," I continued. "It would certainly make things easier for me."

"This have something to do with Josephine?" Valdo asked as he snapped the case shut.

"Actually, no," I said.

"Elise," Bastion said, a tone of warning in his voice.

"That's why you're going to Cirilla, right?" Valdo said. "Why you had me help with Vert? You want the bodyguard out of the way so you can do something to Josephine?"

"You're not wrong," I said. "But you're only half right. I'm also going to access the most secure room on the entire planet."

Valdo's face screwed up in obvious confusion.

"Elise, don't," Bastion said. "The Offworld Relay isn't your priority right now. And you shouldn't involve this young man any more than you already have. Just let him go to his mother."

I heard Bastion and understood his argument, but this was something that had been nagging me. I still saw Theo's face in my dreams, his last words haunting me. No matter what anyone said, I felt responsible for his death, so I needed to find out what was so important that Theo used his final breath on it. *Five companies.* If I was able to take care of personal business under the official business of removing Vert from my life, why not go after the Relay while on the official business of going after Vert's boss?

"Most secure room?" Valdo finally said.

I nodded, smiling as I watched curiosity play across Valdo's face. I wanted him to ask, wanted him to need to know. "Are you going to tell me?" he asked.

"The Offworld Relay," I finally said.

"The Off…wait," Valdo said, stuttering. "The Offworld Relay? Why?"

"Do you really need to know why?"

"Well, that tower is literally the only thing connecting Little Sekmet Settlement to the rest of Earth Space, so yes. I need to know what you would expect me to do. I'm not going to shut it down or crash it or whatever."

"Whoa, whoa," I said, placing a gentle hand on his shoulder. "Nothing like that. I just need information. I'm not looking to shut down the relay. Could you even do that?"

"I don't know!" Valdo shrugged out of my reach. "This all sounds like a bad idea."

"That's pretty much how I live. One bad idea followed by another. But it works for me."

Valdo shook his head, staring at the green case of Preg Vaxxus B. "I still can't believe you got this."

"Of course you can," I said. "You helped me in Josephine's office. You got me out of the Deus Quarter. Mother of Corto, you even helped me secure that case. No way you would have done all that if you didn't think I could get what you needed."

"I…" Valdo looked up from the case and into my eyes, his face completely serious. "Nothing in my life has ever made much sense. My dad is a career guy. He was always in the office or at some office prayer or whatever. When my mom wasn't working, she was praying or attending prayer groups, always stressed about sacred balance. I felt like an afterthought, like an accident that they didn't plan for and didn't want to make room for."

"That's a tough way to grow up," I said. "Just let him go," Bastion said.

"They never needed me for anything," Valdo said. "Never cared what I was doing. Top marks in school? I'm not even sure they read the email. They've never attended a weightlifting or debate tournament. I won a medal for academic achievement last year. There was a ceremony and everything, but they didn't come.

"Then I ran into you in that hallway. And suddenly you needed me. You saw me and saw what I could do and you needed me. And I helped. Maybe that was the stupidest thing I've ever done in my life, but it felt good. I didn't think you would get this for me, for my mom. But I thought, maybe there was a chance. And now I have it."

"I'm glad," I said, not sure what else to say.

"I can help you again," Valdo continued. "I'm sure I can. But, but there are things I won't do."

I nodded. "I understand. I do. You have what your mom needs. I'm not going to coerce you or make you grand promises I can't keep. You can go now, go back and give your mom her first dose. You more than earned it."

"But you can use my help."

"I can. I really think I can."

"You have no idea if you can," Bastion said. "You'll be putting him in harm's way potentially for no reason."

"It might be dangerous," I said, hoping that would appease Bastion. "And maybe what I need is just behind a bunch of locks. Locks I can handle. But you have skills. Skills I just don't have. And I like having you around."

Valdo's eyes sparkled a little, but he quickly looked away. "What do you need from the relay?"

"Information."

Valdo chuckled under his breath. "You're really good at not answering questions."

I sat back down on Poe, sideways so I was still facing Valdo. "Nature of my job, my business. I tend to learn things that would be dangerous to know."

"I need to know what I'm getting into, who I might anger if we screw this up."

"We?" I asked.

He shrugged. "Maybe."

"I do not give you permission to tell this young man about me," Bastion said.

I rolled that around. The truth was a lot. And I couldn't tell Valdo about Bastion, not without Bastion's permission. I'd promised him that. What to tell and what to leave out?

"A few months ago," I said. "I did a job that went sideways. Very long story very short, an Intel Operative from another company died. It was my fault. He said something to me just before he died, though, something that I can't shake."

Valdo's eyes were wide, but he said nothing.

I took a deep breath. Then another. "He said something about the five companies, about a connection between them."

"And you think whatever that connection is, it must be at the Offworld Relay," Valdo said, picking up speed as the sentence progressed until he was just rambling to himself. "Of course you do. All five companies send and receive information to other worlds, but since there's only one relay, they all have to push their information to the same place. Each one has its own trunk line, probably two for redundancy, running under the bay, but there's only one relay. The information for all five is probably coming and going nonstop. A single chokepoint for all of Jayu City."

"To put it in so many words," I said. "Yes."

"But why do you care about this connection? Sure, this other operative died, but what does it have to do with you?"

I swallowed and ran a hand over my shellacked hair. I knew the answer, but at that very moment realized I'd never put it into words. "I don't think that man was my enemy, not really. He was a puppet. A very strong, very dangerous puppet, but someone was pulling his strings. I think those last words of his, before his neural implant literally blew out of his head, were him trying to tell me about the puppeteer. He never got the chance."

"And you're not afraid of going after this puppeteer?"

"I am," I said. "But I have to do it. Anyone who can manipulate people across two companies like that, who can do what they did, they're a threat to me and the entire city."

"And I can help?"

I nodded.

"Help you stop a threat to the entire city?"

I nodded again.

"And all I have to do is hack the most secure facility on the entire planet?"

"Correct."

Valdo's face broke wide open again in an enormous smile. "You're right. That does sound fun."

"Then we have a boat to catch," I said.

"Now?"

I nodded. Then I saw him stare back down at the case. "Do you need to get that to her now? To your mom?"

Valdo nodded, still staring at it. His jaw was working and he was blinking back tears. "I do. The more the disease progresses, the more damage to her nervous system."

I got off Poe and hugged Valdo. It felt right in the moment. His short, muscular body crumpled against me, and he quietly cried. He didn't hug me back. He didn't need to. But he let me hold him while he cried for several long minutes.

"This is a bad idea," Bastion said. "And I know it frustrates you when I talk and you can't respond, but I have to say it. I know the kid is talented. Useful. But you can't just go around pulling broken toys into your circle of trust. Now I have to babysit two of you."

Behind Valdo's back, I used one hand to make a crude gesture toward my own face, knowing Bastion would see it.

"Very mature of you," Bastion said.

"Sorry," Valdo said, finally pulling away. He brusquely wiped his cheeks with the back of one hand. "Sorry, but I can't go. I need to get this to the hospital."

"Tell you what," I said to him, while with my hands, I started texting a courier. "I'll send the meds on to the hospital."

"How?" Valdo looked suspicious.

"A very, very high-end courier who owes me a favor. She usually works for C-suite executives, but she'll make an exception."

"I don't know…"

I looked at Valdo, really looked at his slumped shoulders, his worried gaze, his quick glances between the case and me. He wanted to go with me. Then a solution came to me.

"Did you say your dad is all about fate?" Valdo scrunched up his face and nodded.

"How would he interpret you showing up with that case full of millions of credits of meds?"

The color drained from him. "Now, if a high-end courier delivers this to the hospital, anonymously, with instructions to give your mom all the meds she needs and use the rest however they choose…" I let the rest of the thought linger in the air.

A smile slowly broke across Valdo's face, then he said, "That might feel a bit like the hand of Shainette at work."

"Happy to stand in for fate, as needed." I was probably more like chaos, but whatever worked. I finished sending the text. "Courier will be here in three minutes."

"Wow," Valdo said, looking around and bouncing on the balls of his feet. He gazed at the nearby yacht. "A boat?"

I nodded.

"Fancy. Yours?"

I scoffed. "Hardly. The captain owes me a favor."

"The captain of a fancy boat moored at a Toinette dock owes a Corto Intel Operative a favor."

I smiled.

"And a high-end courier."

I kept smiling.

"This just keeps getting stranger."

"You have no idea," I said. "And everything you know about me, all of that is completely secret when we're around other people."

"I figured," Valdo said. "You're an Intel Operative. What about your bike?"

"Her name is Poe," I said. "And she's coming with us."

"And you trust this boat captain with your bike?"

"He owes me a VERY big favor. Or three."

"Your selective hearing is astounding," Bastion said. "This is a terrible idea."

I disagreed but said nothing to him. I noticed Valdo looked worried again, so I said, "You're with me. So long as I'm around, I'll do my best to make sure you get home to see your mom open her eyes again.

"Nothing's going to happen to you, though," Valdo said. "Right?"

"That is the idea. But no matter what, your mom needs those meds. And she'll get them."

"Thank you."

I put a hand on one of Poe's handlebars, and the thrusters hummed to life. She lifted a few centimeters off the ground into a hover. Then I started walking, gently pulling my bike alongside me. "You're welcome. Now let's get on board. The courier will meet us there. I want to be sleeping in a cabin before that boat leaves the port."

"You'll have to let me look at the servos in that arm first," he said.

This kid was full of talents. "Deal."

Chapter Twenty-Two

I'D BEEN TO THE ISLAND of Cirilla three times before. I was nine the first time, on vacation with my parents. I remember being obsessed with the multitude of swimming pools, wondering if it was possible to swim all the way around the island without ever leaving a pool. The waterpark captivated me too. It seemed to go on forever. In particular, there was a waterslide called Drakon Dive. I must have gone down that slide a dozen times in a single day, splashing down in the pool below and immediately running back to the stairs to go again. The second time I vacationed on the island, I was twenty. Almost twenty-one. I went with a dozen friends on break from Intel Academy. We stayed in the cheapest resort on the island, practically on the wind farm side of Mount Nefertem, the singular peak at the center of Cirilla, perpetually shrouded in a cloud of rain. My friends and I partied, swam, and drank our days away. I had my first and only sexual experience there with a boy my age from Nexus Neuronics. It was awkward and I nearly vomited three times. That was enough to confirm that sex wasn't for me. I had been pretty sure before, but wanted to try it at least once, and did. Even thinking about it now gave me nausea.

The third time I visited Cirilla was with Quynn on our second anniversary. We saved for a very nice resort with an all-inclusive package. We indulged in salon treatments, couple's massages, and fruity drinks brought to us whether we were at the pool, on the beach, or relaxing in our room. It was perfect. I hated to think how this trip might ruin Quynn's memories of that one once they discovered I was also on the island.

What I'd never really paid much attention to on any of those trips was the Offworld Relay. While I was still on the yacht, only a few kilometers out, I could see the relay towered into the sky like a scorched fang jutting up from a lopsided jaw. Tall, sleek, and black, it tapered as it rose almost a kilometer from the shore closest to Jayu City. Massive solar panels covered it, providing part of the prodigious power required to transmit and receive data twenty-eight hours a day. A silver-blue shimmer topped the tower, the lotus-shaped relay glimmering and spinning, too small to make out from here, but I knew what was up there. If everything I'd read and heard was correct, then just below that glimmer was where I wanted to be.

"So cool," Valdo said. I hadn't even realized he was standing next to me. It was the twentieth or thirtieth time he'd uttered those words on the trip, at least that I'd heard. And I slept for more than twelve restful hours after he got my left arm back to ninety percent functionality. He really liked the yacht, apparently.

I stepped off the boat onto the shores of Cirilla for the fourth time in my life. The island was just as impressive and inviting as ever. Before I'd even reached the end of the ramp from the boat to the dock, several people in floral shirts and linen skirts were smiling and waving. Once I stepped foot on the dock, a young person, shirtless and tan with their face painted as a joyful white and red skull, pressed their fingers into a bowl of red paste and then pressed those fingers to my forehead, drawing a small star.

"May your troubles wash away with the tides," they said.

"And may they never find another shore," I replied, as was tradition. If only they knew I was here precisely because of my troubles, that I was following them here and bringing some with me. I stepped past the welcoming committee and took the heady smell of flowers deep into my lungs. Huge pots of flowers dotted the edges of the docks every couple of meters. Every building was covered in climbing ivy, floral vines swinging in the ocean breeze, and window boxes bursting with blooms. The structures looked more grown than built, blooming on the island year-round.

"Wow," Valdo said from behind me. Then he sneezed.

"Yeah," I said. "You never get used to it."

"I should have worn cooler clothes."

"We'll buy you some. And they'll be floral."

"I don't really like prints." His beige pants and plain, charcoal button-up had already told me that.

"Neither do I," I said, twirling in my billowing black pants and floral black and white, sleeveless top. "But it's the Cirilla way. We need to look like we're on vacation."

"I still don't understand why," Valdo said.

"Your evangelist will know I'm here eventually, but the longer I can put that off, the better. Surprise is a powerful tool."

"You're assuming she doesn't already know."

"The young man has a point," Bastion said in my ear.

"I am making that assumption," I said. "While also preparing to be wrong."

We entered the nearest building, the receiving center, and verified our identities and reservations at the Cirilla Sands Resort. After a clerk embarrassed himself by assuming Valdo was first my lover and then my son, we were ushered into a luxury bus and were soon flying to our resort with half a dozen excited strangers. Valdo stared out the window the entire time, mesmerized by all that Cirilla had to offer.

"Thank you for choosing Cirilla Sands, everyone," the customer service representative from the front of the bus. They wore an immaculately pressed gray suit with a vibrant purple and white, floral-print shirt. "How many of you are staying with us for the first time?"

Nearly everyone raised their hands.

"How exciting! And are any of you visiting our little island for the first time?"

Only Valdo raised his hand this time. The rep then launched into a well-rehearsed speech on the history of Cirilla as a refueling station for cargo ships and its position on the equator and isolation making it the ideal choice for the Offworld Relay only twenty years after the founding of Little Sekhmet

Settlement. He talked about the island forming millions of years ago from the volcano we now know as the dormant Mount Nefertem. He went on about the wind farm on the eastern side of the island, how it powered the rest of the island, and about Cirilla's independence from the corporations of Jayu City, falling under Earth Space jurisdiction.

"If you look off to our left," he said. "You'll see Memphis Monsoon, the waterpark that is open year-round and is the largest in all of Earth Space. It boasts forty-two water slides, sixty swimming pools, four wave pools, and over two hundred bars and restaurants. Cirilla Sands offers complimentary shuttle service to the southwest gate of Memphis Monsoon every hour that the park is open."

It was hard to miss the park, several square kilometers in size, sparkling blue with its many pools and the squiggling waterslides in every color imaginable. Even though I was so much older and taller than I'd been as a child, the size of the park still seemed to defy imagination. Too bad we weren't here for the water slides.

Before heading up to our rooms, we bought Valdo proper Cirilla attire from the hotel shops. Lightweight, navy linen shorts that came down to the tops of his kneecaps, a white tank top with enormous pink flowers printed on it, and a serviceable pair of sneakers. He'd initially picked out a pair of sandals, but I had to remind him that with what we were doing, close-toed shoes were always a better choice when you still had biological feet.

Before heading to the cashier, I spotted a silvery statue of the Offworld Relay, roughly sixteen centimeters tall.

"What's that?" Valdo asked when I sat it in the checkout bin to be scanned.

"A souvenir," I said. "For you. To commemorate our partnership."

Valdo grinned.

We headed to our rooms so I could drop off my luggage and Valdo could change. Before doing anything else, I secured my room. Hotel room doors were possibly the easiest locks on the planet to bypass, so I had a kit for just such occasions. First was a portable AmpLock that attached to the inside of the door and doorframe. Not as good as a full biometric or cybermetric lock, but light years better than the default keycard lock. Next, I took four small tripods out of my kit, opening each one and placing them in the four corners of my room. Using my AR interface, I activated them, setting up an anti-intrusion field. It was designed to only allow signals I designated as acceptable through the perimeter. Signals like my comms array or Bastion, for instance. The perimeter also offered a measure of soundproofing. Finally, I disconnected the room's built-in communications.

We ate the kind of hearty breakfast you only get on vacation, and then it was time to start our reconnaissance. We took another of the hotel's complimentary shuttles to the Little Sekhmet Convention Center, sprawling out from the Offworld Relay like the shadow of a mountain. The Convention Center wasn't very tall, maybe six stories, but it was as big as several large resorts put together.

"A video game tournament?" Valdo asked as the shuttle approached. Every enormous screen on the sides and even on the top of the Convention Center was advertising the *Dregs of Osiris* tournament that started tomorrow. Cartoon drawings of hulking, multi-armed gods and goddesses were locked in combat. Holographic busts of some of the big-name competitors rotated in 3D accompanied by their professional records. Even the day before the tournament, the place was buzzing with thousands of people, many dressed up as characters from the game.

"I still don't fully understand it myself," I said.

"Thousands of people in attendance," Bastion said to me. "Hundreds of millions streaming from across Earth Space. Seems to me like an ideal platform for an evangelist. Or a con artist."

"It is a popular game," Valdo said. Then, like an echo of the AI in my ear, "I guess it would be a good way to spread the holy word of Ibhalism."

"You just worry about the Relay," I said. "I hear they give tours."

"Not to any of the sensitive parts," Valdo said.

Our shuttle landed on one of the many landing pads surrounding the enormous building. The doors of the shuttle opened immediately and I stepped out. "Of course not, you can still case the place while on the tour if you know how to look."

"How do I look?"

"Look where the tour guide tells you to look. Act like a tourist, impressed by the stupidest things. But use your peripheral vision to look for cameras, memorize the hallways and check out how doors are locked. And which doors are locked."

"That's it?"

"That's it."

"What are you going to do?" he finally asked.

"I have to do my own recon." I checked the time on my display. Just after 10:00. "I'll meet you back at the hotel for dinner. 20:00?"

"So late."

"Are you ninety? I gave you money. Take the tour, learn what you can. Go to the beach, have lunch, meet somebody. If you get in trouble, don't hesitate to call."

Valdo smirked. "Same to you."

That made me smile, but the entire reason he was on this island was to help me. "Be careful."

He shook his head playfully and walked off, his head still swiveling as he took in all the new sights and sounds.

"Now are you going to tell me how you plan to help Solomon and Valdo in the same weekend?" Bastion said.

"If I had a plan," I said. "I would definitely tell you."

"This is exactly what Quynn is always going on about."

"Quynn!" I'd forgotten, and their name was like a slap back to reality. "Mother of Corto. Where is Quynn?"

"I do not know."

I walked toward the Convention Center, slowly taking in everything. Security cameras. Entrances and exits. Landing pads. Everything I might need to know later. "How do you not know? You two talk. Don't you keep track of her like you do me?"

"I do not, per Quynn's request," Bastion said. "Besides, I am not living in her shoulder as I am with you."

"Can you find out where they are? I really don't want to accidentally—"

"Elise?"

I turned around and sure enough, there was Quynn, looking confused to see me on their vacation that was definitely partly to get away from me.

"Quynn!" I said, doing my best to smile this was exactly how I'd planned to announce my arrival to the love of my life.

Quynn's expression baffled me. They didn't look angry or overly happy to see me, but somewhere in between. Certainly surprised. Shocked, even. I'd been with Quynn long enough that I thought I knew every expression they made, but this one was new. They said, "What are you doing here?"

"Well," I said and took a deep breath. I knew this moment would come, that I would have to tell them I was here even though they'd expressly told me they needed the time apart. But between taking down Vert and suddenly including Valdo in my plans, I hadn't had time to formulate exactly what I was going to say.

"You look more surprised than me," Quynn said.

"Quynn, I meant to tell you," I finally blurted out, not sure how to continue.

To my even further surprise, Quynn smiled, their mismatched eyes I loved so much squinting up in joy. "You came to me. I...I never expected this." Quynn took my hands in theirs and a warmth spread across my chest like they were doing it for the first time.

"I—"I sputtered but didn't know what else to say.

Then Quynn's lips were on mine. My head swam and if my knees had been biological, I think they would have buckled a little bit. They had totally misread my presence here, but it felt so good and so right to be back in Quynn's arms, their lips on mine. I wrapped my arms around them and kissed back like we hadn't seen each other in weeks, not hours.

Eventually, they pulled away, but held my face in their hands, the violet and aquamarine eyes shimmering with the faintest trace of tears. "I'm so glad to see you. You know me so well. Better than I know myself. I said I needed time apart and I really thought I did, but seeing you here, now. This means everything to me.

Everything.

Everything.

Being here, now, where I wasn't supposed to be and definitely wasn't here for Quynn, meant everything to them.

Mother of Corto.

"I hated the silence," I said. "Hated being apart from you.Even seeing you the other night, there was still this distance. You were angry. You had every right to be, and I hated it."

"Me too."

"So here I am," I said. It technically wasn't lying. I hadn't said anything that wasn't true, nothing that hadn't been racing through my heart and head for the last few days. Maybe I implied a false cause and effect, but I wasn't lying. Definitely not.

Quynn kissed me again, then grabbed my hand. "So did you get a ticket for the tournament yet? I don't think they have any Elite passes left, but maybe we can talk security into letting you sit with me during the semifinals and on."

"I don't have a ticket," I said.

"We'd better hurry," Quynn said. "Online general admission sold out a while ago, but I know they held some back for in person. Those might sell out, too, if we don't—"

Quynn pulled me around to face the Convention Center as they spoke, and there was Solomon. He looked as gruff and uneasy as always, but the blue shirt covered in enormous orange flowers took the edge off his grim expression.

"Elise," Solomon said. It sounded like a greeting, an accusation, and resignation all at the same time.

"S—" I started to say his name.

Solomon's expression changed in a blink. He reached out a hand and grabbed one of Quynn's in an animated shake and said, "Steve! And you must be the famous Quynn!"

"Oh, hello," Quynn said and shook the hand of the Cloak of Corto, not that they had a choice. "How do you know Elise?"

"He's a friend!" I half-yelled before Solomon could answer. "He's big into…" I glanced up at the banners again to make sure I had the name right. "…*Dregs of Osiris*."

Gone was Solomon's hard exterior, and here was the Cloak of Corto, glad-handing and smiling like he was the most agreeable man on the planet. Of course, Quynn had heard of Solomon, but they'd never met face-to-face.

Quynn certainly didn't know Solomon was the Cloak. Solomon said, "So great to finally meet you, Quynn! I've heard so much about you. Elise just goes on and on, particularly about your eyes, and they really are just as marvelous as advertised."

"Oh, thank you," Quynn said, blushing a little and smiling at me. "I thought I knew all of Elise's friends. How have I not heard of you before?"

I barely opened my mouth, my mind still spinning between a dozen different and equally terrible lies. I felt those violet and aquamarine eyes searching me, curious and confused. I absolutely hated lying to Quynn, but the hole was already dug beneath me.

"I've helped Echo find parts for Poe," said Solomon.

My mouth dropped of its own accord, not because Solomon had so easily spun a plausible connection, but because I didn't think anyone in the Corto Corporation Intel offices knew about Echo, my Mistwalker mechanic and supplier. Thankfully, Quynn had turned their attention back to Solomon when he spoke, so they didn't see me gaping.

"So you're not part of Corto Corporation?" Quynn asked.

"I am," Solomon said without missing a beat. "I work in R&D. We work closely with Kawasaki, testing engine prototypes and suggesting updates to their design schematics. I'm a propulsion specialist."

"Really?" Quynn asked and then looked back at me. I smiled and nodded in dumbfounded reply.

"No wonder you two hit it off. Elise would do just about anything for that bike."

"And I'm not surprised she didn't tell you about me," Solomon continued. "Our interactions are infrequent and short. Poe is an incredible machine, though. I keep hoping Elise will let me ride her one day."

Quynn barked out a little laugh. "By yourself? No chance. She won't let me do that. I've only ridden with Elise a few times. It makes me nervous with nothing between me and The Myst but an engine and air. Especially with how Elise flies."

Solomon laughed along with Quynn, an incredibly believable laugh, too. Even I was almost convinced that Solomon was a guy who worked on propulsion instead of the Cloak of Corto. I could crack a lock or bypass security as well as anyone, but I still had a lot to learn about the human aspect of being an Intel Operative. Before I knew it, Solomon had launched into an in-depth conversation about *Dregs of Osiris*, the tournament, and their favorite competitors. Solomon seemed entirely at ease and even put Quynn at ease, offering up the extra ticket he had for me. Extra. Right. As in the ticket the Intel office had acquired for me. But Solomon was so good at taking truths and spinning them into believable lies right on the spot. It took me days of preparation to create stories and rapport like that, and he did it in seconds. We walked into the convention center, checked in to receive our swag bags, and walked around the foyer for several minutes, Solomon and Quynn making witty conversation the entire time.

"It has been an absolute joy to meet you," Solomon said to Quynn, taking both of their hands in his for a warm shake. "But I have to meet up with some other friends for lunch. I hope I see you around the tournament."

"That would be great, Steve!" Quynn said. "We should have you over for dinner sometime once we're all back to real life, too."

"That would be perfection," Solomon said. Then he turned to me, still with that jovial attitude, and said. "Let me know when you want to test those new thrust regulators. I can get them to Echo in two days once you let me know."

"Will do," I said.

Solomon smiled one last time and then strode off.

"So how many other incredibly nice people do you know that you aren't bringing around the house?" Quynn asked.

"In my line of work," I said. "Most people I meet either don't know who I really am or would rather throw me out a window than come over for dinner."

"All the more reason to cherish people like that."

"Yeah," I said, remembering the talk Solomon and I'd had at the hospital. That led me back to Nox, laying in a hospital bed in a coma while little robots tried to put him back together.

"Is Quynn going to be a problem?" appeared on my display. A message from Solomon.

I called up my AR keyboard and typed back, "No." Though I wasn't really sure. I hated lying to them, but things finally felt normal between us again. I didn't want to give that up. But that meant adding an additional layer to this already difficult weekend. Stop Tazia from whatever she had planned here on Cirilla. Work with a teenage hacker to break into the Offworld Relay. Make my partner and love believe that I was only here for the benefit of them and our relationship.

What could go wrong?

Chapter Twenty-Three

QUYNN WAS SO THRILLED TO share everything about the tournament and the other activities at the Convention Center. There were matches to watch leading up to the tournament finals, of course, but there were also demos for unreleased characters for *Dregs of Osiris* that Quynn was hyped for. There was the tournament shop that would be selling exclusive merchandise. On and on they went, bubbling with excitement. I smiled and tried to ask compelling questions, but it felt like I was dragging a weight behind me the whole time. I needed to tell Quynn the truth but didn't know how to start.

I was also ignoring texts from Valdo and Solomon, which Bastion kept reminding me about. Solomon was used to that. As Intel Operatives, we regularly had to keep focus and reply when we were free and able. Valdo would likely take some offense, but I could handle that later.

After three hours which seemed like three days of lying to Quynn, we sat down on a low stone wall outside the Convention Center. Quynn said, "I'm so glad you're here and that you surprised me, but I do have plans that I made for this weekend."

"Of course," I said, trying my best to hide my relief that I wasn't going to be plastered to Quynn's side the entire weekend.

"Are you sure? Because I can—"

"I'm here, but that doesn't mean I'm suddenly a *Dregs of Osiris* fan. Go. Enjoy the tournament."

"The tournament doesn't start until tomorrow," Quynn said. "There's a meet-and-greet with the game's director and other developers for VIP and Elite pass holders."

"Look at you and your fancy Elite pass!" Quynn blushed.

"Anybody you know going to be there?"

"You remember Rodrigo and Pitta from work? Raphael from when I was just a developer?"

"I think so," I said. "Rodrigo is the incredibly short guy with the tall mohawk, very chatty? And Pitta has curly red hair and seems like she's always whispering. Raphael, that rings a bell, I think."

"Raphael and I haven't worked together in years. He went into video production, so he's working the tournament. Rodrigo and Pitta bought Elite passes like me. We all made plans to meet up, go to some of the off-site parties together, have dinner at Beluga at least once together."

"Oh, Beluga!" I said, my mouth watering at the memory. It was the best restaurant on the island, hands-down, and notoriously difficult to get into.

"I'm sorry, but Rodrigo made reservations for three months ago. I'm only going because he broke up with his boyfriend a couple of weeks back."

"Sorry for Rodrigo," I said, throwing an arm around Quynn. "But lucky for you."

"But I want you to go to Beluga, too."

"Quynn, I'm on Cirilla, surrounded by beaches and great restaurants and every luxury. You go have fun with your friends. I'll be fine."

"You're sure?"

"I am." I kissed Quynn and wanted to punch myself in the face at the same time.

Quynn was beaming and their eyes sparkled with barely suppressed tears. "Breakfast on the beach tomorrow?"

"That sounds delightful."

"Okay. I should be back at the hotel around 24:00."

"I'll be there," I said. I really hoped I would be.

Quynn kissed me again, squeezed my hand, and practically pranced away back into the Convention Center. Just inside the glass doors, I saw them hug Rodrigo and Pitta. Quynn glanced back one more time before disappearing into the bustling crowd.

"Mother of Corto," I whispered to myself and then said to Bastion, "Catch me up, please. What's going on with Valdo and Solomon?

"Valdo is back at the hotel," Bastion said. "The hotel you booked with him, not the hotel you are to be sleeping at with Quynn."

"You don't have to play the part of my conscience," I said. "The one I already have is yelling at me enough."

"I was merely stating facts."

"You know you weren't. What about Solomon?"

"He does not seem at all happy. You missed a planning session he wanted to have at his hotel. You are to call him as soon as possible. He wants you dressed and ready to work immediately."

"Then I'd better get back—"

"To your hotel room," Bastion said, interrupting me. "Yes. I've already called the hotel shuttle, which should be landing at Pad 9 in less than one minute."

I glanced around and quickly found pad 9, so labeled by a tall sign, the number circled in blue and lit up bright even in the late afternoon. I started jogging toward it and said, "Connect me to Solomon, please."

CONNECTING TO SOLOMON had barely blinked on my display before the Cloak's gruff voice answered, "That took too long. Your partner is going to be a problem, aren't they?"

"They're going to take a little of my time, but I'm here. I'm running back to my hotel to switch to my work limbs now, then I'll—"

"Plaza del Mar Resort," Solomon said with obvious impatience. "Tower three rooftop. I'm sending you schematics and leaving some specialized gear where I want you to be. Text me when you're there, which had better be in less than fourteen minutes."

The call disconnected before I had a chance to say anything else. The hotel shuttle was landing, and I squeezed in once the door was open just enough for me to fit. A chipper recording started to play as the shuttle sat idle on the landing pad with the door open even though I was already aboard. A minute had already passed.

"What is wrong with this shuttle?" I said aloud.

"It is a courtesy vehicle," Bastion said. "I believe it is waiting to see if any other guests need to use it."

"Can you override it?"

"If you can find a data port, I can likely take complete control of it. The firewalls for courtesy vehicles are notoriously weak."

In less than ten seconds, I found an access port underneath one of the seat cushions. I plugged in, and in moments, the shuttle was lifting off as the door closed, all much faster than usual. Twelve and a half minutes to go. It was going to be tight.

#   #   #

The Plaza Del Mar was nicer than the hotel I was staying at. Smaller, with five identical towers surrounding a lush central courtyard. Three large pools, several hot tubs, and a pair of nice restaurants kept the courtyard busy. The sun was setting now, throwing half of the courtyard into shadow, though it was still quite warm.

I arrived on the roof of tower three a few seconds after my fourteen minutes were up despite Bastion and I ruffling the staff at my own hotel with the hot landing and takeoff right outside my room. The roof was simple, black polymer asphalt. Large solar panels on motors took up much of the space, along with a monstrous air conditioning unit. My hair was still loose and blowing about as I found a large, white duffle bag Solomon left for me near the edge facing the courtyard.

"I'm here," I texted him. "Take inventory," Solomon texted back.

I opened the bag to find a long-range, laser listening device. It was disassembled, but once I put it together, it would look like a sniper rifle with an enormous dish on one end. Around our office, we called them Boredom Sticks, since using one usually meant hours of pointing it in one spot and just waiting. Also inside was a crossbow, half a dozen bright green crossbow bolts, and several meters of very fine wire.

SOLOMON CALLING appeared on my screen. I opened the

communications channel.

"Questions?" he asked.

"Many," I said. "What's the plan?"

"Tower five is directly across the pool from your location," he said. "Tazia's room is somewhere between the seventh and seventeenth floor. Poolside."

"So I'm supposed to listen to each room?" I started putting the Boredom Stick together.

"Correct."

"That's a neophyte job."

"Between the two of us," Solomon said. "You ARE the neophyte. And you were late."

I gritted my teeth and finished putting the Boredom Stick together, screwing the dish onto the end, and connecting the last plug. "What about the crossbow? And the thread?"

"The thread is an experimental bungie. Three-point-two meters exactly. It will stretch to a length of sixty-four meters, the stretch slowing as it reaches maximum length, and then it will dissolve."

I glanced over the side of the building. If I had to guess, it was twenty stories. "Let me guess, this building is sixty-four meters tall."

"Correct again."

"And the crossbow?"

Solomon chuckled a bit on the other end of the line. "Let's hope you don't have to use the crossbow. If you do, remember: the pointy bit goes away from you."

"You can't expect me to—"

"The bolts are self-welding. Use them to anchor the bungie if you need it."

"Very funny."

"I thought so. Get to listening." I shook my head and disconnected the call with Solomon.

"Bastion?"

"Yes?"

"Any chance you can access the Plaza Del Mar's guest records so I don't have to spend all night listening to the side of a building?"

"No," Bastion said. "I suspect that Solomon had the same problem. The Plaza Del Mar underwent a well-publicized cybersecurity upgrade two months ago. They have made it a focal point of their recent marketing campaigns. No doubt this is why Tazia selected this particular resort."

I sighed. "Worth asking." I plugged my data cable into the Boredom Stick, pointed it at the far left window of the seventh floor of Tower 5, and turned it on. An advertisement for the waterpark was playing, the sounds from a viewscreen filling the room, vibrating the air, which in turn vibrated the window. A biological ear against that window wouldn't have been able to make out any distinct sounds, but the Boredom Stick was built to do just that. I kept listening as the advertisement ended and a cooking show came back from a commercial break. I kept listening, not to the program, but for any voices of people in the room. For all I knew, Tazia could be a fan of cooking shows. It could also have been a family with three kids who forgot to turn off the viewscreen when they left the room.

After several minutes, a toilet flushed, and a deep voice I didn't recognize commented on how they'd made that very pie filling just last week. Not Tazia. I moved the laser from window to window, crossing four before the landscape of sound suddenly vanished. Okay. Now I knew each room had four windows. I listened for more than five minutes without hearing a thing.

"Bastion, can you make note of rooms that appear to be empty?"

"Yes," Bastion said. "But why?"

"Some of these rooms might be vacant. Nobody checked in. Others might be empty because people are at dinner or something. I can't spend hours listening to an empty room. I'll give each one five minutes, then I'll cycle back through the empty ones."

"A reasonable plan," Bastion said.

"Careful now," I said. "I don't know if I can handle such effusive compliments."

"Shall we talk about your inappropriate behavior with Quynn instead?"

I pointed the Boredom Stick at the next set of windows. A small, young voice was making vroom sounds as Quynn's joyful surprise tumbled through my head, bringing the guilt back up like bile. I quickly moved on to the next room.

"I know I'm messing things up with Quynn," I said to Bastion. "I do. I just…They were so happy to see me here. When they said they needed this weekend to get some space, I just took that at face value. Really, it was more convenient for me with all this going on."

"But you are lying to them," Bastion said.

"I know. And I know I had a moment, right when I saw them in front of the Convention Center, to come clean like I'd planned. To give them the space they wanted. But they were so happy and surprised. Now I don't know how to start telling them the truth."

"It would seem the simplest way to tell the truth is simply to do it. There is no ideal time to reveal that you have been lying."

He was right, of course. And he was echoing thoughts that had been rattling around in my own brain. "And the longer I wait, the worse it will be."

"Also correct," Bastion said.

After a full five minutes of silence, I moved the Boredom Stick to the next room. Bastion highlighted the one I'd skipped in yellow on my display. As I kept listening, lights in a room three stories up and one unit over came on. I pushed my ocular implants to maximum zoom. The figure wasn't perfectly clear, still too far away for that, but looked familiar. I could keep going like normal, which would take forever, or I could take a chance. Move the stick. End this ridiculous task. I aimed the Boredom Stick at those windows, and in a rare moment of luck, Tazia's voice rang in my aural implants.

"…know that. I'm not asking you to bring them out here. I'm asking you to be patient," Tazia said, and then fell silent for a while. I watched her pace her hotel room. She was alone, obviously talking to someone over her comms. "If all goes well, I'll be able to come home after this. Actually home. Spend some time with you all, at least for a while."

Again, she paused, listening to whoever was on the other end of the line. "I know it's been hard. You know it's worth it. You knew what you were signing up for when you married me."

Married. And from the sound of it, had a family, too. I didn't think anyone in Corto knew about that. Hopefully, when all this was done, Tazia could go back to her family and never bother us again. But first, we had to shut down this big Josephine con of hers and whatever she had planned for this weekend. I turned off the Boredom Stick and called Solomon.

"I found her," I said once the call connected.

"Where?" Solomon said.

"Eleventh floor. Poolside. Third room from the northeast corner."

"1122. Good. Now get to the lobby of that building."

"Where are you?" I asked, but Solomon disconnected the call without another word.

"He does not seem happy with you," Bastion said.

"Hard to tell," I said. I took the strange thread out of the bag along with a crossbow bolt. There didn't seem any obvious way to attach the two. No socket or loop to tie, nothing. At least I knew how to load the bolt into the bow, so I did that and spun up the magnetic launch system on the crossbow. I turned my attention back to the bungie, turning it in my hands and trying to look for something I'd missed. As I did, one end wound up close to the end of the loaded bolt, and it magnetized to it hard.

"Couldn't have given me an instruction manual, could he?" I said aloud.

"At least you figured it out," Bastion said.

I fired the bolt into the metal railing on the edge of the roof. It made a loud clang and a bright flash, welding as advertised. I held firm to the other end of the bungie with my right hand. "This makes me nervous. Do you know anything about this stuff? Is it really going to carry me to the ground?"

"I cannot find any information about it online. I suppose you will have to trust Solomon."

"I suppose so," I said and jumped off the roof. After a few meters, I felt a slight tug on the thread, but my cybernetic handheld firm even as my descent continued to accelerate. About halfway down, I felt a definite slowing. Slowing. Slowing. Like a parachute, but even gentler, I touched down on the ground, the thread still in my hand, barely visible. As I pulled the end down to eye level and then a little farther, it just vanished.

"Fascinating," Bastion said.

"No kidding," I said. A few people milling about looked at me strangely but were far too mellow for just watching a woman gently fall from the sky. Then I smelled the distinct aroma of THC vape. Even outdoors, it hung slightly in the air all around this particular swimming pool. So yeah, they weren't very surprised by my unexpected arrival. They wouldn't have been terribly surprised if a starship had landed in their pool.

I walked out of the fog and into the central courtyard of the Plaza del Mar Resort, weaving around the large central pool, the swim-up bars, patio dining, and dozens of people in swimsuits mingling with fruity, umbrella-adorned drinks in their hands.

I entered Tazia's tower to a lobby identical to that of tower three, where I had entered before I ascended to the roof. Dark wood flooring, plush carpets in the scattered seating areas, and a long bar carved to look like a wave frozen in time. More people were here, all enjoying themselves, most with drinks. The bar was half-full of people in evening wear.

INCOMING CALL FROM SOLOMON appeared on my display, so I answered it.

"Take a seat near where you are now. Don't look toward the bar. Order a drink when a server comes. Look casual. Don't touch your ear."

"Hello to you, too, S—"

"Don't say my name. Or my title."

"Okay," I said, following his instructions and dropping the playful tone. "I'm guessing you have a plan?"

"Given what we know about Tazia and who we think she is, what we think her title is," Solomon said. He meant the Ghost of Toinette but didn't say it. "We have to assume that she knows everything someone like me would know. Every trick and every play."

"So breaking into her room isn't an option," I said.

"No. Even in a hotel, she'd do what any of us do when we first check-in."

"Attach a portable AmpLock to the door, kill the phone, and set up an anti-intrusion perimeter," I said, rattling off the list I'd already done in my own hotel room."

"And put laser grids on the vents, magnetically seal the windows, and bug the room with her own closed-circuit system, yes. She'll also know every manipulation trick we try. Even if she didn't know your face, she would see through every persona and lie in our arsenal."

"So why are we even here? In this hotel? On this island?"

"To stop her, but you know that. We also have at least one advantage that I'm choosing to assume. We have me."

"Letting your title go to your head?"

"Very funny," he said but didn't laugh. "I'm assuming that she doesn't know who I am. Given how impenetrable it is to discover my equals in other companies, even when we have a strong suspicion as we do with Tazia, we cannot confirm it."

"She's done a lot of things, known a lot of things we don't."

There was silence on the other end of the line for several long seconds.

"We don't, right?" I asked.

"That's not entirely true," Solomon finally said. "What she's done is impressive. None of it is outside of what I have done to others in the past."

I whistled softly through my teeth. "Wow. That's—"

"Not relevant at this time. Welcome to the real division."

"Fine," I said. "But we're definitely going to talk about that later. For now, let's go with your assumption. You're a mystery. What's my part in all this?"

"You're going upstairs."

"Right. I figured that much."

"You're going to knock on her door and start telling the truth."

Chapter Twenty-Four

THE TRUTH. I HAD A passing familiarity with the word, like coworkers who nodded to each other in the hall but didn't know each other's names. It was a real problem in my relationship with Quynn, but an advantage in my work. Truth and my work happening at the same time? It felt wrong in every way.

But now I stood in front of the door to Room 1122, just staring at the numbers, shiny and the color of upscale doorknobs. With my aural sensitivity dialed up, I could just barely hear Tazia talking. I couldn't make out any words, but I knew she was still in there. The instructions were simple. Put my knuckles forward and just knock. Tell the truth. Actually doing it felt scarier than jumping off the tallest buildings in Jayu City.

"Are you all right?" Bastion asked.

"Not really," I said. "This all seems like a terrible idea."

"I agree."

"That isn't helping."

"You are the bait," Bastion said. "That means I am also the bait, even if Solomon does not realize it."

"I don't like being bait."

"I also think that Solomon's plan is sound. It is the best chance for success, even if it is a terrible idea.”

“This is one of the few times I wish we weren’t thinking along the same lines.”

I took a deep breath and knocked on the door, three solid, but casual knocks.

The barely audible trace of Tazia’s voice stopped. I could just make out some shuffling from the other side of the door. The peephole darkened. Then, with the door still closed, she said, “I have a gun trained on you through the door.”

I slowly raised my hands. “I’m unarmed.”

“I very much doubt that. What do you want?”

“To talk.”

“Why?”

Half a dozen lies came to me in an instant. Three were somewhat believable. One was pretty good. Just like I’d been trained to do, I sorted through possible lies almost as fast as I picked locks. It took a concerted effort on my part to push them all aside, to discard the lies and say, “Those are my orders.”

“Then talk.”

“You must really trust your neighbors. The doors certainly aren’t soundproof. What do you think they’ll do when they hear me speak your real name?”

“What are you talking about?” Tazia said. She was maintaining her lie, but even through the door, I heard the doubt in her voice.

“You’re going to make me say it, aren’t you? You have a gun, my hands are up, and you’re going to make me say it.”

Tazia said nothing. Down the hall, I heard a doorway click open. I turned my head to see a young face poke out, staring at me in wide-eyed curiosity. I smiled. They just kept staring. Maybe it was what I’d said or maybe it was me obviously looking toward a spectator to our talk, but Tazia finally opened the door.

She didn’t look the evangelist now. Gone were the robes and the sparkling golden makeup. For two years, she’d only appeared publicly in that Ibhalism blue and gold. Clothes, makeup, shoes, bags. Now, she was standing there in an oversized t-shirt printed with a cartoon duck, her stick-thin legs covered almost to the knees by the shirt. Her feet were bare. Her blonde hair was wet, plastered to her face and leaving wet spots on the shoulders of her shirt. In her hand, pointing at me, was a small pistol.

I kept my hands up. "Are you going to invite me in?"

"I am not," Tazia said, her eyes narrow.

"Fine," I said in a much quieter voice than I'd used when the door was closed. "I don't know exactly what you're up to, why you're here, but you should just stop. Go home. I know who you are. My people know who you are, your position in Toinette. Your real position. The sooner you stop this, the easier it will be for you. For everyone."

A smile crept across Tazia's face. "You don't know anything."

"I know—"

"Nox was a clever move. He was too new to your ranks, so I didn't know who he was. He's going to make a great Intel Operative if he survives. But he blew that cover wide open, and now you said you don't know why I'm here. All you have is my hotel room, which I guarantee will change once you leave. You came here, unarmed, to tell me what? To stop? Pretty please?"

"I know plenty."

"If that were true, you wouldn't be the only one here. If that were true, Gustin would have sent every operative he has. When I'm done, the lines of power in Jayu City will be irrevocably changed. You don't send some second-rate operative all by herself for that. Even if she does have a strange tendency to get in the way."

Now it was my turn to smile. "I know your name."

"Another lie."

"I get it. We're operatives. Lying is what we do. As weird as it feels, I haven't lied to you once tonight."

A laugh escaped Tazia's lips but died in an instant.

"Believe what you want," I said. "Tazia Toin—"

Before I could finish saying her company name, my throat was suddenly crushed, my entire neck wrapped up in cold metal. I grasped at the object around my neck, but before I could even begin to understand what it was, I was lifted off the ground. Tazia backed up, and I was moving into her room, being carried.

I couldn't breathe. I kept grabbing at whatever had me, and then I was thrown to the ground against the wall below the windows. The room was spinning and I was coughing, my throat spasming as I tried to get air into my lungs.

Then I looked up. Standing next to Tazia was someone who wasn't supposed to be here. Not in this room, at this hotel, or on this island. Vert Toinette-Deus towered, flexing his enormous metal knuckles, looking ridiculous in a floral-print shirt and khaki shorts.

"How?" I said between coughs.

Tazia didn't smile exactly. Her severe features brightened for just a moment, but not in a good way. Not good for me, at least. "That stunt you pulled over Kotega wasn't half bad. Blocked satellite communications. Timed everything just right. Even had just the right enticement to lure in your prey."

At being called prey, Vert glanced down and away briefly, his eyes narrowing a few millimeters. Barely a flutter.

"It must have taken dozens of people to pull that off. And now you use someone from my own company to make sure you were purged from the video? That was an artist's touch. Once I discover who did that, I'll be sure to send them your regards."

"Valdo," Bastion said.

It took everything I had not to shudder or wince. I wouldn't let Tazia have the pleasure of seeing how much that bothered me. Instead, I rose to my feet, ignoring the pain in my throat.

In response, Vert took half a step to his right, moving between me and Tazia.

"You accounted for almost everything," she continued. "Almost. You didn't consider that I have more friends than you. Better friends. Friends in every part of Jayu City. Even Kotega Systems. I made a call. One little call. Vert was back in the Toinette borough in two hours."

"There is nothing online about his release," Bastion said. "People are still talking about him rampaging through the sky."

"Couldn't be without your hired muscle, huh?" I said.

"For you?" Tazia practically purred. "No. I could have handled you on my own. But after you brought so many people to bear on taking Vert out of play, I had to assume Corto Corporation wanted me alone."

I said nothing, staring daggers at her over Vert's shoulder while I used my peripheral vision to take in the rest of the room, to look for an escape. Tazia and Vert were right in front of me, the door back to the hall behind them. A large bed smothered in fluffy, white linen was to my right, the open door to the bathroom on the other side of that. Behind me was a wall of windows.

"Nothing to say to that?" Tazia said. "No reinforcements?"

"She would not come here alone," Vert said, finally breaking his fuming silence.

"She shouldn't come alone," Tazia said. "That's not the same thing. Her apprentice is in a coma. Gustin and all the other operatives are still back in Jayu City."

"All the operatives you know of," Vert said.

Behind Vert's back, Tazia threw him a glance of disgust. It was brief but definitely unhappy. She crossed behind the enormous man, grabbing a pair of white pants off the bed. She kept talking as she shimmied them up her legs. "You embarrassed me. You embarrassed Vert, and therefore me. Now everyone in Jayu City is talking about how Josephine Toinette-Deus works with dangerous people, how her judgment cannot be trusted." She grabbed a lightweight, blue jacket off the bed. "It will take me months to repair this."

"Oops," I said with maximum sarcasm.

Tazia smiled a little as she looked to the ceiling. "Oops," she whispered. She looked at me again and nodded. "Oops indeed. Now you'll pay for your mistake."

"We're not done," I said.

"Vert," Tazia said, turning to him. "I'm going to site B after I meet with the kid. Kill her. Meet me there in an hour." Then she was walking away. "You won't succeed here, Tazia Toinette-Intel!" I yelled.

Tazia stopped. She didn't turn around. "You'll die with my name on your lips. How fitting."

Vert glanced over his shoulder as Tazia closed the door behind her. I didn't wait. With a twist of my wrists, I engaged the tasers on my knuckles, full charge. I leaped and flew at the bigger man with both fists. Almost half a meter taller than me, heavily armored, and easily twice my weight, he just turned a little, one of his bulky hands grabbing my forearm as he did so. Still, in mid-air, the room spun and I was instantly slammed back down to the same spot I'd landed on before. He'd dodged, caught me in mid-air, spun, and threw me back down. The tasers on my fists uselessly unloaded on the thin carpet, leaving black burn marks.

I came to my feet and spun on Vert just in time to see one of those fists flying at my face. I had dived to my left, narrowly avoiding the punch. I got my feet under me and tried to stab my extended hand at his shoulder, between two of the biggest armor plates. Vert shifted slightly, just enough for my hand to ram directly into his chest plate, several of my cybernetic fingers making strange popping sounds with the impact.

I'd barely registered the damage when Vert's torso spun. His feet stayed planted, but his torso spun independently, insanely fast, and the back of one massive hand slammed into my chest, my back hitting the windows behind me an instant later. All the breath flew out of my lungs as I crumpled to a knee. I fought to breathe again, my brain panicking before I finally sucked in air.

"I killed three people in the ring," Vert said. "Never on purpose."

I nodded, which hurt. I was still breathing, which was good but also hurt. I was pretty sure most of my ribs were broken.

"I regretted each one," Vert continued. "Each one so tragic. So preventable. Those people should never have stepped into the ring with me. I wept for them."

"Then just let me go," I said. "You don't need to—"

The blow came across my cheek faster than all the others, but also lighter. Truly, if he'd hit me across the face as he'd done to my chest, I was certain my jaw and neck would have shattered.

"This is personal!" Vert bellowed. "You embarrassed Josephine."

I wanted to correct him, make sure he remembered her name was Tazia, but I didn't want another slap across the face.

"She saw to my freedom, but I doubt I will be able to stay by her side after this. I will take the fall so that she can continue her good work. You have ruined me."

Finally, I got my breathing under control, though it still hurt. My cheek stung, too, piling on.

"I will kill you tonight," Vert said. He drew back his right fist and for the first time, I saw a sequence of red lights softly start glowing along his forearm. I didn't know what they were, but they couldn't be good.

As he did that, I crossed my hands over my chest, trying to make it look like I was hugging myself in fear.

Vert said. "I will not weep for you." His glowing fist flinched.

I closed my fists, bringing up the sparkling, yellow shield in front of me like a half dome.

Vert's fist stopped. He tilted his head a few degrees. "Interesting." Without resetting his cocked fist, the lights on his arm glowed brighter, and my world exploded in sound, burning metal, and broken glass. It was all too fast. His punch, the contact with my shield accompanied by a boom that must have sounded like a bomb going off for several kilometers. The windows behind me blew out as did the shield mods in my forearms, both of which instantly melted the carbon polymer around them, smoking and warped.

Vert was unscathed. His fist only showed the slightest burn marks. He'd seen the shield and knew exactly how to overpower it. I was a thief with a few tricks. This was a professional fighter who had survived and won against dozens of people far more dangerous than me.

But there was now an open window behind me. The drop wasn't enough for my glide wings or any of my normal tricks, but I liked my chances of falling better than standing up to Vert.

I was too slow. The moment I started to rise, that big left hand was around my throat again. He lifted me off the ground, his eyes on mine, full of fury. The metal fist started to squeeze, the pain flaring up anew in my throat. In moments, I couldn't breathe. I flailed. My fists and feet flew at the bigger man, bouncing uselessly off his armor. His arm fully extended. I couldn't even reach his face, the only unarmored part of him, not that I had another fistful of anesthetics. I grabbed his thumb and fingers, pulling as hard as I could, but my cybernetics were no match for his.

I stared at Vert, at his eyes. They were brown. Medium brown. I'd never noticed before. They were bloodshot, too. Maybe it was his anger or maybe that was normal for him, I wasn't sure. I wanted to cry, to scream, to beg, even. I wanted Quynn. I didn't want to die in this hotel room, Quynn wondering where I was, thinking I was only here for them. I was going to die and the last thing I'd told my love was a lie.

My vision was blurring, shrinking. But then something shifted. I thought it was me and my oxygen-deprived brain, but Vert had loosened his grip. A little at first, and then a moment later, he let go. I fell to the floor gasping and coughing once again. Tears streaked my face. My broken ribs protested each breath, but the air tasted sweet and cold and I couldn't get enough of it.

Eventually, I looked up. Vert was still standing there, looking down at me. He closed his eyes and shook his head. "I would weep for you, too. I don't want to, but Shainette has other ideas. You deserve death, but I cannot give it to you. Not like this. Not with my blood cold. Death in the ring is one thing, but murder… Not even after everything you've done."

"Thank you," I croaked.

"Leave this island. Stay away." I vomited like it was some kind of answer.

He said, "What we do here doesn't affect you. Doesn't affect Corto. It is none of your concern. Don't let me see you again."

Slowly, I rose to my feet. "You know I can't do that."

Vert's serene expression suddenly changed to a look of pain, as though after all my flailing and fighting, I'd finally wounded him. "Why? Why can't you just leave it? Why? I don't…I don't…"

"You don't want to kill me," I said. "Then don't. What she's doing here, what you're helping her do, will affect all of Jayu City. Spreading Ibhalism to different companies will upset the balance of power in the city. Maybe it's only Kotega today, but when will Corto be next?"

Vert looked at me, still pained. "You're right. Josephi… Tazia will bring balance to all of Jayu City and beyond. It's only a matter of time. I cannot let you stop that."

"You can."

The pained expression deepened. Wetness gathered in the corners of his eyes. "I won't," he said.

I blinked. In the time it took for my biological eyelids to close and reopen, one of Vert's enormous fists made a journey from loose at his side to right in front of my face. But it didn't stop. His fist connected. My head snapped back as my nose exploded in wet heat. My whole body was in the air, moving, tumbling. Light and dark were spinning. Up and down didn't make sense. A voice was screaming in my ear, but I couldn't make sense of it. My eyes uncrossed and focused just in time to see bright, blue water rushing toward me, and then everything went dark.

Chapter Twenty-Five

I WAS SURROUNDED BY WATER, drowning in it, the acid burn of chlorine in my eyes. A swimming pool. I couldn't tell which way was up and which was down. Tiny bubbles filled my vision in every direction, swirling. I kicked and reached out, trying to find the bottom or a side of the pool. Just water and bubbles. Water and bubbles.

In the distance, beyond where I could make out anything definite, I saw a green glow. Small. Undefined.

But that was impossible.

I was on Cirilla, far away from the Huginn Industries yacht where I'd fought Theo. This wasn't the same pool. Couldn't be. I blinked, trying to focus through the turbulent haze of bubbles and chlorine. The green glow moved, side to side, then it was growing larger. A glowing, green hammer on the side of a dark face. Impossibly, a dead man was swimming toward me.

I turned and kicked hard, swimming with everything I had, my legs kicking and my arms windmilling away from the dead man. I stretched with every stroke, reaching for a wall that had to be there somewhere. In the haze of bubbles and the effort of swimming, the dull ache of muscle fatigue came to me, shooting from the tips of my fingers and toes, through my arms and legs, and up to my brain. Biological fingers and toes. Arms and legs. These weren't cybernetic limbs. I was swimming frantically, inefficiently, with the limbs I'd been born with and surgically replaced a decade ago. I glanced over my shoulder. The bubbles were swirling more intensely, like a vortex all around me. The green glow of the Mjolnir tattoo was closer. I turned and started swimming again, pushing and kicking water. Only at that moment did I realize I wasn't breathing. A new panic took hold of me, nonetheless. Not due to lack of air, but because it suddenly seemed that my world was nothing but water. Meters, kilometers, galaxies of swirling, hazy water.

In front of me, I saw the green glow of Theo's face tattoo. Still too far to make out all of Theo's features, but it was him, floating in front of me, a dark, human-shaped form with that glowing tattoo. I looked back, and he was there, too. Two Theos. No. Not just two. To my left and right as well. I turned in the water, treading my way around. Five Theos. None were advancing on me, just floating in the endless water.

Five Theos.

Five companies.

The Theos reached their hands out to me. Not beckoning, but like they were telling me to stop. With his five times five digits outstretched. Then one by one, his five fingers started to evaporate, like the swirling bubbles were carrying away bits of him, spinning up and away. His fingers, then his hands, the outline of his head and body. I reached out my own hand to him, but my own fingers were flying apart, bubbles grabbing my flesh and painlessly floating them away. I opened my mouth to scream...

...and took a breath of clean, cold air, tasting vaguely of flowers.

"Are you awake?" Bastion said in my ear. His voice was uncharacteristically tinged with worry. Before I could answer, he said, "Don't answer. Don't say anything. Don't move. Vert is looking for you."

I held still, doing as Bastion told me. Every biological part of me ached with fresh wounds. Every breath moved ribs that were certainly broken. Rocks were digging into flesh that was already bruised. I tried to ignore the pain and take in my surroundings. I was wet. Drenched with chlorinated water, which unsettled me. As though everything I'd just dreamed had been real. But I wasn't in the water now. I was lying on my back, on the ground, in the dirt, really. A red stone retaining wall ran along my right side and I was pressed up against it. To my left and above me was a canopy of bushes and tall flowers.

Feet were moving nearby, sandals slapping against the pavement on the other side of the retaining wall. Heavy breathing with each passing pair of feet. Some whispers that I couldn't understand. How did I get here? What happened?

"You fell into a swimming pool," Bastion said as though he was in my head. "You blacked out. I took control of your limbs to swim and crawl us out, hiding us here. It was the best I could do."

I hated that he could do that, take control of my cybernetic parts like I was a marionette, but I had to be thankful now. I would have drowned in that pool, or Vert would have easily found me and made sure I drowned. Silently, I deployed my fiberoptic camera, running up to the top of the retaining wall to look out. I was still in the main courtyard of the Plaza del Mar hotel. There were far fewer guests here now, and the few left were running, glancing around nervously. I guessed seeing a woman fall out of a window had that effect.

After looking around a bit, I found Vert. He was still wearing that ridiculous floral-print shirt and khaki shorts. He was searching for the pools and restaurants and everywhere. Searching for me.

"How long since I fell?" I asked in a whisper. "Twelve minutes, forty-two seconds," Bastion said.

"Has he already been over here to look?"

"I don't know. I couldn't see through this wall."

Vert, still on the other side of the pool, turned his head quickly, like he'd heard something. He crouched down, sneaking slightly, and then suddenly grabbed a large bush and ripped it out of the ground, throwing it a dozen meters away. The exposed roots rained down soil as they flew. This shelter was not going to be sufficient once he made it over here. I glanced around, looking for something, anything that would provide a better hiding place. But this was a high-end resort. Well-lit. Open. Designed to be inviting and decorative, not dark or rife with shadowy corners.

And of course, Vert turned in my direction and started heading my way. His head on a swivel, scanning everywhere, looking deep into the swimming pools, across the courtyard, and even up and down the resort's towers.

"Call Solomon," I whispered to Bastion.

Calling Solomon appeared on my display, but then vanished an instant later.

"Did he just reject my call?"

Can't talk. Tailing my mark. Appeared on my screen then, a text from Solomon. Right. I was just the bait. I'd done my job, sending Tazia off thinking her only problem from Corto had been handled. Had he stuck around at all to make sure I was safe? Had he seen the windows blow out of the hotel room or my fall to the water? Did my presence on this island even matter anymore?

Those questions didn't matter right now. I just needed to survive the next few minutes. I retracted my camera. Frantically, I started shoveling dirt over my torso, and my face.

"What are you doing?" Bastion asked.

"Hiding more." I wiggled down into the soil and muck, trying to blend into the ground.

"This is ridiculous," Bastion said. "A few inches of dirt aren't going to save you. Run."

But those footsteps were approaching, heavy metal thumping against the concrete walkway in a slow, methodical cadence. He was too fast anyway, assuming my limbs weren't malfunctioning from the fall.

I was as buried as I was going to get, listening. Then the next footfall didn't come. Had he seen me? Spotted some sign of my presence? Was he about to leap over the retaining wall, an enormous fist driving down onto my head?

"What?" Vert said almost in a whisper. Several seconds passed before he said, "Yes, of course. Where are you?"

He was on a call. Probably Tazia, beckoning him.

"I'll be right there." He paused again, obviously listening to her say something. "Of course it's done. She won't be a problem."

I didn't deploy my camera again. I didn't move. I barely breathed. Could I actually get so lucky?

"Elise," Vert yelled. My shoulders and stomach shuddered. "My offer stands. Leave this island. Consider this an opportunity to keep living. Don't interfere. If I see you again, I will put you in the ground. I don't care who is watching." Then his heavy footsteps started again, quick now and heading away from me.

I exhaled a shaky breath. I stayed still until I couldn't hear his footsteps before I deployed my camera again and checked to make sure the courtyard was clear. Finally, I sat up, soil falling off me as my ribs protested.

"Are you all right?" Bastion said.

"No," I said. "Not really. Everything hurts. Damage?"

"Your shield emitters are burned out entirely. Everything else is in working order. He definitely focused his attacks on your biological components."

"That he did." I stood, threw my legs over the retaining wall, and sat there for a moment.

"You have several missed messages and voice calls from Valdo and Quynn."

"Tell Valdo I can't see him tonight," I said. "I'm sorry. Send me what he found out and we'll talk tomorrow."

"He won't like being put off."

"He won't, but Quynn is my priority. I need to come clean with them."

"Quynn will not be happy."

"No, but I need them in my corner. In my life. The rest of this doesn't matter if I lose them."

"Calling you a shuttle," Bastion said. I sat there for a few minutes, quietly brushing off dirt.

It was hopelessly stuck to my limbs and jumpsuit, though.

"Landing pad number eight," Bastion finally said. "Between towers four and five. It will be here in three minutes."

#   #   #

"I lied to you," I said to Quynn. I'd walked into their hotel room less than a minute ago. Quynn had gasped at the sight of me, and I'd just blurted out those four words.

262

"I know," Quynn said. Their voice was flat, though I could hear the edge to it.

I was surprised but didn't have the energy to show it. I said, "I'm sorry. I'm so, so—"

"Take a shower," Quynn said without an ounce of sympathy. "I don't want you tracking dirt everywhere. We need to deal with your nose, too."

"My nose?" I said. I touched it, just barely, and pain erupted there. The shape of it didn't make sense, either. With everything else, I'd somehow forgotten it. Now it was throbbing, making sure I couldn't forget it again. Before I could say anything else, Quynn left the hotel room. I took my overdue shower.

Clean clothes were set out for me on the toilet. A plain, gray shirt and black sweatpants. I toweled off, dressed, and found Quynn sitting on the king-sized bed with an emergency medical nanobot kit open next to them. Three large syringes swirling with shimmering silver fluid. Antiseptic wipes. A scanner and a keyboard.

"Sit," they said, picking up the kit and pointing to where it had been.

I sat.

Quynn squinted as they stared hard at my disfigured nose. "The nanobots can't fix this until it's set. I don't know how to do that. Do you?"

I shook my head.

"Your face is bruising. And your neck. Anywhere else?"

"My ribs," I said. "My chest. Pretty much every part of me that isn't cybernetic."

Quynn nodded, their face still stern. They became very task-oriented when they were angry, very get-stuff-done. "Take the shirt off. And start talking."

I took a deep breath, which hurt everything from my nose down to my diaphragm. Then I started telling Quynn everything that had happened since that first job at Tazia's office. Everything. Quynn slowly waved the scanner over my torso as I described that night, running into Valdo, Tazia, and Vert. The falling Stryder and how Nox and I followed Vert to the docks, to his son's fight, and Nox's gambit. Quynn proceeded to scan my neck and face as I described my halo jump to Tazia's apartment and the secret room I found.

My introduction to Necropolis Alpha, my accidental promotion in security clearance, the mind-melting revelation of Tazia as Josephine and possibly the Ghost of Toinette. I walked through Nox and I infiltrating Elizabeth Huginn-Sec's apartment as Quynn emptied the first syringe into a vein in my arm. The fire that put Nox in a coma as they injected the second. I caught Quynn up to now as the third syringe emptied into my blood.

"That should take care of your ribs and all the bruising," Quynn said as they placed the empty syringe next to the others. "You'll need a doctor to set the nose, though."

"Thank you," I said.

Quynn stood and walked to the window. They looked out for several silent moments, and then spun on me. Tears were running down their reddened cheek. "Why didn't you tell me the truth when you saw me here? You said you planned to. So why didn't you?"

I stared at my hands. "You were so happy. I'd been disappointing you over and over again, and suddenly you were happy to see me. I got so caught up in that. It was stupid, but I wanted that more than anything, that happiness." Quynn mopped up tears with a fist. "But you lied to me."

"I did. I'm sorry."

"You can't keep saying that," they practically yelled. "Sorry. Sorry. Sorry. You can't keep betraying my trust and expecting things to be okay just because you say that word."

"I know."

"Do you? Do you really? Ever since Bastion came into our lives, it seems like there's always something you're keeping from me, something you're running off and doing that you know is dangerous. Then when you get caught, you break down and say you're sorry. That isn't enough."

"That's not fair," Bastion said in my ear.

I winced.

"He had some comment about that?" Quynn said. I'd never seen them so angry, so openly emotional.

I nodded, not sure how else to react.

Quynn went to their luggage with long, angry strides. After rummaging around in it for about a minute, they pulled out a portable speaker. They turned it on and slammed it down on the dresser.

"Bastion, if you would?" I said. A moment later. *External Audio Device Connected* flashed on my display.

"If you have something to say, Bastion," Quynn said. "Say it to the whole damn group."

"I don't feel that I am to blame for any alleged duplicity on Elise's part," Bastion said through the speaker.

"I didn't say you were to blame," Quynn growled. "I said she started behaving this way when you showed up. Funny that you feel the need to defend yourself."

Bastion started to say, "I—"

"It's on me," I said. "All me. Quynn, we built this relationship on trust and honesty. You knew about my job from the moment you signed on. It's always been dangerous, but you knew that and I told you everything. Then Bastion showed up and I was afraid."

"Afraid of me?" Bastion asked.

"No. Afraid of what your existence could mean for both Quynn and me." I turned my attention fully to Quynn. "On a planet without laws, we're breaking one set by Earth Space by hiding him. For a little while, it was just on me, not you."

"We've been through all that," Quynn said. They appeared unmoved.

"Then some Toinette operative hijacks my Stryder and almost kills me. All I can think about is if she was able to track me like that, to know I'm an Intel Operative and exactly which rideshare I was going to step into, wouldn't she be able to find out about you? Come after you?"

"And how did hiding that from me help?" Quynn's voice raised even more.

I opened my mouth to answer, but I had no answer. "You're right," I said.

"If I had known your fears," Quynn said, their voice quieting just a smidge. "I could have taken measures to protect myself. If you had talked to me about half the things you've done the last few days, I could have helped. Helped you plan. Helped you see the bigger picture. You always rush off without really thinking through how everything you do will ripple out."

I nodded but said nothing.

Quynn sat down next to me on the bed. They took three enormous breaths, blowing out each one shakily. "What you do is dangerous, but I'm with you because I trust you to think things through, plan, and make smart decisions. For our entire relationship, you did just that. You trusted Hessod and your research. You planned everything out. But recently…"

"I've been in over my head and reacting," I said. "Not planning. Not thinking."

"Exactly. You've gotten by on your skills and your instincts, but it's almost gotten you killed more than once."

"I'm sorry. You're right."

"And you," Quynn said, turning their gaze to the little speaker on the dresser. "For some artificial intelligence that is supposed to be so advanced and intelligent, you're really not helping enough. You could have told me about all this, too. There are speakers all over the apartment."

"Elise told me not—"

"You're not a robot," Quynn snapped. "You can think for yourself. If Elise's well-being is really your highest priority, then act like it."

Bastion didn't say anything. Several long seconds passed.

"We both need to do better," I finally said. I looked at Quynn, whose face was still hard. "We will do better. We'll slow down. Talk to you. This whole thing doesn't work unless we're all working together."

"I concur," Bastion said.

Finally, Quynn's face softened a little. "I still love you. I'm mad at you, but I still love you. And so help me, Mother of Corto, if you lie to me or leave me out again…"

I didn't want to know how that sentence was supposed to end. I reached out and wrapped Quynn up in the biggest hug ever, my ribs be damned. My cheeks were wet as I whispered, "I promise. Never again."

We stayed that way for a while, me holding them. After a long minute, Quynn put their arms around me, too. I cried, letting the damn that had kept my emotions in check crumble. We didn't say anything. Bastion stayed blissfully quiet as well.

Eventually, Quynn pulled away and held me at arms' length. "You need to sleep. I can see you're exhausted and those bots will work better if you just rest."

"I can't," I said. "I need to fill in the Cloak on what happened in the hotel room. I need to make plans for Vert since we failed to get rid of him in Kotega."

"The Cloak is here?" Quynn said.

I nodded.

"Wow. This really is a big deal. Not an excuse, but wow." I nodded again.

"And you have information to review from Valdo," Bastion said.

"Sparks," I whispered. "Right. He went to tour the Offworld Relay. I need to talk to him, make sure—"

"He is asleep," Bastion said.

"Then we should—" I started to say as I stood up from the bed, but the room spun around me. Funny thing about cybernetic legs: while they are vastly more stable than biological legs, they are still ruled by the human brain and the human nervous system. So even though both of my legs were technological feats, when my brain went all dizzy and my nervous system carried that message south, both of my cybernetic legs wobbled, and I sat right back down on the bed.

"This is definitely one of those times to listen to me," Quynn said. "You're sleeping. Now."

"Agreed," Bastion said.

Through the fog of pain throughout my body and the buzz of the nanobots getting to work, I nodded. I was no good in this condition and was going to sleep whether I wanted to or not. I allowed Quynn to help me from the foot of the bed to under the covers. My head barely touched the pillow, and I was asleep.

Chapter Twenty-Six

THE SUN WAS TOO BRIGHT when I finally awoke, needing to pee worse than I had at any time in my life. I stumbled out of the bed, confused for a few seconds as to where I was. A hotel room. Not my hotel room. Quynn's hotel room. I glanced back at the bed, but Quynn wasn't there. The covers were tossed like they'd slept next to me, though. I scurried into the bathroom, filling the toilet with sparkling urine. That was part of the deal when you injected nanobots into your blood: they eventually left you in the form of sparkling pee.

I remained seated on the toilet longer than I needed to, trying to wake up and get my bearings. Nearly 10:00. Almost four kilometers from my hotel, the hotel in which Valdo was staying.

"Any messages?" I asked Bastion.

"Valdo said good morning two hours ago," Bastion said in my ear. "He requests that you contact him when you awaken."

I grunted.

"Solomon has also requested that you contact him."

"Did he say it like that?" I asked. "Request?"

"He did not. His tone is rather more demanding and combative."

"Still not happy that he ran into Quynn, I take it?"

"I should say not."

The door to the hotel suddenly swung open and I kicked the door to the bathroom closed as my stomach jumped into my throat.

"Elise?" Quynn's voice called from the other side of the door. "That you in the bathroom?"

"Yeah," I answered. "You okay?"

"Yeah." I pulled my pants back up and flushed the dead nanobots away. I washed my hands.

"I have coffee and some fruit."

"That's great," I said as I opened the door. "I should really meet up with Valdo. Find out what he learned."

Quynn didn't say anything, just set out the fruit on the dresser without looking at me.

"Are you coming with?" I asked.

"I'm here to enjoy myself," Quynn said, still focused on the fruit.

I held up my hands in surrender. "I'm trying to keep you in the loop. You're welcome to come with me and meet Valdo, but you don't have to. I can fill you in later."

Quynn worked their jaw for a moment. "Oh, that's exactly what's happening. I have plans. Without you. So go. Work. Just keep me informed."

"Okay," I whispered.

Quynn looked up at me then, anger and pain playing across their face. "I hate being mad at you. I love you, and I want you to be safe. But I really don't want to be around you right now."

I put my hands on Quynn's shoulders. They flinched a little but didn't pull away. "If I need you, if I even think you can be helpful, I'll tell you. I'm just going to have breakfast with Valdo and find out what he learned." Quynn looked worried.

"I promise."

"I want to be kept informed. I want to know where you are, where you're going."

"You hear that, Bastion?" I asked.

"I do," Bastion said over the speaker.

"Don't just leave it to him," Quynn said in a whisper. "I need to hear your voice sometimes to know you're really okay." I nodded.

"How are you going to deal with Vert being here?"

"I'm not sure yet," I said. "I'm not going to fight him, if that's what you're worried about. I know when I'm completely out of my depth."

Quynn nodded this time and sighed. "Good. Okay. Go meet Valdo. Check in often." They glanced at the speaker. "Both of you."

"Of course," Bastion said as I nodded.

#   #   #

"Where have you been all night?" Valdo asked when I found him at a little beachside café near our hotel. "And what happened to your face?"

"The short answer?" I said as I sat down across the small table from him. "Vert."

Valdo's eyes went wide.

"Josephine has friends in high places all over the city, apparently."

"Are you okay?"

"I'll need a doctor for my nose, but three doses of nanobots are keeping me upright," I said. I glanced at the menu but already knew what I wanted, a stack of pancakes as big as my head. And coffee. I turned my attention to the beach, the waves gently rolling back and forth a dozen meters away. Birds circled in the air, calling to each other softly. A couple was walking along, bare feet in the sand, hands clasped tightly. I wanted to be there, walking along that sand with Quynn, not a care in the world. Once this was all over, maybe Quynn and I could take a vacation. Probably not here, though. I already wanted to be done with Cirilla.

A server walked over and took our orders, coming right back with coffee for me and a tall, green juice for Valdo.

"It's weird seeing you in those limbs," he said after a big gulp.

I nodded. "You've only seen me in my work limbs. These were the first I ever bought." Before coming to meet Valdo, I'd gone back to my room, inspecting my work limbs once I swapped them out and changed clothes. The shields were completely burned out, leaving two scorched circles on the forearms. Despite the popping, the fingers were all right, just a bit loose in their joints. The limbs were charging now.

I took a long sip of very good coffee before I asked him, "How did your evening go?"

Valdo smiled broadly. "Better than I'd expected."

I smirked. "Good."

His smile shifted. Became more devious, which worried me.

"See for yourself," Valdo said as he pushed a small data drive across the table.

"What's this?"

"I recorded everything. That should give you a VR playback of my little adventure."

"Recorded?" I asked as I took the data drive. "I thought you didn't have optical mods."

Valdo reached into his front shirt pocket and pulled out a pair of glasses. They looked like antiques. "I don't need these to read, but the cameras I installed in them come in handy sometimes."

"You might make a great Intel Operative," I said as I plugged the data drive into a port in my arm. These limbs didn't have all the bells or whistles of my work limbs, but they weren't useless. "Too bad you don't live in Corto."

SCANNING FILE appeared on my display, blinking softly until it was replaced by VR FILE FOUND. PLAY?

I acknowledged, and the real world faded from my vision, replaced by the visitor's entrance to the Offworld Relay. A tour guide in a navy suit was taking tickets. Valdo glanced up at the towering relay briefly before looking back to the tour guide, which in VR, meant it looked like I glanced up and looked back to the tour guide. A hand reached out and handed the guide a ticket. They smiled and gestured in through the doors.

I paused the playback and flipped my vision back to the here and now. "Can you just tell me the highlights? I don't need the whole tour, just—"

"I already edited the file," Valdo said after wiping juice from the wispy little hairs on his upper lip. "Just stick with it."

I dived back into the recording. After milling about in the waiting area with a dozen other tourists, the video skipped forward. The entire group was standing next to a single set of elevator doors, stylish gleaming brass.

"This," the tour guide said in a chipper but over-rehearsed voice, "is the elevator to the control room at the very top of the Offworld Relay. There, our team of engineers makes sure the immense stream of data going to and from Little Sekhmet Settlement is never interrupted, never slowed. More data goes through this relay in a second than any one of us will generate in a lifetime."

The crowd responded with the expected oohs and ahs.

"The elevator also goes down," the guide continued. "All the way to the turbines submerged the ocean water below, constantly turning to move water across the enormous heatsinks that keep the system from overheating. So you see, this tower isn't just for show, but the entire structure supports the critical transfer of data to and from our world."

A hand went up in the crowd. The guide nodded toward the person attached to it, who said, "Why is the Offworld Relay so tall?"

"What a great question! While I don't want to get into all the specifics of how the Relay works, it does need to be on the equator and at least two hundred meters above sea level to maintain constant contact with the rest of the relays across Earth Space. All relays on all planets work the same way."

The video skipped forward again, this time to a large, circular room. The perimeter of the room was covered with enormous viewscreens, all displaying various factoids and historical information about this and other Offworld Relays. Complicated control stations were spaced out in front of those viewscreens, and there were three even larger control stations in a circle near the center of the room.

"This is an exact replica of the control room at the top of the Offworld Relay," the guide said. "Three shifts of over a dozen engineers work around the clock, each engineer at their station, working diligently for all of us. None of them have Jayu City company alignments but instead work for the Earth Space government, which oversees the Offworld Relay program. "These control stations, however, are for your education and information. We're going to stay in here for the next forty-five minutes. Please feel free to try each station, as each one provides different information on the history of this relay, the entire Offworld Relay program, and the history of Little Sekhmet Settlement as a whole."

As the various tour customers started chatting and heading to various stations around the faux control room, the tour guide was suddenly waylaid by one particular tourist with some very urgent questions that I couldn't make out. That was when Valdo did something I would have done. He skirted around the edge of the large room, glancing back to the tour guide several times before opening a heavy door and moving back out into the hallway I'd seen earlier.

I stopped the recording. "What did you do?"

Valdo looked downright cocky. "I thought to myself, what would Elise do?" He spread his arms wide. "As you can see, I made it out just fine. Watch the video."

I shook my head but couldn't keep the smile from my face. Back in the video, he moved quickly, still checking behind himself occasionally, before stopping at a door labeled *Employees Only*. There was no handle, but a basic ten-digit keypad next to the door. I didn't recognize the brand, but it looked simple enough. Simple for me.

Valdo's hand grabbed the keypad and popped the cover right off. He was lucky it wasn't equipped with an anti-tamper sensor. I hadn't taught him anything about short-circuiting a keypad like this one, but he seemed to already know his way around. He disconnected a couple of wires, stripped them with his fingernails, and touched them together briefly. The keypad made a two-tone ring and the door popped open. Valdo stuck a foot in the open door, put the keypad back in place, and entered the room beyond.

Lights near the door came on when Valdo entered, but only illuminated a few meters around him. He was in an enormous server room. Rack after rack at least three meters tall formed a corridor that sprawled off into the darkness. Valdo proceeded forward slowly, his head swiveling so much that it made me a little dizzy in VR. They all looked the same to me.

"Products of Earth Space," Bastion said. "Very similar to the quantum processing servers that Huginn started manufacturing last winter."

The video jumped forward. Valdo was standing in front of a terminal. The screen looked like a wall of gibberish to me, at least half a dozen different programming languages on over a dozen different windows. Valdo glanced to his right and left.

After a few dozen more keystrokes, a security interface appeared. It was very similar to the Corto Centurion program, but the branding was all wrong. In place of the paired Cs of the Corto Corporation logo, there was a stylized, gold "GH." The H lower than the G, the corners of the letters merged.

"GH?" I asked, still watching the VR.

"No idea," Valdo said from the real world. "I spent a couple of hours last night looking it up, but nothing."

Bastion stayed silent on the logo. He was better at searching the Net than any human, but it might take some time if Valdo hadn't found anything.

I watched Valdo move through the security program almost as fast as me, though in an entirely different way. I knew those programs, and how to move within their existing structures. Valdo was manipulating the program like he'd built it, opening debugging panels and other windows full of code. Bits of security footage popped up. The tour group with Valdo moved through the halls only minutes before, all of their faces clear. A moment later, Valdo's face was missing from that footage. As instructed, he was scrubbing himself from the security videos.

"I need you to teach me how to do that to videos," I said.

"I can do those things," Bastion said. "You just have to plug in and I can take care of the rest."

"It's not that hard," Valdo said around a bit of food. "What's harder is setting up a filter to search out and continue blurring any instance of a given face. I did that. It's basically a virus, but one that no antivirus can detect. Not for a few years, at least."

That must have been what I was seeing him do now. More code. He inserted a data drive into the terminal. Images of him appeared, and then blue wireframes traced over the images of his entire body. He worked so fast, it was impossible for me to keep up with him. It was truly impressive. It was also boring when I couldn't understand what I was seeing. I pulled his data drive out of my port. There in front of me sat my pancakes while Valdo was chewing his food.

"Is the rest of that video just you doing your computer magic?"

Valdo swallowed. "Not all of it. I rejoined the tour group, asked some very insightful questions. Nobody even knew I'd left."

I nodded as I stuffed two big bites of syrupy pancakes into my mouth, chewed, and then swallowed. "What did you find out?"

He pointed his fork at the data drive. "It's all on there."

"I'm hungry," I said. "So just tell me."

"You saw the elevator on the tour?"

I nodded.

"That elevator hasn't moved in three years," he said with a wicked grin. He'd been waiting to reveal that little tidbit.

"So how are the engineers getting to the top?" I asked.

Valdo's grin eased at my lack of shock. Sorry, kid. "There's another elevator on the back of the tower. But nothing about it makes sense."

"Goes sideways instead of up and down?"

"No," he said, missing my joke. "It rarely moves. Right now, it's at the top of the tower. Has been for three days. Every four days, it comes down and opens on a sub-level. It stays down there for a few hours, and then it goes back up."

"Do the engineers live up at the top? Are they just making grocery runs?"

"I don't know. I was able to find schematics, though heavily redacted, especially the top level. It looks like an entirely empty floor. The big data lines run up to it through the tower, along with a lot of power and some basic plumbing lines."

"Given the sensitivity of the information that passes through the Offworld Relay," Bastion said. "It would make sense for the engineers to spend their time at the top. Though the size of the control room does not allow for comfortable quarters and working space for that many people."

Nothing was making sense about this setup. I asked Valdo, "And the elevator only comes down every four days? Exactly every four days?"

"Usually four," he said. "Sometimes three or five. Not always the same time, either."

"That makes things harder," I said. I took another bite and chewed it slowly, thinking about this. "How do we get to the sub-level where this elevator opens?"

"There's a back entrance facing the ocean," Valdo said. He took a drink of his juice. "Looks like a door big enough for a car to fly into."

"What else?"

"What do you mean?"

"I mean," I said. "What else can you tell me about the building? What about that big space between the tourist area and the control room at the top? Any stairs? Maintenance access?"

"Two elevator shafts. Massive power and data lines. Plumbing. I didn't see any stairs, though those could have been redacted from the schematics. One maintenance hatch, yeah. The schematics showed it on the sixth floor. If there are stairs, there must be almost two hundred floors between that hatch and the control room."

I shrugged and took another bite, but then remembered that Valdo didn't have modded legs. "If the middle is really empty, I can get us to the top faster than climbing steps."

"So what's the plan?" Valdo said.

"WHERE ARE YOU?" appeared on my display, larger than it should have been, a message from Solomon.

"Hold on," I said to Valdo. I brought up my AR keyboard.

"I do not know how he was able to display the message like that," Bastion said.

"It's Solomon," I typed to Bastion. "Just make sure he can't hack into me and find out about you. Tell him I'm at my hotel, please."

"Message sent," Bastion said.

Only a few seconds passed before "WHO IS THE TEENAGER?" appeared on my display.

I looked around, searching for the Cloak. He obviously had eyes on me.

I didn't see a reason to lie, so I said, "The kid from Toinette who helped with the video feed."

"SO YOU GAVE HIM A VACATION?"

My hands hovered above my AR keyboard as I debated how to respond to the question, whether to be honest or as snarky as Solomon had been, but another message appeared before I could make a determination.

"GET TO A SECURE LOCATION AND CALL ME. NOW."

I sighed and dismissed the keyboard. Valdo was looking at me like he expected me to leave, which was accurate. "I have to go," I said. "I'm going to make a run at that maintenance hatch. Hopefully today."

"We," Valdo said.

"What?"

"We're going to make a run at that maintenance hatch."

"You did your part, there's no need—"

"Do you know what a variable quantum protocol is?"

I stared at the kid blankly. Each of those words made sense in my mind but strung together like that, I had no idea.

"Right," he said. "That's part of the encryption their computer was using in the server room. Very high-end. There are two hundred floors between that hatch and the control room upstairs. Two hundred floors for their cameras to see you. And you don't think there will be any computers in there? No computers you'll need to hack in the actual control room? Can you even imagine what the encryption is like up there?"

"I could get us past any encryption we run into," Bastion said in my ear.

I kept my face still, trying to betray nothing. Both of them were right, but Valdo didn't know about Bastion. Plus if Bastion was hacking into a system, it meant I needed to be plugged into that system. Stationary. With Valdo doing the hacking, it would leave me free to move, to react to anything that came our way. I finished my coffee with one long swig before I stood and said. "Okay. You're in. Send me the tour schedule. I don't want to run into a tour group. I have to take care of something, but I'll be in touch. Wear something you can move in."

Valdo smiled wider than I'd ever seen, like a kid seeing a roller coaster for the first time. "Yes. Yes. Absolutely. I'll be ready."

"Charge breakfast to my room. Try to relax." Then I walked away, back into the hotel.

"You are putting him in danger for no reason," Bastion said.

"I have my reasons," I whispered.

"Any reason that Quynn would approve of?" I thought about that for a moment, and it came to me. "Yes. Someone else to watch my back."

Chapter Twenty-Seven

I MADE SURE MY HOTEL room door was locked and dampeners were running before I called Solomon. In less than a second, his voice was in my ears.

"What happened last night?"

I sighed. "Why can't we just sit down face-to-face?"

Then there he was before me, dressed in a pink linen suit and a wide-brimmed, white hat, sitting on a chair I couldn't see. Apparently, he could override my display to appear before me in AR. That wasn't at all terrifying. He gestured vaguely at himself and said, "Better?"

"Not exactly."

"We're still working under the assumption that Tazia doesn't know who I am. She knows you're here, though. We can't risk me being seen with you."

"Does that mean your evening was successful?" I said.

"I asked you first."

"Fine. Tazia made calls and cashed in favors. Vert is here on Cirilla."

Solomon didn't react. Of course he already knew. I told him the rest, about my whole interaction with Tazia and Vert from knocking on the door to Vert leaving me hiding in the landscaping. I left out no detail. Solomon winced a little when I described the fight, but he didn't interrupt me. "That explains your nose," he said, his tone still gruff. "How are you?"

"Great," I said. "I feel like I've gone through a meat tenderizer and I'm still peeing nanobots, but great."

Solomon smirked. "She went to meet a kid?"

"That's what she said," I said. "Pretty sure it's not her kid, though."

"Her kid?"

"I heard her on a call through the Boredom Stick. She was talking to and about her family."

"Fascinating. Are they here on Cirilla?"

"Not from the sound of it."

Solomon mulled that for a few moments before he said, "We don't have time to leverage them if they're not here. Would you stop pacing?"

I hadn't even realized I'd been doing it, walking back and forth the three or four meters next to the hotel room window. I pulled the chair out from the desk and sat.

"I followed Tazia to the Shogun Heights Resort." Solomon paused, watching someone I couldn't see. He waited several long seconds before continuing. "She went up to the eighteenth floor. I wasn't able to get any closer. After ten or so minutes, Vert joined her."

"When she called him away."

"Right. Tazia and Vert came back down together twenty minutes after that. They took a shuttle to the Orion, the fancy new hotel by the convention center. Stayed there the rest of the night."

"Site B, I'd guess. So who were they meeting at Shogun Heights?"

"I don't know exactly, but it's a favorite of Kotega residents," Solomon said.

"The hotel is at full occupancy right now," Bastion said in my ear. "Seventy-one percent of the reservations are from Kotega Systems citizens. The hotel has surprisingly poor system security."

"Probably someone young. Under eighteen? Sixteen?" Solomon said.

"There are no reservations to anyone in that age range," Bastion said.

"Anyone that age might be there with their parents, not under their own reservation," I said to both of them. "Tazia is in her mid-thirties?"

"She is forty-two," Solomon said.

"Remind me to ask for her skin-care routine," I said. "She could be referring to someone in their early twenties as a kid."

"Good point," Solomon said.

"There are twelve reservations made to people under age twenty-five," Bastion said.

"I'll head over there and get a look at their—" I started to say.

"I'm already here," Solomon said. "They have excellent pina coladas. I'll get into their system. We need to deal with our Vert problem, though. Again."

That was a bigger problem. Literally. My nose was throbbing and despite the nanobots, my ribs were still aching from our last encounter. I had zero chance against him in a fight. I ran through the normal list of ways to turn someone. Money wasn't an issue. Tazia was paying him very well if our research was correct. Ideology was a nonstarter. Vert was a true believer and really put his faith in Tazia's grand plan to evangelize Ibhalism. Coercion was laughable. And despite everything, he seemed to have very little ego. He took no joy in fighting or anything, really. He was focused on doing what he could for his faith. I shook my head and spread my helpless hands.

"I'm open to ideas," I said.

Solomon furrowed his brow. Then he glanced around in what could almost be mistaken for nervousness. "We have some very violent people we keep on retainer."

"Violent enough to take down Vert?" Solomon seemed to consider that question before answering. "Perhaps if we employ several of them. Or if we can surprise him. Then how do we do it without making a spectacle?"

A spectacle. Something about that pulled at my memories. A certain video I'd seen a couple of days ago came to mind, of a young girl hiding while her parents were slaughtered by strangers. How that young girl had grown up to become one of the deadliest people I'd ever encountered. Roxy. An idea started to form, one that I'd rejected not long ago on a Huginn yacht but was making more sense by the second now.

"I think I have something," I said. "Someone, really."

"Who?" Solomon asked.

I waved off the question. "Someone who might be able to take Vert down. At least hurt him. They're not Corto, and they'll want the spectacle, want it enough to pull focus from us."

"And with any luck," Bastion chimed in, obviously inferring who I was thinking of. "Maybe they will kill each other."

Solomon leaned forward in the chair I couldn't see. "Who?"

"I doubt you've heard of her," I said.

"Try me."

"Roxy," I said. "A Mistwalker."

Solomon sat back in his chair and smiled. "Hoping you can get her off your back in the same stroke?"

I couldn't hide the shock on my face. "How could you possibly know—?"

Solomon stood. "Knowing things is what I do. Finding. Knowing. Taking. Call her. Get her here today, if you can. You have official backing and financing for it. I'll leave Vert to you. I'll focus on Tazia and this so-called kid. We don't have time to waste."

I opened my mouth to reply, but the call disconnected. I guess I had my marching orders.

"This might be the most strategic idea you've ever had," Bastion said.

"Purely by accident, I assure you," I said. "Do we have Roxy's contact information?"

"We do. She would be an ineffective assassin-for-hire if I were not able to find that. Should I call her?"

"Not yet," I said. "Send Quynn a rundown of the plan. Send Roxy the video you found, the one of these two people killing her parents. We'll let her call us."

"What do you expect that to achieve?"

"Confusion. Maybe a willingness to talk. Maybe even goodwill. It's the best I've got."

After a couple of seconds, Bastion said, "File sent."

I fell onto the bed. Despite sleeping hard last night, I could have closed my eyes and slept more. But there was no time for that. Roxy might call any minute. If she didn't, I was going to have to call her, which wasn't going to be fun. There was also the small matter of the Offworld Relay, the maintenance hatch I needed to pry open and the two hundred floors of open building to ascend. I needed to get on that, get it done so I could focus on Tazia. I wondered what I would find up there at the top of the relay. A dozen engineers living up there, and some solid connection between the five companies. Where that connection would lead, I had no idea.

Then Quynn was calling. I took it, and they appeared in front of me in AR.

"You got the plan?" I asked.

"I don't like it," they said.

"I don't, either."

"I do," Bastion said.

"I understand your feelings on Roxy, Bastion," Quynn said. "I just see a lot of risk bringing two people who want to kill Elise into the same room."

"Do you see a better plan?"

Quynn sighed and looked around. I couldn't see their surroundings, so I didn't know what they were looking at. "No. And the upside is huge. I know you've been losing sleep over Roxy."

I didn't say anything. I didn't have to.

"Watch your exits," Quynn said. "Be ready to bolt and call Solomon if things go sideways."

"You have an incoming call," Bastion said. "I believe it is Roxy."

"Right on cue," I said to both of them.

Quynn smiled, a forced expression that showed more worry than anything else. Then they nodded and disconnected the call.

I stood, preparing myself as best I could for the next conversation. Then I connected the call.

"Who is this?" Roxy growled.

I swallowed, hoping my voice would remain steady. "Elise Corto-Intel."

"What kind of trick is this?"

"No trick," I said as calmly as I could.

"You lie for a living, Corto. I have no reason to believe you."

"That's true, but that video doesn't lie. Did any of that line up with your memories?"

Roxy growled like a beast stamping at the ground, like she wanted to reach through the comms system and tear my head off.

"My job is also to acquire things, if you recall," I said. "Like I acquired that video. I didn't have to share it with you."

"How…?" Roxy snapped. "No. What was that video? How did you get that?"

"That video is of you, of your parents." I didn't need to describe what happened. She'd seen it or else she wouldn't have called.

"How did you get it?"

I took a deep breath. "From the private files of Josephine Toinette-Deus."

"The evangelist?"

"The evangelist."

"Why would she have something like this?"

"Probably because she's not just an evangelist. She was a job. I wasn't even after that video but found it along the way."

"Is it real?" Roxy asked, suddenly quiet. "Is any of it real?"

"As far as I can tell, yes."

The other end of the line was silent for a minute. Then another. Finally, Roxy said with newfound steadiness, "Who are those people? The people who did that to my parents? To me?"

"I found a couple of personnel files along with that video. I'm not sure they're the masked figures, but they're likely a good place to start looking."

"And let me guess," Roxy said with a hiss. "If I want the files, I have to leave you be?"

The thought had crossed my mind, sure, but as Quynn told me, that would be thinking tactically, not strategically. I needed more from this assassin than just leaving me alone. With a few taps of my keyboard, I pulled up the files Bastion had found and read off the names. "Aurelie Toinette-Cyber and Hode Toinette-Deus. Sending you the files now."

I knew Bastion was listening, and as expected, started sending the files to Roxy.

Another silent minute passed before Roxy said, "Why would you give me this? Do you think it will buy my mercy? Do you think I'm that easy to buy off? To dismiss?"

"No," I said. "Not at all. I'm hoping it will buy me enough goodwill for you to hear a proposition."

I swore I heard another growl from the other end of the connection before Roxy said, "Out with it."

"I have a two-meter-tall problem named Vert Toinette."

"The fighter? Oh, he does work for the evangelist now, doesn't he?" She sounded hungry. "How pathetic. What about him?"

"I can't beat him in a fight. I can't even scratch him. He broke my nose and most of my ribs when I tried. But you can do better."

"Why would I?" Roxy said, but I heard what I was hoping to hear. There was an excitement in her voice, something different from the unbridled vitriol she usually threw my way.

I took another deep breath before I continued, organizing my thoughts. I didn't want to remind her exactly why she hated me. No need to bring up how she'd failed to kill me. Twice. Finally, I said, "In your line of work, your reputation is everything. How better to bolster that reputation than by fighting and beating Vert 'The Hurt' Toinette?"

"Interesting." I swear I heard a purr in Roxy's voice.

Before she could ask questions or reject the idea, I plowed ahead. "I can make sure there's an audience. A big one. And I'll cover your transportation costs."

"Transportation?"

"Cirilla."

"Hmm…" Roxy said. The sound morphed and elongated until Roxy was laughing in a way that made my skin crawl. The laugh lasted too long, was too loud and too deep. It fell away slowly, like aftershocks after an earthquake before she said, "Keep your money. If you can do as you say, get me in a ring with a big enough spotlight, I'll consider our slate clear."

My knees nearly gave out in relief, but now I had to make a plan, one that would get Vert where and when I needed him and put enough eyeballs on the fight to make this work. I started talking, planning out loud, and Roxy kept listening.

Chapter Twenty-Eight

"THEY'RE HERE," I SAID TO Quynn, animating my face and hands more than I normally would.

"And you're sure Roxy will do her part?" Quynn asked.

"I guarantee she'll try. There's no way she'll do anything else with all those cameras on her." That's what I was counting on, at least. From what I understood, reputation was everything as an assassin. Fending her off had hurt that reputation, which was why she was still after me. Defeating Vert publicly would launch her into a new echelon, assuming they had echelons. I would just be happy to get her off my back.

As Tazia and Vert walked into the convention center, Quynn and I stood 30 meters away. Not hiding, but not obvious amidst the sea of excited faces. I was in my work limbs again but wearing a cosplay poncho/cape thing that Quynn had picked out. No need to draw attention with the black, carbon-polymer limbs or the circular burns on the forearms.

I was counting on Vert doing his job as Tazia's bodyguard, his eyes cautiously scanning the room as they entered. Quynn had their back to the doors so Vert would be able to see my face, though I kept my own eyes trained on Quynn's. My fiberoptic camera was resting on Quynn's shoulder, invisible from Vert's point of view, but allowing me to watch the doors without looking at them.

"I still don't trust her," Quynn said.

"Neither do I," I said. "But I trust her nature and that I've given her an opportunity she won't refuse." Before Quynn could say anything else, I saw Vert notice me. My stomach bobbled a little, and I had to work very hard to not look directly at him. He leaned down and whispered into Tazia's ear. Tazia looked in my direction for several seconds before she, too, recognized me. She said something to Vert, and then he broke off from her, weaving his way straight toward me. I took a deep breath as he squeezed between people. I took another as he advanced three more meters. When a slight convention-goer in an elaborate costume yelled at him to be more careful, I moved my eyes from Quynn to Vert, gave him my best surprised face, and started playing prey to his predator.

I spun, moving through the crowd with roughly the same speed Vert was, though my smaller frame made it much easier to navigate the masses. I positioned my fiberoptic camera on my own shoulder now, giving me a rear view, which was slightly disorienting on my display, but necessary. Vert was becoming less and less concerned with remaining inconspicuous, however, and was gaining as he pushed his way through the crowd.

"Second escalator on your left," Bastion said.

I turned and dropped to a squat the next time I saw Vert glance sideways to move someone, vanishing from his line of sight and changing my vector. I couldn't see him while I did this, but I knew how to disappear in a crowd. I was better trained for stealth than purposely leading a chase. I kept moving while in a squat, and once I reached the escalator Bastion had pointed out, I popped back up, looking back at Vert with false panic on my face. After a few seconds, he found me and resumed his pursuit. I'd put distance between us, though, which was the point. Now I started bounding up the escalator, two steps at a time, as I weaved between people who were casually riding up to the next floor. I was nearly at the top when Vert reached the bottom, tossing someone off as he started to climb after me.

"Raphael is ready," Quynn said over comms, using the same channel that Bastion was using.

"Thank you," I said. I kept weaving through the crowd, following

Bastion's directions and making sure Vert saw me just often enough to stay on my trail, but never catch up. The anger became more and more apparent on his face as the chase continued along the massive windows of the convention center. I passed one, two, then three hallways that led away from the windows, looking for the fourth. I made the sharp turn down the hall, disappearing briefly from Vert's view to slow him down, but making sure he saw where I went before I completely turned the corner.

I spied the wide metal doors to room 2402. The screen next to it was blank. Nearly every room had a screen like this, listing the events happening in that room throughout the day. This room wasn't going to be used until tomorrow, or at least that's what everyone thought. I grabbed the handle, hoping that it had been left unlocked as promised. I gave it a tug, and it flew open. I let out a breath, kicked down the doorstop, and walked it, leaving the door open a few inches. I turned on my night vision and saw Roxy standing in the middle of the stage ahead of me, a hooded robe over her. I ran up the aisle that ran under the stands facing the stage. The stands were empty for the moment, but I could see a dozen camera drones hovering. The cameras were here. Roxy was here. The crowds would come.

"You ready?" I asked as I approached her. My stomach tumbled a little being this close to her, smelling her sweat. Too many bad memories there. "Just make sure those cameras are streaming," she growled.

I nodded and ran off toward the left wing but stopped before leaving the stage entirely. Then all the lights came on. I was temporarily blinded until I switched back to normal vision. Vert was standing a couple of meters in front of the stage, at the mouth of the aisle I'd just run through. Roxy was directly in front of him, dead center of the stage. Upstage to her right and left were a pair of glass booths that contained high-end gaming stations, monitors, and expensive gaming chairs. An enormous viewscreen at the back of the stage suddenly lit up, showing the streams from four of the cameras that were watching Vert and Roxy.

"Give Raphael my thanks," I said to Quynn over comms. Raphael Corto-Nano used to work for Quynn before their promotion to director. He was also a big-time gamer and moonlit as an emcee and convention technician. He was flipping all the switches and pushing all the buttons in this theatre right now.

"You can tell him yourself," Quynn said. "We're buying him and his husband dinner next week."

"No more running," Vert yelled.

"I'm not running," I said to him. "I'm leading."

He took two heavy steps before Roxy threw back her hood and yelled, "Vert."

Vert stopped and looked at Roxy like she was an insect. "Who are you?" He shook his head. "It doesn't matter. Don't interfere."

"But that's exactly why I'm here," Roxy said.

Vert ignored her and started walking toward me again, trying to move around Roxy, but she leaped off the stage and into his path.

"I don't know who you are," he said, "but I'm not here for you."

"I am Roxy, formerly of Toinette. Deadliest assassin on Little Sekhmet. I'm here for you, has-been fighter."

Vert's jaw set and he seemed to see Roxy for the first time. "There is much more to life than violence, Roxy. My fight isn't with you, and you should be grateful for that. This is not the path to balance, to happiness. Throw no punches here. Go and I will forget I ever saw you."

Roxy's head tilted slightly, looking up to the bigger fighter. I saw a flutter under her robe as she said, "I'm not here to throw punches." Then the robe fell away in shreds as her spider-like limbs blossomed from her back, ripping cloth and shining in the theatre's lights.

Vert shook his head in disappointment, glanced at me, and then focused back on Roxy. "This is foolish. Why would you fight for her? For that coward behind you?"

"I fight for me," Roxy said and then launched herself at Vert. Roxy was fast. A scar on my cheek reminded me just how fast she was and how lucky I'd been to survive her. Twice. Vert was fast, too, though. Roxy launched a clawed hand at Vert's face, but he deftly moved her hand aside with one forearm and stepped around her. But then two of her spider-limbs were flying at his face and neck, and the big man barely rolled out of the way in time.

He came back to his feet and put all his attention on Roxy for the first time. She grinned with all of her teeth.

"*Dregs of Osiris* fans," Raphael said with his smarmy announcer voice over the theatre speakers. "Do I have a surprise for you!"

Vert looked around like he was trying to find Raphael. Roxy just kept on grinning.

"Right now in the Rosendahl Theatre, legendary fighter Vert 'The Hurt' Toinette is about to square off against the deadliest assassin on Little Sekhmet Settlement, the Mistwalker, Roxy!"

Vert flashed an angry look at Roxy.

"What's wrong, big man, afraid you can't perform in front of a crowd?" Roxy called.

"Is that what this is about? You want the entire planet to watch you lose?"

"I want the entire galaxy to see who I am," she purred. "To watch me kill you."

People started filing into the theatre then, excited voices and pointing fingers quickly jostling for the best seats. Vert backed up onto the stage, one eye on the growing crowd and the other on Roxy. Despite his anger, he looked excited. The man who had fought in front of thousands obviously liked some part of that. Roxy climbed onto the stage, too, focused on Vert, but waiting for the crowd to gather. She was doing this all for the attention, so of course, she was waiting. Within a few minutes, the thousand or so seats in the theatre were going to be filled. I slunk back into the shadows backstage. Roxy needed everyone to see her match up with this legendary fighter, but nobody needed to see me lurking around the edge of the fight.

"Raphael's live stream is already at nearly ten million views," Bastion said. "Including live streams from the audience filing in, over fourteen million and rapidly climbing."

"Good," I said.

"Your plan appears to be working."

"My plan includes Roxy actually beating Vert, not just making him mad."

Raphael continued to pump the crowd up as they filled the arena and his live stream numbers climbed. Roxy and Vert circled each other on the stage, maybe two meters apart. After several minutes of this tense pacing and crowd jostling in, both fighters moved at each other like they were answering some unseen cue.

Vert took a half step like he was tentative but then flew forward toward Roxy's midsection. Roxy launched skyward, one of her copper-colored metal feet clanging off Vert's armored head. Vert rolled when he failed to take Roxy down, coming back up to his feet and putting his eyes back on Roxy in an instant. The last-second impact with Vert's head seemed to make Roxy tumble as she arced through the air, but she landed easily and already facing her opponent again.

"Sizing each other up," I whispered.

"No doubt Roxy has seen many of Vert's fights," Bastion said. "But she is an unknown quantity to him."

Then Roxy lunged at Vert, her spider-limbs jutting straight forward like a quartet of spears. Vert spun, grabbing one of the limbs with one hand and bringing his other in for a powerful punch, the lights on his forearm aglow, but Roxy wasn't there. It was a feint. Even though Vert had one of her spider-limbs in his hand, Roxy had gone into a slide while Vert was focused on those limbs. She launched up now, raking her clawed hand across Vert's chest and up to his cheek. Vert threw her off, spun, and kicked at where Roxy was, but she dodged that, too.

Vert and Roxy faced off again, Roxy smiling that wicked smile. Vert wiped a trickle of blood from his cheek. He looked at the smear of red on his fingers like it was a foreign object. Then his face went cold, but I didn't get to see it for very long. Just like my own helmet, nanobots assembled a plate of armor over his face, so there was absolutely no visible flesh on the big man. It was an unremarkable plane of metal except for two perfectly round, red, glowing spots for his eyes. The crowd cheered in recognition. My stomach dropped when the glow on his forearms extended up to his shoulders, across his chest and back, up his neck, and down his legs. One glowing arm had been enough to blow straight through my shields. I couldn't imagine what his entire body glowing would do, but I felt Roxy's chances diminishing by the moment.

Roxy, however, seemed to grow even more excited. She didn't wait for the glowing Vert to attack, either. She lunged again, two of her spider-limbs extended. This time, Vert smacked the coppery spears away and backhanded Roxy before she had a chance to bring her clawed hands to bear. The big hand hit her across the chest and neck, sending her sprawling away.

Vert leaped, flipping forward in the air and suddenly accelerating down toward Roxy with one enormous fist leading the charge. Roxy kicked up to her feet, and as she saw Vert coming down, her cockiness broke for just an instant, but she deftly swept sideways before Vert's fist hit the ground. The concrete stage splintered and the entire theatre shook with a deep rumble. The crowd quieted for a breath before erupting into even louder cheers.

Vert roared and spun to face Roxy as she landed on him, both her clawed hands and all four of the spider-like limbs flying at his face. She grabbed him by the shoulders and let loose with all of her blades, stabbing at him a hundred times a second. Sparks flew off as the blades hit Vert's armor. His big hands slammed into her back once, twice, three times and Roxy winced with each blow, but did not release her grip on Vert's shoulders. Finally, he moved one huge arm between his face and Roxy's body and flung her aside, her spidery limbs raking across his back and head in one final protest before she was flying through the air again.

Roxy landed four meters away from Vert, rolling backward and springing back to her feet. Vert rolled his shoulders and jets of steam blew out of his joints with a loud hiss.

"He's using so much energy and producing so much heat," I said. "There's no way he can go very long in that glowing state."

"Professional fighting matches have ninety-second rounds," Bastion said.

"Giving him time to cool down between them."

Roxy must have already known this because she was running back toward Vert while he was still enveloped in a cloud of steam, but Vert was ready. He looked like he was winding up for one of his huge punches, but sidestepped Roxy at the last moment, grabbing one of the thin limbs attached to her back instead. Roxy twisted and tried to pull out of his grip but lost her footing as Vert used his height to pull her off the ground. Then he launched one foot into her back while yanking on her limb. Roxy went flying across the stage, crashing into one of the gaming booths, but the limb remained firmly in Vert's grip, twitching slightly as sparks leaped from the severed joint.

Vert threw the limb aside, and it skidded to a stop only a meter in front of me, dead and dull in the backstage shadows. Lubricant leaked slowly from the frayed end, making a dark puddle amidst twisted metal and obliterated wires. My heart was pounding, wondering how many more limbs would wind up at my feet, blood mixing with lubricant. Popping bones to go with snapping metal. First Roxy's lifeless body, and then my own. This plan was a terrible, terrible idea.

Roxy's seething roar brought me back to reality. Somehow, while I looked away, she had resumed her attack, now latched onto Vert's back. Despite all his incredible modifications and unimaginable brute force he'd managed to pack onto his frame, he was unable to grab her, his arms reaching and twisting, but unable to grab directly behind and above him. Roxy's clawed hands were dug into his shoulders, finding purchase between two different plates of armor, and two of her remaining spider-like limbs were feverishly working at his neck. She wasn't blindly stabbing at him this time. Her face was focused. She found something there and was determined to attack it.

A small piece of metal flew into the air and dropped next to the flailing fighters. It wasn't copper in color, but the bright metal of Vert's armor. He glanced at it, and I wished I could have seen Vert's expression. He stopped when he saw it and then did something that seem impossible given his size. He jumped, not straight up, but tucked his knees to his chest and somersaulted forward, Roxy still attached as the big man landed on his back. Right on Roxy. The noise was tremendous. Concrete cracking, metal buckling, and the dual screams of the two combatants.

Vert kicked up to his feet and spun on Roxy, who appeared dazed. He grabbed one of her feet just to yank her close enough to take hold of her neck with the other enormous fist and raise her off the ground. He slammed a fist into her body six times in as many seconds. The sound was thick, metal-on-metal, but even mods couldn't stand up to the kind of power that Vert put behind his punches. In an instant, Roxy gasped for air, coughed blood, and seemed to come out of her daze. She focused on Vert again right as his grip visibly tightened on her throat. He cocked his other arm back as the glowing intensified and the crowd noise grew to a deafening roar.

Roxy did not panic, though. Her face was full of rage, but also focus, a look that sent chills down my spine. Whether pouncing on helpless me outside Echo's shop or facing one of the greatest fighters our planet had ever seen, there was that face. Two of her spider-limbs flashed forward, slamming into Vert's face plate, right into those red eyes, which shattered and went dark.

Vert tossed Roxy aside, hard. She bounced on the concrete stage before getting to her feet. While she took deep gasps of air and massaged her throat, Vert grabbed the faceplate and wrenched it free. To my great surprise, his own eyes were undamaged. The plate had done its job, though it was now useless. He crushed it in his hand before dropping it and focusing his own baleful glare on Roxy.

The next three minutes were the most exhausting I'd ever witnessed in my life. Vert jabbed at Roxy's face. She dodged to the side and brought one clawed hand to bear at Vert's now-exposed face. He blocked it with a forearm and threw a hook at her ribs. She dodged again. On and on they went. Attack and dodge. Attack and block. Feints, rolls, flurries of limbs with neither making any meaningful contact. I counted more than a dozen ways I would have died in the first minute had I been fighting either of them. I definitely needed more training if I was going to keep clashing with people like these. Or more to Quynn's point, I needed to stop clashing with these people.

Vert and Roxy finally broke away from each other, both breathing heavily but still focused on one another. Steam was pouring off of Vert and the air around him seemed to boil. Roxy didn't give the big man more than a few seconds to cool down, though, she darted toward him again, her clawed hands drawn back for another swipe. At the last moment, Vert dropped to a knee and jabbed forward with both fists. It was a smart move, one that would have broken Roxy in half if it had landed. But Vert was slower, had been constantly slowing throughout the fight, probably overheating. Roxy leaped away, twisting through the air and landing right behind Vert.

In the span of a heartbeat, one of Roxy's spider-limbs launched upward at the back of Vert's neck, at the very spot she'd been working at earlier. The big Toinette man barely tilted his head when the bloodied end of that copper limb was suddenly sticking out of his left eye, jutting skyward and bloody. She'd made a gap in his armor. The back of the neck, probably an access panel for neuro mods. In and up went her blade, almost vertical. For a few devastating seconds, Vert's other eye darted around, confused, before it rolled up in his head and his jaw went slack. Roxy yanked her limb back and the big man fell in a heap on the stage, still steaming. Dead.

As though every molecule of oxygen had been sucked from the theatre, the crowd was silent.

Chapter Twenty-Nine

VERT'S REMAINING EYE WAS STILL open, rolled up while blood poured out of the other socket, pooling around his head like a red-black pillow. I knew this was a possibility, one I had been half-hoping for when I called Roxy. She'd promised this outcome, but actually seeing it was something different. I felt like I had on that Huginn yacht when Theo died right in front of me. Because of me. If I hadn't fought Theo, hadn't unleashed my shield in that pool, he would still be alive. If I hadn't called Roxy here to Cirilla, so would Vert. I was relieved, too, relieved that the big fighter would no longer be throwing me out of buildings, but my relief brought on even more guilt.

I did this. I was responsible. And there was no fixing it.

The crowd was booing now, hissing at this strange woman who had so brutally killed the famous fighter. She didn't bow or raise her hands in victory. She stared at Vert's lifeless corpse for several long minutes, folding her spider-limbs into her back before looking out at the crowd. Just looking, sweeping her gaze across them slowly. Then she turned and started straight for me.

"You did it," I muttered. "Of course I did," she said. "Thank you," I said through gritted teeth.

Roxy stopped and looked at me like I was an insect who somehow found its way into a sealed room. "We're not friends, Corto. We're square. That's it." Then she walked past me, bumping my shoulder as she went.

"You need to go back out there," I called after her.

She stopped. She didn't turn around but turned her head slightly toward me.

"They need to know who you are."

"I don't care about those people," she growled.

"The people watching," I said. "The people you want to impress. Tell them your name, at least. Silence the crowd for everyone to see."

Roxy growled. Then she strode back past me to the stage. The boos intensified until Roxy yelled at them to shut up while unfolding her spider-limbs again. Other than some gasps, the crowd went silent.

"As the old Earth saying goes," Bastion said. "You appear to have killed two birds with one stone."

Roxy started talking to the cameras. I didn't pay attention to what she said. I stared at Vert, that open eye gazing at nothing. "Killed. Yeah," I whispered to Bastion.

Roxy came back to me. She stopped less than a meter away and it took everything in me not to flinch.

"Thank you," she grumbled.

"For…?"

She grunted and moved past me. At least she didn't bump my shoulder this time. The crowd was moving now, some climbing the stage and talking, probably to their own live streams. I couldn't stay here any longer. I glanced at the big man's face one last time and said, "I will weep for you. I promise."

I turned and left, weaving through the giant boxes and other backstage detritus and out the door that led to another hallway of the convention center. I checked my corners, but Roxy was nowhere to be seen.

"How do you feel about that?" I asked Bastion.

"About Vert's death?"

"About Roxy just walking away. After what she did to you, to your friend back in the Corto lab."

Bastion was quiet for a moment before he said. "We're not done with her. She'll get what's owed. Just not today."

I let that sit with us for a few moments before I said, "Call Valdo, please."

"Are you alright?" Bastion said.

His question caught me off guard. I sputtered for a moment before I said, "I don't have time to not be."

"Vert is dead and Roxy is no longer after you. You should be relieved."

"You're right. I should be. And I am. But if I could have found a solution for my Vert problem that didn't end with his blood all over that stage, I would have taken it in an instant."

"But then Roxy—"

"Could have been a problem for another day," I spat, cutting him off. "Call Valdo now, please."

Bastion said nothing. CALLING VALDO appeared on my display.

"Hey," Valdo said.

"Are you ready?" I asked.

"I am," Valdo said.

"I'm on my way to you."

"Are you okay? You sound…off."

"People need to stop asking me that," I said in a huff. "Main entrance."

Valdo sighed, then said, "Main entrance."

"See you soon," I said and disconnected.

I took another deep breath and tried to clear my head, to focus on the task in front of me, but Vert's face was burned into my vision. Nevertheless, I put one foot in front of the other and started walking toward the side exit of the convention center, the one closest to the main entrance to the Offworld Relay.

"Hey," Quynn's voice called from behind me. They trotted to catch up and fell into step next to me. "That was brutal."

I nodded. We walked in silence for a couple dozen meters, Quynn slipping their hand into mine and squeezing gently. They knew. They were there on the yacht when Theo died, too. Now they'd been in the booth as Vert died.

"When all this is over," Quynn said after we'd stepped onto the escalator going back down to the ground floor. "We're going to work through it. See a therapist."

"You think I'll be able to tell a therapist about all of this?" I asked.

"Yes, I do. I guarantee there are other people in your line of work that see therapists. Therapists that know how to help and keep secrets."

I shrugged. I certainly wasn't opposed to therapy, I just didn't know how to process everything I was feeling right now, how to talk about it. But Quynn was right, I needed to. I'd barely been able to sleep since Theo died unless I was beaten and exhausted, and that was likely to get worse now. I said, "I'm with you. We'll talk about it when we're home, find someone to help."

"Good," Quynn said. "Off to the relay now?"

"Valdo is waiting for me there."

"Be careful."

"You always say that."

"Oh, so you do hear when I tell you that? Because based on what you tend to look like when you come back "

"Yes, yes, I know. I'll be careful."

"And keep the kid safe," Quynn said. "Remember, he's not in your line of work. Not your apprentice."

I winced, thinking of my actual apprentice comatose in a clinic back in the Corto Corporation borough. I wasn't able to keep him safe despite his training. How was I supposed to keep Valdo safe?

As though reading my mind, or at least my face, Quynn leaned in closed, holding my entire arm, and said, "You'll be fine. Just talk to him, give him instructions. Don't let him out of your sight."

"You make it sound so easy," I said as we stepped off the escalator.

"From everything you've told me, this kid looks up to you. Listens to you. Silent circuits, he broke into the relay's security and got back out all on his own."

"True," I said. "The kid really should be in my line of work."

Quynn grabbed me harder and pulled me aside. "Maybe, but he's not. Don't go planting that seed more than you already have."

That seemed to come out of nowhere, and the confusion must have been plain on my face.

"I love you. I'm with you. But what you do, it can be hard to live with sometimes. Every day when you walk out that door, I wonder if you'll come back. You're good. Very good. I know that, but it just takes one person who is too vigilant, one alarm system that is too sophisticated. One security guard who aims too well, and you'll never come home.

"Let Valdo be a kid for a little while longer. I'm glad you've helped him and that he's helping you, but you already have an apprentice who really needs your guidance. Keep Valdo safe, and then make sure he makes it back home to his mom, okay?"

"Okay," I said, fighting back tears. I truly was the luckiest woman on the planet to have a partner like Quynn, someone who cared so deeply for me. And they were the wisest, smartest person in any room. I kissed them, savoring that moment. "And thank you."

"Of course," Quynn said. "Now go. Don't keep him waiting any longer."

I kissed Quynn again, squeezed their hands, and reluctantly turned to go meet Valdo.

#   #   #

The kid was standing in front of the doors for anybody to see, despite the pair of cameras watching the main entrance from either side. He even waved when he saw me.

"You do realize we're about to break in, right?" I said to him over comms.

"They can't see me, remember?" he said. "A security guard could be staring right at that camera feed and would only see the doors."

"That's still amazing to me."

"I'll show you the code for my virus if it makes you feel better."

"I would like to see the code for his virus," Bastion said on my display.

"It would be meaningless to me, but thanks," I said to Valdo. "Did you happen to include me in that virus?"

"Do I have a complete VR rendering of you on file?" Valdo asked.

"No?" I said, not sure if he did or didn't. I wasn't sure how someone went about making one of those.

"No," Valdo said. "We're going to have to upload one once we're inside. Come on."

I shook my head at how easily this kid moved through computers and how confident he was in his abilities. Reminded me of myself at that age, though with locks. Reminded me of Nox, too. Maybe that was why Gustin and Solomon had assigned Nox to me: we were more similar than I wanted to admit.

The main entrance to the Offworld Relay was a wide arc like something had taken a smooth bite out of the base of the building. Six glass doors were right in the middle. I studied the two cameras as I approached. Old cameras, not of a make I knew, but close enough to a few different models from Huginn and Corto that it made no difference. They were both aimed at the doors, mounted three meters off the ground to either side, and pointed slightly downward. Between the two of them, there was no blind spot to speak of except directly above them.

Good thing I came equipped. I was closer to the camera on my right, so I aimed myself in that direction and took a running start, leaping slightly to put a foot on the base of the arc and triggering the gel that could stick me to just about anything. I usually used it for climbing buildings on all fours, but I didn't need to be that slow or precise right now. The processors in my legs were fast enough to stick and release the gel as I ran up the edge of the arc, running on a wall, and as I came close to the first camera, I reached down and snapped my fingers a few centimeters away. A mini-EMP fired as I did so, knocking the camera out of commission. I kept running along the arc, my hair sticking straight up as I inverted and then falling down the other side of my head as I kept running, snapping my fingers again to disable the second camera. I disengaged my gel, flipped a little, and landed lightly on my feet. I tossed my hair back into place and strolled up next to Valdo.

"You know I could have deleted you from the footage once we get inside?" Valdo said.

"Do I look like a tourist?" I asked. I had doffed my cosplay poncho as soon as I left the convention center, wearing only my bullet-holed black jumpsuit to go with my carbon-polymer limbs. It was mostly clean now. "If somebody is watching those feeds, they might not react to me like they react to you."

Valdo shrugged and then pulled open a door, waving me inside.

The halls of the Offworld Relay were plain but well-kept, just like in the VR recording I'd seen, though they were quieter now. No tour group was crowding the halls. I followed Valdo past dozens of closed doors, glass cases displaying documents and models, up two flights of stairs before we found the same Employees Only door Valdo had walked through in his recording. Valdo reached to pull the keypad off again, but I silently and gently grabbed his arm. He looked confused for only a moment before he moved aside. I plugged my data cable into the bypass port on the bottom and the door unlocked in less than a second.

Valdo's eyes widened. "I need one of those."

"The price is too high," I said, letting all meanings of the phrase wash over him. Quynn was right, I didn't need to sell him on this line of work.

The server room looked even bigger in person. Valdo walked more quickly now, no longer checking his corners or trying too hard to sneak. My awareness didn't change, however. Just like in the hallways, I was looking around every bend and listening intently for any possible presence other than ours. After we'd walked nearly one hundred meters through the racks of servers, Valdo turned right. A dozen meters down, he woke up a terminal and started typing.

"The higher we go, the closer to the maintenance hatch," Valdo said. "The security gets tighter. Better locks. Lots of cameras. We need to make sure their security system can't see you."

"Like it can't see you?" I asked.

He nodded and kept typing, then he mumbled to himself, "There has to be a scanner somewhere…"

"Scanner? Like biometric and cybermetric?" I extended my data cable toward him. "Because I have my scans on file."

"No. This is a virus I wrote that works on a 3D model. Biometrics look at your body shape, sure, but also your hair follicle pattern, irises, fingerprints. Really advanced ones can even look for internal organ structure. Cybermetric scanners look for your full loadout of cybernetic enhancements.

These cameras are just looking at shapes, colors, and density measurements."

"And you happened to have those files on yourself?"

"Among other things, yeah." Valdo kept typing, dozens of different UI windows appearing and disappearing. Valdo frowned. "That will have to do. Follow me."

He walked past me without pause, and I followed. We wound our way through another forty or so meters of server racks before we came to a different terminal. Valdo pulled a multitool out of his pocket and quickly started dismantling the terminal's display. In less than a minute, the circuits were exposed, and he extricated a small camera from the top of the display. I didn't understand what he was doing as he pulled on other wires in the terminal, changing the connections until the tiny camera had three times as many wires plugged into it. He gently inserted it back into the workstation and then started typing furiously again.

"You act like you've done this before," I said.

"Not exactly," he said. "But you'd be surprised how much different workstations and servers have in common. They can be built yesterday or decades ago, built by Toinette or Corto or whatever this GH company is, but they have more in common than not." With a flourish, he slapped the ENTER key and the camera's view filled the entire workstation display. Valdo pivoted the workstation toward me. There I was from the waist up, all in black, though there was an overlay of blue dots in varying density.

"Not very flattering," I said.

"Back up until you can see your entire body on the display," Valdo said.

I did, and then Valdo hit a key while standing next to the workstation. After a few seconds, he had me turn to the side and he did it again. Then my back, then the other side. Valdo turned the workstation back to himself, typed for another minute, and then started undoing the mess he'd made with the hardware.

"That's it?" I asked.

"We'll have to go back to the other workstation to update my virus," he said. "But that's it."

"And they won't detect your virus?"

Valdo gave a small chuckle. "They should hire me for their

cybersecurity. They have the right hardware in place, but their security software is embarrassing."

"Impressive," I said at the same time Bastion said it in my ear.

"Thanks," Valdo said. He finished his work quickly, checking to make sure everything looked as it had before he tore it apart. Then we made our way back to the other workstation. Within a few minutes, Valdo assured me that I would be absolutely invisible to the building security stations, so we proceeded to the next floor.

Bastion continued, "This young man is proving to be a valuable asset."

Valdo was right, the security systems were more formidable as we ascended floors. But considering how pitiful the lock on the server room was, that wasn't saying much. I bypassed half a dozen locks as we moved through the fourth floor, glancing sideways at every camera I saw. I knew I was invisible to them, but a lifetime of wariness was hard to shake. The fifth floor was nominally more complicated than the fourth, but even those locks were outdated by a few years. The sixth floor, the last before the great expanse in the building before the actual control room, proved to be the hardest. That lock was unfamiliar to me, but close to a design I'd seen in Nexus Neuronics last year. Still, I had it open in less than a minute, and Valdo and I found ourselves in a large room that covered the entire floor. It was stacked with crates, disused computer terminals and servers, dusty furniture, and Corto knew what else.

"Storage?" I asked. "Apparently," Valdo said.

"Then why give this floor the highest level of security?" Bastion asked.

"There must be something worth protecting in here," Valdo said.

"It could just be for the maintenance hatch," I said. "But I doubt it."

We wandered through the vast expanse, which was filled with antique servers and computer equipment, disconnected and collecting dust. Holiday decorations, old displays for tourists, and enough rope and stanchions for a hundred-meter line still didn't fill a third of the enormous space. Valdo was gawking at everything he saw, while I was on the lookout for something worth protecting, for some security measures Valdo hadn't anticipated. As Valdo led me through the refuse toward the maintenance hatch he'd seen on the schematics, I heard a faint, low humming that was growing louder as we walked.

"Your legs are detecting slight vibrations in the floor," Bastion said. "They are in time with the oscillation of that faint sound. Whatever that is, it is not small."

"Get behind me," I said to Valdo.

"But the hatch is just—" Valdo said.

"Behind me." I grabbed his arm and tugged until I was in front of him. I crept around a corner of a large stack of crates. The humming was instantly louder as I saw the source, three enormous, bulbous cylinders that ran floor to ceiling, at least six meters tall, yellow light coursing through them.

"Oh," Valdo said. "Oh?" I asked.

"Those must be part of the power structure for the Relay. Or maybe the data structure?"

"Those are capacitors," Bastion said. "Larger than anything I have ever seen. They are likely the last capacitors between here and the control room at the top, delivering enough energy to power half of Jayu City."

I relayed the information to Valdo, and the young man whistled in astonishment. "Those weren't on the schematics, but the maintenance hatch is right in the middle of them. In the ceiling."

"Are they dangerous?" I asked Bastion.

"How should I know?" Valdo said. "I didn't even know what they were."

I swallowed hard to keep from grimacing at my own lapse, speaking aloud to Bastion when someone else was around.

"They should be shielded," Bastion said. "But to be safe, I would advise not touching them."

"Sorry," I said to Valdo. "Thinking out loud. Just don't touch them, all right?"

Valdo looked at me like I'd grown a second nose. "Sure. All right."

We moved toward the maintenance hatch. There were three meters between each of the enormous capacitors, leaving plenty of room to navigate. Even from that distance, the hairs on the back of my neck stood on end as we approached. "Now it makes sense why this room is guarded," I said. "Imagine what would happen if someone tampered with even one of these."

"Probably kill themselves," Valdo said. "And shut down the entire

Offworld Relay."

The thought made me shiver, but not as much as finally seeing the maintenance hatch. It was mounted in the ceiling, far above our heads, a square two meters on each side. MAINTENANCE ONLY was stamped on it along each edge. In the center were the words WARNING. DO NOT OPEN WHILE RELAY IS OPERATIONAL. An enormous handle ran across the warning message.

"Somebody doesn't want this opened," I said. "Wonder what they're hiding?"

"That's what you get from 'warning' in giant letters?" Valdo asked.

"I've seen bolder language used to deter people like me."

"I have searched extensively for information on Offworld Relays. There is very little beyond some conspiracy theory discussion boards," Bastion said. "There is certainly no official information on what lies between here and the control room at the top. Nevertheless, I would heed those warnings."

I sighed, weighing my options and looking around. First, how to get up there? That was quickly answered when I saw a large button on the floor under a transparent polymer cover. Text around it said, "PRESS FOR LADDER." I bent down, lifted the polymer cover, and pressed the button. A rectangular panel opened, and a vertical ladder started to slowly expand from the floor to the ceiling.

"That's step one." I knew I had a lot of protections built into my jumpsuit and helmet. My mods could withstand a lot as well, but I had no idea what lay beyond that door. I turned to Valdo. "Go stand behind those crates. I'm going to open the hatch."

Valdo's eyes grew wide. "Is that a good idea?"

"I very much doubt this is a good idea," Bastion said.

I tapped the plate on the back of my neck. Nanobots started to form my sleek, black helmet around my head as I said to Valdo, "It's probably a bad idea. But odds are, I can handle it. Can you, no-mods?"

Valdo scrunched up his face, but then shook his head and slunk off, ducking behind the crates before yelling, "I don't like this!"

"I don't either, kid," I whispered. Then I climbed the ladder, reached up, swung the red handle a hundred and eighty degrees, and pushed.

Chapter Thirty

I WASN'T SURE IF IT was the blinding yellowish-green light, the intense heat, or the deafening roar that hit me first. It was like I'd opened a door into the center of a star. My display adjusted to the incredible light as my aural implants adjusted to the sound, only to reveal flashing red radiation warnings and alarms ringing. A Geiger counter on my display was blinking LETHAL EXPOSURE. My carbon-polymer hand, gripping the handle to the hatch, was bubbling and melting like wax in a frying pan. I yanked the hatch back down, hard, and flung the handle back into the locked position. Then I fell to the floor, the wind rushing out of me, but I couldn't wait for it to come back. I rolled onto all fours, vomited into my helmet as I stared at the concrete floor, and only then did I feel the pain rushing through every fiber of my organic tissue.

I tried to disengage my helmet, but instead of retracting into tiny robots, it fell away from my face in one piece, shattering on the floor in front of me along with the sloshing vomit it contained. I found myself surrounded by a gray fog. The Geiger counter on my display decreased over several seconds before disappearing, along with the flashing radiation warnings and alarms, but then I heard alarms going off outside of my mods. I vomited again, my stomach muscles spasming with the effort, but at least my helmet wasn't there to catch it this time. There was blood in my vomit.

The fog dissipated, a chemical obviously designed to clean off radiation, but that didn't get rid of what I'd absorbed. A thick arm was suddenly around me and helping me to my feet. Valdo. The man was young, but heavily built, easily supporting me. We were walking to the door, though I was doing little to help. I was overwhelmingly tired, achy, and disoriented.

"Need," I said. My voice was scratchy and it felt like a file raking across my throat. I took a deep breath and continued, "Adrenaline."

I couldn't think of the name of my onboard assistant program, couldn't be bothered to pretend to type. I needed the adrenaline and I needed it now. I just had to hope the exposure hadn't burned out Bastion's chip, secured as it was in my shoulder.

"What you need," Bastion responded, his voice breaking up," is a hospital. Your emergency nanobots are fried, but I can help with adrenaline."

Suddenly I went from incredibly tired to overwhelmingly conscious, the emergency injection system in my left leg doing its job, injecting synthetic adrenaline into my femoral vein. I straightened up to walk on my own and found the servos in my legs were a little sluggish, but my arms were even worse. The hand that had opened the hatch and most of that forearm were mangled, useless wrecks, barely resembling a hand and arm at this point. The other hand and arm were bubbled, slow, but not entirely useless.

"Are you okay?" Valdo asked. "Of course you're not okay. Your arm, the vomit. Was that blood? I'm pretty sure that was blood. We need to get you to a hospital, don't we? How are you standing? What do I do? Where do we—?"

"Emergency adrenaline shot," I said too quickly. "I'm good to go, but not for long." I pointed to the door through which we'd entered the sixth floor. "Are there any exits other than that stairwell?"

"Not that I saw," Valdo said. "We have to go back down to the third floor before there are multiple points of egress. But then, those capacitors weren't on the schematics, either, so—"

"No time to search," I said and started walking to the door. "We have to go now."

Valdo ran ahead of me and flung the door open without any regard for stealth, which was fair. With the alarms ringing in this enormous room and out in the hallway, our presence was no longer a secret. The light from the windows was bright compared to the room, though nothing compared to the space beyond the hatch. My display took too long to adjust, meaning my optical implants had also been damaged.

Valdo took three steps down, stopped, glanced over the railing of the stairwell down below, and turned back to me. He whispered, "They're coming!"

I couldn't even hear whatever he'd heard down the stairwell. Were any of my mods unaffected from those few seconds of exposure? I'd have to deal with that later. I trotted down the stairs past Valdo, every muscle aching with the movements. I stood in front of the window and pulled back a fist, but it was the wrong fist, the mangled one. I dropped it and pulled back my other fist, and then slammed it into the window. It spiderwebbed but didn't shatter. The arm felt weak, fatigued, and slow.

"Brace me," I said to Valdo. He ran down the stairs and grabbed me by the shoulders.

"For what?" he asked.

I leaned back, lifted a foot, and fired my pneumatic pistons in my leg as I kicked the window. It blew out, shards of glass flying away from the building and onto the roof of the attached convention center.

"What are you doing?" Valdo asked, his eyes wide as he looked outside.

I shrugged him off and turned, looking above until I found what I needed: a substantial metal frame around the door we'd just exited. I aimed my good arm at it and fired my magnetic grapple. Then I looked Valdo in the eyes and said, "Hold onto me tight. My other arm is useless, so I won't be able to help you."

I could see the whites around Valdo's irises, the fear and panic plain on his face. "Are we—?"

"Just do it! Hold tight and we'll be okay."

He grabbed hold of me around the waist, his thick arms squeezing hard and intensifying the pain wracking every part of me, but it was necessary. He held on and moved with me as I backed up to the edge of the window.

"On three," I said. "We jump."

"I am not certain your grapple will be able to handle the extra weight," Bastion said.

"Do you have a better idea?" I asked.

"What?" Valdo said.

"You have no idea what the Offworld Relay's security forces look like," Bastion said. "Given the lackluster security systems, you and Valdo might be able to—"

"One," I said. I knew where Bastion was going, but I was crippled. I could feel it. I was upright only because of the adrenaline, and I didn't know how long that would last. Once it wore off, I was going to pass out. I was in no shape to fight, and I wasn't going to put Valdo in that kind of danger.

"This is a terrible idea," Bastion said.

"Two."

Valdo hugged me tighter, practically taking the wind of out me.

"I'm calling Quynn," Bastion said.

"Three," I yelled. I jumped, firing my remaining pneumatics to clear the window as Valdo lifted his feet. The grapple cable whined, but it controlled our descent enough to keep the two of us from outright falling. We were only six stories up, but they were tall stories, easily twice the normal height, putting more than thirty meters between us and the roof of the convention center.

We arced out from the building, coming back toward it after descending a story and a half, I caught us with my legs, the windows of the tower crackling with the weight and my legs nearly buckling, but they held both of us. We bounced down the side of the building, repelling as smoke started to issue from the grapple. After a stressful thirty meters, we both touched down on the roof of the convention center.

I disconnected the magnet and tried to reel the grapple cable back in, but it wouldn't move. Burned out. "Silent circuits," I whispered and disconnected the grapple device from my arm, throwing it to the roof as the grapple cable fell from the open window high above.

"Come on," Valdo said as he scrambled toward the edge of the convention center.

I ran after him, the edges of my vision blurring and my stomach rolling as I approached.

"How do we get down?" Valdo asked.

I looked over the edge. Three or four meters to the well-manicured landscaping below. No problem for my modded legs. I looked at Valdo, and he was still afraid, glancing between the ground below and me.

"We have to jump," I said.

"Jump?" Valdo swallowed hard. "But I—"

"Bend your knees," I said. "Aim downhill and roll once you hit. Don't stiffen up. It's going to hurt, I won't lie. There's no other way. I don't have any other tricks to help you. My legs can't take your weight in addition to mine in a straight fall."

Valdo still looked afraid, but he set his jaw, looking over the side now not only with a little panic but with analysis. He was figuring it out, preparing himself. He kept his eyes on the ground when he said, "On my count this time?"

"You got it," I said. The adrenaline was wearing off in a hurry. My alertness was fading, everything going quiet and dark.

"One," Valdo said, creeping closer to the edge.

I picked a spot on the ground to land, a spot far enough away to be easy for my legs and out of Valdo's roll.

"Two," Valdo said. He sucked in a breath and blew it out hard.

For my part, I tried not to wobble.

"Three," Valdo jumped. I jumped. As the ground rushed up to meet me, the entire world spun on its axis and went dark.

#   #   #

"…can't expect her to do more. Look at her." The voice was familiar. Very familiar. "Not only is it her job, but this is more important than you could understand." A deeper voice. Gruff. Solomon?

"Don't talk down to me like I'm a child! I can understand a lot if you would bother explaining." Quynn. Definitely Quynn. At least they were yelling at someone else.

"You don't have "

"The clearance. You've said that. But she has the clearance, doesn't she? And since I'm her corporate partner, she can tell me anything, right?"

"Not anything."

"Mother of—!"

\#   \#   \#

"…tube is to make sure she doesn't vomit on herself again."

I didn't know that voice. I tasted plastic and vomit, though. I tried to open my eyes but couldn't.

"Thank you, doctor," Solomon said.

"I can't look at her like this," Quynn said. "I can't."

"She's going to be all right. The doctor said—"

"I heard the doctor! It's your fault she's like this! Your fault she keeps going after these dangerous people, flying out of these buildings and, what, jumping into a nuclear reactor?"

Was that what happened? A reactor? I was so tired. More tired than I'd ever been. The last day, two? Seemed like a blur.

"I assure you, Quynn, I did not send her into the Offworld Relay. Perhaps this young man from Toinette would care to actually speak and tell us why you two were there?"

Silence followed Solomon's question. How many people were here with me? My stomach lurched, but nothing else happened. Maybe I could just sleep again.

"Valdo, isn't it?" Solomon said. "Speak up! What were you two doing there?"

Valdo. The Relay. Of course. My memories were like dreams. Hazy and fluid, not making any sense. "She can tell you when she wakes up," Valdo said.

Wake up? No, thanks. I just wanted to sleep. Sleep.

\#   \#   \#

I opened my eyes, the lids heavy as responsibility. Everything was bright.

Fuzzy. I blinked over and over, the room around me slowly materializing and coming into focus. Valdo was on my left, staring out the window. A meter away from him, dozing in a chair in the corner, was Solomon. I was laying down in a bed. A hospital bed, a white and baby blue checkered blanket covering me. Quynn was on my right, holding my hand, looking at me with a weak smile.

"Hey, love," they said.

I tried to speak, but there was something in my mouth. A plastic taste.

"Don't talk," Quynn said. "You're in the hospital. Valdo called an ambulance. There's a tube down your throat. I'll get the doctor."

Another hand grabbed my left and gently squeezed. I turned back that way, slow like moving through an ocean of slush. Valdo. His eyes welled up with tears as I looked at him. He looked worried. Scared. I tried to squeeze back, but nothing happened. I glanced down at my hand, the ruined one, melted beyond repair.

Solomon stood, as stoic as ever. "About time."

Slowly, I made an obscene gesture toward him with my good hand.

Solomon shook his head and walked out of the room. A moment later, Quynn returned with a tall person with light brown skin, bright red hair, and a white coat over green scrubs. The newcomer smiled brightly, the high-contrast makeup on their cheeks sticking out as they did so.

"I'm Doctor Silvestri, she/her," she said. She looked past me to the wall or maybe some machines, pressed a few buttons out of my sight, and then said, "I think we can take this tube out of you. We've got your rads down to a manageable level. The tube in my mouth jiggled a bit before Dr. Silvestri snapped on gloves and took hold of it right in front of my face. "Hold still. Don't try to swallow or cough until I'm done." She counted to three and pulled, which felt like someone was scraping my insides out. The urge to cough was intense, but I held on until she was done before breaking out into a fit of them.

"Mother of Corto," Quynn whispered.

"This is perfectly normal," Dr. Silvestri said. "Can one of you get her a cup of water?"

Valdo practically leaped and ran out of sight. He returned soon with a translucent polymer cup filled near to the brim with water. Dr. Silvestri took it from him with a slight nod and put it to my lips.

"Slowly," she said, though she was in full control of the speed. The water was cool, sliding down like a salve. "Talking is going to be painful for a few days, and you're going to be very tired for a while."

I nodded, tried to speak, and immediately regretted it.

"Then there's this," Dr. Silvestri said, pointing to a spot high on my chest, just below my right collarbone. I looked and saw a flat, round, black disk attached to me, the skin around it red and raw. "You'll need this or its equivalent built into your mods for the rest of your life for regular doses of anti-cancer nanobots. You're lucky to be alive after that high dose of radiation, but you'll have to stay on top of it to make sure it's not lethal in the long run."

I nodded again and sighed.

"I want to see you eat and keep your food down, then you can leave, okay?"

"Okay," I croaked out.

Dr. Silvestri smiled, patted my hand, and walked out of the room. Quynn resumed their post next to me, their hand around mine, and was surprisingly kind while we waited for my food to arrive. They didn't lecture me or threaten to leave me again. Valdo stayed on the other side of me, worry still written plainly across his face.

"Are you okay?" I whispered to Valdo. He nodded and smiled sadly.

"Hey," Quynn said, pulling my eyes back to them. "You kept him safe. You kept to your word and kept me in the loop. Everyone is safe. You worry about you."

I cleared my throat, which was like swallowing a knife, and whispered, "Solomon?"

"Oh, he's livid. Valdo and I know what you were doing at the Relay, but the old man doesn't. He's probably pacing in the hall."

He was. Everything was so tangled up that I didn't know how to work my way free of the knot. Here I was, nearly unable to move. Quynn knew the whole truth of why I was trying to get into the Offworld Relay, but Valdo was only partway in. Then Solomon was on the outside, wondering what I was getting up to when I was supposed to be focused on Tazia. Valdo knew practically nothing about that, and I still had to keep Solomon's identity as Cloak of Corto a secret from both Valdo and even Quynn. Only Bastion knew everything I knew, though he'd been strangely silent since I'd woken up. All I could think to do was squeeze Quynn's hand and look at them helplessly. "Valdo," Quynn said. "Would you give us a few minutes?" Valdo nodded.

"Thank you," Quynn said to him quickly, like they were afraid he would be offended. "You brought Elise here. Contacted me. Thank you for all of that."

"You're welcome," Valdo said. He looked at me with that sad smile, nodded again, and left the room.

Once the door was closed, Quynn said, "So, Solomon is the Cloak?"

If I hadn't been laying down, my jaw would have dropped.

"That's what I thought," they said as they reached into a pocket in their pants.

"How?" I whispered.

"I'd suspected for a while. A few years. But in the last two hours, the way he talks and moves, why he's even here, it all just started to click for me."

I gave Quynn a pleading look.

"Don't worry, I won't tell anyone." They pulled something small and shiny out of that pocket. Bastion's chip. That explained a few things. Quynn said, "They needed to run some scans on you. I took it out just in case." I reached my left hand over to open the compartment in my right shoulder, but soon remembered that hand wasn't going to be able to open anything anytime soon. "I've got it," Quynn said. With nimble fingers, they opened the compartment on my shoulder and replaced Bastion's chip in the secure, padded compartment I'd added for it. Once it touched my modded arm, it sparkled back to life.

"Elise?" Bastion said in a panic. "Elise? Are you all right?"

"I am, Bastion," I whispered. "At least I will be."

After a few seconds, Bastion said, "Your systems are all damaged from the radiation exposure. The left hand and forearm are total losses. You'll want to replace your—"

I held up a hand, knowing he could see it through my vision. He stopped talking. Then I looked at Quynn and gestured toward them. A moment later, Bastion connected a call to Quynn so the three of us could talk together. Then slowly through my raspy voice and intermittent sips of water, I explained the knot of secrets and lies that I couldn't untie. Who was inside, who was out, and how I couldn't navigate all of it. It took me far too long to tell it all, and my throat ached when I was done. Finally, I rested my head back and waited for one or both of them to throw out some brilliant, bewildering plan.

After several long minutes, Quynn finally said, "The truth."

I didn't expect that, and my face showed that plain.

"You trust Valdo. You trust Solomon. I understand why you're trying to get to the top of that Relay. I also understand why you have to stop Tazia. Give them the information and let them sort it out. They'll side with you, or they won't, but these twisted lies will be out of the way."

"I have to agree with Quynn," Bastion said, surprising me even more. "Valdo has proven an ally you can trust with your life on more than one occasion, someone who seems to value you above many things in his life. Solomon has entrusted you with his nephew, entrusted you to be the only Intel Operative here on Cirilla with him. He is the Cloak of Corto. There is no way to divulge the truth without divulging my existence, and I trust both of them with that secret."

My eyes were wide, drying out in the arid hospital room, but my face didn't know how else to react.

Quynn smiled. "We have to trust people in this life, especially with how muddled our lives have become, the three of us. Bastion is right."

I took another few sips of water and then nodded. Quynn left the room and came back a few moments later with both Valdo and Solomon in tow. They both stood at the end of the bed. Once Quynn took their seat again, Bastion connected a call with all of us. I knew it would appear to them both that I was just calling them even though I was in the room with them. They looked appropriately confused. Then I took a deep breath and said, "I have someone that you both need to meet."

CHAPTER THIRTY-ONE

VALDO AND SOLOMON WERE THE pictures of opposites. Valdo with his dark skin, smooth and young, his mouth hanging open in astonishment. Solomon, his skin much paler, his chin and head stubbled in black and gray, lines and creases of well-earned experiences blooming from the corners of his eyes. He looked on the verge of rage as Bastion and I finished telling the entire story from our chance encounter in a Nexus Neuronics apartment to now.

The two didn't speak, though I could hear Solomon breathing heavily through his nose. After a minute, and then another like that, Solomon rubbed his head, pointed at Valdo, and said, "You do realize that this young man is not a Corto Corporation citizen?"

I opened my mouth to answer, but Solomon didn't stop.

"A secret AI that shouldn't exist, developed by our own CEO. A conspiracy kept secret even from the Intel division, and a Toinette kid is sitting here listening to all of it. Toinette! The company of the very woman we're trying to stop from evangelizing all of Jayu City! Did it ever occur to you that he could be her mole? Her inside informant?"

Valdo redirected his shock to Solomon now, opening his mouth to defend himself, but Solomon wasn't done.

"Even if he isn't." Solomon was pacing back and forth now, gesturing wildly with his hands as he spoke. "He's not one of us! He's some kid you literally bumped into and blackmailed into helping you! You even gave him what he wants and he's still here! Doesn't that seem suspicious?"

"You don't know him," I said.

"I don't! I thought I knew *you*, but all this? Are you out of your mind? You have a good life, a good job that you love. Is it dangerous sometimes? Sure. Are you putting yourself into even greater danger by following the whims of some so-called AI?"

"An AI that our CEO developed," Quynn chimed in. "In secret."

Solomon stopped and eyed Quynn, not saying anything. I couldn't decipher the look.

"What would you have done in Elise's shoes?" Quynn said. "Revealed the AI and threatened to upend all of Corto Corporation? Because that's what would happen if Bastion's connection to Ariela Corto was made public. It would threaten us all."

Solomon fell back into a chair and rubbed his stubbled head even harder.

"I'm not saying I've made the right decision at every turn," I whispered hoarsely. "I've done what I thought was right. Was best. Now here we are, this close to finding if there is some connection between the companies and figuring out what Tazia is after."

"Tazia…" Valdo mumbled.

Solomon waved a hand in the air like he was casually swatting a bug. "I know what Tazia is after."

Now it was my turn to look shocked. I gawked at him, then to Quynn who looked at me in surprise, then we all looked back to Solomon. "When were you planning on letting me in?" I asked.

Solomon worked his jaw and looked around at the three of us, still agitated, but finally said, "That trick you pulled with Vert and Roxy worked. Not just in killing Vert. Good job, by the way."

The compliment felt like a slap in the face. A reminder of my part in Vert's death, my shame in it. The look on Valdo's face echoed my shame as his eyes widened and his jaw clenched.

Solomon continued. "Tazia was so thrown off by the public fight and Vert's very public death, she slipped up." He glanced at Valdo, distrust plain on Solomon's face. "I found out who the so-called kid is, who Tazia has been meeting with here. Everything fell into place once I had that name."

He didn't want to say it out loud, not with Valdo here. I said, "I trust Valdo, Solomon. Don't you trust me?"

The Cloak of Corto looked back to me, several emotions at war on his face. "I did. I thought I did. But everything you just said, it's—"

"More than you could have expected," Bastion said. He was still connected to everyone in the room via comms. "Elise did not believe me at first, either. She thought I was a hacker cleverly reaching out through my chip. You taught her to be wary, as you are now, but she knows I am what I say I am. She knew before Dr. Ariela Corto confirmed it. And Valdo has saved us on two occasions now."

Solomon stared at me. "Only because you promised him something he wanted."

"Needed," Valdo said almost in a whisper, staring at the floor. "Without the Preg Vaxxus B, my mom will die."

"You have it," Solomon said. "Why are you still here?"

Valdo slowly lifted his eyes to me. He looked haggard. "Elise is my friend. Maybe my only friend, the only person who has ever seen me as more than a kid who messes with old computers too much. And she kept her promise. She risked a lot to do it, too." He smiled just a little. "That's what we do, right? Help each other?"

Solomon's face softened the tiniest amount as he kept his eyes trained on the young man.

"Somehow," I croaked. "I've found myself so far in over my head, I can't see the surface, certainly not on my own. Bastion, the CEO, Theo. The man told me one thing before he died. He hated me, wanted to kill me, but he refused to die without someone knowing what he knew. I have to find out if there's something to it. Maybe it's nothing, just some dead-end Theo was chasing, but I have to know."

"And Tazia?" Solomon said.

I nodded. "We have to stop her, too."

"We don't have much time," Solomon said. He looked to Valdo once again, the young man meeting his eyes this time. After several long seconds, Solomon grunted and turned back to me. "Orogen Siwa Kotega, second son of Tenisha Siwa Kotega."

"Tenisha? The CEO of Kotega Systems?" Quynn said.

Solomon nodded. "Orogen Siwa is one of the competitors in the tournament. He's quite good, from what I gather. His gaming handle is Vitamin K."

Quynn nearly jumped out of their seat. "Vitamin K? He's one of the top five players on the planet!"

"What do you two…?" Solomon glanced at Valdo again. "You all know about Kotega's rules for succession for their CEO?"

Valdo and I both shook our heads. Quynn said, "Hereditary, but not automatically given to the oldest child like some old Earth monarchy or something. The CEO chooses the next CEO from their children or close family."

"Exactly," Solomon said. "Tenisha Siwa is rumored to announce her retirement soon, and therefore her successor. Her third child, Miere Siwa is the heir apparent, the most focused of Tenisha's children, but Orogen Siwa is seen as a close second."

It was like the clouds parted and the sun shone through. Vert had mentioned an entire borough joining *the fold*. This was what he meant. "And given the Kotega focus on honor, I'm guessing winning a huge tournament like this one would be a coup for young Orogen Siwa?"

Solomon nodded.

"And Josephi… I mean, Tazia got to him, to Orogen," Valdo said.

"Right again," Solomon said. "I think he's fully converted to Ibhalism. So if he were to succeed as CEO of Kotega Systems…"

"The prophets of Toinette would gain unlimited sway over Kotega through its CEO," Bastion said. "Effectively merging the two companies into one."

"Then it would just be a matter of time before they set their combined strength on taking more," Quynn said.

"Corto Corporation would have to merge with Huginn or Nexus just to have enough capital to stay in the game, fighting over whichever company was left out in the cold," I said. "Assuming we weren't the ones freezing."

Solomon was nodding along as we put all the pieces together. "Exactly what Dr. Ariela tasked us with stopping." Then he looked directly at me. "You still think you need to go up in that relay?"

I worked my jaw. He was right. While I needed to go up there, to find out how the companies were connected, there was a more pressing matter. Tazia's plan would destabilize Jayu City. Corto Corporation would have to merge or be devoured, ending our way of life as we knew it. The idea of becoming a boisterous Huginn or a nonchalant Nexus or some pious Toinette made me nauseous all over again. I couldn't afford to split my attention. I sighed, about to say it would wait, when Valdo said, "I'll go up there."

We all turned to him. "Alone?" I asked.

He shrugged. "Stopping the Ghost of Toinette from making sure Kotega's chosen successor wins a video game tournament? I'm no help to you there. I could hack a gaming rig, sure, but those things are checked and re-checked before every match. But I can make my way to the top of the relay, find out what I can, and get back down."

"Alone?" I asked again.

"Alone," he said with finality. He looked at Solomon. "Though if you wanted to help me with the planning, I wouldn't refuse it."

"I'll go with him," Quynn said.

Solomon shook his head. "We need you as eyes. Unlike Elise and I, you actually look like you belong at this tournament. You know the lingo and the players."

It took all I had not to sigh with relief. Valdo going up the relay alone made me nervous enough, but if something had happened to Quynn because of my obsession, I never would have forgiven myself.

Quynn opened their mouth to protest.

"It's okay," Valdo said to them. "I've got this under control. You three take care of Tazia, I'll see what there is to be seen up the relay."

"You're sure?" Solomon asked, looking back to the kid. For a moment, I swore I saw a glimmer of concern Solomon only directed at Nox, but only for a moment.

Valdo looked at me long and hard. He looked disappointed or sad or some combination of those. Then finally, he just nodded.

#   #   #

After keeping down my bland dinner, the doctor let me leave with detailed instructions on keeping cancer at bay for the rest of my life, including several vials of anti-cancer nanobots, enough to last me a month. Quynn took me back to their hotel room, where I switched to my everyday limbs and got to really survey the damage done to my work limbs. The left hand and forearm looked like a black, mechanical skeleton coated in melted and cooled carbon polymer. The rest of the arm was warped, and most of the internal mechanisms had been exposed to too much heat too quickly. The shoulder was barely functional. The right arm fared better, though it only had twenty percent mobility left. My legs looked fine, though the radiation had damaged the internal parts enough to make them both a little slow and creaky. The nanobots stored in the plate on my neck were burned up. My aural and ocular implants were damaged, making the world look and sound a little muddled. All that damage was going to affect my ability to do anything tomorrow. Solomon gave Quynn and me a little time to get settled, and then joined us to walk through his plan for the next day. It was less a plan than a to-do list since we didn't know any details about Tazia's plan. There was even a chance we were completely wrong about Orogen Kotega, but it was the most logical conclusion. After only an hour of planning, my eyelids grew too heavy for me to contribute.

"I think that's it for tonight," Quynn told Solomon.

Solomon glanced at me. For the first time all night, I thought I saw a glimmer of sympathy on his face, but it didn't last. Especially in front of Quynn, he was all business. But he nodded and said, "Tomorrow, then. You both have as much instruction as I can give you."

Quynn rose as Solomon did, walking him to the door. They spoke too quietly for me to hear, both glancing at me on occasion. I was honestly too tired to even care. I nodded off, waking a little as Quynn was brushing their teeth. They helped me out of my clothes and under the blankets, and I was deep asleep in seconds.

We woke early the next day and ate breakfast in Quynn's room. My stomach argued but kept it down. I felt like I'd been run over. Nevertheless, we geared up as best we could. My work legs were fully charged and functional enough for most things, so I put them on, along with my partially functioning right arm. The left arm would be useless, however, so I kept my everyday limb on the left. I felt off-balance and weak with the mismatched limbs, but I had no other choice unless I wanted to walk around with only one arm. I put on my floral-print shirt and black pants over my work jumpsuit. It was hot and uncomfortable, but I wanted to be ready for anything.

We took the hotel shuttle to the convention center to enter right as it opened. Quynn led me to the official *Dregs of Osiris* merchandise store and bought me an iridescent purple cape designed to drape over my left side, hiding the mismatched arm. The cape cost way too many credits, but I could tell Quynn was excited for the excuse to make the purchase. After this weekend, I certainly wouldn't need it again, so it would be Quynn's souvenir.

Finally, Quynn and I embraced, and we went our separate ways. Quynn was to wander the convention like any other attendee, feeding Solomon and me information. I was heading for the security offices.

"Third floor," Bastion said. "Positioned directly in the center of the building."

"Thanks," I said. I stepped onto an escalator with dozens of convention-goers, trying to look like I belonged. "How are you doing with the big reveal last night?"

"It makes me a little nervous," he said. "Much like I was when I first revealed myself to you. And Quynn. And Hessod."

"But I kept my word, let you decide this time."

"Yes. I appreciate that. And both Quynn and Hessod give me faith in how you judge whom to trust. And you have to admit, it makes today easier."

"That it does." I stepped off the escalator, made a U-turn, and stepped onto another going up to the third floor.

"What is your plan?" Bastion asked.

"You remember that security office in the Huginn brothel?" I asked.

"Vale of the Valkyries. Yes, I remember."

"Pretty much that."

"This is not a brothel."

"No, but the strategy is sound. Pretend I'm a mess of tears. Scream some. Make everybody uncomfortable so they drop their guard. You tell me where to plant our little backdoor device."

"You have so little faith in security personnel."

"That's true."

A family was standing just ahead of me on the escalator. Two adults and three kids, all of them pretty young. I didn't know *Dregs of Osiris* or any other game, really, but everyone in the family was in coordinating costumes like they were a superhero team or something. "Definitely not a brothel. That's not the point. Just variations on a theme."

"If you say so," Bastion said.

I stepped off the escalator and wove through the crowds until I found a heavy set of double doors labeled SECURITY. The hallway leading to it was heavily outfitted with cameras, including a wide-angle lens right above the door. I had to get in character before I approached. I turned away, looking out the enormous windows over the rest of Cirilla, all tropical trees and towering resorts. People were still streaming in for blocks. I set my feet, loosened my knees, and triggered the modified tear ducts behind my modified eyes. I messed my hair, plastered a look of misery on my face, and wailed as I turned and ran directly toward the security doors.

"Where is he?" I screamed. The crowds parted before me, shock and disgust and fear on dozens of faces. Parents yanked their children out of my path. A few just gawked or giggled. I ignored them all and kept running and screaming. "Where is he?"

I flung myself against the door, beating on it while sliding down to my knees, letting the tears pour down my cheeks. I wailed into the metal door, pounding my fists as though the secret to eternal life was on the other side. After twenty or so seconds, the door opened and I tumbled inside, bawling on the floor like a toddler.

In an instant, there were hands on my shoulders, hauling me upright. A concerned face was way too close to mine. Sharp cheekbones and lightly painted eyes looking at me with pity. "Where is who?" they asked. "Where is who? Please, take a breath and tell us who you're looking for."

"My son!" I whimpered, which made the stranger flinch back from me. One advantage to the breathing tube: I already sounded like I'd been crying and screaming for hours. I glanced around like I was a wild animal cornered, but I was examining the room. It was tiny, maybe two meters square. Just a vestibule. Another pair of heavy double doors were on the other end. There was another security guard in the vestibule. They were taller, broader, and staring out the open door into the rest of the convention center. I continued, "I can't find him. He was right there, right with me…" I let my words muddle into unintelligibility from there.

"All right," the stranger said. "All right. Let's sit you down and figure this out."

I let Painted Eyes lead me aside while their partner silently closed the door. Once it was shut, a low buzz sounded, and the partner opened a door on the other side of the vestibule. Then they held the door open as Painted Eyes led me into a room much larger than I'd anticipated. It was similar in design to Necropolis Alpha. Rows of long desks with workstations started near the door and descended, theatre-style, toward the bottom of an enormous screen on the other end of the room. This room, however, was easily three times the size of Necropolis Alpha. Dozens of security camera feeds from all over the convention center were on the enormous screen and the hundred or so workstations, each operated by a security guard.

"Oh my," Bastion said in my ear.

That was an understatement. Most security offices were smaller than my living room. I'd never seen more than four guards stationed in one. This was on a whole different level. I was going to have to keep this ruse going far longer than I liked.

Painted Eyes sat me down near the back wall, farthest from the enormous screen, while their partner walked away. Other guards, all wearing matching navy-blue button-downs and khaki pants, occasionally glanced over their shoulders to see what the fuss was all about, but most stayed focused on their work. The partner returned with a small paper cup, which they handed to me. It was half-filled with water.

"Drink," Painted Eyes said. "Take a few deep breaths. What's your name?"

I made a big show of trying to calm down, shakily taking sips of water, and letting the heaving cry keep welling up and taking over, drawing out the moment as long as I could while slowly scanning the room. I could see a lot, but with Bastion accessing my optical implants, I knew he was capturing images, zooming in, and closely examining everything in my field of vision much faster than I could.

Painted Eyes glanced aside at their partner, impatience starting to show. Time to bleed the moment for all I could. I said, "El…Ellie. My…name…is Ellie. Sh…sh…"

"She/her?" Painted Eyes asked.

I nodded.

The impatience evaporated into a warm smile. "Okay, Ellie. I'm Joanna, she/her." She tilted her head toward her partner. "And that's Gray, they/them. Tell us everything. Your son's name. Age. What is he wearing? How tall is he? Hair and eye color, anything to help us look. Where were you last when you saw him? Every detail could help us."

A dozen different workstations suddenly lit up on my display, highlighted in yellow.

Bastion said, "These are the high-clearance workstations. Place the piggyback within ten centimeters of any of them, and I'll do the rest."

I focused on the one closest to me, three rows down and four meters to my right. Then I glanced up at the giant screen at the front of the room and started screaming.

Chapter Thirty-Two

I SHOVED JOANNA OUT OF the way, practically knocking her to the floor as I flailed about, drawing every eye in the room toward me. I draped myself over the guard working the nearest workstation, grabbing at their shirt and screaming in their face. They leaped out of their chair and backed away quickly. I knocked their chair over and tossed myself about like I was aimless and frantic, though I was moving closer and closer to a workstation that Bastion had highlighted.

"Ellie," Joanna called to me. "Ellie! Please calm down!" She didn't sound very calm herself.

Security guards were jumping out of their seats, trying to get out of my way as I careened across the workstations, playing up a frantic mother out of her mind looking for her lost son, looking desperately for hope and answers in every face she saw.

I held close to my training, exuding overdrawn emotion while staying focused and calm beneath the surface. I knew my target, the workstation only a few meters away now. I knew the piggyback device was in the left pocket of my pants. Every scream and frantic grab was improvised but thought out. My body was on fire after yesterday's radiation exposure, especially my throat. I was short of breath from all the screaming, but it wouldn't last much longer.

Then hands were on me. I whirled on them. Joanna, Gray, and another security guard I didn't know had tried to grab me, but they pulled back with a start when I whirled. Gray was still expressionless. Joanna looked concerned and a little frightened at the same time. The guard I didn't know just looked like they didn't want to be anywhere near me.

"Where is he?" I screamed at them. "Where? Why can't you find him?" I grabbed the chair nearest me and thought about flinging it across the room. But that would elicit too severe a reaction. If I was seen as a danger, they would likely subdue me with far less compassion. So long as I was just frantic, they would merely contain me. I fell to the ground, making it look like I'd stumbled, and then crawled closer to the target workstation, working my way back to my feet as I moved along.

"Please, Ellie," Joanna said. "If you would just calm down and talk to us, I'm sure we could help you. We have cameras all over the convention center and some of the best facial recognition software on the planet. Do you have a picture of him? Of your son? Please."

I ignored her, climbing to my feet with the help of a chair while I palmed the piggyback device from my pocket. It was round, only a few millimeters thick, and about the size of my thumbnail. I peeled the polymer backing off the adhesive side, leaving the backing in my pocket. Thank Corto for the incredible dexterity of cybernetic fingers. Then I fake stumbled again, this time right onto the workstation. I slapped one hand hard on the table right next to it, pressing the piggyback under the table right beneath the workstation in the same instant. Then I fell to the floor, sobbing.

"Testing connection," Bastion said. A hand touched my leg and I meekly kicked it away.

"Connection successful," Bastion said. "I have access to all of their cameras, remote locks, and communications. Now get out of there."

I sobbed even harder to cover the sigh of relief I wanted to let out. Time to leave. Right. Now that I was in deep with this missing-kid bit, I wasn't sure how to get out. I'd done with angle before, but usually with only a few guards. Twice, I knocked them unconscious and left. Playing stupid or forgetful had also worked in the past, guards so anxious to get me out of their office that they didn't even argue. This was different. There were too many guards, I'd caused too much of a scene, and Joanna was still too invested in actually helping me find this nonexistent child.

I let her help me to my feet and then sit in a chair that I'd knocked down. They brought me more water, as if that would help, though my sore throat was thankful for it. I glanced at the enormous screen at the front of the room, looking for a child alone, one I could pretend was mine, but the few I saw were accompanied by adults.

"Gray?" someone said, and Gray walked off toward the voice.

I pretended to hyperventilate as the camera angles cycled on the enormous screen. Professional gamers, convention attendees ranging from their late teens through middle age, staff members, and more security guards, but there just weren't enough children and none that were alone.

Gray returned and said to me, "We've found him, ma'am."

"What?" I blurted out, my surprise genuine this time. How had they found the child I'd made up? It didn't make any sense, and I didn't know how this could turn out well for me.

"He turned up here," Gray said, turning and heading back to the doors and beckoning me to follow. Joanna smiled so genuinely that it made my heart ache a little for her. Gray continued, "He was looking for you, asking for you by name and description."

I didn't know what to do other than play along, so I gasped and started crying again, effusive as I ran ahead of Gray toward the doors. They didn't open until Joanna passed a hand over a black panel on the wall. Then I bounced on the balls of my feet waiting for the first set of doors to close so they would open the second. I didn't know what I would find on the other side, but at least I would be able to run away if things went poorly.

The second set of doors opened, and there was Solomon. He smiled and placed his hands on a young person standing in front of him. About the right height, wearing what I'd described, and matching the vague description I'd given closely enough to be convincing.

"Mom!" the kid yelled and suddenly hugged me.

I grabbed him back, taking his face in my hands and looking him over like this was the child I'd actually lost.

"I found him over on Concourse C," Solomon said. "I figured this was the best place to bring him."

"Thank you," Joanna said to Solomon and then turned to me, "Please be more careful. Enjoy the convention."

I nodded briefly and turned my attention back to the child like the attentive mother I pretended to be. The two guards disappeared back behind the double doors, and I took the child's hand and began walking away, still playing the part. We moved down the hall, the child pretending as well and glancing at Solomon occasionally. Once we rounded a corner, Solomon finally nodded to the kid, who let go of my hand, took off the green windbreaker he'd been wearing, handed it to me, and ran off.

"Who—?" I started to say.

"Bastion told me," Solomon said. "Little Neeraj there looked the part. I bought him a five-year subscription to some game and put that jacket on him."

"Thank you for that," I said.

Solomon nodded once without smiling. Then his eyes changed focus, looking into the middle distance instead of at me. "Piggyback is working. You know what to do." He walked away before I could say another word.

"Yeah, I know what to do," I said to myself.

"Do not take it personally," Bastion said. "I don't think he's angry, just task-oriented."

"I think he's always a little angry."

"That is possible."

I sighed. No point worrying about that right now. I said to Bastion, "Have you found him yet?"

"Orogen Kotega is on the first floor in a room the professional gamers call, 'The Pit.'"

"The Pit?" I headed toward the nearest escalator heading down.

"One moment," Bastion said. "Flailing mother, huh?" Quynn said on my comms.

"Works every time," I said. "What's this pit?"

"The Pit," Quynn said. "Every tournament has one. It's the room set aside for the pro gamers to relax, eat, get away from the fans."

"Pro gamers only?" I asked.

"Pro gamers, coaches, and tournament staff," Quynn said. "But he has a match in twenty minutes."

I reached the bottom of the escalator and stepped aside. "Where?"

"Why?" Quynn asked. "You want to jump him on the way?"

"I can't act against him directly," I said. Solomon hadn't said it last night because he knew I knew. Even in our line of work and with the lack of rules, CEOs and potential CEOs were off-limits. Orders directly from the Intel VP. The blowback was just too much if we were discovered to be working against someone at that level.

Ten minutes later, I watched Orogen walk out of The Pit, which was just another of the large rooms in the convention center. This one didn't have a special banner or any other markings, but security guards were stationed on either side of the doors.

Orogen was immediately swarmed with fans. He was about my height with straight, black hair sticking out from his head at every angle. He had black eyes too close together and an easy smile. He wasn't necessarily attractive, at least not to me, but seemed unassuming and friendly. He was dressed identically to three other people that left The Pit with him. A red, button-up, short-sleeved shirt covered with dozens of product logos. Kotega brands and Earth brands, along with some I'd never seen. Black pants and shoes. Poking out from the shirt were two high-end cybernetic arms that exactly matched his skin, a brown only slightly lighter than my own.

After signing a few autographs, one of his teammates whispered in his ear, and they walked away together down the hall. I trailed 'from a dozen meters away, not that any of them had ever met me. Even if they had, the crowd was so packed in those halls, nobody would have noticed. After only a few turns, they walked past half a dozen guards blocking the entrance to a hallway that led to the stage door for the main tournament theatre.

"He's swarmed with people," I said over comms, a channel that included Bastion, Quynn, and Solomon. "He just went backstage. Is this it? The big final?"

Quynn softly chuckled. "Semifinals. Though if he loses now, that would solve our problem."

"I don't know how to get to him," I said. "Anything on Tazia?"

"She just walked into the convention center," Solomon said. "Other end, though. And she's in no hurry. I'm on her, but whatever she has planned, I doubt it's happening in the next few minutes."

Unless she'd already set things in motion. Not seeing other options, I walked into the main theatre with the rest of the crowd. After going through open doors and heading down a dark tunnel shoulder-to-shoulder with hundreds of other people, I emerged into a space that would have rivaled any professional sports arena. I didn't even know the convention center had a room this size, the two booths in the center for the competitors dwarfed by hundreds of rows rising up all around. Thousands must have been here already, with more and more pouring in every second. Music was thumping, lights were spinning and flashing. Enormous screens kept cycling through images of the two competitors about to face off, along with highlights from their previous matches.

"Where—?" I muttered.

"On your left," Quynn said. "Up about twelve rows."

I looked left and up, scanning the dense crowd until I saw Quynn waving a hand at me. There was an open spot right next to them.

"Thank Corto for you," I said and started pushing through the crowd to join them. They took my hand as I sat, and I gladly held onto it. In a few minutes, the music faded, and an announcer started talking. I didn't understand most of it. Talks about playstyle, coaches, and accomplishments with other games and at other tournaments. Orogen waved to the crowd when he entered the arena, still smiling, before he entered his little booth and connected the gaming rig to his mods. His opponent, a rounder figure whose name I didn't catch, didn't smile before entering their booth and doing the same.

Then they were playing, the crowd roaring and booing at various times while two people in business suits gave a running commentary. I couldn't follow any of it. I played a few video games when I was a child, usually when I visited friends or when they had birthday parties. I just never got into them. I was an adrenaline junkie from the time I could walk, and video games just never gave me what I craved.

All the while, Solomon kept giving updates as he followed Tazia around.

She grabbed a coffee and a pastry, then stared out the window while she ate, obviously distracted. She slowly meandered through the first and second floors, making it look like she was bored and uninterested, but Solomon knew the look of someone casing a location. Eventually, she wandered into the main tournament theatre, walking halfway down one of the entrance tunnels just in time to see Orogen win the semi-finals and earn his place in the final match. Then she left, but not before smiling, likely thinking nobody could see her. Solomon was forty meters away, using better optical zoom than I had in my eyes to watch her closely.

"When is this final?" I asked Quynn as people started to leave the theatre.

Quynn glanced aside for a moment, and then said, "In two hours."

"Two hours for some sabotage," I said.

"Any idea what you're going to do?"

"A few. We'll see what works." I kissed Quynn and then left, moving through the crowd to get out of the theatre in a hurry. "Where is he?" I asked Bastion.

In response, a camera feed appeared in the upper right of my display. Orogen was walking with his teammates, all full of celebration and swagger, back toward The Pit.

"Who is his opponent for the final?" I asked.

"Kala Nexus-Seventeen," Quynn and Bastion said at the same time. "She/her."

Bastion continued alone. "She is an underdog. She entered the tournament with very low odds of winning even the first round. Even now, Orogen is a four-to-one favorite to beat her."

"What were Orogen's odds of advancing to the final?" Solomon asked.

"He was ranked fifth out of all competitors entered in this competition," Bastion said. "But his odds were still one in three. He was not favored to win that semi-final match, either."

"Makes me wonder if Tazia is already pulling some strings," I said. "Bastion, where is Kala Nexus-Seventeen?"

"One moment," Bastions said.

"Orogen advancing despite those odds sounds awfully lucky," I said.

"Too lucky," Solomon said.

"Like maybe Orogen has already been getting help," I replied.

"I do not see Kala on any active cameras," Bastion said. "Searching back through recorded footage now."

"That would also explain why Tazia hasn't done anything since I laid eyes on her," Solomon said. "She's already done it. She's just waiting around in case something needs her attention."

After a few more seconds, Bastion said, "She entered a bathroom on the fourth floor a little over an hour ago. There is no footage of her leaving."

"There's a fourth floor?" Quynn said, echoing the same question in my head.

"The tournament is not using it," Bastion said. "But yes."

I looked around briefly before spotting another escalator and then made my way to it. Up and up and up I went, skirting around a FLOOR CLOSED sign that blocked the escalator going up to the fourth floor. I moved and held my head like I was supposed to go up there, and the crowds barely gave me a second glance. Bastion provided directions, far in the southeast corner of the building. I didn't know what I would find on the other side of the door, so I took a deep breath and softened my expression before pushing the bathroom door open.

Kala Nexus-Seventeen was perched on the long countertop, her back to the wide mirror. She looked so small, light blue eyes set deep in her pale face. Her hair matched her eyes, so long that it pooled on the countertop behind her. She was wearing an outfit just like all the other pro gamers, though hers was grey and had fewer product logos than Orogen's. Her modded hands gripped the edge of the counter, shaking slightly as they did, while she stared off at the floor. She didn't even notice me enter.

"Kala?" I said softly.

She jumped, her eyes darting all over the bathroom before landing on me. She looked ready to panic and run. "Who—?"

I held my hands up to indicate I was no threat. "My name is Ellie. She/her. I'm here to help."

"Help?" Kala asked as her face screwed up in suspicion. I wondered if Tazia had taken the same approach.

INCOMING MESSAGE FROM VALDO appeared on my display, but I ignored it.

"Someone talked to you before the tournament, didn't they? Or maybe right when the tournament was starting?"

Kala just stared at me. I had to be careful. Tazia may have coerced Kala or worse. I took a slow step forward, still holding my hands forward. "I don't work with her. I know what she's after, and it's nothing good. It threatens all of Jayu City. I don't want to help her; I want to help you."

Kala's brow furrowed and she glanced down and away. Remembering. Maybe remembering her conversation with Tazia, maybe someone else who was threatened. Those hands of hers were still shaking. Not just shakes. Tremors. Cybernetic arms were not supposed to do that no matter how emotional their owner was.

"Kala," I said. "Did she do something to your mods?"

Kala glanced at her hands, then at me as tears welled up in her eyes. She nodded.

"May I see?" I asked as I stepped closer still. "I want to help you. I might be able to fix whatever she did."

"You might make it worse," she whispered. "Or she might find out. I can't—" Kala choked on the words as tears fell down her cheeks. Definitely coercion, then.

I stepped forward again and gently took her hands in mine. She didn't pull away, but she didn't look at me. "She said her name was Josephine, right? Did she threaten you?"

Kala didn't react.

"Your family?" Kala winced.

"Kala," I said, kneeling a little so I was in her line of sight. She met my gaze, her eyes full of fear. "Josephine isn't who she says she is. I'm an Intel Operative. I'm working against her and I'm not alone. Not here on Cirilla and certainly not in Jayu City. Tell me the names and locations of your family, the ones she threatened, and I promise they'll be protected."

The promise was shaky at best, though I would do whatever I could to make it real. I knew Bastion and Solomon were listening, so I really hoped that they would do whatever they could to make it true as well. Kala looked at me for a long time, her gaze shifting between my eyes, searching for something.

"You don't know me," I said. "And especially after what Josephine did, you don't trust me. That's good. You should be cautious. But I'm going to stop her. I'm going to help you and your family and we're going to stop her together."

Kala swallowed and wiped her cheeks on her shoulders, then said, "Bella Nexus-Neuro and Sal Nexus-Neuro. Those are my parents. My twin brothers are Jack and Mack. Seven. She said she has people outside our apartment, watching. Please—"

"What building?" I asked.

"Nexus 233. Apartment 25688."

"Calling it in," Solomon said in my ear.

"Sending an anonymous message to the building security," Bastion said.

"My partner heard everything," I said to Kala as I tapped my ear. "We're sending people right now. Your building security, Intel, anybody who will respond. But I can tell you this, too. I know Josephine. She was probably lying to you, but we're going to check it out anyway."

Kala nodded as tears streamed down her cheeks, her mouth almost cracking into a smile.

"Josephine wanted you to lose to Orogen, didn't she?" I asked.

Kala kept nodding.

INCOMING MESSAGE FROM VALDO appeared again. I ignored it again.

"She helped you win, but now you have to lose. And she messed with your mods for insurance."

Kala raised her hands in front of her face. The tremors were slight but constant. They stopped for five or six seconds before resuming. Kala said, "I can make them stop if I think about it. Josephine told me to hide it, make sure nobody saw. They feel so slow, like they aren't connected or calibrated right. Like they aren't mine. She did something with my neck."

"May I?" I asked as I stood again. Kala dropped down from the counter to her feet, turning her back to me and pulling her long, blue hair aside to reveal her neck. It looked pretty normal for someone with cybernetic mods, circuitry running just under the skin, visible to the naked eye. But there was one spot just below her third vertebra that was red and swollen. Right in the middle of it was a black spot like an overgrown blackhead. I zoomed in on it and saw that it wasn't a skin blemish at all, but a tiny circuit.

"I see it," I said. "Whatever it is, she pushed it into your skin, connected it to your circuitry."

"Can you get rid of it?" Kala asked.

"Did it hurt when she attached it?"

Kala shook her head slightly. "She did something to numb it."

"Then it's probably going to hurt when I take it out. I'm sorry."

"Just do it. Please."

I deployed small tools from my fingertips from my one work limb, tools I usually used for picking mechanical locks. They were certainly agile enough to handle this, even if they were sluggish and quirky from damage. I pushed them into her skin just a little, grabbing hold of the black dot firmly. Kala hissed a little as I did but didn't move.

"Ready?" I asked. "Ready," Kala whispered.

I pulled. Blood trickled out of the hole as the black dot started to come away, but there was significant resistance. Kala whimpered and grabbed hold of the countertop with one hand. I pulled harder and saw four thin wires trailing out of the black dot and into the hole. I had no idea how deep they went, but I had to get them out of her.

"I'm sorry," I said. "I almost have it."

"Hurry," Kala said between whimpers. INCOMING CALL FROM VALDO appeared on my display now. Whatever was going on with Valdo, it must have been urgent, but so was the task in front of me. I ignored him again.

I continued to pull, slow and steadily so the wires wouldn't break. Centimeter by centimeter, one hand bracing the back of Kala's neck as blood trickled down through my fingers and onto the top of her shirt. After nearly twenty centimeters, the ends of the wires finally pulled free from Kala.

"Got it!" I said.

"I would advise not letting those wires touch your biological skin,"

Bastion said. "Just in case."

Kala clapped a hand to the wound and turned to look at it, the tiny thing with the bloody wires like some miniature jellyfish pulled from a red sea. Still breathing heavily from the pain, she held her other hand in front of her face, watching it no longer tremor. A smile broke across her face. "Thank you."

I opened a compartment in my left forearm and dropped Tazia's little device inside. I would have it examined by Hessod and the other Intel Analysts later. I didn't like the idea of a tiny device that could mess with mods like that. Then I smiled back at Kala and said, "You're welcome."

Kala's hand came away bloody from her neck, and she put her hand back over the wound.

"There are medical offices on each of the first three floors," I said. "They should be able to fix you up."

"What will I tell them happened?"

"The truth," I said with a smirk. "You had a really big blackhead."

Kala almost smiled again. "That's terrible."

I shrugged. "I thought it was funny. Go on. Your family will be fine. Your mods are good. Go win that tournament."

Kala smiled so wide and bright, it reminded me of just how young she really was. Then with one hand still clamped on the back of her neck, she left the bathroom.

"Well done," Solomon said.

"Thank you," I said. "But I have to wonder how Tazia is going to react when that kid starts beating Orogen in the finals."

"I'll take care of that," Solomon said. "Valdo is trying to call you again," Bastion said.

I nodded and accepted the call. "Hey, Valdo. What's—?"

"I can't get to the back door," Valdo said. Meaning the back door to the Offworld Relay. "I need your help."

"My help? Why?"

"It's underwater."

Chapter Thirty-Three

I FOLLOWED VALDO'S INSTRUCTIONS AS best I could, skirting wide left of the Offworld Relay's front door, climbing over landscaping, and retaining walls until I was walking along the rocky terrain that encircled most of the structure. With each step, I reminded myself that I was making the right decision. Maybe the Offworld Relay wasn't my top priority right now, but I'd taken care of Kala. The Cloak of Corto was watching Tazia. Everything was under control in the convention center. It was.

It had to be.

I stayed close to the building as the rocks climbed higher and the distance to the edge and the drop into the ocean shrunk. After twenty minutes of scrabbling, I finally came around the back of the building and found Valdo sitting, looking down and away from me.

"They really don't want anyone coming this way," I hollered.

Valdo looked back at me, nodded briefly, and returned his gaze. I joined him, sitting on a ledge overlooking a large chasm. As waves bashed against the rocks, they created a violence of water in the chasm below, swirling and crashing and breaking against the side of the Relay like a giant washing machine.

"Down there, huh?" I asked.

"Down there," Valdo mumbled. Then he looked at me and spoke more clearly. "The car left about an hour ago, so I expect it to return in the next twenty minutes."

"And it came from down there?"

"I saw the lights on it before it emerged from the water. About a dozen meters below the surface. I wasn't sure what I was seeing until it flew out of the water and just kept going. Looked like a perfectly normal Mercedes once it was out of the water."

"A car that not only flies but can submerge," I said. "Sounds useful if you're trying to protect a super-secret entrance to the most valuable building on the planet."

"I'm not aware of a single manufacturer on Little Sekhmet that produces such a machine," Bastion said in my ear.

"Must have come from off-world," I said.

"Off-world?" Valdo asked. Right. I'd closed the open channel, so only I heard Bastion.

"Bastion said nobody on the planet makes anything like that," I said. "That just stresses how much they don't want anyone knowing about this entrance."

Valdo nodded and looked back into the water. Something was bothering him, that was obvious. He said, "I don't see any other way into the back entrance. I walked around the entire building three times."

"So we need to go for a swim." All the color drained from Valdo's face. "Can you not swim?" I asked.

"It's not that." Valdo didn't look at me as he spoke. He was quiet and intense. "I watched that video. Vert fighting that woman."

"You didn't need to—"

"I did. I needed to understand. I didn't know he was dead until back in your hospital room. Ever since I met you, things have felt a little dangerous, sure. But fun. The danger never felt real, not to me, at least. But Vert is dead." Finally, Valdo turned back to me and held my gaze. "And you made that happen."

His words dug into me like a knife. All my own thoughts, my own guilt spoken aloud by someone else. I wanted to deny it, to make some great case for why another man needed to die, but I couldn't. No matter how necessary it might have been, how much logic I could apply, it never felt like enough. Not enough for Theo and for Vert. Vert's son would grow up without a father. It didn't matter why.

Valdo turned back to look into the swirling chasm, his silence almost as painful as his words.

"I hate it," I said. "I hate that I'm in this position and that I've put you in this position. I'm not a killer. I refuse to be. I don't know if it's possible to say that when the blood is still fresh on my hands, but I'm saying it. Maybe if I keep saying it, you and I will both believe me. I'm in the business of stealing things, not lives, and I want to get back to that so badly."

Valdo nodded but didn't look at me. I wasn't sure what to make of the gesture.

I took a deep breath and refocused on the task at hand. "Do you think that underwater door closes? Is it always open?"

"I can't tell from here." Valdo's tone was flat and disconnected.

"All right." I stood and walked to the very edge. "I'm going in. A dozen meters down and a dozen meters up the other side, I can hold my breath that long. My legs can move me through the water pretty quickly. I'll check to see if the door is open. If it is, I'll let you know and you can join me. I think I can get us both through in one breath."

"I'm not going with you," Valdo said, his voice barely loud enough to carry over the crashing waves.

"Valdo…"

"I'm out." Valdo stood, glancing at me briefly before looking away. "I helped you. You helped me. We're even. But I can't be part of this anymore. I won't be part of a decision that gets someone else killed. I'll be on the boat tomorrow morning. Please don't look for me." Then Valdo walked away from me, his biological legs wobbling over the rocky terrain.

My gut felt empty. Pulled out and stomped on. Not just because a young man who'd become a good friend had ended our friendship, but because I agreed with everything he said. I wanted to do the same thing with the person I'd been for the last six months. I wanted to run after him and beg him not to leave me, but I couldn't.

"Elise," Bastion said. "I'm picking up faint thrusters in your aural implants."

I turned and looked out across the chasm and toward the rest of the island. Sure enough, I could just make out a car flying away from the rest of the traffic scurrying across the skies, heading this way. A quick zoom-in confirmed what Valdo had seen, a Mercedes that looked like any other.

I closed my eyes and took two long, deep breaths. The Offworld Relay. The five companies. Theo's dying words. I had to get up there, had to make sure his death wasn't in vain. I turned on one heel and dived, hands extended before me, falling the twenty or so meters before slipping into the churning water below. Once the swirling bubbles cleared, I saw the enormous opening in the side of the building. No door. I started kicking. The water pressure was agonizing, pressing hard on my skin and organs that were still healing from the abuse of the last few days. I darted in through the opening and reoriented myself up. After another dozen or so meters, my lungs starting to burn, I broke the surface and took a huge breath.

I was in a metal cavern, for lack of a better term. The space was at least fifty meters wide and a dozen meters high above the water level. The outer wall was transparent, at least from this side, giving an incredible view of the chasm and its frothing, churning waters. It was strange to see that at eyelevel when the water I was treading was so calm. I turned, looked around, and found a single elevator door. I swam over, pulling myself out of the water onto the concrete dock that ran half a dozen meters out from the elevator. I ran a hand through my hair, ringing out the ocean water.

"How much time do you think I have?" I asked Bastion.

"Two or three minutes," Bastion said. "Depending on if that car has to make any mechanical adjustments before diving."

"How is the tournament going?"

"Orogen and Kala just finished the first round of their finals match. Kala won."

I smiled. "And Tazia?"

"She started moving with more purpose a few minutes ago. Solomon is following her."

"Can you give me a visual?"

A rectangle of video appeared on my display, sitting in the lower right of my vision. It was a fisheye security camera watching thin crowds wander over the terrible patterned carpet of the convention center. Tazia walked through the frame, taking long, purposeful strides. A beat after she left the frame, Solomon entered it, blending with the crowds and keeping his distance. The video changed. Another camera. A different angle. The same story. After three more camera switches, Tazia plowed through an EMPLOYEES ONLY door.

"What is she up to?" I mumbled to myself.

"That door leads to any number of places," Bastion said, not catching the rhetorical nature of my question. "Employee break rooms and lockers, bathrooms, administrative offices, laundry, and storage facilities. I believe her most likely destination is the trunk line control room."

"The what?" I asked.

"The trunk line control room. It is a secured room that houses the main data connections between the convention center and everywhere outside the convention center, including the connections to Jayu City and the Offworld Relay."

"Why would she be going there?"

"My hypothesis? *Dregs of Osiris* requires a connection to the game's servers to be played," Bastion said. "There are servers in Jayu City, of course, but the tournament requires the use of the main servers, which are on the Zarabanda Colony, twenty-eight light years away."

"Mess with the connection to the servers," I mumbled. "And the tournament has to stop."

"Hypothetically," Bastion said. "It could also be possible to introduce lag into Kala's connection without affecting Orogen's connection. It would be difficult to do without being discovered, but it is possible."

"Mother of Corto. Does Solomon know?"

"I have told him, yes."

The camera feeds kept changing, now all focused on the back hallways, narrower angles that kept changing faster as they followed Tazia through the winding hallways. Solomon was still following, sticking to walls and looking around corners, no longer able to hide amidst a crowd. The camera angle changed again, an empty hallway leading to a dark door with a number pad. Several seconds passed, but neither Tazia nor Solomon appeared.

"What am I looking at?" I asked.

"I was following Tazia. That is the door to the trunk line control room." The camera angles switched rapidly, briefly showing Solomon down the same hallways and peeking around the corner. No Tazia, though. "I cannot find her."

Solomon came around the corner and was moving fast and low, his head on a swivel. The camera angles changed to follow, still not showing Tazia anywhere. Then three meters before the secured door, Tazia seemed to shimmer into view in mid-stride, landing a solid haymaker on Solomon's jaw.

"What?!" I yelled, my voice rebounding around the enormous metal cavern.

"That is the shimmer of holographic camouflage," Bastion said. "Military tech that she should not have."

"Connect me to Solomon. Now." In moments, my display informed me that Bastion had done what I asked. "Solomon! Are you okay? She has military tech!"

"Get over here and help me!" Solomon growled in my ear as I watched him get to his feet on the security feed. Tazia, however, had vanished again. So not fair. At that same moment, I could see the Mercedes descending from the sky, slow and steady, until it passed from air to water.

"We could take the car," Bastion said.

"What?"

"The Mercedes. Once it docks, I can hack in and we can take it. We could get to Solomon faster. Help him. Stop Tazia."

He was right, but that would destroy my chances of ever getting up to the top of the Offworld Relay. If there was an underwater door down there, they would close it and tighten up security. They would know my face. I would never get another chance.

"Maybe," I said. But maybe between now and the car docking, Solomon would take care of things and I wouldn't have to decide.

Tazia appeared again on the security feed, this time behind Solomon, but he wasn't the Cloak of Corto for no reason. He ducked her next blow, a lazy hook, and slammed his elbow into her stomach. Tazia stumbled back, more from surprise than actual pain.

"I'm guessing you didn't just come upon me by accident, then?" Tazia said, her words to Solomon faintly carried to me by his comms. "One of Kala's friends? Was it you that called her family?"

Solomon positioned himself between the door to the trunk line control room and Tazia, but he said nothing.

"No, that's not it," Tazia said. "You were talking to someone. Asking for help." Her eyes grew wide, and she smiled. "I saw you the same night I saw Elise outside my office. You must know her. She does make strange friends."

Tazia turned invisible again, shimmering into nothing. Solomon was prepared this time, his right forearm opened, lighting up with electricity, and then a three-meter-long whip made of arcing green energy erupted from his right hand. He whipped it in a zig-zag fashion, tagging Tazia as she was trying to sneak past, knocking her into the visible spectrum as she slammed against the wall. Her smile was gone.

"You're more than just her friend," she said. "I don't know your face. Your name."

"I know yours," Solomon said as he retracted the whip, but sparks began to leap from his knuckles.

They stared at each other, sizing each other up. I pushed myself into the darkest shadow I could find as the Mercedes came through the underwater opening and started to rise.

Tazia narrowed her eyes. "Could it be?"

Solomon smirked. "You're the Ghost of Toinette. You tell me."

"The Cloak of Corto?" Tazia chuckled. "In all the decades that our intelligence agencies have played our little games against each other, how often do you think people like us have actually spoken to each other? Looked at each other? Squared off? Ghost, Cloak, Wing, Tsuba, whatever Nexus calls theirs. This might be the first time."

"Fascinating," Solomon said, but his tone was flat and droll.

"I thought I knew every face in your operation, but I guess you were able to keep yours from me," Tazia purred.

"We're just better."

The little smile disappeared from Tazia's face. "A head start doesn't mean you're better."

Then the talking was done. Tazia launched a sweeping kick at Solomon's head. He ducked easily and threw an electrified fist up toward her jaw. She turned and slid back to avoid the blow. Watching Tazia and Solomon fight was like watching a dance. It wasn't like the fight between Vert and Roxy. Neither were professional fighters nor assassins. This fight wasn't as brutal or as fast, but they were both skilled. Solomon bounced on the balls of his feet like a boxer, blocking and ducking, jabbing with those electrified punches, but never landing more than a glancing blow. Tazia flowed like silk on water, sliding her feet and preferring kicks, but never staying in one stance for more than a breath.

The Mercedes was rising from below and moving toward the concrete dock.

A flash of light on the security feed drew my attention back to the corner of my display. Solomon was blinking his eyes rapidly, his arms up in front of his face. I didn't see Tazia. He brought out his whip again, lashing it around, scarring the walls and floor and ceiling, but he didn't make contact with the Ghost of Toinette.

The Mercedes surfaced and the driver's side door opened soundlessly. Someone stepped out, just a single person. Tall and rail-thin, with skin a little darker than mine. They were carrying half a dozen grocery bags in their two hands. They didn't look around, didn't take in their surroundings. Steal their car or press a blade to their neck, they wouldn't see me coming.

I looked back to Solomon just as he grabbed the back of his neck and stumbled forward a couple of steps. His eyes were wide, blinking slowly. He looked confused. Then Tazia shimmered visible again a few steps behind him, standing tall and making no move toward him.

"You should lay down before you fall down," she said.

He turned to look at her and dropped to one knee, the electric arcs from his fists etching black burns on the floor. "What did you do?"

"Neural disruptors," Tazia said. "Developed to treat neural interfaces that are overactive. One of them in a perfectly functioning neural interface causes lag between the brain and the mods. Half a dozen can shut down the connection completely. I just slapped—oh, I don't know— twenty or thirty on the back of your neck. I'm not sure what that many will do."

For the first time in my life, I saw panic spread across Solomon's face.

"You need to help him," Bastion said. "We can figure out the company thing later. We cannot let Tazia succeed."

The person from the Mercedes approached the elevator door and pressed the button. It immediately dinged and opened.

My heart was racing. The door to the car was wide open. I could jump in and be there in minutes. Maybe I could stop her. *Five companies.* Theo's words kept running through my brain.

Whatever damage Tazia had inflicted on Solomon, it was done. He couldn't stop her now, but maybe I could stop her later. Even if she succeeded today, it would be months before Orogen might become CEO of Kotega Systems. But if I drove that car away from here now, that was it. I might never get another chance to go up the Offworld Relay, to follow the single lead I had that might connect all five companies.

I moved forward from the shadows, taking long, silent strides. The tall person with the groceries stepped one foot into the elevator. Tazia stood over Solomon, who was still on one knee, wobbling. The grocery bags vanished entirely into the still-open elevator. I was two meters away. Solomon looked up at Tazia, his eyes rolling, and then lashed out with his whip. He didn't hit the Ghost of Toinette, no, but slashed a deep, burning gouge in the door to the trunk line control room, destroying the keypad in the process.

Tazia let out a guttural scream.

Solomon collapsed.

"Elise," Bastion said, his voice trembling. "Don't go up there. Solomon needs your help. That many disruptors might kill him. Forget the relay. Theo is gone, but Solomon is still alive."

"Tell Quynn," I whispered.

I entered the elevator, grabbing its occupant by the neck and slamming them against the back wall. I'd done what I could to stop Tazia from winning. Now, Solomon had as well. Quynn would make sure Solomon was okay. Kala was going to win. And I was going to the top of the Offworld Relay.

Chapter Thirty-Four

THE PERSON IN MY CLUTCHES squirmed but didn't drop the grocery bags. The elevator doors shut behind me and the elevator began moving up, though I hadn't seen this person press any buttons. After several seconds of gagging noises, I let off the person's neck, though I stayed in a fighting stance just in case.

After several seconds of coughing, they said with an accent I didn't recognize, "Nice to meet you, too."

"What?" I said.

"What did you think I was going to do? Extend claws like a honey badger and maul you to death? I operate the relay. I don't guard it."

I had no idea what a honey badger was, but that wasn't the point. They were far too relaxed for my sudden appearance. "Aren't you scared?"

"Of what?" they said. "Of you? If you wanted to kill me, you would have. If you want to harm me, then fear won't help me. You want to see the control room? Fine. I'd love to show it. I don't get a lot of visitors. Just the occasional inspections, really, but even those are mostly done via hologram. I'm afraid I haven't tidied the place up much since I wasn't expecting you, though."

I opened my mouth to say something, anything, though I wasn't sure what.

"Oh, my goodness," they continued. "How rude of me. My name is Horus. Horus McLaughlin. And you are?"

I didn't know if I should answer them or knock them unconscious, if this was a ruse or if they were genuinely this chatty and disarming. My brain blurted out the first thing that came to it: "Pronouns?"

"Oh, yes!" Horus said. "He/him. Thank you. And you are?"

"Ellie," I said. "She/her."

"Ellie." Horus seemed to roll the name around in his mouth like a fine wine. "Keeping your company name to yourself, I see. Understandable."

We stood in uncomfortable silence for a minute or so, him staring at me like he expected something, maybe trying to decipher more about me.

"Honestly, it's a long ride to the top. And it's rather rude to make someone carry six bags of groceries while your hands are empty, isn't it?"

"I'm not carrying your groceries."

Horus frowned and shrugged his shoulders, adjusting his load. Both of his arms were obviously cybernetic, so the bags shouldn't have been an issue anyway. "You can at least carry some of the conversation, then. I know I don't get out much, don't entertain, but I'm sure you have questions, or else you wouldn't be here. I am curious, though, how did you discover the back door?"

I stared at him and said nothing.

"I'm sure we don't have the best security on the planet, not like some of those buildings in the city, but I thought the underwater entrance was rather clever. All party in the front with the tour and whatnot, business in the back, hidden away. I can tell you, that custom Mercedes was no cheap thing, either. Had to special order it from Earth, if you can believe. Oh, how I miss it."

"The car?"

"Earth."

My eyebrows shot up. "You've been to Earth?"

"El…" Bastion said in my ear, the comms channel breaking up a bit. "Orogen…round…disappear…"

I brought up my AR keyboard and texted him back, "Comms breaking up. Repeat?"

A few moments later, a message from Bastion appeared on my display: "Orogen and Kala are tied. Tazia has disappeared behind her camouflage."

"What was that?" Horus asked, watching my fingers dance in the air.

The question caught me off guard. Most people used AR keyboards to text. It was nothing to see people conversing in person while typing away in the air. But the question and look on Horus' face made it seem like the action was entirely foreign to him.

"Texting someone," I said.

"Fascinating," Horus said. "Augmented reality, haptic feedback, all connected to your communications implants, correct? Yes, that must be. I've seen people doing that when I run my errands, I've just never asked what it was."

"How is Solomon?" I asked Bastion via text.

"Quynn is with him," Bastion said. "As are medics. He is unconscious. Alive. Barely. You can still turn around. Stop Tazia. Keep Orogen from winning. You can—"

I pressed a four-key combination that muted my communications, cutting Bastion off. Solomon was going to be fine. I needed to focus on the task at hand, on this Horus fellow that I didn't trust at all.

"You're going to show me the control room," I said to Horus. "I need information."

"Certainly, certainly!" Horus smiled broadly. "It's really a wonderful system. So much information flying across space faster than light. Truly a wonder!"

"Fine, just—"

"And we've arrived!" Horus said. A breath later, I felt the elevator slow to a stop. It certainly hadn't felt like a long ride. I stepped aside, urging Horus to move toward the doors while staying in front of me. He nodded and moved as though he knew my intention.

The elevator doors opened and Horus moved quickly, too quickly for my liking. I followed him closely, not into the enormous control room like the replica I'd seen in the replay of Valdo's tour, but into a rather large and messy living space. Two well-worn, blue couches lined the far wall, pointed at a large viewscreen several years out of date. On one wall was a flag I didn't know. An eight-pointed red cross, outlined in white, with a blue background. Photos covered many of the other walls, some with Horus in them, but not all. His family or friends, maybe. Horus hustled through, kicking aside blankets and power cords on his way to an adjoining kitchen, muttering apologies under his breath the whole way. He set the bags on the counter with a sigh.

"Do you mind if I put all of this away first?" he asked, already opening one bag and digging into it. "I found a very nice brie and three different cheddars that really should not sit out…"

"None of this looks like downstairs."

"The tour?" Horus said. "No. That's a nice fiction for tourists. Nothing so elaborate up here."

"Is there a control room?"

"Of course. Just let me—"

"The control room, Horus," I said, leaving no room for argument in my tone. "Now."

Horus sighed and looked into the grocery bag as though he'd found an injured bird. "Fine. This way."

Horus led me through the kitchen and into a corridor that was decidedly neater than the rest of his living quarters. It was downright sterile by comparison, ending in a single, heavy, metal door. Above the door was a biometric/cybermetric scanner that was as dated as his viewscreen. He stood in front of it for about thirty seconds before the door slid open with a slight grind.

The control room was a semicircle, maybe three meters wide and as many deep. A gleaming, half-arc workstation took up the center, lights blinking all over. Right in front of that workstation, on the floor, was a hatch that looked exactly like the one I'd opened two hundred floors below. Along the outer wall were a dozen smaller workstations, all covered in a thick layer of dust. Blank viewscreens were mounted above them, all even more dated than the technology inside the living quarters.

Horus stepped forward to the large workstation. His hands changed shape to flat octagons. He then pressed them into spaces on the workstation like custom-built keys. The workstation lit up even more and the viewscreens came to life as well, displaying readouts, graphs, and hundreds of numbers that meant nothing to me.

"What do you need to know?" Horus asked.

I took a deep breath, my chest shaking as I let it out. This was it. I was finally here. It shouldn't be this easy, but I had to take what was in front of me.

"The five companies, they all send their data through here, right?"

"Right." Horus' tone implied that he was waiting for me to ask more.

"Do they connect somehow? The companies?"

"Connect?" Horus looked genuinely confused.

"Yes. Connect. They're so separate, so competitive, I just need to know—"

"I understand what you're asking," Horus interrupted. "It's just strange to me that you see them as disconnected."

My heart fluttered and my throat constricted. They *were* connected. Theo was right, he was onto something. I steadied myself and said, "What do you mean?"

Horus looked into the middle distance for a moment, and the viewscreens all changed. Most of them went blank, but the biggest one in the middle changed to a huge bar graph with only two bars. One was blue and filled most of the screen. The other was needle-thin and red. Numbers fluttered around the edges, but I didn't understand any of them.

"The blue," Horus said. "Is the outgoing data. Red is incoming."

I didn't know how that connected the companies, but that alone was staggering. Given the immense size of the companies and their reach across Earth Space, I would have expected a more even distribution.

"None of the data is sorted by company, though. It's all formatted the same way, encrypted and packaged the same. I couldn't tell you which packet came from which company if I tried."

"An Earth Space standard?" I asked.

"There is no such thing. Across Earth Space, there are hundreds of thousands of different encryption styles for relayed data."

"But the five companies here all use similar ones?"

"No," Horus said. "The exact same one."

That didn't make any sense. The five companies of Jayu City were galactic powerhouses, headquartered right here. They controlled most of the galactic economy. They should be receiving much more data than they were sending, communicating with other offices, and guiding their far-reaching business interests, not the other way around. I spun from the viewscreen and looked back at Horus. The confusion must have been plain on my face.

He said, "Let me show you."

I turned back to the screen. In a second, the bar graph was replaced by a spread of data:

Purchase: Dillon Medium Handbag, Pack Style, Red and Gold

Price: 422 cr

Gender: NB

Sex: Male

Age: 25

Skin Opacity: 62.3

Religion: None

Children: 1

Partnership: Dual corporate certified

On and on the information spooled out. Occupation, years in occupation, generations on the colony, annual income. There must have been more than a hundred data points about one single purchase.

"This is marketing information," I said. "I guess that makes sense. There are probably off-world marketing people. What else are we sending?"

Horus shrugged. "Some corporate communications, HR information, but ninety-nine-point-three percent of everything going out is just this. Every purchase made in Jayu City."

If my legs had been biological, I think I would have fallen down. The Offworld Relay could send and receive three petabytes of information each day. Ninety-nine-point-three percent of ninety-eight percent of those three petabytes were just marketing data sent FROM our planet. Why would five massive companies, all based on this planet, be sending all of that information out? Maybe if they were receiving that information from the hundreds of other planets in Earth Space, that could make sense. But this?

"Wh…" My voice shook. I took several breaths to steady myself before continuing. "Where are we sending all of that information?"

"Gibbingson Holdings, of course." Horus smiled. Something about that smile made my spine tingle in all the wrong ways.

"Never heard of them."

"GH? Biggest corporation in Earth Space. Everyone has heard of them," he said. "Well, maybe not on this little settlement, I suppose."

GH. The logo I'd seen downstairs. "Why not on this settlement?"

Horus shrugged. "I just run the relay."

None of this was adding up. I knew I couldn't trust that happy facade. I said, "You're hiding something."

"I'm hiding a lot. I don't report to anyone on this planet for a reason."

"That's not what I mean, and you know it. You're playing coy."

Horus kept smiling, saying nothing.

"Why did you tell me all of that? Why are you so helpful?"

His smile faded just a shade. "It's not like you're leaving. And it was nice to talk to someone for a change."

I glanced around, looking for signs that Horus had sprung some kind of trap, but I didn't see anything. "Not leaving? What do you mean?"

"Well, you are leaving here, just not on your own. You're certainly not going back to Jayu City to talk to anyone. The moment you stepped on my elevator, you triggered the facility's fail safes. The scanners are old, but they do the trick. They see anyone but me, and everything is automatic. Bring the elevator up, lock down the tower, and call the dozen Earth Space Enforcers who are stationed on the island. We still have at least a few minutes, I'm sure. The failsafe has never been triggered before, so they aren't exactly in a state of readiness around the clock. But they'll get here eventually, fully armed. They'll arrest you or kill you if they have to, ship you off to the nearest prison colony. Gilrock, I think. About fourteen lightyears from here."

I don't know if I'd ever felt this stupid. I made my living bypassing locks and sensors, and yet I'd been so worried about getting up here, so distracted by Solomon and Tazia, I hadn't looked around. I should have noticed the sensors. I could have inspected the elevator while I was waiting for Horus' car to arrive at the dock. Now I was trapped, waiting for offworld military to arrive and arrest me.

But if years of training and pulling jobs all over Jayu City had taught me anything, it's that there was always a way out. Like the hatch that Horus was standing on. Identical to the one far below.

"Horus," I said. "You're telling me the elevator is the only way out of here?"

"Right on the first guess," he said with that insufferable smile.

"Even if there's some sort of emergency?" I said. "Like a fire?"

For the first time since I'd laid eyes on him, Horus' animated face froze. The smile was plastered there, but it didn't reach his eyes. He took a long moment before he said, "The elevator works even during a fire."

"But aren't you the only person on this entire planet that can operate this Relay?"

"Well—"

"So, if there was a fire somewhere between this room and the elevators, they would just let you cook up here?"

"There are fireproof doors. And I'm certain help would arrive before anything disastrous happened." Horus' face softened just a bit, but one of his feet absently slid back, tapping the handle to the hatch without a sound. I was right.

"Of course. Help would arrive immediately. Like they have now. I've been up here, what, ten minutes? Still nobody? And what would happen if there was a fire in this room?"

Horus opened his mouth to answer, but I cut him off.

"Let me try it. That hatch below your feet. I opened its twin downstairs. That was a bad idea, but now I know why. It's not for maintenance. At least, not entirely. It's for you, in case you have to leave in a hurry. Now, assuming you're telling the truth about the automated lockdown, I'd guess the emergency procedures to safely open that hatch are also automated. Am I close?"

The smile faded from Horus' face. "You can't."

"Can't?" I said. "Or shouldn't?"

"Do you know what's down there?"

"I do," I said. "Massive amounts of radiation coming off the power conduits running through the building. Which means for you to open that hatch, the power has to turn off and the radiation has to be vented."

"The entire Offworld Relay would shut down," Horus said through gritted teeth. "For hours. The sheer volume of information lost in that time would be worth billions of credits. I would lose my job."

"And the radiation?"

Horus rolled his eyes. "Vented into storage tanks, what did you—?"

Now it was my turn to smile. "My life and freedom for your job? I'll take that trade."

"They'll find you," Horus hissed. "Earth Space. They'll find out who you are. You've shown your face all over this building."

Except they hadn't, of course, not if Valdo's little virus was doing its job. They would only have Horus' description of me. I could live with that. I held up my knuckles, charging my tasers on a steady current. They glowed slightly in front of my face.

"You won't get away with this," Horus said.

"Everyone always says that." Then I pressed my knuckles to the back of the console Horus was plugged into. He jumped, pulling his hands free and transforming them back into standard hand shapes. The lights blinked, some winked out, and a few sparks flew here and there. I kept the current flowing. A guaranteed way to make a fire was to push electricity somewhere it wasn't supposed to go. Sure enough, after about fifteen seconds, flames leaped out of the console in three different spots. Horus backed away, his hands up in surrender as he watched the flames in abject horror.

"No," he whispered. "No, no, no."

I shrugged and waited. It didn't take long before a siren started to wail. A digitized voice said, "Warning, fire danger. Warning, fire danger. Exit the control room."

Horus turned and ran out of the room with a whimper. Lights flashed. A vapor started pouring into the room through spigots on the ceiling, but I quickly moved around to the other side of the control board, reached up, and crushed the spigots with my hands. I wasn't going to let some fire suppression system keep me trapped. The fires on the console grew, touching the ceiling and sending up showers of sparks as they ruined more and more circuits.

"Warning, fire danger," the digitized voice said again. "Fire suppression failure. Warning, fire danger. Biological presence detected in control room. Emergency shutdown commencing. Stand clear of exit."

I did as I was told, standing off to the side of the hatch. The idea of that thing opening gave me the sweats, even more than the growing heat in the room, but I reminded myself that there would be no wave of radiation this time. No near-death experience. The lights on the hatch started flashing as an enormous hum that I hadn't even noticed faded away. The remaining lights in the control room went dark except for the hatch. After several long and exceedingly hot minutes, the hatch hissed and opened.

No blinding light. No radiation warnings on my display. The enormous chamber was hot, sure, but it wasn't dangerous. I looked over the edge and saw a spiral staircase winding down what seemed like an impossible height. Over two hundred floors of stairs.

"Thank Corto for mods," I said and started down them, taking the stairs three at a time. Down I went for a dozen or so meters, then looked out over the side. I could barely make out the bottom of the chamber below. It was only then that I remembered one of my newest toys I'd had installed only recently. I brought up my AR keyboard and quickly confirmed that yes, the system was still working, unfried from my earlier radiation exposure. I jumped, engaging the sparkling blue light of my anti-inertial field. I landed three meters from the already open hatch below.

I glanced back up once, nearly dizzy at the strange height of it all, and then dropped down the hatch, walking out of the Offworld Relay, still invisible to its cameras thanks to Valdo. As I stepped out of the doors, I re-engaged my comms array.

"Elise!" Bastion's voice was back in my head instantly. "What happened? I lost contact with you! With everything! How…"

I waited for him to finish his sentence, but it didn't come. I asked, "What is it?"

"Orogen," Bastion said. "He just won the tournament."

Chapter Thirty-Five

THE BOAT RIDE BACK TO Jayu City was a somber affair. Despite their tickets on faster, flying transportation, Quynn and Solomon joined Valdo and me on the boat. Solomon was still unconscious, though at least he was alive and stable. Though he never looked at or spoke to me. Valdo helped Quynn and I carry Solomon onto the ship. Then he stayed to himself. Quynn and I sat in our quarters, going over every detail of the fight between Solomon and Tazia, as well as everything I saw in the Offworld Relay.

"Even if I'd left the moment he asked for help," I said. "I wouldn't have gotten to him on time."

"I know," Quynn said. "And I don't know if you made the right decision. But it's the decision we have to live with."

It didn't soothe my conscience, but it didn't make it feel worse, either.

About halfway to Jayu City, Solomon finally came to, so I went to see him in his room. He was unable to move either of his modded legs and could only twitch his arms. Despite all that, he didn't panic. He coolly assessed his situation and then asked what happened. Once Quynn and I broke the news that despite our efforts, Orogen had won the tournament and Tazia had vanished, he became quiet and cold.

"There's still time," I told him. "Orogen isn't CEO of Kotega yet.

We're not beaten."

Solomon looked at me. Really looked in a way that made me feel tiny. Then he said, "I need rest. See yourself out."

I felt as tired and beaten as Solomon looked, for sure. I'd gotten to the top of the Offworld Relay and discovered some information that definitely connected the five companies, even if it didn't make any sense to me. Not yet. Neither Bastion nor Quynn had ever heard of Gibbingson Holdings, but it was a lead, something I could look into. That was a small win.

But Solomon, the Cloak of Corto, was flat on his back. A few days later, I would learn that all of those disruptors had permanently damaged Solomon's motor cortex. Despite all of our technological advancements and our cybernetic wonders, all of them still relied on the brain's ability to send signals through the nervous system. We could even replace nervous systems, but not brains. Solomon would never walk again, though he would regain limited use of his arms.

He could still be a valuable part of the Corto Corporation's Intel division, but not as the Cloak.

On the bright side, Nox had woken up while we were gone. The nanobots had done their job. He was sore but he was going to be okay. I was going to have my apprentice back in short order.

It took me a few hours, but I finally managed to get some sleep of my own on the ship. Quynn woke me just as we were arriving. A Corto medical transport was waiting on the dock to take Solomon. Valdo was already on the dock, the first one off the ship without so much as a goodbye. Just watching him go made my heart ache. His life had been so hard, was still so hard. I hadn't realized how much I'd brought to his life until I unknowingly undermined it. One day, I knew I would think of a better option for taking Vert out of that equation, a way that could have removed him without killing him. It always worked that way, days or months later, in the shower or just as I was falling asleep, it would come to me.

But I hadn't seen that option back on Cirilla. I'd made a decision with the information in front of me, eliminated Vert, and removed the looming threat of Roxy in one blow. It had been the right call. Even if my brain knew that, my heart felt different. Watching Valdo walk away like that only worsened the guilt.

\#   \#   \#

I started unpacking once I got home. Buried in my clothes was a souvenir from Cirilla. A small model of the Offworld Relay, the one I'd bought for Valdo. In the rush to leave the island, I'd packed it in with my things.

"What's that?" Quynn asked as they unpacked their own bag. "Valdo forgot this," I said.

"Oh," Quynn said. They put a hand on my shoulder and squeezed. "Maybe he's not as done with you as you fear. Take it to him but give him space. Give him time. He's hurting and confused. That doesn't mean he wants you out of his life forever."

I nodded and hugged Quynn, my partner and love. I really hoped they were right.

I didn't waste any time before meeting up with Valdo. I took a quick shower. After texting him half a dozen times, I finally had Bastion route a message to him through a dummy ID.

"I don't want to talk to you," his response finally came via text.

"I know. But you forgot your souvenir."

I expected a curse or some quick backpedaling, but instead, all he sent was an address. I changed into plain clothes and hopped on Poe. I wasn't excited to fly back to the Toinette borough, but it was the least I owed Valdo for everything he'd done. Not to mention for the pain I'd inflicted on him. I pushed an antique motorcycle helmet down over my head before I left the garage, just for a little anonymity in a borough that likely still had my picture on screens in their security offices.

After twenty minutes of flying, I found the building. I sat Poe down on a landing pad in front of a large sign that told me it was a hospital. He hadn't sent me to his home, no, but to where his mom was receiving treatment. That made sense. I made my way through the labyrinthine halls of the hospital, the souvenir tucked in a gift-wrapped box, an apology card attached. I had to ask for directions at four different nurse stations before I found the right floor and hallway for Qudrah Toinette-Deus, Valdo's mom. As I approached,

I didn't see anyone in the hallway, but there were chairs where I could wait. Maybe I could knock on the door, but then I remembered everything he'd told me about his father. No, I wouldn't interrupt. If anyone other than Valdo came out of that room, I would ignore them.

The door did have a thin, tall window in it. At least I could discover if Valdo was already there or not. I peeked in, and there was my young friend, standing at the foot of a bed. I couldn't see the rest of the room, a curtain hanging from the ceiling blocking the rest of my view. Valdo was talking to someone, listening intently whenever they were speaking, nodding solemnly on occasion. I could only make out occasional words, augmented by watching Valdo's lips. Mom. Dad. She'll be okay. At least I knew that I'd helped his mother, allowed her to leave the hospital soon, and get back to her normal life. Even if he never spoke to me again, I could give him that.

Valdo stepped slightly to the side and another man walked out from behind the curtain, crossing the small room to dig in a bag that was sitting in a chair. I knew it was a man immediately because I knew him. I knew the cut of his jawline. The dark of his eyes and the brown of his skin. The line of his cheekbone was the same as Valdo's. The same as mine.

That man was my father. Defected from Corto Corporation when I was twelve. Left my mother and me forever.

Valdo told him, "You don't need to do that, Dad."

Dad.

Dad?

Dad.

My father, whose name I could no longer speak, who had defected years ago, though I didn't know where. But there he was, with his new family. His dying wife. His brilliant teenage son.

Valdo was my brother.

Acknowledgements

MY FIRST THANKS, AS ALWAYS, go to my amazing wife, Christy. She is my alpha reader, the one person who knows all of Elise's and Bastion's secrets and where my overall vision is going for this series. Without her encouragement and feedback, none of this would happen.

Big thanks to my agent, Katie Salvo, who holds my metaphorical hand through the slow and challenging world of publishing. Thanks to In Churl Yo and Jason Henderson of Castle Bridge Media for believing in this book, this series, and in me. They take this cyberpunk dream of mine and put it into your hands.

I wouldn't be the writer I am without Hadara Bar-Nadav, Christy Hodgens, Michael Pritchett, and Whitney Terrell. They were my creative writing professors at the University of Missouri-Kansas City, and I will always hear their voices in my head as I write and edit.

Thank you to all of my fans and loved ones who make this worth it. I write because I have stories to tell, and when people love those stories, my heart sings. Your words keep me going, and I have a lot more stories to tell. I see you all. I hear you. You mean the world to me.

CASTLE BRIDGE MEDIA RECOMMENDS...

If you liked this book, you might also enjoy reading the following titles from Castle Bridge Media available on Amazon or by order at your favorite book store:

Animal Charmer
By Rain Nox

Austinites
By In Churl Yo

Bloodsucker City
By Jim Towns

*THE CASTLE OF HORROR
ANTHOLOGY SERIES*
Volume 1
Volume 2: *Holiday Horrors*
Volume 3: *Scary Summer
  Stories*
Volume 4: *Women Running
  From Houses*
Volume 5: *Thinly Veiled:
  The 70s*
Volume 6: *Femme Fatales*
Volume 7: *Love Gone Wrong*
Volume 8: *Thinly Veiled:
  The 80s*
Volume 9: *Young Adult*
Volume 10: *Thinly Veiled:
  Saturday Mournings*
Edited By Jason Henderson
and In Churl Yo
*Edited By P.J. Hoover

**Castle of Horror Podcast
Book of Great Horror:
Our Favorites, Top Tens
and Bizarre Pleasures**
Edited By Jason Henderson

Dream State
By Martin Ott

Dominic
By Lee Guzman

FRENCH DECEPTION
A Forgery in Paris
By Janice Nagourney
A Forgery in Lyon
By Janice Nagourney

FuturePast Sci-Fi Anthology
Edited by In Churl Yo

GLAZIER'S GAP
Ghosts of the Forbidden
By Leanna Renee Hieber

Isonation
By In Churl Yo

JAYU CITY CHRONICLES
The Hermes Protocol
By Chris M. Arnone
Necropolis Alpha
By Chris M. Arnone

**Junk Film: Why Bad
Movies Matter**
By Katharine Coldiron

MID-LIFE CRISIS THRILLERS
18 Miles From Town
By Jason Henderson
Lost Angel
By Sam Knight

**Nightwalkers: Gothic
Horror Movies**
By Bruce Lanier Wright

THE PATH
The Blue-Spangled Blue
By David Bowles
The Deepest Green
By David Bowles

SURF MYSTIC
Night of the Book Man
By Peyton Douglas
Dark of the Curl
By Peyton Douglas

**Yesterday's Tomorrows:
The Golden Age of
Science Fiction Movies**
By Bruce Lanier Wright

Please remember to leave us your reviews on Amazon and Goodreads!

THANK YOU FOR SUPPORTING INDEPENDENT PUBLISHERS AND AUTHORS!

castlebridgemedia.com